T0106156

Bus Ride to an Old Beginning

Mitch's Travels

REBECCA SOWDER

iUniverse, Inc.
New York Bloomington

iUniverse books may be ordered through booksellers or by contacting:

iUniverse
1663 Liberty Drive
Bloomington, IN 47403
www.iuniverse.com
1-800-Authors (1-800-288-4677)

ISBN: 978-1-4401-4562-9 (sc)
ISBN: 978-1-4401-4565-0 (ebook)

Printed in the United States of America

iUniverse rev. date: 6/8/2009

Chapter one

The dark night whisked by the bus windows, raindrops causing streaks of light along the panes of glass. Mitch leaned his forehead against the cool glass and watched the dense, black night slip rapidly by. Every once in a while, the darkness was broken by a light in a farmhouse window or a small, sleepy town. Most of these, Mitch did not even notice. His mind was several hundred miles to the east, a direction he was traveling as fast as his meager funds would let him. His destination was an area just outside his small hometown. He hadn't been there for years but in his mind he could picture the town, the people, the house in which he had grown up, and even the rough, uneven lot near the railroad tracks…his final destination. He much preferred to think of what was ahead of him than what was behind him, but they all seemed to blend. Unfortunately, they were all connected. He couldn't separate one from the other.

As the bus continued on its route, Mitch's mind began to wander…back to those days when it was just a nice hometown; where the people all knew your name and would call to you as you passed their well-kept yards surrounding small, comfortable houses. People were good then. But, things changed…or maybe some of the people changed…or maybe only he changed. When did it all begin to go wrong for Mitch? Maybe if he relaxed and took a good look at his life, he could tell…and possibly fix it.

Things were good when he was in grade school. He walked the same route to school every day, played ball with the same group of boys, teased the same girls, and fought with his older brother on a daily basis. Even that was good. Mitch smiled to himself as he thought about that time. He remembered the good smells coming from the kitchen where his mother was cooking and baking lots of yummy things. He really didn't ever think about being either rich or poor. He just knew that the warm, welcoming home would always be there for him. His mother always made sure they had clean, well-mended clothes; plenty of good food; regular baths (no matter how much he and his brother complained) and enough extras to keep them happy. His father worked hard, but back then Mitch did not know what kind of work he did. Later, he learned his father toiled many hours in a factory making a minimum wage, just so his family could be safe and secure. That really wasn't anything to be ashamed of…most of the men in the area worked at the factory…but as Mitch got older, he wanted more in his life than this kind of spirit-breaking, boring work and such a minimum amount of money.

All of these thoughts began in high school when he met Peggy. The first time he saw her was on the first day of his senior year. She had just transferred into the district and was standing near the principal's office with some of the girls in his class. He knew all of the girls and had even taken a few of them out a time or two, but he had never found a girl he was really interested in or one that would encourage him to think about a future. The minute he saw Peggy, he knew this was the girl for him. She had long, dark hair that hung almost to the middle of her back and she kept sweeping it back with her hand or tossing her head; big, deep blue eyes with long, dark eyelashes; a light flush on her smooth alabaster skin; full, red lips; and a smile that was dazzling.

Mitch took all of this in and felt his breath actually burst from his body while a white-hot streak shot down his groin. He had never felt like this before. She wasn't just beautiful, she was a goddess. Realizing he must be staring, he looked around quickly to see if anyone had noticed. The other guys were still talking and laughing with each other and did not seem to have noticed. Thankfully, Mitch turned his back to Peggy and tried to begin to interact with his friends. Still, he felt a pull that was almost physical to turn around again and the heat kept building. With a will he did not know he possessed, he kept looking away.

With much will-power, Mitch joined his friends on their way to their first class. It was good the other guys were talking and laughing so much they did not even notice how quiet Mitch had become. Definitely not natural for Mitch, the "class cut-up." As Mitch took his seat at a desk near the window in his first class, he found himself unable to think of anything but Peggy. He had never seen any girl that exuded pure sexual magnetism like she did. It radiated just like heat. Some of the girls in school had pretty good figures, many with big breasts, something that guys like to talk about, but she went beyond that. Unbelievable, was the only way Mitch could describe her. Then it hit him! He did not have a chance with this goddess. He was popular enough with his classmates because he was a "Good-time Charlie;" he kept them laughing and joined in all the crazy things teenagers could get in to; but she was not the kind of girl that would go for that. Somehow, he knew that. In fact, he couldn't believe she did not already have a steady guy. Surely someone had tied her down. Even the guys he palled around with would not pass up this chance, and none of them were in her class either.

Mitch felt deflated. He had been as high as if he had been drinking or doing drugs. But with the reality that had set in, that she was way out of his league, he felt as if he had fallen so far he had hit rock bottom. Even as class started, he had trouble mustering enough energy to listen to what was going on.

He had struggled to complete the day. After all, this was the first day of his last year in high school. He had to keep going. Without a diploma, he'd never have a chance to get away from the factory...to get somewhere.

He was so glad to hear the final bell ring and he headed quickly to his locker to drop his books. He knew well enough that he had no energy to put into studying tonight. He just wanted to crawl into a hole and pull it in after him.

His friends yelled to him, asking him to join them at the malt shop, but he waved them off with a lame excuse that he had to get home.

And home is where he went. He did not even head for the kitchen for his usual after-school snack. He went straight to his room and flopped on the bed.

His mother knocked on the door and asked him if everything was all right. All right? How could he ever be all right again? Fighting off the dregs of depression, he told her that he was just fine; just tired. After all, this was sort of an emotional day... first day of his senior year.

As his mother went down the hall, Mitch turned his face to the wall. If he hadn't been so old and a boy, he thought he would have cried. Thankfully, no tears came. After all, that would have really culminated his failure...his life.

He must have dozed off because the next thing he heard was his brother hammering on his door and yelling that supper was on the table.

Supper. How could he ever eat again? The lump in his throat was just too big. He couldn't even swallow, and they were bound to ask him questions about school.

Wow! It looked to Mitch as if he was getting what he had given. After all, he had teased a lot of friends when they had fallen head over heels for a girl. Now he wished he had been more understanding.

As Mitch took his place at the table, he tried to act normally. Maybe he could get away with it if he could just put on a good act.

He knew his luck was bad, though, when his father asked him how the first day of school had gone. Gulping, Mitch tried to tell them it was just an ordinary day. He noticed his brother stopping with a fork of food halfway to his mouth. He knew! Mitch knew that his secret wouldn't remain a secret too long.

His parents didn't seem to notice, so Mitch quickly finished his meal and asked to be excused. He hurried back to his own room and shut the door.

Soon he heard Carl coming down the hall and stopping outside his door. He held his breath, but Carl soon continued down the hall to his own room. Would Carl understand? After all, he'd been really popular and had lots of girlfriends. But had he ever felt this way? Carl seemed so satisfied with his life. He worked at the factory and seemed to be happy. Would he ever understand Mitch's feelings? After all, this girl seemed to represent what Mitch wanted in life. The girl that didn't belong in a factory town; the girl that would need and deserve a better life than his mother had ever had.

The sun had gone down and the room had grown dark. Mitch reached for his bedside lamp, then pulled his hand back. It was too painful. He had to talk to someone, and Carl seemed his best bet. Hopefully, he wouldn't see him as just a silly little brother any more.

Mitch went down the hall and knocked quietly on Carl's door. He could hear the radio playing softly in the room. Carl yelled for him to come in and Mitch entered, closing the door behind him. Again he felt that lump in his throat. What was he doing here? Was he making a mistake? Well, he wouldn't know until he tried.

Mitch pulled out the desk chair and sat down near Carl who was stretched out on his bed. He looked at the floor and wrung his hands.

Carl then did something Mitch never thought he would do. He got up, came around the chair, and put his hands on Mitch's shoulders.

"What's up kid?" asked Carl.

When Mitch heard this question it just all spilled out. He told Carl that he wanted so badly to get out of this town, to leave the factory behind. Carl didn't seem to feel that he was being put down by this, so Mitch continued.

"And then, today, I saw the girl that I know would give me the incentive to do that," said Mitch. "She is a goddess."

Carl laughed slightly and sat back down on his bed.

"So, little Mitch is growing up," he said. "I wondered when the love bug was going to bite you. Well, my man, it has."

Mitch looked at Carl and suddenly he knew that Carl was a real friend who cared about him and what he thought. How had he missed this before? Had he wasted all these years? Or did it just happen when everyone reached a certain place in their lives. Did he have to grow up before they could be friends and not just brothers?"

"Look, Buddy," said Carl; "You are good enough for any girl, and don't you ever forget it. And as far as the job goes, just because I wanted to do what Dad does, he won't expect you to do it too. He never pressured me and he won't pressure you. Believe it or not, he will understand. Just give him a chance."

Mitch looked at Carl and actually smiled.

"Thanks, Carl. I really appreciate the time you took with me. I guess I always thought you were a jerk but I was wrong. You are not only a great brother but a good friend. I hope I can be just as good."

Mitch let himself out and went back to his own room. This time he did turn on the lamp. He sat at his desk and took out a pad of paper and a pen. Writing quickly, he started to list the things he felt he needed to do, not only to get out of this town and make something of himself, but to show Peggy he was the right guy for her.

Suddenly he laughed. He hadn't even talked to her yet and he had them being a couple. Well, only time would tell, but he could at least control where he ended up even if he couldn't control Peggy's decisions. But he would try. He would try as hard as he possibly could.

After he finished his list, he put it in the top drawer of his desk, undressed, and went to bed. Much to his surprise, he went to sleep quickly and slept deeply, all night. It was really nice to have a big brother.

Chapter two

"Fifteen minute stop," the bus driver yelled, bringing Mitch back to the present. He sat up, stretched, and, for the first time, looked at his fellow travelers.

The bus was only about a third full; people didn't seem to be traveling this rainy night. Mitch was the last one off the bus and hurried to the awning outside the combination bus depot and restaurant.

Entering the building, he went to the counter and ordered a cup of coffee. Maybe this would keep him more alert during the next leg of the trip.

After getting the coffee, Mitch left the building, feeling the need to stretch his legs. Besides, the depot felt cramped and stuffy to him. The rain had slacked off and he took a short stroll out of the parking lot to the highway and back. It helped to breathe in the cool, fresh air. Maybe he just appreciated it more now, but it seemed so sweet to him.

As he approached the bus, he saw the driver leaving the depot and returning to the bus. He boarded and again found his seat. As the other passengers reboarded, he kept his head down, not wanting to make eye contact or have to speak to any of them. He just wanted to be left alone. After all, he had a lot of thinking to do the rest of this trip. He was just beginning to face the past.

Mitch finished his coffee and put the empty cup in the knapsack on the seat next to him. Then he stretched his legs out in front of him and again placed his forehead against the window pane, just as the driver closed the door and resumed the route.

It didn't take Mitch long to get back to his memories. He was soon back in high school, trying to work on his "list."

He remembered vividly the second day of his senior year. He had decided that he had to approach Peggy and at least introduce himself. He knew he was not bad looking and the other kids liked his personality and sense of humor. The biggest drawback to Mitch seemed to be that he was "just ordinary." He made average grades, was a follower and not a leader in any organization he belonged to, and did not take part in any team sports. All in all, he was Mr. Average. Many times a Mr. Average can be overlooked. In some ways this is good because he is not getting into trouble, but neither is he distinguishing himself in a positive way.

Mitch realized that if he had any chance with Peggy, this would have to change. He would have to be a producer and quit gliding through life. In fact, if he was to get the factory out of his future, he needed to produce, so maybe Peggy coming to the school was just the incentive he needed.

He looked for Peggy before school but did not see her anywhere. Refusing to let himself get down again, he concentrated on his morning classes and surprised most of his teachers by participating in class discussions.

At lunch time, Mitch headed to the bleachers near the football field to meet his friends. They always bought sandwiches and drinks and met there for lunch. It was a time of laughing and talking and Mitch always enjoyed this time with his friends.

That day it was really special. As he arrived at the football field, he saw that most of his friends had already arrived and were talking to some of the girls from their class. Mitch knew all the girls and felt comfortable around them, but as he approached, he saw that on the far side of the group stood Peggy. He almost stopped but willed himself to continue. After all, he had wanted to meet her.

As he approached the group, one of the guys called out,"Hey, where you been man?"

"Just slow today," answered Mitch.

When he got closer, Janie, a girl that Mitch had dated a few times who was still a good friend said, "Hey, Mitch. This is Peggy. She has been wanting to meet you."

Mitch couldn't believe what he was hearing. She wanted to meet him. This was just unbelievable.

"Hi," said Mitch. "I saw you yesterday. Your first day here?"

"Yes," said Peggy, "and everyone has been so nice and friendly to me. I feel as if I've known everyone for ages."

Mitch felt himself holding his breath. She seemed as nice as she looked and her voice was very sultry, much lower in pitch than most of the girls his age; he could even say it was sexy... and enticing.

Then Mitch surprised even himself. He actually asked Peggy if she would like to sit with him to eat their lunch. None of the guys ever asked a girl to join them during this time of 'male bonding' but he asked her before he even gave it a thought. Actually, he was surprised the words had come from him, but they had.

Peggy smiled and said, "That would be nice. I'd really like to know more about you."

She'd like to know more about him? That was really funny. What was there to know about him? He was just Mr. Average.

Well, maybe at least he could use this time to find out about her. Then he would decide if he needed to revise his list to improve himself enough to be the kind of guy she would be interested in.

Taking hold of her elbow, Mitch helped Peggy climb the bleachers. They went almost to the top row before they sat down. Some of the guys gave out some hoots, but they quickly stopped and began eating their own lunches.

As they unwrapped their lunches, Mitch wondered if he could swallow with Peggy being so close. Now that he saw her up close, she was even more perfect than he had thought. He tried not to stare and he didn't want her to think he was studying her, but it was hard. Peggy crossed her legs, causing her skirt to creep slightly above her knee. Mitch knew that she was absolutely the sexiest girl he had ever seen…and her scent was causing him to have trouble breathing.

During their lunch, they talked almost non-stop and Mitch was surprised to find that she was so easy to talk to; easier than any girl he had ever known. In that short period of time, he learned that she and her family had just moved here and that her father was a surgeon. They had lived the last seven years in Albany, New York, and although she had liked it there, she was happy with the way she had been received in this new town. Unbelievably, he found out she did not have a steady boyfriend and actually had never had one. She said she thought her mother was worried that she would never settle down. When she said that, she laughed a bright, bubbly laugh that lit up her face. When she asked about his family, he reluctantly admitted that he had lived all of his life in this town in the same house and that he had never really been anywhere. He told her about Carl but when she asked about his parents, he became uncomfortable. He finally told her that his mother was really nice but she was 'just a housewife,' and that his father worked in the factory. In fact, his grandfather had worked in the same factory and now his uncles and even his brother worked there. She surprised him again when she said that her uncle worked in a factory in Detroit and that he had been there his whole life.

She seemed to feel there really was no difference as long as you did a good job at whatever you did in life. When Mitch showed his surprise, Peggy frowned.

"What's the matter?" she asked.

"I guess I thought you would think working in a factory was below most people," Mitch said.

Suddenly Peggy sat up very straight and her cheeks got very flushed.

"I can't believe you think I am that kind of girl," she said. "That makes me sound so shallow." Her eyes were flashing with anger.

"You're right," said Mitch. "I'm really sorry. Maybe it's just my own feeling."

Mitch apologized again and hurriedly went on to say that he really wanted to do something else, but he wasn't sure what that was.

Thankfully, Peggy took a deep breath and began to relax and even laugh a little.

"I don't know either," said Peggy. "I think I will just plan on going to college and maybe by that time I will know what I want to do."

Her next question really caught Mitch off guard.

"Do you know which college you are going to attend?

Mitch stopped chewing right in the middle of a large bite of his sandwich. Was he going to college? He had never even thought about it. He didn't think anyone in his family had ever gone to college. Besides it cost so much money it was probably out of the question. When he told Peggy this, she said there were lots of ways he could get financial help if he really wanted to go to college. Then she made a suggestion...one he should have put on his improvement list. She told him he should go see the school counselor and talk over his future options.

That sounded like a great idea to Mitch and he told her he would do that as soon as possible. Then, without even thinking about it, he asked her if she would like to go to a movie over the weekend. The minute he opened his mouth he thought he had made a mistake, but she said yes.

Mitch spent the rest of the day on cloud nine. Not only had he met the girl of his dreams, she seemed to like him and they had a date. He also had an idea about what to do to get him out of the factory. Life was beautiful.

Chapter three

As the bus continued to travel through the night, Mitch smiled as he remembered that day so long ago…but was it really so long ago? Time seemed to have stood still for him over the past few years. Actually, it was only seven years since that wonderful day when life was so good. When did it change? How could he have fallen so far in just seven years? Now, life was the pits.

Again his mind wandered back to those happier days.

Within a week, Mitch had not only seen the counselor but was in the process of looking over career choices and also some college program brochures. They looked like they belonged to a different world than he had always lived in. Was it really possible? Was this just a wild dream? Maybe he wasn't meant to get out of this town and the factory. Anyway, it was great to dream, but the only person he talked about it with was Peggy. He still hadn't told his family that he wanted to go to college. He didn't know why he couldn't tell them. Maybe he was afraid they'd laugh at him, or maybe it would make them angry…or sad. Why? He couldn't decide what was holding him back. Maybe it was the fact that he still hadn't told his parents he didn't want to work in the factory.

He studied hard and his teachers were all surprised that he

was showing signs of liking and understanding his schoolwork. He was almost always the first to volunteer in class…something he had never done for the first eleven years of schooling. Some of his buddies teased him, but he didn't care. They never dumped him, and in reality he thought they might just admire him.

Outside of school his life had never been better. He and Peggy were a definite 'item.' They spent every minute between classes together, studied together at the library several afternoons each week, shared sodas and malts at the local teen hangout, and spent hours on the phone talking when they were apart. At least once a week, they went out to a movie, a ballgame or a dance. Mitch knew he had never felt so good. He only had one small nagging worry and he didn't let it enter into his thinking very often; but when it did, it was really puzzling. So far, Peggy had never let him meet her family. In fact, she had declined even to meet his family. Mitch couldn't figure this out, but he was so happy with his 'perfect life' he tried to keep from thinking about that.

With all the extra studying, looking into college programs and ways to fund them, and Peggy, Mitch's senior year flew by. Before long it was Christmas and they faced two whole weeks apart. It was especially bad since Peggy and her family were going away for the holidays. Mitch spent most of his time in his room, brooding, but told his parents he just had a lot of studying to do. One special memory he played over and over in his head was the last Friday night they had been together. It was only a few days until Christmas and Peggy was leaving the next morning. Instead of going anywhere with other people around, they drove to the football field and parked in the parking lot. It was cold but the car heater was good.

There they exchanged gifts…he had bought Peggy a tiny gold locket with a diamond chip and her initial on the front. Inside he had placed their pictures and, on the back was engraved, "together forever." That was the way he felt and

Peggy said she loved it and cried when he put it around her neck. Maybe she felt the same way. It had taken most of his savings that he had left from his summer job, but it was worth it just to see her face. She put her arms around his neck and held herself tightly against him. Mitch thought he would never be able to breathe again, but then she pulled away, looked into her face, and kissed him softly. Remarkably, he was able to breathe again normally almost instantly.

Peggy then brought out a small square box, beautifully wrapped, and handed it to him. His fingers were all thumbs. He had such a time opening it, she gave a little laugh and then said, "Here, let me help."

Sliding her long fingernails under the flap, she neatly pulled the paper away from the box. Mitch took a deep breath when he saw the box was from the classiest jewelry store in town. As he slowly opened the box, he saw a gleaming gold id bracelet lying on a dark-blue velvet base. As he picked it up, he saw his name etched into the gold. It was the most beautiful thing he had ever seen. It was heavy…much heavier than it looked…and he couldn't take his eyes off it. Finally he looked up at Peggy. Her eyes were glistening.

"Do you like it? she asked.

Did he like it? What wasn't to like? This small bracelet probably cost more than anything in his house. Mitch's smile quickly faded when he looked at the tiny locket, now nestled between Peggy's breasts. It rose and fell with every breath she took. But it looked so cheap next to the bracelet.

Suddenly, Peggy began to look very sad. "You don't like it," she said.

"Oh, no," said Mitch. "I love it."

"Then what is the matter?" Peggy asked.

"It is too nice, too expensive. I couldn't begin to buy you anything this nice," said Mitch.

Peggy took his face in her hands, lifted it so he was looking directly into here eyes, and said, "I couldn't love anything as much as I love this locket. What it cost does not matter. I believe you gave it to me because you love me; that is why I gave you the bracelet."

Suddenly Peggy was in his arms; kissing him all over his face, pushing her body close to his. He felt the heat from her body, the tenseness against him, the beating of her heart. He felt her breasts...those beautiful, full breasts...pushing hard against his chest. He smelled the scent of her hair, the scent of the light but memorable perfume she had dabbed behind her ears, and, more than anything, he smelled her woman scent.

At that moment, they were the only two people in the world. Quickly, he pulled her coat off and then his, throwing them into the backseat. She clawed at him, opening his shirt all the way to his waist and began to kiss him from his throat to his waist. Chills...from the excitement, not from the cold, went through his body. In his mind he was telling himself to stop. This wasn't right. They had been so controlled. But his body was aflame. The ache in his groin felt as if it would make him explode. Taking her firmly with both hands, he pushed her away. For one second she had a look of bewilderment on her face, but then, as he quickly pulled her sweater over her head and reached behind her for the snaps of her bra, she sighed and smiled and pulled his face down between those beautiful, full, warm breasts. Mitch couldn't remember anything but the feel of those warm, soft globes smothering his face. Again he drank in the smells of her body; her sexuality was palpable. It was Heaven. He felt Peggy arch her back and he knew that she too was feeling the incredible desire. He was so comfortable with his face buried deeply into the breasts of this goddess. It seemed too good to be true. Reluctantly, he pulled his face back slightly, enabling him to gaze at these wonderful mounds of joy. He couldn't believe that she was here with him, Mr. Average, when she could be with any guy.

"Come on Mitch," said the small voice in his head. "Count

your blessings and get as much as you can because it may be over at any moment. You know you aren't in her class."

In spite of the joy he was feeling, that is all Mitch could think about. It would not last. Period. They were truly the odd couple.

Just then, Peggy leaned forward again, pressing her breasts against his face and started to fumble with his belt and the hook on his pants. Small groans were coming from deep in Peggy's throat. Mitch pulled her hands away from his buckle and held them behind her back in one of his hands. Then he began to mouth her breasts, licking and nipping closer to the hard, dark nipples. She shuddered as he slipped the hard round nipple into his mouth and began to suck deeply. Her moans increased and her body writhed. She reached behind his head pushing him harder and harder against her body. Her back arched and she pushed her leg against his groin. Mitch ran his hands down the small of her back, reaching the top of her skirt. He fumbled with the button, but was unable to open it. Hurriedly, he slid his hands down her thighs, finding the hem of her skirt, and pulled to get it up. Suddenly, her skirt was up around her waist and the beautiful forbidden area of this rare person beckoned him. He leaned forward to kiss along the line of her panties. His breath caught...he was in dreamland.

Then, for a reason he would never understand, he thrust her willing body away from him. He pushed her skirt back down and pulled her sweater over her bulging breasts.

Peggy looked at him with shock...maybe even a little hurt. He was rejecting her. She was willing to give herself to him and he was turning her down.

"I'm sorry," said Mitch. "I want you more than I can ever say, but this is not right. This seems so cheap and I would never consider you cheap. Someday, when the time is right, our love will lead us to a beautiful and wonderful fulfillment, if it is real."

Mitch couldn't believe this was him talking. Where and

when had he developed such a conscience, such a moral code? He loved Peggy more than life and she was his for the taking, and he was saying no.

Peggy finished putting her clothes back into place and Mitch buttoned his shirt. He couldn't bear to look at her. Would he find her eyes filled with hate, revulsion, or maybe even pity? That would be the worst. Then he would know that they would always be on different levels and wrong for each other.

Straightening his shoulders and reaching for the switch to turn on the headlights, Mitch took a deep breath. Without turning toward her, he said, "Can you ever forgive me?"

"What?" asked Peggy. "What do you mean? There is nothing to forgive."

Turning toward her, finally looking into her eyes, he saw tears glistening there and a beautiful smile on her face.

"You aren't mad at me?" asked Mitch.

"Mad?" asked Peggy. "Of course not. You have really made me feel so special and so safe. You even protected me from myself. How could I ever be mad at you. I love you, and, to me, you have told me in the most special way just how much you love me." Peggy scooted close to Mitch and laid her head on his shoulder.

"Let's go get a malt," she said. "I want to show off my locket…the second best gift I ever received."

"By the way," she whispered, "did you look on the back of your bracelet?"

He hadn't so he quickly turned it over. There, in bold letters was 'Peggy and Mitch; the perfect couple.'

Mitch smiled, then leaned over and gave her a soft kiss on that perfect mouth. He was such a lucky guy. 'The perfect couple.' Could it really be true?

Suddenly lights flashed across the front of the bus. Mitch stirred out of his reverie and looked down at his bare wrist. Why hadn't he kept wearing that bracelet? It still represented the best time of his life…when life was perfect.

Chapter four

Mitch stretched his arms over his head. The bus was moving quickly through the night toward his goal. He didn't know if he was happy or sad…maybe a little of each.

Returning to his thoughts, he tried to return to those wonderful days during that final year in high school. It was hard to think of that time, of what might have been.

During the rest of the year, Peggy and Mitch were never far apart. They spent lots of time together planning their future. They were looking forward to college in the fall and planned to go to the same school. Of course, it was easier for Peggy. Funding wasn't an issue for her. They had even decided that they might major in business so that they could work together in the future. Besides, to Mitch it looked like a great way to break the mold.

One thing that continued to bother Mitch was the fact that Peggy still kept him away from her parents. She had given in a little and had met his parents. His mother adored her; his father thought she was too good for him. He told his father he agreed, but that he was going to earn the right to have her in his life. That caused his father to smile, but he didn't say anything.

Finally the last month of school started. Both Peggy and Mitch had been accepted to nearby State University and they were very excited. Mitch had applied for funding and that too had been approved. Even his father seemed excited that one of his sons was going to college. He never said anything, he just had a look of pride whenever they talked about the future.

Everybody was busy. There were finals to finish, caps and gowns to order, invitations to send, and, of course, their Senior Prom. Mitch was as excited as Peggy. He was renting a tuxedo and, along with his friend, Josh, he had rented a limousine for the evening. They had even made dinner reservations at one of the fanciest restaurants in town...one Mitch had never been to in his life.

On the day of the prom, Mitch went to pick up Peggy's corsage and his tuxedo and then came home to get ready. He was so nervous he needed help tying his bow tie. Carl came to the rescue. Mitch was afraid that Carl would tease him, but he didn't. All he did was tell him to have the time of his life.

Finally the time arrived. He joined Josh in the limo and they sped off to pick up Janie, Josh's date. While Mitch waited in the limo, Josh went in to get Janie. Of course they had to wait while Janie's parent took pictures for posterity but soon they rejoined him.

Janie looked so grown up. In fact, so did Josh. Janie was wearing a beautiful gown and her corsage matched perfectly. For the first time Mitch began to wonder what he was doing here...but here he was. Just then they the arrived at Peggy's house.

It wasn't the first time Mitch had seen Peggy's house...he often brought her home, but she had never let him come to the door. Tonight it was going to be different. He was supposed to meet her parents for the first time. As he walked toward the door, his mouth became dry and he thought he couldn't breathe. In one hand he held the orchid he had bought for Peggy. With the other hand he straightened his tie, then knocked.

Peggy's mother opened the door.

"Hello, Mitch," she said. "I'm Peggy's mother. Please come in."

"Thank you, Mrs. Johnson," said Mitch, following her into the biggest living room he had ever seen.

There, standing near the fireplace, was Peggy's father. He wasn't smiling and Mitch began to feel as if he should run. He wanted to pull on his collar which seemed to be getting tighter.

"Hello, sir," said Mitch. "I'm here to take your daughter to the prom."

"Yes, I know," said Dr. Johnson. "I understand you and Peggy have been seeing a lot of each other. It's nice to finally meet you."

"Thank you, Sir," said Mitch. "I really like Peggy a lot. She's a neat girl."

At that, Dr. Johnson smiled, and Mitch began to breathe easier.

"Please have a seat," said Mrs. Johnson; "Peggy will be right down."

Mitch sat on the nearest chair and found himself fumbling with the ribbon on the florist's box. He hoped Peggy would hurry, and then, Peggy came into the room. She looked like an angel. Her dress was a beautiful cloud of white that accented her beauty and her figure and her head was crowned with a mass of dark curls, cascading down her back. She actually took Mitch's breath away. He never knew that anyone could look so beautiful.

Then she smiled at him and everything was all right. Quickly, Mitch stepped forward. "You look so beautiful," he stammered. "Ah, here. I brought this for you." He handed her the orchid and she smiled radiantly, reached up and kissed him on the cheek and said, "Thank you. It is beautiful."

Peggy removed the orchid from the box and handed it back to Mitch.

"Will you pin it on?" she asked.

"I don't know if I can," he said, fumbling with the pins.

"Here, let me help you," said Mrs. Johnson, showing him where to pin the orchid on Peggy's shoulder.

He succeeded, even if his hands were trembling, and it looked perfect. In fact, she made the orchid look even more beautiful.

"Shall we go?" asked Mitch.

"Of course," said Peggy.

"Oh, wait. The pictures," said Mrs. Johnson.

After the obligatory pictures, they left the house, Peggy's arm tucked safely in his. When he looked at her he felt as if he was smiling like the Cheshire Cat.

"Bye," said Peggy.

"Have a wonderful time, dear," said her mother.

As they reached the limo and were escorted in by the driver, Mitch realized that no one had said anything about a curfew. When he whispered this to Peggy, she replied that they trusted her to use good judgment.

Inside the limo, everyone was very excited. The girls looked beautiful and the guys looked remarkably handsome and grown-up in their rented tuxedos. This would certainly be a night to remember.

Just walking into the restaurant would have made Mitch nervous before, but with Peggy on his arm, he felt like he owned the world and could go anywhere.

The four of them laughed and talked throughout dinner. As Mitch looked around, he thought that they were the best looking couples there…they belonged.

At the prom, they danced the night away. When Peggy got her dance card, she put Mitch's name down and drew a line through all the lines. She smiled coyly over this, and Mitch almost burst with pride. She wanted to spend the whole night with him. At least the better part of it. He really loved this girl.

The evening went too fast. Mitch and Peggy were lost in

their own world, dancing to one song after another, not even noticing there was anyone else around. But just as good things must end, so did the music.

As they walked to the limo, Mitch couldn't tear his eyes away from Peggy's face. She looked at him with such love and caring, he thought his heart would burst.

After the dance, they had planned to go to a post-prom party at the home of one of the teachers. As the limo headed to the party, Peggy whispered to Mitch, "Do you really want to go to the party? Why don't we have our own party?"

Mitch felt his heart jump into his throat. Could this really be the night they actually pledged themselves to each other? He hadn't told any of the guys but he meant to be a 'one-woman' man...and Peggy was the woman for him

Leaning forward, Mitch asked the driver to drop them at his house on the way to the party. As they got out of the limo, Janie and Josh asked where they were going.

"Just to get my car," said Mitch. We'll need wheels after the party...remember we only have the limo for another hour. I think we might be there longer."

With that, they got out of the limo, waving goodbye to their friends as they drove away.

Laughing as they hurried up the driveway to Mitch's car, they felt like thieves in the night. Mitch helped Peggy into the car and, even before he could start the engine, she had thrown her arms around him and was kissing him more passionately than she ever had before. Her lips were soft and moist and gave off great heat as they clung together. Reluctantly, Mitch pushed her away as he started the engine and put the car into reverse. He did not turn the lights on until he was in the street, hoping he wouldn't wake his family. After he turned the lights on, he smiled at Peggy.

"This feels so right," he said. "You make me the happiest person in the whole world. Actually, tonight I feel as if I own the world," Mitch said, smiling broadly.

"Let's go to the football field again," Peggy said. "I always feel as if that is our 'special spot.' Okay?"

Mitch smiled to himself. He felt the same way. As he headed for the football field, his pulse quickened. It looked to him as if he and Peggy were finally going to pledge themselves to each other. That was important to Mitch. He loved her so much.

When they arrived at the field, Mitch parked in the darkest corner, turned off the motor and sat very still with his hands continuing to clutch the steering wheel.

"Are you sure this is what you want?" he asked, still looking straight ahead.

He felt her hands on the side of his face, turning him to face her. He really gave no resistance as she looked deeply into his eyes and then gave him a deep, passionate kiss, her tongue forcing its way between his welcoming lips. He knew the answer.

"Yes; definitely," she replied. "You are all I will ever want. I love you more than I ever thought I could love anyone."

With that, all his doubts and his resolve to wait left him. Turning his body to face her, he held her tightly in his arms, pressing her body against him. The heat he felt was unbelievable. His arms ached holding this special treasure, his breath was ragged and his groin ached with such heat he felt as if he was on fire. There was no going back now.

His kisses covered her face, her neck, the hollow of her throat, and into the cleavage showing above her ball gown. Her skin was so silky and soft and he noticed the faint scent of spring rain as he continued to kiss and caress her. Above that, he smelled 'her'...this woman he was holding. He couldn't stop and she made no effort to stop him. In fact, she melded her body against him and he could feel her shiver slightly. He knew it was not from cold, but from the passion they were both feeling.

Finally, he was able to pull himself away from her and held

her at arms length, drinking in her beauty. She was too perfect to be true, but here she was, and she wanted to belong to him. And he wanted her too.

"Peggy, we need to take care of your beautiful dress," said Mitch, feeling almost silly saying this.

"You know Mitch, you are the most thoughtful person I ever knew. Most guys wouldn't care," said Peggy, smiling at him.

Peggy removed her orchid and put it on the dashboard. "I don't want to damage this either," she said with a coy smile.

"Turn around," said Mitch. "Let me help you with the zipper."

How was he being so cool? He couldn't believe it but it was only on the outside. Inside he was so excited he was shaking.

As she turned around, Mitch couldn't help but lean forward and caress her creamy shoulders with his lips. At the same time, he slowly slid the zipper of her dress down, feeling it pull away from her body, inch by inch.

Peggy turned to him and he reached out and pulled her dress away from her breasts. Then, with her help, he lifted it over her head and laid it in the back seat, safely out of the way. While he was laying it out, Peggy was busy undoing his bow tie and pushing his jacket off his shoulders and down his arms. These items soon joined Peggy's dress in the back seat.

He took her in his arms and pressed her to him. While kissing her lips he fumbled with her bra. As he released the clasps, her breasts sprung forward, firm and inviting, with dark circles surrounding hard, stiff nipples which drew him forward.

While he stared hungrily at these bulging nipples, Peggy took his hands and slid them into the waistband of her panties. With her encouragement, he pushed them down her long, luscious legs and removed them and her shoes. Now she was wearing only a garter belt and stockings. It made Mitch want her more than he could have ever believed possible. He reached for her and started kissing her from her lips down to her toes. He didn't miss an inch and the way she responded made Mitch know that she wanted him as much as he wanted her.

As he continued to kiss her, he lingered over the thrusting nipples, taking them into his hungry mouth. They were rock hard, and he ran his tongue over them as he hungrily sucked on them.

After tearing himself away, quite reluctantly from those thrusting breasts, he continued to travel down her body, kissing her stomach and ending at the beautiful dark triangle between her legs. This was the promised land that Mitch had waited so long to claim. This was the night…they would belong to each other and they would never forget this night.

As Mitch kissed her body, Peggy was squirming with delight and desire. She had waited for so long for the right person to give herself to, and she knew Mitch was the right one. After tonight, they would belong to each other, forever, and no one or nothing would come between them.

She shuddered as he stopped kissing her body and began to run his tongue over her vagina. He slowly began to push his tongue deeply inside her while burying his face inside the lips of her vagina. She moaned and thrust her body forward to meet him. Her legs wrapped around his head, pressing him forward. She had never felt such yearning. Such response. She couldn't wait any longer.

Hungrily, she raised him up enough to again kiss his willing lips. While she was drinking in his hot kisses, she quickly unbuttoned his shirt, pulling it out of his waistband and sliding it down his arms. It, too, ended up in the back seat and, before it even landed, she was tearing at the button and zipper of his pants. She fumbled with the button hook, but Mitch reached down and helped her. She was more than able to open the zipper and then she began to push his pants off. Mitch raised up from the seat so that she could slide them over his buttocks and off his feet. By now the backseat was getting full. Next she hooked her fingers into the waist band of his briefs and pulled them off, quickly. Now he was as nude as she was and it felt good. They caressed and kissed each other's bodies from top to bottom. Mitch felt his penis getting hot and stiff, a condition Peggy did not miss.

From that moment, the rest of the evening seemed like a dream. Mitch had never imagined anything could be so good. They were so right for each other.

As their heated bodies came together, Peggy brought her legs up around him, enclosing his body and holding him close. He waited with a heightened expectation as he entered her... and he was not disappointed. As he pushed his hard, thrusting penis into Peggy's vagina, she moaned and squirmed beneath him. As he began to rock, trusting himself as deeply as he could into this warm, moist paradise, she pulled him close, raking her long nails across his back. Her moans continued and he was surprised to hear his own moans intermingling with hers. He worked harder and faster, feeling as if his body was going to explode. Just when he felt he couldn't stand it any longer, he felt Peggy's body arch and push even harder against him. Her nails dug into his back and she let out a loud scream and her body shuddered just as he felt himself explode inside her. He suddenly realized that he had been holding his breath and he began to gulp in large mouthfuls of air as he felt both of their bodies relax. She was covering his mouth with hungry kisses and he found it almost impossible to drink in enough air. Sitting up, he leaned against the driver's door and pulled Peggy on top of him. As their bodies relaxed against each other, he began to kiss her beautiful face.

"You are so beautiful," he said, "and I love you more than I can ever tell you."

Peggy buried her face in Mitch's bare chest and he felt the hot tears falling down his body.

"What's wrong?" asked Mitch, pushing her away from him. "Did I hurt you? Are you upset? Disappointed?"

Raising her tear-streaked face to his, Peggy smiled, and said, "Oh, no. You didn't hurt me and I am not disappointed. It was so beautiful...even more than I had dreamed about. I know we're right for each other because it was so right. You were the one I was saving myself for. I love you Mitch, now and forever."

Smiling broadly, Mitch leaned forward and kissed her firmly, tasting her salty tears.

"You are mine, forever," said Mitch. "Nothing could ever be better than us and this."

Later, after carefully restoring their clothes, they drove silently back to town, Peggy's cheek resting on his shoulder.

"Do you want to go to the party?" Mitch asked.

Resting her hand on his arm, Peggy said, "I don't think so. I just want to go home and remember forever this night."

Mitch smiled and headed for her house. He walked her to the door and their kiss was tender and warm but still held the passion of their evening. As Mitch drove home, he couldn't stop smiling. He thought that nothing could be better than this night; maybe this would be the ultimate in his life. What could begin to match these feelings?

That night he slept soundly, dreaming of a girl in a cloud, reaching out to him and taking him into her arms with such tenderness and love, he cried, even in his sleep.

Chapter five

Mitch suddenly jolted out of his reverie; the bus was slowing down. When he looked out he could see the lights of a small town. Maybe this was another stop...but, no. Soon the bus started moving again.

As they again picked up speed and the sound of the wheels on the pavement began to hum rhythmically, Mitch stretched out, laying his head against the seat back. He stared at the ceiling of the bus, but soon he was not seeing anything. He was again thinking of those years so long ago.

The morning after the prom, Mitch slept late. In fact, he did not want to face his family. He knew everything from the night before must show on his face. Finally, however, he got up and went to the kitchen to look for some breakfast. He didn't see his brother or his father, but his mother was busying herself in the kitchen, probably preparing lunch.

Mitch counted this as a blessing because he knew she would never ask him anything...she waited until he wanted to talk. Not wanting to talk, he sat at the table and ate a bowl of cereal. It was funny to Mitch now that the bowl of cereal was so clear in his mind.

When he finished his cereal and put the bowl in the sink, he told his mother that he was going to return his tuxedo to the rental shop. He left the room, but then, because he felt a little guilty, he returned to the kitchen, gave his mother a kiss on her cheek and said, "the prom was wonderful, mom. And Peggy looked beautiful. It was a night I will always remember."

Mitch's mom smiled and said, "I'm glad, son. I hope things keep going good for you."

Then, unexpectedly, she reached up and took his face in her hands, and said, "You know, Mitch; your father and I are very proud of you."

Then she looked embarrassed and turned back to the food she was preparing.

Mitch smiled, but left the room, picked up his tux, and headed downtown. He still felt like he couldn't quit smiling.

When he was going into the rental shop, Josh was on his way out.

"Hey, Mitch," called Josh. "What happened to you guys last night? You missed a great party. We didn't get home 'til 4:30 this morning."

"We just didn't feel much like a party," Mitch replied. "We were home long before that. Besides, the prom itself was enough excitement for anyone."

Mitch pointed into the store and said, "As soon as I return this, do you want to go for a burger and coke?"

"Yeah," said Josh. "I'll wait for you here."

Mitch returned his tux and then he and Josh went to the malt shop.

As he thought about it now, this was one of the last times he and Josh had spent any time together. He wondered why that was. Josh had been his best friend, but time seemed to have slipped away. It shouldn't have happened that way.

Mitch spent the weekend after the prom studying for finals. After all, it was important to get good grades so he could go to college with Peggy.

The only time he left his room was to eat or talk to Peggy on the phone. Those were the best times. He couldn't believe he found it so easy to talk to a girl, but with her, nothing seemed strained. The memories and joy of their passionate night were evident in their voices...if not their words.

The next week passed in a blur. There were exams every day and he spent every spare minute with Peggy. They never talked about that night at the football field, but Mitch was sure it was on her mind, just as it was on his.

After finals came graduation. As he picked up his diploma, it made him happy to see the pleased looks on the faces of his parents. But, now it was all over. No more regimented high school...now he had to discipline himself. And he knew he could do it.

During the summer, he and Peggy both worked as many hours as they could at their respective summer jobs. After all, when school started, they needed to have as much money saved as possible. Even though his student loans would cover his tuition and part of his living expenses, he had to come up with the rest. Even so, they stole as many hours to be together as possible. Once they had opened the door on their sexuality, they couldn't stop it. That summer, the sex between them was fantastic.

Maybe that is when it all started to come apart.

Mitch resettled in the uncomfortable bus seat and returned to his thoughts. Maybe if he looked real hard, he could understand why he was here, traveling through the night on a bus, heading back to his childhood home.

He and Peggy had driven to school together that first day in her car. He unloaded her things at her dorm and then she took him to his.

His roommate was already there. His name was Jim and he too was a Freshman. Jim had come from a family of jocks. He was on the football team and would be going out for basketball or wrestling, whichever he felt would be best. He had his walls covered with posters of girls in bikinis and jocks. Mitch's side of the room looked a little barren; he hadn't thought of anything for the walls. Maybe he didn't need it. Beside his bed was a framed picture of Peggy.

She was his pinup...the only one he needed.

Even though they were so different, Jim and he became friends. Jim even got permission for Mitch to attend football practice and one day the coach asked if he would like to be a student manager. What a deal. He would get money toward his living expenses and he could hang out with Jim and the other guys. Of course he took it. What Freshman wouldn't.

The only problem this caused was he had less time to spend with Peggy, but she said she understood. After all, she knew he needed the money. They still were able to get together for study dates and at least one date every weekend. When the team played a home game, that date would be on Saturday night; but when they played an away game, they planned their date for Sunday night.

Then two major things happened. Peggy got invited to join a very prominent sorority. She was so excited, he couldn't tell her he didn't want her to join. But sorority girls are supposed to hang out with fraternity men, and that is one thing he was never going to be. He wasn't important or wealthy enough. She assured him that she would always be his girl and that this wouldn't change anything. He told her he believed her, but deep inside, he knew things would never be the same.

The second thing that happened was that, at about the same time Peggy joined the sorority, the group of jocks he was hanging with decided it was time to have more fun. They cut back on studying. Maybe this wouldn't have been so bad, but he always had trouble catching up if he let his work slide. They also decided they should 'enjoy' more girls, often sneaking them into the dorm, along with all sorts of alcohol. He had never had a drink, but he soon learned that he loved it. In fact, he loved it so much that he always drank more than anyone else. Many mornings he awoke, usually in his bed, with a terrific hangover. He couldn't remember the night before and, even worse, there was often a strange girl in his bed.

He kept telling himself that he wasn't cheating on Peggy. After all, he never remembered even talking to these girls; certainly he didn't remember having sex with them. But even he knew this was a weak excuse. Because he felt so guilty, he canceled more and more dates with Peggy. He always told her he had too much school work or he had to work in the locker room, but those excuses got old after a while.

Finally, near the end of October, Peggy told him that she thought it might be good for them to date other people. When she told him that, he knew it was the only thing that was fair to her; but it hurt. He looked down at the id bracelet still on his wrist. He couldn't think of anything to say.

She leaned close and kissed him softly on his lips. He looked at those luscious red lips that had been his and he ached with what he was losing.

"Call me sometime," she said. "I will always love you. You will always be the one for me."

With that she turned and ran quickly across the campus. As she turned, he thought he caught sight of tears in her eyes. But…he couldn't go after her. Yes, he still loved her. He still wanted her. But he was no longer good for her.

When he got back to the dorm, Jim and a bunch of their buddies were already partying. Of course, he jumped right in with them. In his current state of mind, it was the worst thing he could do, but he partied with a vengeance. He had no idea how many drinks he had that night. At one time he remembered several girls stopping by and, since they were all pretty bombed, they all started grabbing them and tearing their clothes from them. Some of them were even crying, but that didn't matter to him. In fact, he felt like he wanted to hurt a girl…just as Peggy had hurt him.

That night was the beginning of a downward spiral for Mitch.

The next morning he woke up stretched out on the floor, completely naked, with two naked girls lying on top of him. When he began to stir, they woke up. They looked as dazed as he felt.

"You girls better get out of here," he said. "We don't want the dorm monitor to catch you."

They grabbed their clothes, dressing quickly, and left, scurrying down the hall like thieves. He didn't even know their names...and he didn't want to know them.

Jim was still sleeping in his bed. Mitch staggered into the bathroom, took one look in the mirror, and decided there was no way he could get himself ready for classes.

After all, he told himself, he had attended almost every class 'til now. One day wouldn't hurt.

Unfortunately, one day became two, and two became three and so on until he couldn't remember the last time he attended classes. Jim was in the same condition. He finished football but never went out for another team. They just partied, partied, partied.

They never wanted for girls, booze or drugs. They were all plentiful for them. He kept telling himself that he deserved this. After all, Peggy was partying with all her sorority and fraternity friends. But that wasn't really true. He knew it wasn't true. Because he had messed up so badly, she was dating other people, but he had heard there was no one special. Everyone said she seemed to be sad and waiting for someone. He couldn't even respond to that...the girl of his dreams and he was not just losing her, he was driving her away.

Just before the Christmas holiday break, they completed their final exams. Jim and he managed to get to the exams, but they were hopelessly behind in their work. They didn't have a chance to pass any class. It was time to face the music... but they were so bombed all the time, it still hadn't hit them. They were still flying...after all, they were the coolest dudes on campus.

When he left for Christmas break, he still hadn't heard about his grades. He even talked himself into believing that no news was good news and he had, in some way, succeeded in passing the exams. Jim and he both left on a high, planning to room together the second semester and resume their twenty-four hour a day parties.

When he arrived home and took one look around, he couldn't believe he had ever lived in...let alone enjoyed...this sleepy, boring, little town. He now knew for sure that he was meant for bigger and better things. His biggest question was how was he going to stand spending a three-week Christmas break here.

Mom and Dad were waiting as he walked into the house. They both looked at him with such pride.

"Well, here is the big college man," said his dad. "You look great son. It is so good to have you home, and we are so proud of you. You are going to be the biggest success ever in this family."

He smiled weakly then headed for his room, telling them he was a little tired.

"Call me for dinner, Mom," he said as he went down the hall.

As soon as he closed the door, his smile faded. Sure, they would really be proud if they knew how he'd spent the last few months. For the first time he felt a little guilt.

But that soon passed. After all, it was his life. Besides, they weren't paying his way. It was with loans he got and money he'd earned. Besides, he just knew he'd passed, and he had had a terrific time.

Right now, he could use a drink, but in this house that was out of the question. Maybe he could slip out later and find a liquor store. He had a fake id that had worked so far.

As he stretched out on the bed, feeling angry and depressed about having to come back here and leave his exciting life behind, he tried to think of some way he could go back to school early without hurting his folks. He'd have to give it some thought. Gosh, he sure could use a drink.

He must have dozed off because he was startled by a knock on the door.

"Come on in," he yelled.

"Hi, Joe College," said Carl. "Hey man, you look great. Well, maybe a little tired. Too much studying, huh?"

"Oh, yeah," he said. "That's it."

For the first time in a long time, he felt uncomfortable with Carl. He wasn't going anywhere, stuck in that factory.

"Hey, man. How is school? Do you and Peggy get enough time to see each other?" asked Carl.

"Oh, we don't see much of each other anymore," he said. "She and I sort of found that we had different interests. Besides, there are girls coming out of the woodwork up there, and they are all so available. Why should I saddle myself with one girl."

"Sure," said Carl, but Mitch noticed he frowned a little as he started to leave the room.

"Hey, Carl. How about you? Anything happening? Got a girl?" he asked, surprising himself.

Carl turned back, gave him a strange look, and said, "Sort of. There is this really nice girl that works at the factory, in the front office. She and I have been seeing each other. I hope you can meet her. After all, I kind of hope she is going to be your sister-in-law."

"Who is she? Do I know her?" Mitch asked.

"Grace Richardson. Do you remember her? She was in the class right after me. I always used to think she was cool, but I never thought I'd have a chance with her. Anyway, she is fantastic, and we have been talking about a summer wedding. If it happen, man, you are the Best Man."

"Sure," said Mitch.

After a couple of uncomfortable seconds, Carl left, closing the door behind him.

It sure was sad. He had grown so much more than Carl, they could never have anything in common again. Carl's greatest plan was to marry a girl from the factory. Blah! That was really thinking 'small.'

Now he knew he had to leave early. He couldn't spend three weeks here. He had to get back to the real world. Back to the parties and the fast lane. Soon.

Chapter six

The sound of the airbrakes of the bus brought Mitch back to the present. He looked about, wondering if this was the next stop, but soon found that it was only to slow for a small town. He looked around and saw that most of his fellow passengers were sleeping. It looked so easy for them. He wished he could sleep that easily. It had been a long time since he had felt that relaxed, or safe. Would he ever feel that way again? He wondered...and really doubted...that he ever would. It really was true that you could not go back...back to the simple, safe times.

With a wry smile and a small shake of his head, he resettled into his seat and returned to his thoughts of that past that seemed so long ago...back in that bedroom during Christmas break.

He remembered how jumbled and anxious his thoughts had been. How was he going to escape? He didn't want to hurt his family, but he didn't belong here any more. He had outgrown them. But he didn't hate them. How could he leave?

As he was thinking about this, Carl knocked on his door and yelled, "Hey, Joe College; supper time."

Supper. It had been a long time since he had heard that word. In his circle of friends they called it dinner. Supper was so unsophisticated.

Slowly, Mitch raised himself from the bed and found his way to the kitchen. His parents and Carl were already at the table. He took his old place, keeping his head down while he put his napkin on his lap.

Finally he looked up and glanced around the table. His mother was smiling and as he looked around he saw that even Carl and his father had happy looks of anticipation on their faces.

"What?" asked Mitch. "Is something wrong?"

"No son," said his mother. "Nothing is wrong. We are so glad to have you home. See, I even cooked your favorite meal."

For the first time, Mitch looked at the table. It was true. His mother must have worked all day. He was a little ashamed as he looked at the brimming bowl of mashed potatoes and the large roast. He knew this had been an expensive meal, one they would have to sacrifice to afford.

"Thanks, Mom. Thank you all," said Mitch. "I do appreciate it. It has been a long time since I had a home-cooked meal."

As his dad piled food on Mitch's plate, he wondered if he could even swallow a bite. He really didn't have an appetite and, besides, he never ate heavy food like this any more. His tastes had changed to junk food and alcohol…especially alcohol, and it seemed to have lessened his appetite.

Struggling, he ate more than he ever had eaten. At least while he was eating, they weren't expecting a lot of conversation from him.

As soon as he finished, he asked to be excused.

"Of course," said his mother. "Are you going to see Peggy?"

Peggy!

Just her name caused his stomach to tense up. He hadn't seen much of her since that day on campus. A few times he had seen her walking with some of her friends between classes, but he had made sure she didn't see him.

"You bet," answered Mitch.

He glanced at Carl but he was still eating. At least this would give him an excuse to leave the house. He knew if he didn't get away, he would lose his mind.

He grabbed his jacket and headed for the door.

"See you later," he yelled. "Don't wait up."

As he left the house, he finally took a deep breath. The air felt good and he was glad to be free. The worst part was that his mother made him think about Peggy. He was sure she wouldn't want to see him, and it still hurt. Especially when he was sober. Alcohol numbed that feeling. That's what he needed…a drink.

Mitch headed into town. Where could he get a drink? His fake id was pretty good, but so many people in town knew him. That was something else that was bad about a small town. He had to be careful.

"Yes," he said, with excitement. "I know where."

He headed west, across the railroad tracks to a seedy part of town. He had not been here before. It wasn't a particularly safe place, but they had bars almost wall to wall. He had to be able to find a drink down here.

He passed up the first bar but went into the next one. It was dark and musty and everyone looked as if they had been there for years.

Mitch pulled his jacket close around his neck and went to the far end of the bar. The bartender looked tired and disinterested. He put a small wrinkled napkin in front of Mitch and said, "What'll you have?"

Mitch thought. A beer would be easy, but he needed something stronger. He finally ordered a boilermaker. That was a drink that seemed to fit the setting.

The bartender walked away, not even questioning him about his id.

When he returned with the drinks, Mitch thanked him and asked him to start a tab. For the first time, the bartender appeared to look a little closer at Mitch, but he finally nodded and went off toward the other end of the bar.

Mitch took a deep breath. It had been much easier than he had thought it would be. He grabbed the whiskey and gulped it down. It was hot and strong as it went down, but it felt great. He quickly followed it with the beer chaser and felt even better. A wry smile crossed his face. This was the way it should be.

He put the glass down on the bar and, when the bartender turned his way, he signaled for another round. The bartender nodded and started to pour.

Mitch wasn't sure later how many 'rounds' he had consumed, but he knew he felt a lot better when he left the bar than when he had gotten there.

Feeling refreshed and braver, he decided he would go past Peggy's house. He started to walk, a little unsteady, but at least he knew where he was going.

When he got to Peggy's house, he stood across the street under a tree and just stared at the front of the house. He really didn't know what he had expected. Did he think she would just come out, see him, and run into his arms? Of course she wouldn't.

She was too good for him. She was a sorority girl…and he was a dorm rat. Ha! That's what she thought. He was a big man in the dorms. Everyone knew him and wanted to party with him. Maybe he was too good for Peggy. Yes, that was it. He was too good for her.

With that thought in mind, he turned away and started home. When he got there he was very careful not to wake anyone else. After all, they were small-town people. Late nights weren't their bag.

Mitch threw himself across his bed, not even bothering to undress. In no time, he was snoring loudly.

Chapter seven

So, Mitch thought, as he opened his eyes. That point had been the real beginning of his downward slide. See, the answer did lie in the past...with home...and with Peggy. He had finally turned everything around. Peggy, the goddess of his dreams, wasn't good enough for him. How had he ever convinced himself of that? He must have been really drunk.

Mitch turned his head and looked again at the dark landscape sliding past the bus window. Now that he had found the key, maybe he could see how he got to this point and find his way back. Was it possible?

Mitch remembered that the next morning had been really rough. He was really hung over and he didn't want his parents to know. He washed his face, almost drowning himself in the basin, hoping to clear his mind and get his brain working again. Finally he felt he looked good enough to meet the scrutiny of his family.

He ambled into the kitchen and went, as usual, to the cereal. His mother, who was washing dishes, smiled.

"Just the same as always, isn't it?" she said. "Nothing really changes, does it son?"

"No mom, it doesn't," Mitch replied, knowing he was lying.

He ate his cereal and put his dish in the sink.

"I think I'll go look up some of the guys," he said. "Don't worry about lunch. I'll get something downtown."

He left quickly, hoping his mother wouldn't say anything else. He hated lying to her. She was the one person he really hated hurting.

As he headed downtown, Mitch vowed to really try to see some of his old friends and to stay away from the bars. He just had to try to walk a straight line. Nothing good could come of these lies.

He wandered into the mall and was surprised when he found it crowded with holiday shoppers. He had forgotten. It was so busy, he had a sudden pang of remorse. He hadn't even thought about gifts for his family. He had gotten so caught up in his new life, he had neglected everything about his old life. He realized that his mother had already begun to decorate the house, and he hadn't even noticed.

Well, that was going to change. He decided it was time to start buying gifts. The first stop he made was at a counter filled with beautiful scarves. His mother would never spend money on something so impractical for herself, but he wanted her to have one; a really pretty one. Boy, a bad conscience could really affect your thinking. With the help of a very nice saleslady, he picked out a beautiful blue and white chiffon scarf and then, thinking he should be a little practical, he added a new pair of gloves. He had both of them wrapped and started off with his packages to find something for Carl. It was hard to think of anything for him. They had become so different, he wasn't sure Carl would like the same things he would like. Of course he could always use warm socks. It got very cold in the factory in the winter and the men always talked about their feet getting cold. So...socks it would be. He spent some time trying to decide on the right ones, finally deciding on three pair of thermal socks he could wear under his work shoes. As a special addition, he decided he would stop by the movie theater and buy Carl a gift certificate for two tickets so he could take his girl. Now, the hardest of them all. What would he get for his father? Mitch wandered through the men's wear department but didn't really see anything that he felt his father would like. Finally he decided to take a break and have some lunch. Maybe he would even run into some of his friends at the food court.

As he settled down with a burger and fries, he heard someone call his name. It was a soft, female voice and his heart leapt. Was it Peggy? As he turned, he tried not to show his disappointment as Janie approached him.

"Hi, Stranger," said Janie. "How does it feel to be a college man?"

"Great," said Mitch. "What are you doing, Janie? Still hanging around with Josh?"

"Sure am," said Janie, proudly extending her hand to show a sparkling engagement ring with a small diamond.

"Congratulations," said Mitch. "When is the big day?"

"Oh, not for another year," said Janie. "I am working in an insurance agency and Josh is working as a mechanic. We hope to save some money before we get married. We'd love to put a down payment on a house before then."

Mitch tried to look happy, but, in reality, it made him sad. Here was his best friend settling for this small town and a dull life, just like their fathers had endured. Mitch was so glad he was getting out. He would show them. He would make something of himself and then they would know that they had settled for too little.

While he was thinking this, he smiled and said, "Gee, that's great. I wish you all the best. Tell Josh 'Hi' for me. I had hoped to see him while I was home, but I am going back early so I may miss him."

"That's too bad," said Janie. "I know he'd love to see you, but I'll tell him I saw you. By the way, how is Peggy? I haven't seen her since she got home."

"Oh, she's great," said Mitch. "We're both really busy with school, though."

Mitch noticed that Janie gave him a strange look, but she quickly stood and told him she had to get back to work.

Mitch was glad she had left. He didn't want to answer any questions, especially about Peggy. No one would understand how much his life had changed; how much he had grown.

Deciding he did not want to run into any more old friends, Mitch quickly finished his lunch and went to look for a gift for his father.

After all his worry, Mitch found the perfect present for his father, and it was so easy. Why hadn't he thought of it earlier?

As he left the food court, heading for the exit door, he came across a hardware store. Great. His father loved tools. Now if he could find just the right one. What would he need? What would he want? And then he thought of it. Not only did his father like tools, he loved the chance to have an outing, and there was no place he would rather spend an afternoon than browsing in a hardware store. He approached a salesman and asked if he had any suggestions on how he could present this to his father. The guy was fabulous. He helped Mitch pick out a leather key holder and inside the box they placed a gift certificate. After it was wrapped, Mitch left the store feeling very good. He had to admit that after the afternoon of shopping, he felt less guilt about the way he had been feeling about his family.

Since he hoped to avoid any more encounters, Mitch took the closest exit from the mall and headed toward home. The good feelings he had experienced at the mall quickly vanished as he walked along the streets and looked around at what he feared was a trap he could easily fall into. Mitch couldn't ever think about returning here to live…not since he had tasted life away from here. Yet, in the back of his mind, he wondered if he was strong enough to resist the easy rut.

Mitch shuddered and pulled his jacket closer around his

body. It wasn't really cold, but he had a sudden chill as he continued along.

Looking up, he realized he was on the street where Peggy lived. Why had he come this way? What if she saw him? Quickly, he turned and took a side street, leading away from Peggy. Was it also leading him away from the life he wanted?

No, Mitch thought. Remember, he was a big man at school, a world that was much removed from this town. He didn't need Peggy or anyone. He was going to make it big. Just wait and see.

With this new feeling of confidence filling him, Mitch walked a little faster, even smiling to himself. Looking around, he saw that he was again in the area of neighborhood bars.

Why not? thought Mitch. It was cold, he had finished his shopping, and he wanted a drink. Why should anyone care.

Entering another dark, depressing bar, he thought again about the differences between his life here and his life at school. Here he felt as if he was skulking around, hiding as he looked for a drink. At school, everyone came to him. It was fun, right, and exciting to drink with his buddies. Here, it seemed almost sinister.

Even so, he wasn't going to pass up a drink. He climbed up on a barstool, dropping his packages on an adjoining stool.

"What'll it be?" asked a surly looking bartender.

"Make it a whiskey, straight," replied Mitch looking into the bartender's face. "Hey, make it a double," said Mitch as the bartender started to turn away.

The bartender turned and started to pour the whiskey.

Mitch felt his mouth begin to water. He could almost feel himself shaking inside. He really wanted that drink. He knew, though, that he wasn't an alcoholic. He could take it or leave it. It was just that being home was driving him up the wall and he needed this to help him relax...even survive.

The bartender came back and set a glass filled with the inviting golden liquid in front of Mitch.

"Thanks, man," said Mitch.

"Sure," answered the bartender as he turned back toward a customer at the other end of the bar.

Mitch sat looking at the inviting, almost glowing liquid before him. He started to reach for it but found that his hand was shaking. He quickly pulled his hand back into his lap, grabbing it with his other hand, and glanced around to see if anyone else had noticed.

No one seemed to be paying any attention and Mitch tried again to reach for the whiskey. This time, his hand was steady and he pulled the glass to his lips, tilting his head back and letting the liquid flow quickly down his throat.

As he set the empty glass on the bar, he felt a warm feeling flow through his body. That was good. Maybe just one more.

Mitch signaled the bartender who brought him a second double. This time, he had no problems with shaking hands and drank this one as quickly as he had the first.

Now he was feeling great. He could probably even face his family...if he had to.

Mitch left some money on the bar, picked up his packages, and headed out the door, nodding to the bartender as he passed him.

Out on the street, Mitch realized it was getting dark, and colder. He decided it was time to get on home. Besides, he had to work on a way to get away and back to school. By the time he reached home, he had decided what to tell his folks.

That evening, he made every pretense of making a telephone call to someone at school. When he hung up, he turned to his parents with a somewhat pained look on his face.

"What is it son?" asked his father.

"Nothing really," said Mitch. "I just found out that the guy covering my job while I was here had to leave. If I go back, I can earn some extra money before school starts."

Seeing the hurt look on his mother's face, Mitch said, "Look, I can just tell them to get someone else, but the money would be really good."

"Of course you have to go," said his dad. "We understand. I'm just sorry you even have to work. I wish I could just give you the money."

Taken back, Mitch almost blurted out that it was all just a lie and that he really didn't need to go back early. The old guilts were coming back...but the desire to get away was even stronger than the guilt, so he said, "Thanks, Dad, Mom. I'll try to get back soon for another visit."

Heading for his room before he lost his nerve, Mitch quickly threw his clothes back into his bag, ran a comb through his hair, grabbed his jacket, and headed for the front door. He sure could use a drink right now.

Stopping in the living room he handed his mother the bag containing the gifts he had purchased. "Here, Mom; pass these out on Christmas. I'll try to call that day."

Hurriedly, he looked away as he saw tears coming into his mother's eyes. He didn't want to hurt her and he hated lying to her, but if he stayed, it would probably be worse. He just couldn't hang on any longer.

He gave his mother a quick hug. He felt her sobs. He hurried to the door, turning to take a last quick look, then hurried out into the night air. Now all he had to do was decide how he was going to get back to campus. When he originally left for school, he had ridden with Peggy. A dorm mate had dropped him off at the start of vacation. But now, he had two choices...the bus or hitchhiking. Well, he hated the bus, so he'd better get started looking for a ride.

Chapter eight

This memory caused Mitch to smile. Imagine, he hated the bus, and now he was traveling half-way across the country on a bus. Things really had changed.

Hitchhiking that night had been a little frightening. He had walked out to the highway, hoping to catch a ride. Traffic was fairly light and it was getting even colder. In fact, it felt like it might even snow. Boy, that was all he needed.

He kept walking, turning to face every approaching vehicle, but by walking he kept himself warmer. After about a mile of walking, he thought his feet were becoming blocks of ice. It was just then that he saw a truck stop in the distance. Hurrying, he reached the lights of the parking lot and then went into the diner. It was bright and cheery, filled with music and Christmas decorations and a lot of happy chatter. Several truckers were sitting on the stools at the counter or in booths along the wall. A friendly, bubbly waitress was taking orders, pouring coffee, and carrying on lively conversations with all of them.

As he entered, it got quiet and everyone turned toward him.

Grinning, he said, "Gettin' cold out there. Going to be a long night, I think."

This was greeted with smiles and polite responses.

"How about some hot coffee?" asked the waitress.

"Sounds good," said Mitch, heading for the nearest stool.

The waitress set a cup of steaming coffee on the counter in front of him and, looking down the counter, he asked the trucker next to him for the sugar.

Pushing the sugar toward him, the trucker asked, "Where are you going?"

"Back to school," replied Mitch. "I was hoping to find a ride, but traffic is fairly light tonight."

"Sure is," replied the trucker. "Everyone is trying to beat the weather and make it home for the holidays. I'm going east if you'd like to ride along."

"Fantastic," said Mitch. "I'd really appreciate it."

"Just finish your coffee," said the trucker. "Then we'll leave."

As he climbed into the warm cab of the big rig, Mitch thought he had been lucky to find a ride. It looked more and more like snow.

Neither of them talked much during the ride, each seeming to be lost in his own thoughts. Just before reaching his destination, Mitch turned to the trucker and asked, "Are you heading home for Christmas?"

"You bet," said the trucker. "I can't wait to see my family. I have three little girls and we always love this time of year. How about you?"

"Oh, I just came from home," said Mitch. "I'm heading back to campus early."

"Oh, a serious student," said the trucker, grinning at Mitch.

Mitch smiled and nodded. No need to tell him the truth. After all, it was a little embarrassing.

As they came to the edge of town, the trucker asked, "Where should I drop you?"

"You can drop me at the next exit," said Mitch. "It is just a short walk to the campus from there."

When they reached the exit, the trucker pulled over and Mitch grabbed his gear, opened the door and climbed out. It had just started to snow. He would have to hurry to the dorm. "Thanks, man. Merry Christmas."

"Same to you. Keep warm," he said, and then he pulled away.

Mitch watched as the taillights disappeared into the snowy night. Glancing at his watch, he noticed it was almost two o'clock in the morning...already Christmas Eve.

As he approached the dorm, he found the going harder and harder. The snow was really coming down now and if it kept up much longer, the roads would be impassable by dawn. He hoped he could get into the dorm. He didn't know what he would do if he was locked out.

Luck was with him; the front door of the dorm was unlocked. As he let himself in, he was struck by the quietness around him. Even in the middle of the night there was usually lots of noise. Of course, most of the students were gone. Jim was with his family. Mitch thought wistfully of his own home but quickly got over that and headed for his room.

The hallways were dimly lit and he found himself feeling his way tentatively along the wall. Finally reaching his door, he put the key into the lock and really felt like he was home.

The room he entered felt good. Putting on the lights, he threw his gear on Jim's bed and headed into the bathroom. He felt as if he was really grimy. A hot shower would feel good and then a good night's sleep.

As Mitch stood in the hot, steamy shower and let the stinging streams of water bounce off his skin, he felt as if he could stay there for a long time. Soon, however, he turned off the faucet and grabbed a towel, toweling his body and hair as dry as possible.

Tying a dry towel around his waist, he went into the warm, welcoming dorm room, crawled into bed and turned out the light. Just before he nodded off he thought how funny it was that he didn't even think he needed a drink tonight. No pressure. He felt good.

Light entering the window woke him the next morning. He moaned, stretched and looked at the alarm clock. It was almost eleven o'clock and yet it didn't look very light outside. Mitch slowly set up then pushed himself up off the bed, letting his towel drop to the floor, and walked, naked, to the window.

No wonder it looked dark. It had snowed all night and snow was really piled up on the street and even on the window sill. Mitch pushed the window open, knocking the snow off the sill and leaned out.

"Brr. It was cold out there. Shutting the window, Mitch walked across the room and opened the door to the hall. Sticking his head out, he looked up and down the hall, but didn't see a soul. He closed the door, crawled back into his bed, and pulled the covers over his head. It didn't take him long to fall asleep again.

The next time he woke, it was almost one o'clock. Now he felt much better and even a little hungry. He got up, walked into the bathroom and looked at his image in the mirror.

He looked pretty good, but he could use a shave.

After shaving, Mitch put on a pair of jeans, a heavy sweatshirt and boots; then grabbing his jacket and gloves, he headed downstairs, meaning to search for some food.

When he got to the main floor, he ran into the dorm monitor.

"Hey, Nelson. When did you get back?"

"Late last night," said Mitch. "Thought I could get a good start on next term."

As he said this he felt a little pang. That wasn't the reason for his being here. Why couldn't he tell anyone? He wasn't ashamed of his life style. He liked to party. It wasn't anything to be ashamed of...was it?

Mitch headed outside and found that at least the paths had

been cleared so he could get out to the street and head for a restaurant nearby.

He entered the first bar and grill he came to and sat down in a booth near the back. When the waitress approached, he asked her for a whiskey, double. She looked at him a little strangely, but then went to get his order. When she returned, she asked him if he had any id.

"Of course," said Mitch, producing his nicely faked driver's license.

"Thanks," she said as she set the whiskey in front of him. "Can I get you anything else?"

Mitch thought a minute and then said, "Bring me a cheeseburger, make it two, and another whiskey."

Again, he thought she gave him a strange look, but he ignored it. After all, he was the customer, and the customer is always right.

As Mitch sat slumped in the booth sipping his whiskey, he suddenly felt terribly alone and almost scared. What was he going to do now that he was back on campus? He wondered if any of his party friends were around. Well, if not, he would find some new ones. And then, after Christmas, he would go over to the administration building and try to find out about his grades. After all, he needed to know where he stood before he decided on the classes for next term.

When the waitress reappeared, carrying his cheeseburgers and whiskey, he gave her a smile. After all, she was kind of pretty. She smiled back and after putting his food down she asked if he needed anything else.

"You can bring me another whiskey when you get time," he said. This time, he didn't even look to see if she reacted. He just picked up the whiskey, took a gulp, and then dove into the cheeseburgers. He was surprised at how hungry he was, but it had been a long time since he had eaten. He gulped the burgers down and glanced at his empty whiskey glass. Just then, the waitress returned with another whiskey.

He looked around the bar and saw that there weren't many customers.

"Kind of quiet today, isn't it?" asked Mitch.

"A little. Most of the campus is empty now," she answered.

Again he smiled and she smiled back. Now that he took a good look, she was really quite pretty in a dowdy sort of way.

"What about you?" he asked. "Do you live here or are you going to school?"

"No, I'm not in school but I just moved here a few months ago," she said. "I thought it would be nice to live in a college town."

"Can you sit a minute?" asked Mitch.

She looked around at the empty room, nodded, and slid into the booth opposite him.

"My name's Mitch," he said. "What's yours?"

Smiling shyly, she replied, "Cindy."

"Where you from Cindy?" he asked.

"A little farming community in the northern part of the state," she said. "I couldn't wait to get out."

"Boy, do I know what you mean," he said. "I couldn't wait to leave home either. Life is sure better now."

Suddenly, he wondered if he really meant that, or was he just trying to convince himself. Why was he so confused? Regardless, he turned back to Cindy.

"Are you staying here over the holidays?" he asked.

"Yep, couldn't get much time off and it was too expensive to go home for such a short time. I have tonight and tomorrow off, then it is back to work until New Year's Eve," said Cindy.

"Do you have any plans for tonight and tomorrow?" Mitch asked.

"No, not really," she replied.

"How about going out with me tonight? asked Mitch. We could go out and eat and then take in a movie, or if you didn't mind, we could go back to my dorm room and watch television.

"That sounds great," said Cindy. "I was feeling a little sad about being alone."

"Great," said Mitch. "Would seven thirty be okay?" Cindy nodded, and he noticed she had a beautiful smile on her face. He really had made her happy. That made him feel so much better.

"Where do I pick you up?" Mitch asked.

"I'll write my address down," said Cindy. "It isn't far, since I have to walk to work all the time."

"Good," said Mitch. "I don't have a car, so wear your boots."

"I will," said Cindy, laughing as she handed Mitch a piece of paper with her address and telephone number written on it. "I'd better get back to work. See you tonight."

With a small wave, she was gone. Mitch set back and smiled. It wasn't going to be such a lonely holiday after all.

Mitch looked at the check, dropped some money on the table, and, sticking Cindy's address in his shirt pocket, headed outside. He waved to Cindy as he left and she smiled at him.

Outside, it was still cold, but the snow seemed to have stopped. Mitch certainly had more of a bounce in his step as he walked back to his dorm. He was thinking about getting in some liquor. After all, this could be a great night. Cindy looked very interesting.

Passing the dorm, Mitch went to a corner liquor store that they always used for their stash. He knew the clerk that was on duty and they exchanged greetings and holiday wishes when he entered the store. He picked up several bottles of booze...vodka, gin, whiskey...and some beer and put them on the counter. The clerk obviously knew the boys had fake ids, but he never hesitated to sell them anything they wanted. He had even been known to have a little weed to sell on the side. As an afterthought, Mitch asked him if he had any of his 'private stock' on hand. The clerk grinned and reached below the counter. He brought out a small cellophane bag of finely crumbled weed. It looked real good. Mitch handed him some extra money and stuck the bag in his jacket pocket. After all, they might have a real party tonight.

When he got back to the dorm, he passed very few doors that appeared to have people behind them. Most of the rooms were empty and quiet. He went to his own room and took a good look around. Maybe he'd better clean it up a bit. He hoped he was going to have company tonight.

He picked up the clothes thrown around the room, straightened the furniture, made the bed and then tackled the bathroom. After scrubbing the sink and putting out clean towels, Mitch took another look around. It looked great for company. Now, one last touch.

He pulled the small couch around so that it faced the television and put a small watt light bulb in the lamp nearby. Then he put a romantic CD on the player. Next, he set the liquor up on the small refrigerator in the corner and checked to make sure they had ice cubes. The ice bucket was with the liquor and he would fill it when they got home.

After he finished setting the scene, he laid down on the bed to rest before getting ready to pick up Cindy. Funny how much better things looked since he had met her. He didn't need Peggy. There were plenty of girls around and most of them were glad to spend time with him. As he lay there, feeling good about the prospects of the evening, he drifted off to sleep.

Suddenly, Mitch was startled out of his sleep. It was darker in the room and he sat up and looked at the clock. It was almost six o'clock. He had better get to his shower because he would need about twenty minutes to walk to Cindy's apartment.

Mitch found himself singing in the shower. He hadn't done that for some time. Life was beginning to feel good again.

Mitch dressed carefully. After all, his mother always told him to have respect for women. He tried to do this, but he

knew that his mother wouldn't think he always had respect...
especially when he didn't even know their names. Quickly, he
put that thought out of his mind. Nothing was going to spoil
this evening.

Mitch put on his jacket, locked the door behind him, and
headed for Cindy's apartment, located just two blocks from the
campus. Yes...life was good.

Chapter nine

Again Mitch felt the bus come to a stop. This time they were having a break. He unfolded his lanky frame and headed for the door. His legs felt cramped and he could use some fresh air.

Instead of heading inside with the others, Mitch decided to take a walk. He walked quickly, breathing deeply, so that the fresh, clean air seemed to fill his lungs. After about three blocks, he crossed the street and turned back toward the terminal. Nobody seemed to be awake. All the houses were dark. He looked at his watch under a streetlamp and saw that it was almost three in the morning. No wonder everybody was sleeping, especially in a small town.

When he got back to the terminal, he saw that everyone was still inside. He opened the door and went looking for the restroom. As he passed the counter, he noticed a pretty young waitress. She reminded him of Cindy.

Mitch asked her if she could get him a cup of coffee, black, to go; then he went to the men's room.

When he returned, he picked up his coffee and headed outside. The driver was just returning to the bus so everyone else started that way too. When they started to move again, Mitch looked at the cup of coffee in his hands. As he looked at it, his thoughts returned to that Christmas Eve almost seven years ago.

He had arrived at Cindy's apartment about ten minutes early. He decided to walk around the block so he wouldn't seem too anxious. In fact, he was surprised that he was so anxious and was looking forward to this evening with Cindy. Why?

He hoped it was because he really thought she was pretty, nice and would be fun to be with; but he was afraid he just wanted any girl around to make him feel like the big, important man again. That scared him. He had never been that way before. Remember how strong he was with Peggy? What had happened to that Mitch? He no longer existed. Now, he took what he wanted and never even thought about the effects on anyone else or even on himself.

Shutting that thought out, he knocked briskly on Cindy's door. When she answered, he almost turned and ran. She no longer looked frumpy to him. She had let her blond hair down and it framed her face like a cloud. Her skin was fair and clear and she wore little makeup, except for that accentuating her green eyes and light pink lipstick on luscious lips. Her figure was much better than he had thought. Her waitress uniform and the bulky sweater she had worn over it had hidden her well sculpted, voluptuous body that was now encased in a short, snugly fitting black skirt and a closely-fitted black sweater with silver flecks throughout. Around her neck she wore a silver medallion on a chain which left it resting just at the top of her cleavage. She smiled at him and her eyes were sparkling like emeralds.

"Come on in," she said. "Let me take your jacket."

"You look great," Mitch stammered. Why was he stammering? He had seen lots of beautiful girls before. But, she had, for some reason, surprised him.

"Would you like a drink?" asked Cindy. "I think I have some wine and a little whiskey my roommate's boyfriend left here."

"Oh, that's okay," said Mitch. "I'll wait until we go to dinner. Is your roommate here?"

"No, she left for the holidays," she replied. "She won't be back for about ten days."

"Won't you have a seat?" she asked.

Mitch followed her into a small, comfortable living room and took a seat on the sofa. Cindy sat in a chair just across from him and as she crossed her legs and her skirt slid further up her thighs, he again thought that her beauty had been hidden, including that lovely, enticing triangle which was now barely hidden by her skirt. She was gorgeous and desirable and he was beginning to wonder if he could keep his hands off her until after dinner. She sure wasn't just a 'fill-in,' she was the 'real thing.'

Mitch finally pulled his eyes away from Cindy who appeared to be slightly flushed by his attention, and looked around the room. There were Christmas decorations around the room and a small tree in the corner. He noticed there were two small presents under the tree. It almost looked sad...it was so bare.

"This is nice," said Mitch. "It makes my dorm room look pretty bleak."

Cindy laughed, a lilting laugh, and said, "Yes, but at least you are going to school. Look where I am."

Mitch noticed she looked a little sad when she said this so he hurriedly changed the subject.

"Do you have a preference for dinner?" he asked. "Any particular restaurant or kind of food?"

"Oh, you choose," she said. "I know it will be fine."

Mitch knew he was making a mental switch in his choice for dinner. This girl deserved a nice restaurant.

"Shall we go?" he asked.

"Just let me get my coat," she replied.

As she stood, her skirt slid down her creamy thighs and stopped about two inches above her knees. Mitch licked his lips and watched as she gracefully glided across the room.

She returned with her coat and his jacket. He took both of them from her, laying his jacket on the back of the sofa while he helped her into her coat. Then he picked up his jacket and put it on as they started toward the door. He took her arm as he opened the door and assisted her through the doorway. He pulled the door closed behind them and checked to see if the lock had caught. Then he smiled at her, took her arm and pulled it through his and they began their walk to the restaurant.

When they entered the warm, quiet atmosphere of the little, family-owned Italian restaurant, the smells of warm bread and pungent, spicy sauces almost overwhelmed them.

The wife of the owner came to meet them with a smile and holiday wishes. She took one look at them and escorted them to a small private table in the corner. The only source of light was candles on the table and there were Christmas carols playing softly on the stereo system.

Mitch helped Cindy with her coat and then took his seat across from her. He found it difficult to take his eyes off her. The candlelight was glinting in her eyes and it looked as if sparks were flying from them.

The waiter appeared and asked if they would like a cocktail before dinner. Mitch turned to Cindy who said she would like a glass of red wine. Mitch ordered a shot of whiskey and the waiter left to fill their orders.

They picked up the menus, and Mitch asked, "Do you know what you want?"

"Boy, it is hard to decide," said Cindy. "Everything looks delicious. Maybe I will just have a small house salad and their baked spaghetti."

"That sounds good to me too," said Mitch.

When the waiter returned with their drinks and a basket of hot bread, he asked if they needed more time.

"No," said Mitch. "I think we know what we want. We'll have two small house salads and two of your baked spaghettis."

"Wonderful," said the waiter. "Good choice."

When he had left, Mitch raised his glass and held it toward Cindy, saying, "How about a toast?"

"How nice," said Cindy.

"Here's to a new friendship and a wonderful Christmas for both of us," said Mitch.

"How lovely," said Cindy, clinking her wine glass against Mitch's glass, and sipping her wine.

Mitch took a swallow of his whiskey. It still felt good going down, but looking at Cindy felt good too.

They talked quietly while waiting for their meals. They talked about their families, how they had wanted to get away from home, and how they had dreams about big futures. The only difference seemed to be that Cindy was very close to her family and not really glad to be away from them, just from their life. He didn't tell her that he did not feel close to his family or that he might be just a little ashamed of them at times.

When their food came, they concentrated on eating, adding only small talk here and there.

When they had finished, the waiter approached, asking if they would like an after-dinner drink, coffee or dessert.

They declined, saying they were absolutely full and bragging on the delicious meal they had just eaten. Mitch was surprised to notice that he had not even finished his first drink. That was unusual for him.

After paying the bill, Mitch helped Cindy into her coat and, after donning his own, guided her toward the door.

"Good-night, and Merry Christmas," said the hostess.

"The same to you," Mitch and Cindy said, almost simultaneously. They laughed over this as they left the warm, cozy restaurant and went back into the cold night air.

Mitch put his arm around Cindy's shoulder, holding her close.

"Are you okay?" he asked. "Not too cold?"

"I'm fine," she said.

They walked quickly. It was too cold to stroll, although Mitch found he would have enjoyed doing that with Cindy.

Over dinner, they had agreed that it would be nice just to go back to his dorm room and watch television. They thought it would feel sad going to a movie on Christmas Eve.

As they approached the dorm, Mitch hoped that they would not run into anyone in the hall. He was sure nothing would be said, especially during the break, but he didn't want the hassle.

Luckily, the halls were empty.

Mitch opened the door to his room and held it open for Cindy and reached in and flipped on the light. He was glad he had straightened up the room. He wanted Cindy to be impressed.

"This is very nice," said Cindy, as she looked around and gave him one of her dazzling smiles.

"Let me take your coat," he said. As he helped her remove it, he again noticed her firm, pointed breasts thrusting out. He carried her coat and his jacket across to Jim's bed, laid them there, and returned to her.

"My roommate is gone for the holidays, too," he said. "We can use his bed as a coat rack."

"Come on, have a seat," Mitch said, directing Cindy to the sofa. He leaned over and switched on the soft light of the lamp next to the sofa.

"Would you like a drink?" he asked. "It'll warm you up after that walk."

"Sure," she replied. "What do you have?"

"Whiskey, gin, vodka, beer. What would you like?"

"I think I'll have a little gin with water over rocks, please," said Cindy. "Please make it light."

"Coming right up," said Mitch.

Hurriedly, he got glasses and ice and mixed her drink then poured himself a whiskey, tall. He quickly gulped down the whiskey and refilled the glass before returning to Cindy.

He handed Cindy her drink, shoving a coaster on the end table and set his own drink down.

"Do you know what you want to watch on TV?" he asked.

"No, let's just channel surf," she said.

Turning the set on, he handed Cindy the remote. "Find us something," he said.

Cindy began to channel surf while Mitch moved over and turned out the lights except for the lamp by the couch. Just then, Cindy came across the old movie, 'It's A Wonderful Life.'

"Oh, let's watch this," she said. "I know it is sort of sappy, but I love to watch it for Christmas."

Mitch laughed as he sat down beside her. Sliding his arm around her shoulders, he said, "That's fine with me. I agree. It really is a Christmas staple."

They both picked up their drinks and sipped them as they watched quietly, but Mitch knew his mind wasn't quiet. He had a difficult time watching the screen, wanting instead to look at Cindy. She was so gorgeous and he loved how it felt as she cuddled into the crook of his arm and the heat his hand felt as he gripped her shoulder. She was a very 'hot' woman...and he wanted her...badly. Her hand lay lightly on his thigh and he felt the heat spreading to his groin. He knew he was getting hard and hoped she wouldn't notice.

What surprised him was the fact that he also respected her. He did not want to hurt her or make her feel cheap. This was a change. No girl he had ever had in his dorm room had caused these feelings in him. But Cindy was different. He didn't know why, but she was.

He finished his drink and looked at hers. "Do you want another drink?" he asked. "At least let me freshen it for you."

He took both glasses to the bar and filled them again. He returned to the couch, put the drinks on the coasters and sat next to her, pulling her into the crook of his arm again.

When the movie stopped for a commercial, he felt her body stir slightly. For some reason, he took this as a signal and reached under her chin with his fingers, tilting her face up toward him, and kissed her firmly, passionately on that beautiful mouth. He felt her respond and found that their tongues were intermingling and that their bodies were turning to each other with what felt like electric shocks occurring between them.

Breaking away, he looked deeply into Cindy's eyes and saw desire and passion equal to what he felt she must be seeing in his own. He drew her to him again, seeking her luscious mouth with his tongue and running his hands down her warm, trembling body.

In that moment, everything else was forgotten, even his love for Peggy. The movie played on, but no one was watching. He again pulled away from her and began to kiss her all over her face. She moaned softly and arched her back. He slid his hand up her sides, pushing her sweater up around her neck. Cindy responded by holding her arms up and allowing him to slip it completely over her head. Dropping the sweater to the floor, Mitch buried his face into the cleavage showing above her bra. Her large breasts literally seemed to burst out of the top of her black, lacy bra. More moans followed and Cindy began to squirm in his arms. As he continued to push his face into her cleavage, he reached behind and unhooked her bra. It pulled away easily from her body and her firm, rounded breasts sprang forward. They were large for the rest of her frame but very firm and had no sag. The round areas surrounding the nipples were large, dark, and smooth and the nipples were large and inviting. As Mitch put his lips to them, he found they were hard and that when he sucked them, it caused more squirming and moaning in Cindy. Going from nipple to nipple, he kept her in an almost frantic state for several minutes. Then, as he pulled away to again look at her face, she threw herself against him, pulling at his shirt and forcing it off his shoulders. In her passion, she became stronger than he thought she could be and pushed him back onto the sofa and threw her body against him, grinding her breasts into his bare chest. This caused her to quiver and moan and he found, to his amazement, that it also caused him to shudder and feel an overwhelming desire to get even closer to this beautiful, passionate woman.

Knowing he could not wait any longer, Mitch sat up, picking Cindy up in his arms, and carried her to the bed. As he laid her down, she again began to squirm and moan. Her eyes were closed and she had such a strong look of desire on her face, she appeared to be in pain.

Quickly, he bent over and pushed her skirt down her legs and over her feet. Before it hit the floor, he was sliding her pantyhose and panties down her legs where they too dropped to the floor. While he was doing this, she was greedily unbuttoning his pants and pulling his zipper down. Then, with a sudden thrust, she pushed his pants and underwear down his legs. He quickly stepped out of them and stood over her, his quivering body aching for her but almost unable to move forward as he looked at her silky, desirable body there for the taking. His desire was certainly there for her to see.

For some reason, he hesitated. Sensing his hesitancy, she looked up at him with questioning eyes.

"What's wrong?" she asked. "Don't you want me?"

"Oh, God, I want you so much," he said.

And with that he mounted her beautiful body and she squirmed to adjust her position so that they seemed to blend as one. As he entered her, he felt tight pressure but moistness that welcomed him. He caught his breath. He thought he had had the best, but now he wasn't sure. This girl could send him to the heights of Heaven or the depths of Hell, probably both at once, with her body. Her body was the most beautiful, wonderful instrument he had ever had the privilege to try to play.

Suddenly, Cindy used her unexpected strength and flipped him over to his back; straddling him, she looked down in his face. Her blond hair still framed her face and made her so beautiful, so desirable, she took his breath away just by looking at him.

Continuing to straddle him, she began to rock back and forth, causing her large, beautiful breasts to come close to his face and then pull away. It was enough to drive him crazy. He felt his desire become so strong and hot that he felt like an erupting volcano. Still, she continued to rock back and forth, her eyes closed and her pointed red tongue pushing in and out of her mouth. She seemed to be so far away...and yet they were sharing a moment of unforgettable, indescribable joy and fulfillment.

Cindy began to moan, but her moans were only part of the sound. Mitch too was moaning loudly and bucking his hips up and down on the bed. With one sudden thrust, he again flipped Cindy on her back and remounted her. He thrust his body back and forth, entering deeply into Cindy who was thrusting her own body upward to meet him. The power of these meeting bodies was unimaginable. Now both of them were screaming out with the pain their bodies were feeling...and their need to erupt. With one solid downward thrust, meeting Cindy's body at the apex of its thrust, Mitch felt his body erupt, spewing forth all the hot liquid his body had been building up. Continuing to push hard against each other for several seconds and letting out one last scream of pleasure, they felt the result of their bodies eruptions flowing down between their bodies. With a suddenness that neither could have expected, they collapsed onto the bed, Mitch still on top of Cindy's beautiful body. After several deep breaths, he rolled over onto his side, still holding tightly to Cindy and pulling her body against him. In spite of this eruption and the exhaustion of his spent passion, Mitch still found Cindy's body to be the most beautiful, exciting thing he had ever held. He did not want to let go of her and continued to hold her tightly against him. However, with the exhaustion he was feeling in his body, he was afraid that he would not even have the strength in his arms to continue holding her. Finally she moved her face up to his, gave him a deep, loving kiss, and said, "thank you."

That surprised him. Even in his exhaustion, he had to know what she meant.

"What for?" he asked.

"For making me feel special and desirable, and not cheap," she replied. "You did not make it feel like a one night stand, even if that is what it turns out to be."

"But it won't," said Mitch. "Not unless that is what you choose. You are so wonderful that I never want to let you leave my arms."

Cindy laughed. "That would be a little impractical, but we will see. Now, why don't you take a nap. I think you are tired."

Again she gave him a light but passionate kiss, pushed his hair back from his forehead, and scooted down so that she was curled up in his arms and against his chest. He realized he had a big smile on his face as he closed his eyes, but that is all he remembered. He fell into a deep, contented sleep, and dreamed of beauty and love and total fulfillment.

Hours later, Mitch stirred. As he opened his eyes, he saw that it was very early; light was just starting to hit the window. He looked down at Cindy, quietly sleeping in his arms, breathing gently against his bare chest. She was so beautiful and desirable, he couldn't help but touch her. With his finger, he moved a tendril of blonde hair from her temple. Then, he reached down and kissed her lightly on her forehead. She stirred, but did not awaken. Deciding he was a little disappointed, he ran his finger gently down her arm and onto her silky side, ending on her firm buttocks, which he squeezed gently. This accomplished its purpose...Cindy opened her eyes and looked up at him. She smiled and he noticed there was love and desire shining in her eyes. He knew that she was seeing the same thing in his.

He leaned forward and kissed her firmly on her lips and felt her response, not only in her lips but in her lithe body which shuddered slightly and moved closer to him. That was the only signal he needed. He knew that his desire and lust were strong, even as strong as they had been last night. Cindy felt the lust and desire coursing through her own body and responded, pushing him onto his back and pulling her own body on top of his. As she lowered herself onto him she began to squirm, pressing her breasts with their hardened nipples into his chest and beginning to rock gently back and forth. Again Mitch felt as if he was going to explode. He never imagined he would feel so much desire so shortly after the fulfillment he had experienced just a few hours earlier. Cindy was almost a witch when it came to lust and desire. She inspired these feeling in him so easily that he felt he had absolutely no control. He had never known anyone so forceful...nor so desirable...in his whole life.

Cindy's mouth covered his and her tongue probed deeply into his mouth. His body ached so badly that he wanted to scream. In some ways he wanted her to stop because the pain was so great, but he knew that if she stopped, he would want to die. Grabbing her by the waist, he pulled her even closer, if possible, to him and began to rock up and down, pulling her against him with every thrust. He heard her begin to moan quietly deep in her throat and she arched her body, pulling her head away from him. Again, he quickly thrust his body off the bed and pulled himself around, ending up on top of Cindy. She seemed not to even notice when he mounted her. She seemed to be in a world of her own, squirming and moaning, with her head, eyes closed, lolled back as her stiffened body arched and lurched against him. Suddenly, he too felt that nothing existed except the heat he felt in his groin and the extreme need to erupt. He rocked harder and faster, grinding himself into her. With a loud moan, he felt his body released of its' pent-up desire. Cindy too screamed and went limp in his arms. For some time, they laid just as they were, his body resting on hers, breathing deeply, eyes closed. As his breathing returned to normal, Mitch kissed Cindy softly on her lips and all over her face, and continued down her body to her beautiful breasts. Cindy sighed deeply as he took her nipple in his mouth and began to suck in hungrily. He rolled to his side, continuing to grasp her nipple with his teeth, and, while lying beside her he started to suck, first one and then the other breast. Cindy continued to moan softly, but she leaned forward, kissing him and stroking the back of his head.

Mitch could not even guess how long this continued, but when he finally drew back and looked into Cindy's face, he saw a glow of contentment. He pulled her face down to him and kissed her deeply. She responded, then slid again into his arms. It felt so good to hold her body next to his. He believed he could stay like this for the rest of his life.

Surprisingly, both Mitch and Cindy fell asleep again, holding each other tightly. When they awoke, the sun was shining brightly through the window. It must be late, Mitch thought. He looked into Cindy's face and he smiled.

"Merry Christmas," she said. "I'm sorry but the only gift I can give you, is me."

Mitch laughed.

"What more could anyone want," he said. "That is the most perfect and useful gift I ever received. You are the one that is getting short changed. I have nothing to offer but myself, and that is a gift of much lesser value than the one you have given me...one beyond price."

Cindy looked at him with tears in her eyes. "That is the most beautiful thing anyone ever said to me. You are so special. Thank you."

Mitch smiled, but for a brief second the picture of him and Peggy exchanging Christmas gifts crossed his mind. He shook it off, quickly.

Since the day seemed to be passing quickly, they decided they should get something to eat. After some discussion, they decided to order pizza to be delivered. Surely someplace was open on Christmas day.

After several calls, they found a place open that made deliveries and ordered an extra large pizza. Since it was going to be about forty-five minutes until delivery, they decided to take a shower…together.

As they soaped each other's bodies, lingering over some of the more exotic areas, Mitch thought that he had never had a more romantic experience, even with Peggy. Cindy certainly exuded sex but she also was filled with romance. Never before had sex been more than physical needs. He never knew what it was to really feel love and caring so deeply that he would do anything just to be near this beautiful, romantic, sexy woman. She was really a deep person with so much hidden below the surface.

Finally, after a long languid shower, filled with many caresses and kisses, they stepped out and began to dry each other. Cindy's hair was plastered in blonde ringlets around her face and neck. She stood in front of the mirror, completely nude, rubbing her hair with a towel which she finally wrapped around her head. Mitch just stood and watched her. He couldn't take his eyes off of her.

Mitch grabbed a pair of jeans slipped them over his nude body. Since Cindy had only the clothes she had worn last night, he gave her one of his shirts which she put on, buttoning the front and rolling up the sleeves. Mitch thought his shirt had never looked so good. As she buttoned the last button, she straightened up and the shirt hung almost to her knees. She looked like such a little girl, but that was a facade. Underneath was a sizzling, enticing woman that offered more than any man could deserve. And, at least for now, she was his. After all, she was his Christmas present. Mitch smiled to himself. If Peggy could only see him now.

Suddenly Mitch quit smiling. Why had he thought about Peggy? After all, she had wanted to leave him. And, remember, she wasn't good enough for him. She couldn't measure up to Cindy in any way. At least that is what Mitch told himself.

Shaking his head, he returned his thoughts to Cindy. She had removed the towel from her head and was looking so desirable, he had a hard time keeping his hands off of her. He could not believe that after the hours of love-making he could still feel so much desire in his body. She seemed to play his body like a fine instrument, bringing more out of it than he had ever thought it contained.

"How about a drink?" Mitch asked, mostly to break the mood and curb his desire, at least for a little while.

"Sure," she replied. "Another gin and water would be good. Can I help you?"

"No, just relax," said Mitch. "Why don't you see what is on television. Or you could pick out a CD or a video.

While Mitch fixed the drinks, Cindy looked through the CDs. Finally, she put one on the player and turned it on. He couldn't believe it. She had chosen a romantic Beatles album, his favorite. He didn't think anyone else his age would have chosen that album. Mitch shook his head. She just kept getting better and better, and he had almost failed to even ask her out.

Just then there was a knock at the door. Mitch left the drinks and went to open it. Their pizza had arrived.

He paid the man, giving him an extra big tip, wished him a Merry Christmas, then turned back with the hot pizza.

Cindy took the pizza and put it on the coffee table. Mitch picked up the drinks and napkins and joined her on the couch. For some time they were quiet; eating their pizza, sipping their drinks, and drinking in the romantic music coming from the CD player.

Cindy had a far away look in her eyes. She seemed a little sad and this concerned Mitch. If she was getting tired of him, he didn't know what he would do. No man would want to lose such a jewel.

"What's the matter, baby?" Mitch asked. He had called her that to test her reaction. He held his breath to see how she would respond.

"Nothing, really," said Cindy. "I guess I am just thinking

about my family. This is the first time I haven't been home for Christmas. Oh, I guess I am just feeling sorry for myself, but I shouldn't. I couldn't be happier than I am with you. Darling, you make everything seem so good."

Mitch would have burst his buttons if he had been wearing a shirt. She liked him, in fact, she might even love him; and he made her happy. Now he thought his heart was going to burst. This girl had a very strange affect on his body. Maybe she was touching his soul.

Mitch reached over, took her in his arms, and kissed her tenderly.

"I know it is hard on you," he said, "but I am so glad you are here with me. Would you like to call your family? Maybe that would help."

"Oh, could I?" asked Cindy, a happy look on her face.

"Of course," said Mitch. "Help yourself to the phone. Can I fix you another drink while you make the call?"

"Yes," said Cindy. "This is a day to celebrate, isn't it? Besides, I'm not driving." She laughed, and he was glad to see that she no longer looked sad.

While Mitch took his time fixing the drinks, hoping to give her some privacy. Cindy called her family. He could make out a word here and there and it seemed as if they were concerned that she was spending the day alone. He heard her say that they shouldn't worry because she was with a friend and really having a wonderful time. If they only knew, thought Mitch.

When she hung up, Cindy sat quietly for a few minutes. Mitch picked up the drinks and carried them over to her.

"Here," he said. "This will make you feel better." Clinking his glass against hers he said, "Here's to a great holiday and to many more happy days...and nights...together. And nothing ahead for us but blue skies and smooth sailing."

Cindy's smile told him that he had hit just the right note. As he thought about the toast, he was surprised. He remembered that just forty-eight hours ago he would never have thought about the future with such hope and anticipation. It was a new beginning for him, he just knew it.

Mitch and Cindy spent the rest of the day, cuddling together on the sofa while they listened to music and watched some television. It is possible neither of them could have told you what they heard or watched. It seemed as if they had eyes only for each other; and, of course, their hands were only used to enhance the feelings of the other. Since they had not turned on any lights, the room got dimmer and dimmer as the day passed, and it soon was so dark that they would not have been able to see anything if it had not been for the light coming from the television screen.

It wasn't long before they felt their desires begin to take hold again. Their hands and mouths began to carry more urgent messages and their bodies began again to writhe and squirm, pressing hard against each other. Again, the depth of his desire surprised Mitch. This beautiful woman could get more of a rise from him, in every way, than he had imagined was in him. Their mouths began to carry the urgency of the desire between them and their hands roamed all over each other. When their desire threatened to pull them away from the real world, Mitch lifted Cindy from the couch and carried her to the rumpled, unmade bed that had become their love nest. Laying her on her back, he quickly unbuttoned the shirt she was wearing and pulled it away from her quivering body. Then, he immediately dropped his jeans, leaving them where they fell, and returned to his own place of ecstasy, Cindy's body.

Later, Mitch again slept peacefully and soundly. He couldn't believe it, but the love making they experienced that night was even wilder and more satisfying than that of the first night. Yessir! Life was, again, beautiful.

Chapter ten

Mitch smiled to himself. Those days seemed so long ago, but remembering them now almost brought back the exciting and satisfying feelings of that time. He was right. Life, then, was beautiful. If only it had continued that way. Too bad he had been so immature…or maybe just stupid. As he continued thinking about the past, he began to see why his life had gone so wrong. The reason was…him.

The day after Christmas, Cindy was scheduled to work again. Her schedule called for her to work from eleven until five. Mitch hated to see her leave him; he wasn't even sure he could stand being without her. Maybe he should go with her and hang out at the bar and grill. After all, if he sipped slowly, he could make a whiskey last a long time. When he told Cindy about this plan, she laughed.

Hugging him, she said, "Mitch, darling; I love you so much. You make me feel so special, something I never felt before. But you don't need to go to work with me. Why don't you just go to my apartment with me while I get ready for work and then you can hang out there until I get off work." He thought about this and decided it wouldn't be too bad. At least he could spend a little more time with her before she went to work and he would be with her immediately afterward. In fact, maybe he could go over and walk her home.

After they had showered, another wonderful experience, at least to Mitch, they dressed, Cindy putting on the clothes she had worn to dinner on Christmas eve, and headed across campus to Cindy's apartment.

When they arrived, Cindy hurriedly changed into her waitress uniform and added a bulky sweater. She hurried so she could get to work on time. Mitch looked at her and couldn't believe she was the same beautiful, sexy woman he had spent the last two days with, enjoying her body to its fullest. It really was a wonder he had asked her out if she looked like this, but he was sure glad he had and that she had accepted.

Mitch grabbed his jacket and left the apartment with her. He intended to walk her to work so he could spend every possible minute with her. As he thought about it, he was glad she looked so plain in her uniform. Maybe the other guys would keep their hands off of her. He sure hoped so.

When they arrived at the bar, Mitch kissed her and she smiled as she went inside. She had given him a key to the apartment so he could go back there to hang out. However, since he was so close, he thought he might drop by the administration building to see about his grades and his classes for next term.

At the administration office, he gave them his name and student number and they looked up his record. He noticed a frown cross the face of the woman looking up the record. When she returned, she said that he should stop down the hall to talk to a counselor.

He decided to get that over with too and proceeded to the counselor's office. When they called him in, the counselor looked very stern.

"Young man," he said, "you are hanging on by your fingertips. Just look at these grades. All D's. That means you can enroll for next term, but you will be on probation. If your grades don't improve, I am afraid you won't be able to return for your sophomore year. Now, is there any way we can help you succeed?"

Mitch looked at the report he held in his hand. He knew that the reason he had done so poorly was because of his study habits and the lack of class attendance.

Finally, he looked up at the counselor. He really seemed concerned.

"No, sir," said Mitch. "I just have to spend more time studying this term. I know I can do it. Thanks."

With that, Mitch got up, shook the man's hand, and headed for the door. He took a deep breath. At least he had passed and he could stay this term. That was really important now that he had met Cindy. He would have to get his schedule set up so that he had time off when Cindy was off. He just had to see her, whenever possible. But, for her, he decided he would try, really try, to succeed.

Mitch walked slowly back to Cindy's apartment. He sprawled out on the couch, deep in thought. He was trying to form a plan in his mind. He would have to attend all his classes and study in between so that he could be with Cindy in the evening. That didn't leave much time for work. How would he get enough money to pay his dorm fees and take Cindy out? There had to be a way.

As he was thinking, Mitch reached into his pocket and felt the small, cellophane bag he had picked up at the liquor store on Christmas Eve. It was funny. He hadn't needed the weed to get a high the last two days. All he had needed was Cindy. Cindy. Just thinking of her made his body begin to ache and it was still over four hours until he could pick her up. Almost without thinking, Mitch rolled a cigarette of the fine grass. He lit it and laid back on the couch to inhale deeply and think about a plan. What could he do to earn money?

As the smoke flowed through his body and he began to relax, he started to form a plan. It was risky, but it was worth the risk just to be able to spend a lot of time with Cindy.

By the time he had finished the smoke, he had formed a perfect plan...at least it seemed so to him. He reached over and pulled the phone toward him. He also picked up the phone book and hurriedly found the number for the liquor store. With any luck, the right guy would be working.

Mitch was relieved when the clerk answered the phone to hear the voice he was hoping to hear.

"Hey, man; this is Mitch. Can you talk?" asked Mitch.

"Sure," said the clerk. "What's on your mind?"

"Well, I was hoping you could get me a job," said Mitch.

"You mean here?" asked the clerk.

"No way," said Mitch. "I mean with your supplier."

Mitch listened, hearing nothing. He hoped the clerk would at least listen to what he had to say.

"Look, man; I won't cut in on your deals. I won't even try to sell to anyone who ever bought from you. I just need a job with flexible hours where I can make some quick cash...and real money."

Again there was silence. Mitch waited. What would he say?

Finally, the clerk said, "Okay, Mitch. The Man was just asking me the other day if I knew anyone who might be interested in supplying. It seems as if his business is really growing...and more than just weed. I can't really chance anything stronger than weed out of here. Maybe you are just the one. At least I know you can keep your mouth shut. After all, you've been buyin' long enough.

Mitch let out a breath. He was so glad to hear what the clerk said.

"Great; I'm ready, anytime," said Mitch. "When can I meet him?"

"I'll call him today and try to set something up. Are you available the next few days?"

"Anytime," said Mitch. "Just let me know. I'll meet him anywhere at anytime. Thanks. I won't forget this."

As Mitch said this, he wondered if he meant it. It seemed as if his promises didn't mean anything any more.

"You bet you won't," said the clerk. "I'll call you tomorrow. Give me your number."

Mitch gave him Cindy's number. He hoped that is where he would be today, tomorrow, and...

Just in case, he gave his own number as a back up. But if luck was with him, that wouldn't be necessary.

Mitch hung up and lay back on the couch. He smiled. Now he thought he would be able to accomplish everything. He could concentrate on classes and studying and there would still be plenty of time for Cindy. But, he was sure the money would come rolling in, as soon as he got his customers set up. Yes, now he could smile.

And smile Mitch did. He lay out on Cindy's sofa and dreamed about their future. He was sure it was going to be wonderful. After all, what more could they ask to make it better. Cindy was the answer to every man's dream. He knew he could never do better. Funny, he had thought that once before...about Peggy. But Peggy was not right for him. There were too many differences. She would never have been good enough for him but Cindy was going to be. He really couldn't help but thank Peggy, though, because she started him on the right road. If she hadn't introduced him to the idea of college, he would never have met Cindy. Now, when he graduated with a degree in business, he could take care of Cindy, and she would meet every emotional need he would ever have. Just thinking about her body and the way she caressed him, caused him to want her again. That in itself was unbelievable. She had turned him into a sex maniac. He'd never had a sex drive like this in his life...and he still couldn't believe he contained such a drive. It took a real woman, Cindy, to bring the real him out. Because he loved her so much, it was wonderful. Life could never be any good without her. And he was going to make enough money to support her in a wonderful way. She was going to live like the princess she was, at least if he had anything to say about it. And that was going to start right now. No need to wait until he received his degree. Once he met The Man, he knew he would start making money. He refused to think how illegal this endeavor would be. After all, someone had to be the supplier. Why shouldn't he be the beneficiary. He didn't make people use...he just met their needs. After all, it was the old story of supply and demand. And he would supply.

Mitch looked at the clock. Still over two hours until Cindy got off work. Maybe he should get some carry-out food so she could relax when she got home. There was a deli not too far from the apartment and he decided he needed to walk anyway. He was very antsy just thinking about what was happening in his life.

Leaving the apartment, he walked swiftly along the icy sidewalks, getting to the deli without meeting anyone on the street. The town really was empty...but the most important person was here.

Inside, he looked over the salads, sandwiches, soups and entrees that were available. He was having a difficult time deciding. Actually, he was just so high he couldn't settle down to make such mundane decisions. He knew the weed was partially responsible, but mostly it was Cindy, and the future he envisioned them having together. Taking a deep breath, he told himself he would have to make a decision. He finally decided on some salads, a couple of entrees, and some snack foods, including chips and pretzels. He thought about getting some liquor but didn't know if his id would pass here. He decided to make a trip to the liquor store for the drinks.

After paying for his purchases, Mitch headed back to Cindy's apartment. He put the food away and headed out again. They just had to have something to drink. After all, they had a lot to celebrate...even if Cindy didn't know it yet.

Walking into the liquor store, he was glad to see his old contact was still on duty. They nodded to each other as the clerk finished waiting on another customer. While he was doing that, Mitch collected some bottles of booze, including gin and whiskey, and a six-pack of beer.

When he got to the counter, the clerk said, "How you doin'? I left a message for The Man. I should hear from him tonight or maybe tomorrow. I'll let you know as soon as I do."

"Thanks, man," said Mitch. "I really appreciate it. This is important to me." He reached into his wallet and pulled out the money for the liquor. After getting his change, he left, waving goodbye, as the clerk started to wait on a new customer.

Mitch walked with a light step all the way to Cindy's apartment. After all, things were really going good.

After he deposited the liquor and put the beer in the 'fridge, Mitch decided it was time to head to the grill to meet Cindy. He noticed his breath got a little quicker, just thinking about seeing her again. She had really cast a spell over him, and he loved it.

Mitch went into the grill, looking around to see if he could spot Cindy. He saw her at a table near the front window, serving a couple of guys who looked like jocks. He frowned a little as he saw them reach for her hand and one of them even tried to pat her on the butt. Just as he was going to go and stop it, he saw that she was quite capable of taking care of herself. She playfully slapped his hand, laughed at him, and moved away from the table.

As she turned back toward the kitchen, he caught her eye. She flashed him such a dazzling smile, he knew it went straight to his heart, and he felt the pain as if he was stabbed.

She passed close to him and said, "Hi; I'll be done soon. Just have a seat. Do you want a drink?"

"Sure," said Mitch, and she was gone.

Soon she returned carrying a tray of food in one hand and a shot of whiskey in the other. She set the whiskey in front of him, again giving him a fabulous smile, and went to deliver the food.

Mitch sipped his drink as he watched her move gracefully around the restaurant from table to table. He sipped his drink, thinking of her. Then suddenly, he felt a soft touch on his shoulder.

"Are you ready to go?" she asked.

"You bet," replied Mitch. As he got up, he leaned forward and gave her a light kiss. He wanted to grab her to him and give her a passionate kiss, but he didn't think this was the place for that. He would just have to wait until he got her home.

After helping her with her coat, he shrugged into his own jacket, and then held the door for Cindy to exit. When they got outside, he put his arm around her shoulder in a protective and proprietary way. After all, she was his woman and he didn't mind telling the world. In fact, he wanted to tell the world. If it wouldn't have embarrassed her, he would probably have shouted it from the rooftop. But, he tried to play it cool.

When they got to the apartment, Cindy asked what he wanted to do about dinner.

He was glad he had picked up food, for two reasons. One was that Cindy looked tired, and the second was that he wanted her all to himself as long as possible. Yes, he was selfish, but he didn't care…as long as she didn't mind.

"No need to worry," he said. "I did some shopping today. I think we have plenty of food and drinks, at least for a few days. Now if you just didn't have to work. Then we could stay here, together, all the time."

Mitch laughed, just so she would know he was kidding, but he really wasn't. He would have loved to spend every minute with her.

"You are terrific," she said. "I am a little tired, so I appreciate it. I think I will change into something more comfortable," she added with a mischievous grin.

She disappeared into the bedroom and Mitch dropped onto the couch. He picked up the remote and turned on the television. Maybe he could find out what was going on in the world.

Suddenly, Cindy reappeared. She was dressed in a filmy, sheer, pink gown that swirled around her feet. It had a deep vee neck and narrow shoulder straps. He couldn't believe his eyes. Her bare feet peeked out from the hem of the gown and he could tell she had absolutely nothing on underneath. He really couldn't see…it was just a feeling…but he knew it was true.

Cindy was looking at him in a way that seemed to ask what he thought. He knew she could tell what he thought if she just looked at his face.

Mitch reached out and drew her to him. She collapsed in his arms and he felt her body mold to his. This was the way he wanted to always feel. They were no longer two…they were one. He really had never imagined he could feel this way. What a treasure he had found…and in a little bar and grill, at that.

With his mouth intertwined with Cindy's, he slipped one arm around her back and one arm under her knees and lifted her onto his lap. They continued to kiss each other deeply… and Mitch had no idea how much time had passed. When he was with Cindy, time seemed to stand still.

Knowing his desire was growing and that he had to have this woman again, Mitch started to push the narrow straps off of her shoulders. Her shoulders were so smooth and soft. Every time he touched her, he was amazed at how she felt to his touch. It was unbelievable.

As the straps dropped down her arms, the gown dropped away from her breasts. Again, they took his breath away. He couldn't wait any longer. He had to feel them in his mouth. He laid her back on the sofa and buried his face in her breasts. Seeking the hard nipples with his mouth, he smothered her breasts with tiny licks from his tongue. Cindy's breath quickened and she entwined her fingers in his hair, pushing his face more firmly against her breasts. While he continued to search her breasts with his mouth, she began to undo the buttons of his shirt and work it off his shoulders and down his arms. With both of them naked to the waist, he could not contain himself any longer. He picked her up in his arms, kicking off his shoes, and carried her into the bedroom. This was the first time he had been in her bedroom and he quickly took in his surroundings. It was a feminine room with soft colors and lots of ruffles. It looked like her. He liked it.

He noticed that she had left a soft light on in the bedroom when she came to change her clothes. It looked warm and welcoming. He carried her to the queen-sized bed piled high with ruffled pillows and stuffed animals. Laying her on the bed, he pushed away some of the pillows and animals so that they had a cozy nest for their bodies. As he stood over her, looking down at this beautiful person, he quickly discarded his jeans and underwear and then, kneeling on the bed, he covered her with soft kisses from the top of her head down to her waist where her diaphanous gown still rested. As he reached this area, he continued to go down her body, pushing the gown in front of his mouth. He continued kissing her body, covering her flat stomach and continuing on down past the beautiful, passionate area he found supplied him with such joy, and on to her thighs, legs, and down to the tips of her toes.

With every kiss, her body shuddered slightly and he knew that the desire was building in her as it was in him. He couldn't wait to fulfill her needs, because in doing so, his own needs would be met. That was a wonderful and special part of their relationship...their needs were alike in every way.

Pulling her toward him by her ankles, he pushed his hard, pulsing penis against her and she threw her long, lovely legs up and around his body, entrapping him in this beautiful area of pleasure. Their bodies began to rock back and forth, meeting each other at the apex of their movements. They meshed so easily. It was as if their bodies were reading each other. Their movements were almost choreographed...in fact, some dancers didn't move so well together. This unforced, natural movement just increased their enjoyment and their satisfaction. They ended up, falling into each other's arms and sleeping curled up together. Nothing felt more natural.

When they awoke a couple of hours later, they realized they were hungry. They were so comfortable with each other, they walked, completely naked, into the kitchen where they picked out the food and drinks they wanted and then went to the sofa where they enjoyed their meal, and the sight of each other's firm, young bodies. They didn't even notice the television was still playing.

Chapter eleven

As Mitch continued to lounge on the bus, he remembered that the week between Christmas and New Year's Day seemed to fly by.

Mitch and Cindy spent every night entwined in each other's arms, fulfilling all the sexual fantasies either had ever had. While Cindy was at work, Mitch was working on his own employment plan.

He met with The Man and talked to him about the job he wanted him to do. It turned out that the need for drugs on and around the campus was increasing faster than he had been able to supply them. The clerk at the liquor store could handle all the marijuana, but he wasn't in a position to handle anything harder. That was what he really needed...a front man for the hard stuff. Mitch was delighted with the opportunity. All he could think about was the major money that he would be earning. He refused to think about how the stuff he was supplying could hurt and even destroy people. After all, it was their choice. Someone was going to get rich; it might as well be him.

He had received a good recommendation from the clerk so all he had to do was tell The Man yes, and he did so, immediately. The Man spent some time going over the process with him. He would receive his supply once a week, at a different location every time, and he would be notified about twenty-four hours prior to delivery. The Man would usually not be present, but his representatives were able to make decisions for him. Mitch was to collect the money and turn it over to the representative when he got his new supply. The next week, at delivery time, he would receive his pay in cash. He would receive fifteen percent of his total sales. If he wanted any of the supplies himself, he would receive a wholesale price for personal use.

All of this sounded great to Mitch. He was told that he would receive the names of several customers, but he was encouraged to cultivate new customers whenever possible. He was never to take a chance at exposing himself or his supplier to any authorities so The Man expected him to use his head. After all, he was a business student. You didn't do anything to cut down your profits.

After the meeting, Mitch was told to meet a representative the next morning, at eleven, at a bar on the far side of town. He would be sitting in a booth in the back, wearing a black leather jacket, and drinking a mug of beer. The representative would give Mitch his first supply and his first list of customers. It was up to Mitch to contact these customers and arrange for delivery. All of these were old, established customers, so they would pay him on delivery. If there were any new customers he thought he could cultivate, he was encouraged to give them their first hits for free, and then start supplying them with additional hits at a reduced price until he had them hooked. He was to keep a record of these supplies and he would not be expected to pay full price for them. None of this sounded too hard to Mitch. He could work his own hours and the money would be big. In fact, the more customers he could hook, the more money he would make. This sounded exciting to him. He never even gave serious thought to what he was thinking...that he was hoping to "hook" some new customers.

That night, Cindy spent the night at the dorm with Mitch. He seemed a little quiet and Cindy asked him what was worrying him. He told her not to worry, that he was just anxious because he was starting his new job the next day as a representative for a big company. When she had started to ask more questions, he had taken her into his arms and they were soon making passionate love, and all the questions were forgotten.

New Year's Eve was a special celebration for Cindy and Mitch. They went out that night to a dance at a local bar. It was noisy and crowded, but the music was good and he and Cindy danced the night away. At midnight, they sealed their love with a long, passionate kiss. This was going to be a good year.

By the time Cindy's roommate and Jim returned from their holiday break, Cindy and Mitch were a real item. They were inseparable and spent every night together, either at the dorm or the apartment. Both roommates soon accepted this arrangement since they saw that this appeared to be the 'real thing'. In fact, both of them noticed that Cindy and Mitch seemed to blossom with their relationship. They were both more focused and stable since they had met and Jim, particularly, noticed that Mitch was doing much better with his classes. Cindy, evidently, was a good influence.

And Mitch had money. He had a large contingent of customers and was developing more every day. He tried to keep his business away from the dorm, thinking that would be the easiest way to get caught. Even without looking for customers in the dorm, he had plenty of candidates. By the middle of January, Mitch was needing to get two deliveries a week. The money was rolling in and his bank accounts, spread out at different banks at the suggestion of The Man, showed healthy balances.

In order to meet all his deliveries, Mitch decided he needed a car. Buying it would be no problem, so he asked Jim to go with him to look for something. They found a flashy Red Pontiac firebird that Jim really liked. Mitch liked it too, but he thought it was too flashy for his purpose. He finally decided on a black, two-year-old Ford Thunderbird. It was classy and sporty, but not too flashy. It was perfect.

That night, he drove to the bar and grill to pick up Cindy. He had her close her eyes and then led her outside. When she opened them, she couldn't believe what she was seeing.

"It is beautiful," she said. "I'm so glad your job is going so well. This must make you feel so good."

"It does," said Mitch. "I finally am beginning to feel successful. This good job and lots of money on top of the most perfect girl in the world; what more could I want?"

She reached up and kissed him and he found himself clinging to her, right there on the sidewalk. When he realized where they were, he pulled away and helped her into the car.

"Let's go out and really celebrate tonight," said Mitch.

"Well, I need to change, but it sounds great. Just run me by the apartment."

"Why don't you pack a bag, including that sexy see-through gown you have, and let's check into a great hotel for the night."

Cindy smiled, shook her head as if she didn't know what to expect next, but said, "It sounds great."

And it was.

They went to the swankiest hotel in the city and check in as Mr. and Mrs. Nelson. Mitch was sure the desk clerk knew they weren't married, but he didn't say anything.

After they checked in, they decided just to order room service. After all, how better to celebrate their good fortune, and they really didn't need anyone but each other.

After Mitch placed their order for the fanciest food on the menu, he removed his jacket and tie and stretched out on the sofa. He unbuttoned the first button and looked around the suite. This was the way to live, and he never wanted to live any other way. Besides, this was just the right setting for him to show off Cindy to the world. She belonged here. And so did he...at least he wanted to believe he did.

Cindy returned from the bedroom, dressed in the gown he had grown to love. It was elegant but sexy; it made him want to devour her immediately. He was trying hard to learn patience and pacing himself with Cindy would be the best practice possible.

She smiled at him and twirled around so he could get a good look at her. It made his heart beat faster and he knew it would be very hard for him to be patient. Even as he tried to be patient, he felt heat begin to fill his body. She really mesmerized him.

"Can I fix you a drink?" she asked, going toward the full bar that was part of the suite.

"Sure," said Mitch. "You know what I want."

Cindy went to the bar and poured him a double whiskey and then poured a small gin and tonic over the rocks for herself. Picking them up, she literally glided toward the sofa.

Mitch started to sit up, but she hurriedly pushed him back onto the sofa.

"Don't move," she said. "Just relax."

She sat on the edge of the sofa and set the drinks on the coffee table.

"Mitch," she said, somewhat hesitantly. "Can you really afford this suite? I know you are making good money, but I hate to see you waste it on me."

Sitting up suddenly, Mitch grabbed her by her shoulders.

"You're hurting me," said Cindy, a pained look on her face.

Mitch put his arms around her holding her close. He buried his face in her neck and mumbled, "I am sorry. I never want to hurt you. Oh, Cindy; nothing I ever spend on you is wasted. It is only the fact that I have you that makes working worthwhile. Don't you see, you are my whole life."

Mitch found he was even crying. That really surprised him, but the very thought that he had hurt Cindy or that he could possibly lose her, was just unthinkable.

Cindy pulled back from him and raised his face up with her hands. She looked deeply into his eyes, and said, "Darling, I love you. I wasn't really complaining…I was just concerned. You know, you don't have to buy me. My love does not depend on what you can give me…only my Christmas gift…yourself.

Mitch pulled her close and hugged her so tightly he was afraid she would break. He felt so powerful with her by his side and so safe with her in his arms. With her, he would always be a success.

A knock at the door broke the spell of the moment and Mitch pushed himself off the sofa and went to the door. Cindy slipped into the bedroom, not willing to have a stranger see her in this special gown meant only for Mitch's eyes.

The waiter pushed a cart of food into the room. Mitch wasn't sure he had ever seen anything more elegant. The glasses were crystal; the tablecloth and napkins, linen; a bottle of very good champagne was in a silver bucket; and the table was set with fine china. There was one long-stemmed rose in a crystal bud vase gracing the table and two tall, white candles in silver candlesticks. Mitch signed his name to the tab, adding a generous tip, and closed the door after the waiter.

Stepping to the bedroom door, Mitch knocked softly.

"All clear," he said, returning to the table and picking up the champagne.

Cindy seemed again to float across the floor and Mitch suddenly felt very important. What feelings that woman could cause within him.

Popping the cork on the champagne, they laughed as it bubbled over, running down Mitch's hand to the floor. As Mitch poured the champagne into the crystal glasses, Cindy lit the candles and turned the room lights low. The romantic glow of the candles made everything perfect.

Mitch handed Cindy a glass of champagne and they clinked glasses.

"Here is to a life filled with nights like this," said Mitch.

"Oh, that sounds wonderful," said Cindy, "but I can't believe it is possible."

"Hey," said Mitch, "just have some faith in me."

"Oh, I do," said Cindy. "I have so much faith in you that you are my very life and breath. That is almost scary."

They sipped their champagne and then Mitch pulled a chair out for Cindy. As they seated themselves at the table, he looked across at her and thought his heart would burst with the love he felt. Much more than he had ever felt for Peggy. Whoa! Why did he even think of Peggy? What was wrong with him? He had an angel right here in this room. Why would he think about someone that rejected him…and she wasn't even good enough for him. He had to keep telling himself that.

These thoughts had caused Mitch to become a little quiet, so they ate in relative silence, appearing to be enjoying each other's company and the magnificent meal.

After they finished their meal, Mitch pushed the cart outside the door, but Cindy retrieved the candles and set them on a table near the sofa, choosing not to turn the lights up. Mitch sat on the sofa and Cindy curled up against him, his arm held tightly around her. Neither one spoke. They felt comfortable just to be together and felt no need to communicate with words. Mitch was thinking that he could stay right here, like this, for the rest of his life and be extremely happy. Cindy was thinking about the feelings of contentment and safety with Mitch holding her. She too felt that life could go on like this forever.

Because of their comfort, they dozed off just holding each other. When they awoke, it was really dark outside. Smiling, they blew out the candles and walked slowly into the bedroom. Their love-making that night was as intense as it had ever been, but not as frantic. They knew each other's bodies so well and they knew what each needed to feel fulfillment…and they desired to supply that.

When they awoke the next morning, they again made love. Mitch continued to be surprised at how often he could make love with Cindy and still feel so wonderful, excited and fulfilled. He had never believed that to be possible...but now he knew it was. No matter how often he made love to Cindy, it took only her touch to bring him back to the brink again.

Afterward, they took a shower together and dressed. After all, Cindy had to go to work, and he had classes. Life did go on.

Chapter twelve

Sitting alone on this half-empty bus, Mitch smiled and nodded to himself. Yes, that was where the end really began. From that point which seemed so perfect, he began to spiral downward at a frightening rate...and he lost everything that ever really meant anything. This part of the memories would be painful, but if he ever had a chance to pull it together, he had to face it, and there was no time like the present.

Mitch remembered that the second term had seemed to speed past. He was a completely different person. He missed no classes; kept up on all his studies; became a dependable friend to Jim, even if their time together did diminish; and was the most attentive lover he could be to Cindy. He loved seeing her smile and making her happy. To him, the best thing was just holding her and feeling her body against his. He knew that she had told her family about him, and that made him feel very important. He hadn't met any of them but that could come later. For now, he just needed to keep her happy. Of course, in his mind, one component of that was to have enough money to take care of her. He used Cindy as an excuse to continue dealing drugs and even expanding his list of customers...but that wasn't really the truth. The truth was, he liked to deal drugs. It made him important, at least to those he serviced. He held their future in his hands. Power was intoxicating. He had become the biggest supplier in the area in only a few short weeks and, before the end of the term, he had become the biggest supplier The Man had working anywhere, and he did cover a lot of territory. This made Mitch feel even more important. After all, now he was important to The Man. In fact, he had done so well, The Man was meeting with him more and more on a face-to-face basis. The Man liked Mitch's enthusiasm, his work ethnic, and his ruthlessness in turning his customers into die-hard users.

One day, near the end of the term, The Man asked Mitch to meet him for lunch at a very swanky man's club. This really impressed Mitch and he dressed carefully in his best slacks, sports coat, shirt and tie so that he would look as if he belonged. He even shined his shoes until he could see himself in them. When he looked in the mirror, he saw a very important, successful businessman, peering back.

Jim noticed the care he took in dressing and said, "Must be a really important date. With Cindy?"

"No," said Mitch, "but don't worry. No woman; just my boss."

"I'd really like to meet that boss sometime," said Jim. "Maybe he has a place in his business for me."

Mitch really didn't know what to say. He knew that Jim did not know what he did for a living. All he knew was that he was an area rep for a company and that he cultivated sales and made deliveries.

"Maybe sometime," said Mitch, quickly heading for the door. "I'll check it out and see if there are any openings. See you later."

With that, he shut the door and headed down the hall. He took a deep breath. That had been close. He wondered how Jim would react if he knew what he was doing. Jim wasn't squeaky clean but he had cleaned up his act this term. He was trying to get into shape for football in the fall and was really taking care of his body. The knowledge that Mitch was dealing drugs might really freak him out. He would have to be careful.

As he drove out of the parking lot, he completely forgot about Jim. In fact, he didn't even think of Cindy. All he could think of was The Man. He wondered what he wanted to see him about. It made him a little nervous.

Driving up to the exclusive club, Mitch felt very important. A valet came forward to take his car and Mitch flipped him the keys. Although his car was neither flashy nor new, it certainly fit anywhere he drove it. Pride was becoming a big part of Mitch.

A doorman opened the heavy wooden door for Mitch and upon entering, he found himself in a large, dimly lit hallway, elegantly furnished with highly polished antiques, and what he knew must be a real Oriental carpet. He hardly felt right walking on it, but he did. As he proceeded toward a large room straight ahead of him, he could hear the sounds of men's voices. They even sounded important.

Then he saw him, The Man. He was talking to a shorter, stockier man and they were in deep conversation. Not really knowing what to do, Mitch just stood near the entryway. A man dressed smartly in a tuxedo approached and asked if he could help him. He explained that he was waiting to speak to his friend who had invited him to lunch. He nodded toward The Man and the greeter just nodded and walked away.

Soon, The Man turned and saw him.

"Mitch, come on over here," he said. "I want you to meet a friend of mine."

Mitch walked over, extending his hand to The Man who shook it and said, "Mitch, the is Monsieur Roget; he is the head of an international banking consortium with which I have done a great deal of business. Monsieur, this is Mitch Nelson, one of my most trusted and productive employees."

Mitch mumbled something, he didn't really know what, as he shook the banker's hand. He was having trouble just taking in what The Man had said. He had actually said he was important…Mitch. He couldn't believe it, but he was very happy and excited.

"Will you excuse us, Monsieur; I think our table is ready."

"It was a pleasure meeting you sir," said Mitch, as he followed The Man to a table in the back corner of the room.

"Have a seat, Mitch," said The Man.

"Thank you, Sir," said Mitch, sitting in a chair opposite The Man.

"Look, I think you should call me Sam, or at least Mr. Watson. After all, we have been doing a lot of business together, and I hope there will be more in the future."

Mitch couldn't believe what he was hearing. He had never even heard his name before, and here he was asking Mitch to call him by his first name.

"Thank Sam," replied Mitch. "I have enjoyed our business arrangement and I too hope it continues."

"Well, I hope it doesn't," said Sam.

What? What was he saying? Had Mitch really heard what he thought he had heard? But before he had a chance to ask him, the waiter appeared, ready to take their orders. Mitch was so upset, he could hardly see the menu. He stammered something and it must have made sense because the waiter left with their orders.

Now what did Sam mean?

"What do you mean, Sam? I thought we had been doing well," said Mitch.

"Of course we have," said Sam. "All I meant was that I hope we can go further. Your talents are being wasted on this level. I'd like you to consider coming into my organization as my right-hand man. What do you think?

Mitch couldn't believe his ears. Right-hand man, to the big boss. Who could have ever dreamed this would happen. Now he knew he would never go back home. Those days were over.

"I'd love that," said Mitch, trying to sound relaxed although his heart was beating rapidly. This was almost as good as sex with Cindy...almost.

"Good, let's do a little preliminary planning now. Okay?" asked Sam.

Okay? It was perfect.

"Of course, Sir," replied Mitch.

"Sam, remember?" Sam reminded him.

"Oh, yes, Sam," said Mitch, with a smile.

Before the luncheon, which Mitch ate without even tasting, was over, Sam had arranged for him to meet with a new young supplier to turn over his customers and route. Then he told Mitch that he would be expected to meet with him at least once a week to help him keep his business affairs straight, his suppliers in line, and his supply of product moving smoothly. He would receive a salary of $2,000.00 a week to start with in this new position. Mitch couldn't believe it. He was sure to have a lot of extra time and maybe he could get Cindy to either quit her job or cut down on her hours. Then they could spend even more time together. In fact, maybe they should consider just getting married. If things continued to get better and better in his job, he would, no doubt, move up in the organization and a beautiful wife wouldn't hurt his cause.

When he left the club, shaking hands with Sam, he felt like he was floating. He couldn't wait to tell Cindy.

Driving directly to the bar, he went in, looking for Cindy. He saw her at a table on the far wall. She was laughing with two young guys seated at the table. He took a close look at her. She was even looking more beautiful here at work. Love seemed to be agreeing with her. Even so, the wonderful beauty she possessed never could get through that dowdy uniform. That was good, he thought. Then he might get really jealous when she joked with customers. It was hard enough now, but he knew she loved him, and only him. Jealousy had no place in their relationship.

As she turned, he waved at her, and took a seat in a booth. Before long she appeared, already holding a double whiskey for him.

"Hi," she said. "I didn't expect to see you."

"I couldn't wait 'til tonight. I've got the best news. I met with my boss at lunch and he promoted me. Now I am going to work in the organization as a junior executive. No more sales and deliveries. And, believe it or not, it will be shorter hours and better pay."

All of this came tumbling out so fast he wasn't sure she could understand it, but when he looked at her face, he knew she had understood every word.

"That is so great," she said. "I am so proud of you. I know you have earned this, and I know you will do a great job in the new position. You are terrific, Mitch."

Mitch smiled at her. She was so good for him. She accepted him as he was, but she encouraged him to reach his potential. That made them a perfect match.

"I'll wait 'til you get off," he said. "I can't wait to get you home. I can't think of any better way of celebrating than just showing you how much I love you."

Cindy blushed a little, reached down and kissed him lightly on the lips, and then hurried back to work. Mitch was again surprised that his body responded so quickly to her. He breathed deeply as he watched her walk away.

Mitch sat slumped in the booth, nursing his whiskey. He was so lucky. What more could any man want. A success in his job and a success in his relationship with a sexy, beautiful woman. He would show everyone. He wasn't a nobody; he wasn't even a Mr. Average.

Thinking of that old nickname made him think of Peggy. He really didn't want to think about her, but she kept slipping into his thoughts. He couldn't understand why.

After all, what could she possibly offer him that Cindy didn't offer him in spades. In fact, she couldn't hold a candle to Cindy, either in beauty or in her sexual prowess. But, then, why did he keep letting her creep into his thoughts? He had to stop. It wasn't fair to Cindy…and she was the best ever for him. Right then he promised himself that he would not let Peggy slip into his thoughts again. Ever.

When Cindy finished work, she joined him in the booth.

"Are you ready to go or did you want another drink?" she asked.

"No, let's get out of here," he said. "I can't wait to get you alone."

He hustled her out of the bar and to the car. When they were safely inside, he took her in his arms and kissed her so deeply he thought he would get lost and never resurface. The sexiness she exuded just overwhelmed him. Every time he thought he had reached the depths of her sexual appeal, he found another level that he had never touched. He felt like tonight he would find another one if this kiss meant anything.

"Where should we go?" asked Mitch, pulling his mouth away from her, reluctantly. "Either place is good for me. Just as long as we can be together."

"Let's go to the apartment," Cindy said. "My roommate won't be home tonight. She is out of town on an interview."

No question then. The apartment it was. Mitch drove there as quickly as he could. It is hard to drive when you are quivering with desire. He couldn't believe it. He and Cindy had been together just about every night for almost five months and he still wanted her as much as he ever had. It was almost unbelievable. In fact, Jim couldn't believe it either. He, too, didn't think any one could stay that fascinated and in need of any other person that long, but he knew that Mitch had. In fact, Jim had told him he was a little jealous because he had never found anyone that meant half as much to him. Thinking of this caused Mitch to smile.

As soon as they closed the door, Mitch grabbed Cindy and pulled her to him. He immediately began to cover her mouth with his, drinking in her sexuality. They struggled, still engulfed in each other's arms, to the sofa where they fell together, now intertwining their bodies together. They were completely lost in their desire for each other and all they could think about was fulfilling that desire. It was unimaginable that they still felt such strong desires, considering the many times they had fulfilled them, but they did. Each time seemed almost like the first time, except they knew each other's bodies so well by now they knew just what it took to provide complete fulfillment for the other. That they did...gladly.

Mitch remembered this night particularly. They made love three times before dawn and once again just before they got up to start their day. Each time was better than the time before and Mitch tucked this memory into the corner of his mind and of his heart. He really didn't know what made him try so hard to keep this memory, but he did. It was a good thing that he did. Time would show him that desire might last, but the willingness to give up the time to fulfill it, might not.

When Mitch returned to his dorm room after dropping Cindy at work, knowing he had a couple of hours before his first class, he found a note from Jim. Sam had called and wanted to talk to him as soon as possible. The number was scribbled at the bottom of the note.

Mitch hurriedly called the number and waited while it rang several times. Finally it was answered by a gruff-voiced man, definitely not Sam. Mitch asked for Sam, telling the man he was returning Sam's call. He gave his name and waited while he heard him walk away from the phone.

When Sam came to the phone he didn't seem upset. That made Mitch feel better.

"Hey, buddy," said Sam. "Do you have any time today?"

Thinking quickly, Mitch realized he could easily miss his class today.

"Sure," he replied. "What can I do for you?"

"Great," Sam said. "First, meet your replacement at noon

at the liquor store. You can take him around and show him the ropes. Give him your list and introduce him to any of your customers that you can. Then, I'd like to see you about four this afternoon. You can come by the office."

Mitch felt very excited. He had never even thought about there being an office and he really had never thought he would see it. Now he was going there as a 'big shot' employee. Sam gave him the address and he wrote it on the bottom of the note containing the phone number.

After he hung up, Mitch tried to decide what to wear. He didn't want to stand out too much as he was showing his replacement around. Maybe just slacks and a shirt. That should fit in anywhere. Maybe he'd better go by and tell Cindy he might not be there to pick her up after work. Oh, better yet, he would just call her.

Mitch showered, shaved and dressed as quickly as possible. Then, just before leaving he called Cindy. She was accepting of the news, but he could tell she was disappointed. Oh, well, she would understand later. After all, he was doing this for them. Their lives were going to be so much better because of this.

Mitch headed for the parking lot and, after retrieving his car, drove to the liquor store. The kid wasn't there yet, so Mitch loitered around, talking to the clerk. He found he was getting a little nervous and he thought he needed something to calm him down. He picked up a bottle of whiskey and paid the clerk for it. Deciding he needed to have a drink, he told the clerk he was going to wait in his car. He asked that he send the kid to him when he arrived. He checked the clock and saw that there were still ten minutes until he was due.

Mitch slipped into the car and quickly opened the whiskey. Taking one long drink, he immediately felt better as the warm liquid flowed through his body. Even so, he still felt nervous. After all, this was a big day for him and could mean a lot to his future. Unlocking the glove compartment, he pulled out a cellophane bag filled with pills and capsules of every imaginable shape and color. He sifted through them, looking for the ones he wanted. In spite of supplying so many of them to his customers, he had not made a habit of using many drugs himself. In fact, because of Cindy, the whiskey had been enough. But this was different. He picked out three different pills and returned the others to the glove compartment, locking it securely.

Mitch leaned back against the seat and felt his body relax. This was the combination he needed to pull off today. All at once he saw a face peering into the window. At first he was startled, but then he realized this must be the guy he was expecting.

Mitch motioned for him to open the door. He looked at this kid…and he really was just a pimply-faced kid. He didn't even look old enough to drive. How could he ever turn his customers over to him? Could he really trust him? Well, it really wasn't his decision. Sam had picked him, so he must be okay.

Opening the door, the young man asked, "Are you Mitch?"

"I am. Get in." said Mitch.

"My name is Walter; I'm sorry if I kept you waiting."

"No problem. You're right on time. We'd better get started. We have a lot of information to cover in a very short time."

Mitch decided they should drive to a nearby park where they could talk without being interrupted. Walter made small talk as Mitch drove. Mitch decided Walter was a little nervous… he remembered those days.

When they reached the park, Mitch parked his car in a secluded parking lot and turned off the engine. Then he turned to face Walter.

"How much did the boss tell you?" asked Mitch.

"Not too much," said Walter. "He told me that I would be taking over your customers and that you would tell me the procedures and also give me a list of users."

Mitch found himself wincing a little. He did not like to

think of them as users. They were, of course, but not using that word had made him feel less guilty about being a supplier.

Shaking off the feeling, Mitch decided to start at the beginning, just like they had with him. He told Walter about picking up the supplies, turning over the proceeds, and how he would get paid. He also explained the cut-rates for personal use drugs. Next, he set about telling him about the customers. He had a long list of those he currently serviced and decided to start with that.

Mitch patiently went over each name, giving Walter all the information he could about each of them…what they liked to use, how much they needed, how they liked to take delivery, and how they were at paying. Walter, to his credit, paid strict attention to all that Mitch was saying. He made notes as Mitch talked and seemed to be able, despite his youthful look, to understand and organize information easily. He never even asked Mitch to repeat anything. The final bit of information was the delivery locations and telephone numbers for the clients. Mitch would be contacting them all to let them know that Walter would be their new supplier. If any of them did not want to continue using a new supplier, he would notify Walter.

"Do you have any questions?" asked Mitch.

"Not really. You've been very thorough. One thing though, when and where do I get the delivery of my supplies?" asked Walter.

"You will be contacted about that, probably tomorrow," said Mitch. "My customers will not need any deliveries until the end of the week. That will give you a couple of days to get organized. I know you will do well. By the way, did I tell you about developing your own clients?"

"Not yet."

"Well, if you find any potential clients that you feel you can cultivate, you have some leeway with the supplies." Mitch then told Walter about free and cut rate drugs to use for this purpose. As he was saying this, he again felt a small pang of guilt. After all, he had literally hooked some of his friends and acquaintances. He didn't want to think about any bad results that might occur.

When Walter felt that he understood the process, Mitch drove him back to the liquor store. Thanking him, Walter walked away from Mitch's car, never looking back.

Mitch glanced at his watch. It was almost time for his meeting with Sam. He decided he should just go to the office. It wouldn't hurt to be a little early. In fact, Mitch wanted to get there early. He was very excited about what was about to happen in his life.

When he arrived at the office, he was surprised to find a guarded gate leading to the parking lot. He stopped next to the guard who asked his name. Mitch told him and he checked his list, then let Mitch proceed. He told him to park in the third row and go into the nearest door. Mitch was impressed.

When Mitch entered the office, he was again startled. He found himself in a beautiful lobby with plush carpet and comfortable chairs and couches lining the walls. There was a huge fish tank straight ahead filled with colorful tropical fish. Just in front of this tank, at a highly polished desk, sat a beautiful woman, neatly and professionally dressed, surrounded with telephones, computers and an intercom.

Mitch approached her and told her his name, stating that he was a little early for his appointment with Mr. Watson.

She checked her books then told him to take a seat. While he was lowering himself into a comfortable chair, he heard her use the intercom to notify Sam that he was here.

In a few minutes, a buzzer sounded, and the receptionist said, "You can go in now. Just go through that door and go to the third office on the right.

Mitch hurried down the hall, trying not to look too anxious. After all, he was going to be the right-hand man.

When he entered the office, Sam was seated behind a fabulous glass and brass desk. It was covered with papers, pens and folders. It also held three telephones and an intercom, just like the one on the receptionist's desk.

"Come on in," said Sam, getting up, coming around the desk and holding out his hand.

Mitch shook his hand and tried to find his voice.

"Sit down, sit down," said Sam. "Can I get you a drink, a cigar, a cigarette?"

"No, nothing right now," said Mitch as he settled himself into the nearest chair. He crossed his legs and tried to look business-like.

"Well, how do you like the set-up?" asked Sam.

"It's great," said Mitch. "Much larger than I had anticipated. I am really excited that you are willing to give me a chance to work here."

"It's my pleasure and my gain," said Sam. "You are going to be a great addition to our little family. Now, I'm sure you'd like to know what your duties and hours will be."

"Yes, Sir," said Mitch.

"I thought we were past that 'Sir' stuff," said Sam with a grin. "Okay, I will try to make it as clear as I can. You will be acting as my eyes and ears in a lot of meetings, many of which I will not be able to attend. You also will be my 'enforcer'... keeping people in line for me. Your other duties will be here in the office. We will set up a private office for you and you will work there whenever you are in town. I will want you to keep a close eye on our supplies. How much is coming in; how much is going out; and where I might be getting ripped off. You will be very important to me."

Enforcer? Is that what Sam had said? What did he mean by that? Mitch had never been a fighter. He always kidded people into doing things, never forced them. He hoped he could do this job.

"Sam, what would my duties as an enforcer be?" asked Mitch. "I don't know if that is something I would be good at."

"Oh, sure you will," said Sam. "I will expect you to use your brain most of the time. It there is ever any need for rough stuff, I will get someone to do what you want done. Don't worry. You will do fine."

"It sounds real good then," said Mitch, relaxing and smiling for the first time since he had entered the building. "Did you say something about my being out of town?"

"Oh, yes. There will be many out-of-town meetings in your future. You will use the company jet for most of these trips and we will furnish transportation for any others. I think you will enjoy the education all of this travel will give you."

"I'm sure I will learn a lot, Sam, but I am a little concerned about being out of town too often. What about my classes? If I don't finish well this term, I can't enroll again."

"Don't worry, kid," said Sam. "Your duties regarding out-of-town meetings won't begin until this term is over. Then, if things go as I hope, you may not even want to enroll for another term. Time will tell. Well, do you have any questions? Concerns?"

"No, not that I can think of right now. I will probably have lots of questions after I leave here. In fact, I think it will take me some time just to take all of this in. I hope you won't mind if I give you a call later, just in case I do think of something."

"That will be fine. Look. I have a meeting in a few minutes, but feel free to contact me at any time. By the way, you start work tomorrow. What time do you get out of class?"

"Tomorrow my classes end at two. Would that be okay?"

"That will be just fine, Mitch. Come in then and you can spend time setting up your office and getting used to us."

Sam again came around the desk and shook hands with Mitch. He walked with Mitch down the hall and into the lobby, making him feel really important. As Mitch left the building, he felt as if his face was going to break he was smiling so big. Things were really going well. Now maybe he and Cindy could think about getting married.

Cindy! Oh, gosh. He had to see her, to explain more fully why he couldn't meet her after work. He would go right now to her apartment. He knew she would understand, after he explained. After all, this job would mean just as much to her as it did to him...it would mean a lot to their future.

He drove as quickly as possible to Cindy's apartment. He was still on cloud nine...he couldn't believe his luck...but when he pulled up in front of Cindy's, he found that he was a little nervous. That was unusual...especially considering how he and Cindy felt about each other.

Bounding up the stairs, he knocked on the door. It took some minutes for her to answer, and this just seemed to add to his apprehension. When she did open the door, she wasn't smiling and he thought she looked as if she had been crying.

Reaching for her, he asked, "What's the matter, baby? Did someone hurt you?"

Moving away from his touch and seating herself on a chair in the living room, Cindy sniffed, then said, "Just you."

"What?" asked Mitch. "I hurt you? How?"

Sniffling some more, Cindy put her head down, wiping away tears with a tissue. "I guess I am being silly, but when you called at the last minute, I thought you had found someone else. I guess I just fell apart. I love you just too much."

Quickly approaching her and kneeling beside the chair, Mitch took her hands, pushing her chin up so she was looking at him.

"No way, baby," said Mitch. "I told you it was business. My boss, Sam, had left a message for me with Jim. I should have called you as soon as I knew but I had some things I just had to do. Can you forgive me? I love you, Cindy, and only you. I guess I just didn't think. Really, it was work."

Cindy looked deeply into his eyes and then he thought he saw the start of a smile. Smiling at her, he stood, pulled her up and put his arms around her. He wasn't sure how she would respond but he wanted nothing more than to kiss her...now.

And, he did. He was delighted to feel her respond to his kiss, searching with her tongue while she molded her body against his. But from now on he would be clearer, and more thoughtful. The idea of losing Cindy made his blood run cold, and he felt himself shiver.

Cindy pulled away. "What's the matter?" she asked. "Are you cold?"

"No way," said Mitch. "You just feel so good to me."

Leading her to the sofa, Mitch pulled her onto his lap and held her tightly. She snuggled against him, and it felt so right.

"Let me tell you about today," Mitch said. "It was a terrific day...for us. I really believe our future is set."

Cindy looked up with a puzzled look on her face. "What do you mean?" she asked.

"Well, I told you that Sam called me. He asked me to meet with him today. But first he had me meet with another guy and turn over my route and customers to him."

"You gave your route and customers away? Why? Didn't he think you were doing a good job? You seemed so happy and I thought you were doing a good job. Oh, darling, I am so sorry."

As she was saying this, Mitch noticed such a look of concern on her face. He couldn't imagine anyone caring this much about him, but she did.

"No, no, honey," he quickly responded. "He just had me give up my route so I could take a promotion. I am going to be a junior executive in the organization. I will even have my own office. And, the pay is great. I start at $2000.00 a week."

"$2000.00 a week?" Cindy was astounded.

"You bet," he said, "and I have no place to go but up. I know this is the answer for our future. Sam likes me...and the organization is so classy. My hours will be erratic, but most of the time, I will work even less than I have been. The only bad thing is that sometimes I will have to go out of town for meetings. I will be representing Sam at some meetings so

I may be away overnight sometimes. But it will be worth it, Honey. Please hang with me. It is our future."

"Oh, Mitch, of course I will," said Cindy. "Just remember you are on business trips; no other women," she said with a teasing grin.

"Only you," said Mitch. "You are the best and all that any man could want. Why would I look at anyone else?"

There it was again. Just as he said that, a picture of Peggy popped into his mind. Would he ever get her out of his life and memory? He had to. If Cindy ever knew, it would hurt her.

"No other women," he promised, solemnly. And he meant it. He really did. But a strange feeling came over him as the words left his mouth.

He felt like he wanted to change the subject. After all, he was feeling a little uncomfortable and he was afraid that as well as Cindy knew him, especially his emotions and feelings, she would begin to ask questions.

"What about some dinner?" he asked.

"Let's just eat here," said Cindy. "I have some eggs and could make an omelet. I really just want to be with you. I don't think I will ever forget how I felt when I thought I was losing you."

"You will never lose me, Baby. An omelet sounds great."

As Cindy went to wash her face and begin cooking, Mitch stretched out on the sofa. He was surprised at how tired he felt. He really was emotionally drained. He didn't know anyone could make you feel like this…taking away everything with just a few words. He never wanted to go through that again.

He meant to close his eyes for just a couple of minutes but when he awoke, he found Cindy standing over him and saw a tray with their food on the coffee table.

Startled, he sat up. "I'm sorry; I meant to help you. I guess I just fell asleep. Forgive me, Honey?"

"Nothing to forgive. I love you and am so glad that you can

relax once in a while. It is a comfortable feeling. But you'd better eat your dinner before it gets cold."

Mitch was surprised at how hungry he was and he gobbled down the omelet, along with four pieces of toast. Cindy was a good cook. Another talent he hadn't realized she possessed.

Cindy had been daintily eating her omelet and put her fork down with over half of it left on her plate.

"Aren't you hungry?" Mitch asked.

"Not really," she said. "Just having you back with me took my appetite away. Would you like the rest of mine?"

Mitch admitted he was still hungry and quickly finished her omelet too. When he was done, she gathered the dishes on the tray and took them to the kitchen. He crossed the room to the liquor cabinet and poured himself a large glass of whiskey. He could hear Cindy stacking the dishes in the kitchen.

"Hey, honey; would you like a drink?" he called.

Cindy came to the kitchen door, wiping her hands on a towel.

"Yes," she said. "You know what I like."

Mitch filled a glass with ice, gin and tonic…heavy on the gin. This wasn't really her request, but he thought she needed it tonight.

When Cindy came back into the room, for the first time, he noticed that she had changed from her uniform into a silky robe. Now, as he drew her to him, he felt the cool, sleek material slide under his hands and he knew she had nothing on under it. He had to admit it wasn't really any softer or smoother than Cindy's skin, and all of a sudden he felt his desire to feel that beautiful body pressed next to him grow, quickly.

Mitch pulled her close, planting kisses all over her face and ending on her mouth which he kissed deeply. In fact, he again lost himself in this beautiful, enticing woman…how could he ever survive without her? Life wouldn't be worth living. He really had convinced himself that he was working to be able to take care of her. He couldn't admit, even to himself, that he found working for the organization and dispensing illegal drugs made him feel good.

Pulling himself away from his thoughts, he untied the sash of Cindy's robe and let it fall away from her shoulders and down her back. She sat there, unaffected by the fact that her beautiful body was now completely exposed. He liked that about her too. She was in no way ashamed of her body, but she did limit its exposure...only to him.

His kisses covered her body and she began to squirm, wildly. He was so amazed, but extremely glad, that he could still awaken such wild desires in Cindy. He never felt this way around anyone else, and he knew she didn't either. Of course there was Peggy. No! He refused to let Peggy enter into this scene. She didn't belong here. In fact, she didn't belong in his life or his memory. With extreme will, he forced himself back to concentrating on Cindy. Oh, Cindy. What am I going to do, he thought? I want only you. Why can't I think only of you?

Cindy did not seem to notice that his mind had wandered. That was good. She would never understand. She was too faithful. Now concentrating only on Cindy, he found his own desires so strong, he had to act on them. He picked her up and carried her to the bed. There, they spent a wonderful night of love-making, forgetting everyone, thinking only of each other.

When they awoke the next morning, they found they were running late. They hurriedly showered and while Cindy headed for work, Mitch headed for class. He walked since it was so close, and the parking was limited. He enjoyed taking in the fresh late-spring air as he walked across the campus. He felt himself walking even taller and straighter than usual.

His classes that day seemed to crawl past. He had a difficult time concentrating, but he knew he must. He was going to pass this term.

It was just about the end of his last class and Mitch was thinking about how exciting it was going to be to have his own office when he suddenly remembered he had forgotten to tell Cindy that he would be working today so he probably would be late.

When the bell rang, he rushed to the nearest payphone. It was with great trepidation that he dialed the number. Would she ever believe him? Would she be understanding? Well, only time would tell.

When she came to the phone, he said, "Honey, I hope you won't get upset, and, please believe me. I forgot to tell you that I have to go to work this afternoon. I don't know what time I will get off. It may be late. I am so sorry. Do you believe me?"

Mitch heard a little giggle, then she said, "Of course I believe you. I admit we didn't take a lot of time to talk last night after we finally straightened out our relationship. I understand. Will you come by when you finish?"

"I don't know how late it will be. Don't wait up. I'll come by if I can. I will call you when I know for sure."

"Okay," said Cindy, and he thought he detected just a little disappointment in her voice.

After telling her again that he loved her, Mitch hung up the phone and walked rapidly to his car. He needed to go back to the dorm and change. After all, he didn't want to show up in the same clothes for the second day.

Going as fast as possible, he arrived at the dorm and sprinted up the stairs. When he arrived at the room, Jim was there watching television with a girl who looked way underage to Mitch.

"How's it going, Man?" asked Jim.

"Great," said Mitch, "but I'm late for work. Don't mind me."

Mitch glanced again at the girl and wondered if she was stoned or drunk. She didn't act as if she knew what was going on around her. Oh, well, that was Jim's business, not his.

He quickly changed into clean slacks and shirt and grabbed a new sport coat that he had been saving for a special occasion.

His wardrobe, at least, suited his new job. He had stocked up on clothes when the money started rolling in. No more juvenile clothes for him.

He headed for the door. "See you later," he yelled as he passed.

Back outside, Mitch thought about Jim. He really wasn't going anywhere fast. Just look at that girl. He knew she was just a one-night-stand, but he was glad he would never settle for that again. But he had...first term. What a difference one visit to a bar had made.

When Mitch arrived at the entry gate, he stopped to speak to the guard. This time, the guard seemed to know him.

"Go on in Mr. Nelson," he said. "They are expecting you. You can park in any spot next to the building that isn't reserved."

Wow, he was coming up in the world already. No more third row parking now.

Locking the car, Mitch adjusted his jacket than went into the lobby. The same receptionist was behind the desk, but this time she gave him a dazzling smile and said, "Welcome, Mr. Nelson. Go on in. Mr. Watson is expecting you."

Mitch strolled down the hall, trying not to run or appear too anxious. When he reached Sam's door, he knocked, even though it was open.

Sam glanced up and motioned him in. Mitch noticed he was on the telephone so he just took the same chair he used the day before.

Sam seemed to be arguing with someone. He kept telling the person on the other end of the line that he had better get his act together or there would be serious consequences. Evidently, this frightened the person Sam was talking to, because Sam smiled and told him he knew he would see it his way. He quickly ended the call and turned to Mitch.

He came around the desk and again extended his hand to Mitch. Mitch stood up and shook his hand.

"Welcome," said Sam. "We are glad to have you with us. I want you to know that this organization is a family and we take care of our own. If they need to be reprimanded, we do it; but if they need help, they get that too. Now, let's take a look at your new office."

Mitch was escorted down the hall to the left to the room next to Sam's. It was a large office with beautiful paintings adorning the walls. On the far wall, there was a huge picture window that looked out over the rolling lawns and lots of trees. It looked so serene and peaceful. There was no furniture in the room, the only exception being a wet bar built into the far left corner of the room.

"Well, how do you like it?" asked Sam.

What could Mitch say. It was gorgeous...fantastic.

"It's wonderful. I know I'll be happy here."

"We intend to make sure that is true, Mitch. Now, I want you to go with Terrance here and pick out the furnishings you want. The boys will bring them up just as soon as you do, so your office should be set up before you leave tonight."

Mitch looked around. He hadn't heard anyone enter the room, but there, standing just inside the doorway, was one of the biggest men he had ever seen. He was tall and broad-shouldered and he looked uncomfortable in the obviously expensive suit he was wearing. It looked as if it strained the buttons on the coat because his chest was so big, or did he maybe have something underneath? He had dark hair, neatly trimmed, and a dark, heavy mustache. In addition, his nose looked as if it had been broken more than once. When Sam introduced him to Mitch, he smiled, showing yellow-stained teeth and he shook Mitch's hand with one of the biggest, strongest hands that Mitch could imagine.

They nodded to each other and then he motioned for Mitch to precede him through the door.

In the hall, Mitch let Terrance take the lead and Sam stopped at his own office.

"See you later, Mitch," said Sam.

As they walked along, Mitch tried to learn something about Terrance. He asked him where he was from, how long he had worked for Sam, what his job was…but Terrance didn't answer him. Soon Mitch quit trying and just tried to keep up with Terrance's long strides.

When they arrived at the far end of the complex, they entered a large warehouse. Mitch noticed that this was just one of four large warehouses here.

Inside this warehouse, Mitch saw office furniture of every description. He tried to take it all in, but Terrance kept walking. Reaching nearly the center of the building, Terrance finally spoke.

"Just look around," he said. "When you find something you want, mark it with one of these tags. Then go to the warehouse office near the front and tell the guys to bring everything over to your office."

Terrance handed Mitch a stack of bright yellow tags with both tape and ties.

"How will they know where to take it?" he asked.

"They already know," said Terrance. "Just tell them your name." and with that he was gone. For a big man, he moved quickly and quietly. Mitch decided he wouldn't want to make an enemy of that man.

Well, he'd better get busy. He had a big job ahead of him. Walking down first one aisle and then another, he saw style after style and every color imaginable. This wasn't going to be easy.

Finally, he decided he would select a desk first. He found a beautiful, big desk. In fact, it seemed to be almost as big as a dining table, and it was made from teak. It gleamed and he could see his reflection in the top. That would be the centerpiece of his office. Now that he had chosen the desk, he went looking for a desk chair…an executive one, of course. He sat in several but felt so comfortable in a black leather chair with padded arms, he chose it. Remembering the carpet in the office was an off white, he decided he should have some color in the room, either in paintings or chairs, or maybe both. He finally found two barrel-style visitor chairs, covered in cream, black and sea-green fabric. They were beautiful, and so classy. He tagged them and then decided he needed a small sofa and some tables too. It didn't take long to settle on a sea-green sofa with comfortable black and cream throw pillows and two black and white table lamps.

Next he went searching for some tables and maybe another chair or two. After searching, he decided to move the barrel chairs over near the sofa and chose two sea-green colored leather chairs to place hear his desk. The tables he picked were somewhat modern made of teak with gold trim. He also found some paintings that he felt would make the room perfect. They had gold frames and were black etchings, which he would hang over the sofa setting and he also picked out some excellent copies of Monet pieces that he planned to hang on the other walls. As he thought about his choices, he began to get very anxious to see it put together. This was going to be spectacular.

He found his way to the warehouse office, gave his name and then showed the men the color of tags he had used. He also gave them a list of the items so they would know when they had everything.

On his way back to the office, he took the wrong door out of the warehouse and found himself near a second warehouse. He decided he would take a minute and look into it to see what was happening. He opened a side door and stepped into a cool, dark, dank atmosphere. This was strange. Whatever would they use this place for? He inched forward, feeling his way in the darkness. He thought he saw some light further ahead, and then he thought he heard voices. Heading for the light, he came upon an open area filled with long tables. People were seated next to each other along each side of the tables. In front of them, there were bins of vari-colored pills and capsules. The people were bagging them in cellophane. They were working rapidly and seemed to be engrossed in their work. He noticed there were piles of bagged drugs in a bin beside each chair and there were women pushing carts along the aisles picking up the filled bags and taking them to the other end of the warehouse. So this was where his supplies had come from. Mitch couldn't believe it. A drug warehouse right in the middle of town and right in the open. This organization must be big.

He decided it was time to return to his office. After all, the furniture would be arriving soon, and he wanted to be there to place it correctly. Besides Mitch wasn't sure he should be nosing around. After all, this appeared to be a big business, but one that should be kept quiet. Of course, he wouldn't tell anyone. He was a part of the organization now. That sounded good.

Returning to his office, he walked over to look out the window. He loved the view and thought it would be beautiful during any season of the year. He wondered if the organization owned all of the land. He would have to ask Sam. It would be a shame if anyone built back there, and maybe a little dangerous for their business.

He was so lost in his reverie that he did not hear the men as they first entered the room. Everyone seemed to walk so quietly around here, he would have to stay alert.

As piece after piece of the furniture he had chosen was brought into the room, he got more and more excited. It looked as if it had been made to go together. He had made good choices. He took down the pictures that were already hanging on the wall and hung the ones he had chosen. They were perfect. As the last piece was put into place, he took a look around and felt a lot of pride. His first office. He wanted to always remember it just as it looked now.

"Will there be anything else, Mr. Nelson?" asked the warehouse man.

"No, this looks great," said Mitch. "But could you return these pictures to the warehouse for me?"

Mitch handed him the pictures he had removed and he left with them, closing the door behind him.

Mitch went around the desk and sat in the executive chair. It was even adjusted right. He leaned back and swung around surveying his surroundings. Boy, could he get used to this.

As he was looking around he noticed a door in the wall to his left. It looked like it might connect with Sam's office. He would have to ask Sam. Mitch glanced at his watch. He knew it was late because it was getting dark. It was even later than he had thought...almost seven. He went down the hall to Sam's office and knocked on the door.

"Come in," Sam yelled.

Mitch entered and said, "Well, Sam, I got the office set up. I wondered if there was anything else you wanted me to do tonight."

"Have a seat," said Sam. "Would you like a drink?"

"Sure," said Mitch. "Make it a straight whiskey, double."

"Well, a man after my own heart," said Sam. "I like a guy who can handle his liquor."

Mitch took the drink Sam handed him and again sat in the same chair. He relaxed as he started to sip his drink. Sam had poured himself the same drink. They were quiet for several minutes.

Finally, Sam spoke.

"Well, how was your first day?"

"Great," said Mitch, "but I am afraid I really didn't do anything for you and the organization."

"Oh, yes, you did. You got set up so you can go to work. The workplace and its feel is very important," said Sam.

Thinking about that, Mitch agreed.

"Well, if that is true, I am in good shape," said Mitch. "I love the office."

"Good," said Sam. "What is your schedule for tomorrow? When can you come in?"

"Tomorrow is a short day for classes," said Mitch. "I can be here by twelve thirty I think."

"Great," said Sam. "Why don't you plan to have lunch with me. I'll have something brought in. It will be a working lunch and we will get you started on your duties. By the time you get here tomorrow, you will have a telephone and computer hooked up, as well as an intercom. We'll go over how to use everything then."

"That sounds really good," said Mitch. Finishing his drink, he said, "I better get going. I've got some things to do tonight."

"Seeing that little girl again?" asked Sam.

That startled Mitch. He didn't even know Sam knew about Cindy.

"Maybe," said Mitch, "but I've got some studying to do too."

"Well, you'd better go, then," said Sam. "Don't count on leaving this early after you get started."

This early? It was almost eight o'clock.

"Oh, I won't," said Mitch. "Good night. See you tomorrow."

He put his glass on the bar and left, waving goodbye as he did. He was surprised to see that the receptionist was still at her desk. Everyone seemed to work hard and late around here. He hadn't figured he would be working late too often. He wondered what he should tell Cindy. Would she understand? Well, it had to be faced; but tonight he thought he would just go back to the dorm. He would call her later.

Chapter thirteen

A wry, almost sad smile, crossed Mitch's face as he thought about that day. It seemed to him the happiness and euphoria disappeared almost as rapidly as the dark night was slipping by the window of the bus. If he had only known. Memories flooded over him.

Mitch drove home, deep in thought. His life was really going to change...a lot more than he had thought it would. He would have to find time to sit down with Cindy so they could discuss this, but tonight was too soon. He was so keyed up, he wasn't sure he could even handle Cindy tonight. He still loved her, deeply, and he wanted to feel her body next to his, just not tonight.

When he arrived home, Mitch reached into the glove compartment and pulled out the cellophane bag of drugs. Tonight, they might come in handy. He was getting a little short; maybe he should refill his supply tomorrow. He wondered how he would do that, now that he wasn't dealing.

When he opened the dorm door, he found that the lights were out except for the television and he was greeted with giggles.

"Hey, Jim," he said. "Can I come in?"

"Come on in buddy," said Jim in a somewhat slurred voice.

Mitch hadn't heard him sound like this since last term. What was happening to him?

He crossed the room and turned on a lamp, next to his bed. It wasn't as bright as the overhead light, so he thought that would be more considerate. As his eyes adjusted, he was able to make out three people on the couch.

"Come and join us, buddy," Jim slurred.

Mitch walked over to the couch and saw that Jim was seated between two young, nubile girls, and they were all nude.

"What's going on?" asked Mitch. "What about football?"

"Oh, man; where you been? Spring practice is over and I don't need to be in shape until August. This is my time to party," said Jim, smiling crookedly. "Come on in and join us. Get a drink. These girls are Bambi and Thumper, but I don't know which is which."

Jim was really bombed. But he looked like he was having fun...like the old days. Mitch thought about it and then decided he had been toeing the line pretty well. Maybe he deserved a night like this too.

Heading for the bar, he poured himself a tall glass of whiskey. Then he wandered back to the couch.

"I don't think there is room for me," said Mitch.

"Oh, we'll make room," cooed Bambi, or was it Thumper, "but you can't get in this club if you have any clothes on."

Mitch noticed a sly grin and a twinkle in her eye. Well, rules were rules. Mitch quickly shed his clothes and flopped down on the couch next to Jim. The girls had stood up and now sat down on their laps. Whichever one he was holding felt good to Mitch. He tried to concentrate on her, his drink and having fun. If he let himself think about Cindy, he couldn't go on with it.

The drink started to take effect. After all, he had just had a drink with Sam and he hadn't found time to eat today. Even so, he wasn't numb enough and he was sure Jim and the girls were far ahead of him.

Dumping the girl off his lap, he stumbled over to the bar and poured himself another big drink.

"Anyone need anything?" he yelled.

"Yeah, bring the bottles over here," said Jim. "That will be easier."

"Sure," said Mitch, "but I have something even better."

Struggling over to his jacket while carrying the bottles of booze, Mitch fumbled in his pocket and pulled out the cellophane bag filled with drugs.

Setting the bottles on the floor near the couch, Mitch held up the bag and waved it in front of them.

"Look at this. Pretty aren't they? Powerful too. Only the best for good old Mitch."

Mitch had gotten so unsteady on his feet he stumbled and fell to his knees in front of the couch. He was laughing and trying to get his balance. The girls and Jim were laughing too, but they were also interested in Mitch's little bag.

Mitch found that he couldn't get up, so he just rolled over and laid down on his back on the floor. He was still laughing, but he didn't know why.

The next thing he knew, one of the girls was sitting, straddling his body. He thought she was trying to take his drugs but he wasn't sure. He thought he heard Jim ask if he would share the drugs.

Finally, he pushed himself up, dumping the girl on her pretty little butt. They were all laughing now. Then he opened his little bag and started to pass around the multi-colored capsules and pills. He was now unable to distinguish one from the other so he really didn't know what anyone was taking. All he knew was that before long the bag was empty. By then, they were all bleary-eyed and almost catatonic. Wrapping his arms around the nearest girl, Mitch threw her to the floor and threw his own body on top of her. He knew he was too heavy for her and he was not holding any of his weight back, but he just couldn't do anything about it. But, she was still laughing. He tried to kiss her, but it was difficult for them to even find each other's mouths. He thought he was just licking at her and even slobbering. She started to squirm but he knew it was not in a sexually aroused manner. Even through this veil of alcohol and drugs, he knew she was not aroused. Neither was he. She just wanted to get him off of her. His weight was beginning to crush her.

With a great deal of effort, Mitch rolled off the girl, ending up on his side and facing the girl. He wasn't aroused either, but he needed comfort, and this girl really didn't know how to give it, not like Cindy. Mitch started to cry. Tears were running down his cheeks and onto the girl lying beside him. Why did he have to think about Cindy? He wasn't really cheating on her. Remember, he wasn't aroused. He wasn't even interested in this girl...but she was here. To get his mind off Cindy, he tried to develop an interest in the girl, but there was just none there. Then he knew how he could get comfort from her. He reached out and grabbed the breast nearest to him. It wasn't very big and didn't even look sexy, but he put his mouth on the breast, trying to entice a hardness in the nipple. She surely didn't respond like Cindy. But this was all he had available. He gave up manipulating the nipple, and started to suck hungrily and deeply on the breast. At first the girl seemed to fight him, but eventually she became still and he continued to suck deeply. Sometime during this action, he fell asleep.

When Mitch woke up, his muscles felt stiff and he was cold. He looked around and realized he was sleeping on the floor, naked, and was lying next to a naked girl. Talk about de ja vu. He didn't even know her. He had no idea what time it was and he couldn't focus his eyes on his watch. Jim was stretched out on the couch and a girl was lying on top of him. Both of them were snoring loudly. This seemed like old times from the first semester.

Releasing himself from the girl's arms, he struggled to his feet and made his way into the bathroom. He turned on the light and looked at himself in the mirror. He looked terrible. What had he been drinking? And what drugs had he taken? He had no idea. He should be glad he could even walk. Bending forward, he splashed his face with cold water. Maybe that would help. What had he been thinking? Was he crazy? He finally had his world put together and he jeopardized it for a night of booze and drugs and some little nymphet? Shaking his head, he wanted to kick himself. What was he going to tell Cindy?

Oh, God! Cindy! He was supposed to call her. What was he ever going to say?

Well, he would have to get some sleep before he could think clearly or even face someone. He turned the light off, crawled into his bed, and pulled the blankets over his head.

The next thing Mitch remembered was the sound of someone walking around the room. Peeking out of the covers, he saw the girl that had been lying next to him. At first he just wanted to pull the covers back up, but he felt sorry for her. After all, he had brought the drugs.

Sitting up, Mitch asked her if she was okay.

"I don't know," she said. "Boy, do I have a headache."

Mitch looked at the clock. It was almost six and the sun was beginning to rise.

"Where do you live?" he asked.

She told him the name of her dorm but she still looked terribly unsteady.

There was nothing to do but try to get her home. Mitch got up and, suddenly embarrassed by his nudity, he grabbed his pants and put them on. He didn't know what difference it made; he had slept nude against her all night, but that was then, and they were almost sober now.

"Why don't you put your clothes on," said Mitch, "and I will take you home. Does the other girl live in the same dorm?

"Yes," she said. "Is she okay?"

"I think so," said Mitch. "Maybe we'd better try to wake her up."

They started to shake both Jim and the girl. Finally, both of them began to stir.

Jim looked as bleary-eyed as Mitch had when he looked in the mirror. The girl still seemed to be stoned, but she could stand up. With the help of her friend, they were able to get her dressed, and when both girls were ready, Mitch asked Jim to go with him to take them home. Jim threw on a pair of jeans and that is how he went. Mitch had put on the shirt from the day before. Neither one of them looked too great but they hoped they wouldn't run into any one.

Luck was with them. They were able to get out of the dorm and into Mitch's car. When they arrived at the girls' dorm, they helped them out and took them to the door. By helping each other, they were sure they could get to their room, so Mitch and Jim headed home.

When Mitch got back to the room, he headed straight to bed. This would be a day he missed classes, but he wouldn't let it happen again. He hadn't said a word to Jim all the way home and he pulled the covers over his head so Jim wouldn't even try to talk to him.

Mitch woke up when he heard Jim in the shower. He looked at the clock and saw that it was after ten. He remembered he had a luncheon engagement with Sam and knew he needed to get himself together before then. He sat on the edge of the bed, holding his head. He couldn't remember when he had felt this bad. Even in his days of hard partying, he hadn't felt this bad. He couldn't begin to know why, but he felt there were several reasons. He knew he took too many drugs, hard drugs, and he didn't even know what kind. He also had been drinking much more than he was currently used to drinking.

He hadn't been drinking so much since he and Cindy were together. He hadn't needed it. Of course, he did drink some, but somehow it was more social, not because he needed it. And, of course, he was feeling very guilty about Cindy. How could he have treated her this way? He hadn't even called her. That was bad enough, but he had spent the night with another girl. He hadn't really been unfaithful, since they hadn't had sex. But that was only because he had been too drunk and too stoned. He had, though, spent the night naked, curled up to a strange girl who was also naked. Since he and Cindy had been together, he had come to believe that the sight of their bodies was only for each other. How would he feel if Cindy spent the night with another guy? He knew. He would be really mad...even angry. Well, she probably would be too, and he deserved it.

He heard Jim shut off the shower. In a few minutes he came out of the bathroom, not looking any too good himself.

"Morning," said Jim. "How you feeling?"

"Just about the same as you look," said Mitch, venturing a little smile.

"I know," said Jim. "What happened to us? I never went off the deep end like I did last night. Hey, by the way, where did you get those drugs? Those were the real things. Hard... really hard."

"I know," said Mitch. "I'm sorry I ever gave them to you guys. That was really stupid."

"Do you and Cindy use those things? You never seem to be high when I see you two together.?

"No way," said Mitch. "Cindy would have a fit if she knew I even had them."

"Then why did you even have them?" asked Jim.

Mitch thought a few minutes, but didn't think it was the right time to tell Jim the truth. Maybe later.

"Later; I'll tell you all about it later. Right now I've got to get ready to go to work. Sure can't show up looking like this."

"That's for sure," said Jim. "I'll make some strong coffee while you shower. Maybe that will help."

Mitch hurried into the bathroom, feeling as if he wanted to escape. Why didn't he just tell Jim. He kept telling himself that there was nothing wrong with his job, but, if that was true, why did he hesitate telling his friends what he did for a living?"

Well, first things first. He had to get ready. He couldn't be late for work, and he had to be sober.

After a hot, stinging shower and a quick shave, Mitch decided he felt a lot better. He wrapped a towel around his waist and went to search for clothes. Jim had poured him some hot, strong coffee and it was sitting by his bed.

"Thanks," said Mitch. "Maybe now I will feel human."

He dressed quickly, deciding to wear slacks and a new sports coat today, especially since he wasn't going to class first. After all, he had a swanky office; he ought to look like he fit it.

Jim watched him dress but didn't say anything else. When he was dressed, he finished his coffee, waved to Jim, and left.

Driving to work, he tried to take in as much fresh air as he could. He looked better now but he still felt pretty wasted. He would have to put on a good act at work.

Today the guard just waved him through the gate, not even acting as if he should stop. That started him feeling better. Maybe he hadn't screwed things up, at least at work. Cindy might be a different story.

"Good morning, Mr. Nelson," trilled the receptionist. As he listened, he thought she almost sang as she spoke.

"Hello, Miss...ahh; I'm sorry. I don't think I know your name."

"It's Sabrina; Sabrina Franklin; and it is definitely Miss," she replied.

"Hello, Miss Franklin," Mitch said, giving her a friendly, warm smile.

She returned the smile as he continued on toward his office. He went into his own office, noticing that Sam's door was closed. Once inside, Mitch again got that feeling that this all had to be a dream, but it wasn't. He went to his desk and saw he did have a telephone, a computer and an intercom already installed. On his desk, he found a list of numbers of people in the building and those members of the organization at other locations. Glancing through the list, he was surprised to see the people were all over the country and in many foreign countries. It seemed, however, that the majority of the foreign listings were Central and South America and the Caribbean. Maybe Sam would explain it all to him. Thinking about Sam, he checked his watch. He still had fifteen minutes until his luncheon date, so he decided to see what was in his desk. Even though it had just been put in here yesterday, someone had stocked it with supplies before he had arrived. He found a manual that seemed to outline the organization, including its bylaws and the general plans for the business.

Reading the manual, Mitch finally began to face reality about the organization he was a part of…it was connected very high up…there were several politicians listed in the manual as well as several members of crime families. Mitch began to feel a little uneasy. Maybe he was getting in over his head. But he passed this feeling off as being unfounded. After all, Sam was accepted in the best clubs and had friends who were important. He had never seen anything that made him think they did anything but supply drugs to those who wanted them. He knew they were illegal, but, as he had always told himself, if he didn't make the money, someone else would. By the time he joined Sam for lunch, all doubts were gone. He had thoroughly brainwashed himself.

Lunch had gone well. Sam was friendly and seemed quite open with Mitch. He told him that most of their drugs came in from South America or the Caribbean. Most of the money ended up in the Caribbean where it was easy to launder. Even though Mitch knew this was illegal, it didn't seem really terrible. After all, no one got hurt. All the customers wanted what they got.

By the time lunch was finished, Mitch was absolutely and completely hooked...on power and money. That was what he was being offered. What boy from a small factory town who never wanted to go back there could turn it down. That brought a pang of guilt to Mitch. He hadn't even contacted his parents since he left before Christmas. They deserved better, but they just didn't belong in his new world.

The guilt quickly passed as Sam began to outline his duties. He was given a ledger of all the various drugs they dealt and the names of the suppliers in various countries. In addition, a second ledger contained the names of all the local suppliers from each place and their lists of main customers. Mitch was a little surprised at the area the organization covered. He had known it was large, but he had no idea how large. It was spread all over the country with the largest lists of customers coming in college towns, just like this one. Big cities were also full of customers, but Sam told him that they tried to concentrate on the college clientele because they were more likely to be middle and upper class, and once hooked, became much more likely to have jobs that would keep them flush and keep them buying for a long time. Sam seemed really proud of this plan and what it accomplished. Mitch tried to see it in the same way, but he wondered if he ever could. Remember, no one twisted their arms to use; it was by free choice. Mitch had to keep reminding himself of that, because, to him, that made it okay.

Sam explained that Mitch would be expected to keep in contact, at least weekly, with their international suppliers. Their local suppliers, when they had problems, would call Mitch who would be expected to get it straightened out as soon as possible. After all, time was money to the organization. Sam didn't expect Mitch to go personally to meet with the local suppliers; he would have a staff to do that for him. However, he would need to meet personally with the international suppliers. Some of these meetings would take place in locations within the United States. They were usually out-of-the-way places since many of the suppliers entered the States illegally. Other meetings would take place in the countries out of which the suppliers dealt their goods. Sam asked Mitch if he had a passport and he said that he had never had one. That would be one of the first things he needed to do. Sam told him to ask Miss Franklin how to do it. Then he should familiarize himself with the names in the ledgers and their ranking of importance to the organization. That would be a lot of work, but Sam felt that Mitch could do it. Sam explained that they had a large pool of accountants that kept the books so they did most of the records keeping. If there were any problems, Mitch would mediate a settlement. Mitch felt like his head was swimming. This was really a lot of responsibility. For just a minute, he wondered if he was in over his head, but he decided Sam wouldn't have asked him if he didn't think he could do it.

As Mitch left Sam's office, carrying the large, heavy ledgers, Sam stopped him.

"Mitch, I know you are going to do a great job. I have all the confidence in the world in you. If you have any questions or if you get overwhelmed at first, please let me know. I am always here for you."

Mitch smiled and thanked him. That made him feel really good. But he knew it was going to take a lot of time for him to get up to speed as soon as possible. It looked like every spare minute was going to have to be put into this job.

He deposited the ledgers on his desk and sprawled in the chair. He didn't know where to start. Well, at least he could separate things into piles and decide which were the most important. But he already knew that the most important thing was Cindy, and he had some fences to mend with her.

He walked quickly over to Sam's office again, and knocked on the door.

"Come in," Sam called.

"Can I see you for a minute, Sam?" asked Mitch.

"Sure, I told you any time," Sam said putting aside the papers he was scanning.

"Well, it is like this," said Mitch. "I have this girl who is very special to me and I have been so involved in getting started here, I have neglected her and even stood her up. I know it is going to take me a lot of hours to get myself acclimated, so I was wondering if I could take a few hours now to try to explain to her; then I can come back and even work all night, if necessary."

"Of course," said Sam. "I have a wife, so I know that sometimes the woman in your life has to come first. Take all the time you need. I trust you to get your work done."

Mitch suddenly realized he had been holding his breath so he breathed deeply. Now he could get things back on track.

"Thanks, Sam. I will be back later. Will the door be unlocked?"

"I'm sure it will," said Sam. "There are people working here all hours, but ask Miss Franklin for a key, just in case it happens to be locked."

Mitch left, finally feeling that everything would be okay. On returning to his office, he picked up his new phone and placed a call to Cindy. When her boss answered, he said Cindy had called in sick. That surprised Mitch, and worried him. Should he call her or just go over to the apartment? Maybe if he just showed up, she would at least have to talk to him. That's what he would do.

As he left the building, he stopped to pick up a key. He noticed that Miss Franklin, or Sabrina as she insisted he call her, was giving him a very long look. Maybe if he didn't have Cindy, he would have given her a long look back, but he knew she could never be as good as Cindy. And she was too old.

As he drove to Cindy's apartment, he tried to formulate what he could say to her. He knew that he was going to have to beg and to crawl and probably even plead. But it would be worth it. And there was nothing that she could ask him to do that he did not deserve.

When he pulled up in front of the apartment, he looked at her window, wondering if she was looking out. He didn't see her, but he intended to, right now.

Mitch knocked on the door. There was no answer, so he knocked again. Finally, Cindy came to the door. She opened it, keeping the safety chain latched.

"Go away," she said. "I don't want to see you and I have nothing to say to you."

She tried to push the door closed, but Mitch stuck his foot into the opening.

"Please, Cindy; just hear me out," he pleaded. "If you will let me in and let me talk to you, let me explain, then if you still want me to leave, I will."

"No," she said. "I can't believe anything you say."

"Yes; yes you can. Cindy, I love you, and I know you love me. Let's not lose that because I was a jerk. I promise I will leave if you want me to after we talk. Please, Cindy. I love you so much."

He took his foot out of the door, knowing it was now up to her. As he waited, he realized how scared he was. If she didn't let him in, if she didn't let him talk to her, he didn't know what he would do. She really was his life. He realized no matter how important he was at work, without Cindy, it didn't matter.

Finally, after what seemed like an eternity, he heard her release the safety chain. He turned the knob and opened the door. Cindy was halfway across the room, heading toward that stupid chair. He wanted her to sit on the sofa with him. He wanted to be close enough to touch her, but he knew he couldn't touch her until she allowed it. Maybe this was better. He thought it would be impossible to keep his hands off her if he was seated next to her. She probably knew best.

Mitch closed the door and followed Cindy into the living room. He sat on the sofa, facing Cindy. He noticed she didn't seem to want to look at him. Well, he wasn't sure he could blame her. He really had a lot of explaining…and crawling… to do. What a mess he had made of things.

"Where's your roommate?" asked Mitch, thinking that was a crazy thing to ask.

"She's gone for the week," said Cindy, sniffling as she talked. "She has been interviewed and it looks like she's getting a great new job."

Mitch realized they were both talking about nothing so they wouldn't have to talk about the real problem. But, talk about it they had to.

"Look, Cindy, I hope you will at least listen to me. I am not going to try to excuse myself. I just want to tell you what happened and why. I know I was wrong, but if you'll only give me a chance, I hope I can explain it to you. I love you, Cindy, and I hope I can convince you to love me again. I know you did love me; please give me the chance," Mitch pleaded.

Cindy looked at Mitch. He saw that her eyes were red and bloodshot and he realized he had done the one thing he said he would never do. He had hurt her…hurt her bad.

"Okay, Mitch. I'll listen. I guess I think that what we had is too good to throw away without at least hearing you out. Go ahead; I'm waiting."

"Oh, Cindy," Mitch said, feeling tears welling up in his eyes. "I really do love you and I hope that when you said that what we had was too good to just throw away, you really meant that what we have is too good, not past tense. I am sure going to give it my best try."

Mitch took a deep breath and leaned his head back against the sofa. He noticed that Cindy was looking at him through the hair that had fallen over her face. She still looked so hurt; he couldn't bear to look at her. Pulling his eyes away from her face, he looked past her, really looking at nothing. Well, here goes, he thought. It is now or never.

"Cindy, I blew it. I treated you with such disrespect, I don't blame you for feeling the way you do. It all started when Sam gave me this promotion. Really, I don't want to blame Sam. He isn't the one who neglected you; I did. Anyway, as I told you on the phone, I had to go out to the office of the organization, after I spent most of the afternoon working with the guy taking my route. That was pretty intense, just by itself. I didn't know how protective I felt about my customers. Giving them up felt like I was giving up part of myself. Anyway, that's still no reason for my behavior. I went out to the office after that. It was very impressive. In fact, I was almost overwhelmed. It is very big and very luxurious and all the people I met were very professional. I think that scared me a little. After all, I am just a college freshman, and not very sophisticated. I guess I felt a little pressure and was trying to play big man. Anyway, I got caught up in all that was going on there. They even gave me my own office. Oh, Cindy, you should see it. It is really elegant; more luxury in that one room than in the entire neighborhood where I grew up. Anyway, they sent me out to the warehouse and I got to pick out all the furnishings. It was unbelievable. There was anything you could ever want...just there for the taking. If I do say so myself, I put together a pretty snazzy and classy office. So, by the time the warehousemen brought the furniture in and we got it all in place, it was getting really late. I did sit for a few minutes and just enjoyed the room. Remember, it is the first office I ever had, and it is all mine. When I finally noticed the time, I went to see Sam again and set up my schedule for today. I have to admit, I was so exhausted, I could hardly drive home. Why I went there and not here, I can't begin to tell you. Maybe I was just so exhausted and my brain was so fried, I didn't think. Anyway, I meant to call you; really I did. When I got back to the dorm, Jim was there. He was back in his partying ways and he was already wasted. He had a girl with him, and they were really into it. I have to admit, I'd had several drinks during the day and when I joined them for more drinks, I just passed out. I didn't wake up until this morning, and I was such a mess it took every minute I had to put myself together to go to work."

Mitch stopped and looked at Cindy. At least she was listening. He just had to be careful and keep going. He realized he hadn't been completely honest with Cindy but he wasn't sure she could take it, at least not yet. All he had left out was the drugs and the second naked girl...but that was enough.

Since Cindy didn't say anything, Mitch decided he should go on.

"Well, anyway, I mean, listen Cindy, I don't know what I mean. All I know is that I love you. I really do. I only wanted this job so that I could make more money and take care of you. I don't like you having to work in the bar. I know, even though you never say anything, that you get hit on all the time. I know, because I know guys. I'm not jealous, because I trust you completely, but I still don't like you having to go through it all the time. I know, if you will be patient and understanding, and, most of all believe that I love you, that I will be able to get established in my job and we will be living on Easy Street. That is what I want for you. That is what you deserve."

Finally, feeling as if he couldn't say another word, Mitch stopped talking. He couldn't bear to look at Cindy. He had pleaded his case in the best way he could. If she told him to go, he knew he would die. At least life wouldn't be worth living.

The apartment was so quiet that he could hear the traffic outside. The quietness was driving him crazy.

Finally, he asked, "Do you still want me to go?"

Still, she didn't answer. How long was she going to make him wait? Well, it didn't matter if she made him wait all night, he would if it was necessary.

Then, just as he thought there was no hope, he felt Cindy's warm, soft hand reaching out to touch the side of his face.

His head jerked up, and he found himself looking into her beautiful, tear-stained face. He couldn't believe this beautiful creature was reaching out to him. He knew he didn't deserve it, but she was going to give him another chance. She was going to give him his life back; at least that is how he felt. Now he felt tears flowing down his face; and he wasn't ashamed.

"Oh, Cindy," he said. "You are wonderful, terrific, perfect… and I know I don't deserve you, but I do want you, in the worst way. Thank you, thank you, thank you."

He wanted to stop crying, but he couldn't.

Reaching up, Mitch put his arms around Cindy's waist and buried his face against her body. She was caressing his hair and making soft murmuring sounds. He couldn't understand her, but he didn't care. She loved him, and he had another chance.

Finally, as the tears stopped flowing, Mitch leaned back, pulling Cindy down on the sofa next to him. He couldn't keep his hands off her. He almost couldn't believe she was here.

He wanted more than anything to grab her and make wild, passionate love to her, but something told him he needed to use restraint, to take things slowly. He vowed that he would do this right.

After kissing her for several minutes, intermingling their salty tears, he pulled her into the safety of his arms and told her they needed to talk some more.

"What about?" she asked, not raising her face.

"Well, I want to tell you all about this new job," he said. "For a while, I will need to work really hard, just to get myself on the right track. There is really a lot of responsibility in my duties. I don't want to go into it too much; it would probably bore you; but I do want you to have a general idea of what I will be doing. Most of our supplies come from outside the States. One of my jobs will be to meet with these suppliers and make sure the flow of goods keeps going smoothly. Sam says that I will have to travel a lot for those meetings, but I won't be gone long. Maybe, after I get better established, I can even take you along sometimes. The organization has a private jet so I will be traveling on that most of the time. Another part of my job is to make sure that our local suppliers do not have any major problems. After all, if they can't deliver, we don't take in any money. So, as you can see, they really think I can deliver some valuable service."

As he stopped, he realized that Cindy had raised her face to look into his. He noticed some concern and asked her about it.

"Oh, I will just be worried with you traveling so much," said Cindy. "I won't be jealous. I trust you. But I will miss you and I will not rest until you are back here in my arms."

Mitch smiled and kissed her. It hadn't escaped him that she had said she trusted him. Well, from now on, she could; last night never happened.

"Don't worry, Cindy; I will always come back to you, as soon as possible. By the way, when I get established, how do you feel about quitting your job?"

"Let's wait and see," said Cindy. "We will deal with that later. Now we need to deal with the present. If I understand you correctly, you are telling me that you will be putting in a lot of time at work for the next few weeks. Right?"

"Right," said Mitch. "It isn't by choice, but by necessity."

"Will you be able to come here after work?" she asked.

"I will try," he said, "but until school is out, I am going to be very busy trying to balance school and work. I don't want to give up my time with you, but by doing so now; I believe we will have more and even better time later. I think we can spend time after work, late, either here or at the dorm, at least sometime each week. Can you live with this, if I can?"

Throwing her arms around his neck, she said, "Of course I can; as long as I know you love me."

With that, Mitch couldn't keep his hands off her any longer. He found himself kissing her passionately while pulling at her clothing. She too was caught up in the passion and was trying to get his clothing off. After several minutes, they both succeeded, although clumsily, and he looked down again at her beautiful, perfect body. He couldn't wait. He picked her up and carried her into the bedroom where they found they were very anxious to satisfy each others needs, passions and desires.

As Mitch lay looking up at the ceiling with Cindy's head resting on his chest, he found himself thinking about the job. He couldn't believe he could think about that with Cindy right here, but he did. He wanted to think about her but he found his mind was completely filled with thoughts and questions about the job. Besides, he needed to get back there soon. He looked down and Cindy, sleeping softly on his chest. She was so beautiful and sexy, but there was also something intoxicating about the job.

Chapter fourteen

"Effingham. Thirty minute dinner break," yelled the driver, jolting Mitch back to the present. He was surprised that he felt so tired from visiting the past. Maybe something to eat would help. He followed the other passengers off the bus and into the diner.

The diner was clean and bright and Mitch headed for a table for two in the far corner. When the waitress approached, he ordered ham and eggs, toast and coffee. That should give him energy.

When his food arrived, Mitch gave it his full attention, quickly cleaning his plate. Leaving money on the table, he went to the men's room, then straight back to the bus. He felt like he was finally coming to the place in his past that could show him how to go forward.

Mitch remembered that on that night he had finally slipped his arm out from under Cindy. She had stirred slightly but didn't wake. He got out of bed and dressed quickly. He scribbled a note telling Cindy he loved her and that he would call her as soon as he got a chance. Then, he leaned over and kissed her forehead, noticing how her long, fair eyelashes fell on her cheeks and the hair curled softly around her face. Quickly, before he found himself wanting to stay, he let himself out of the apartment, locking it behind him.

By the time he reached the car, Cindy and their passion were far behind. His mind was filled with the intoxicating idea of what was ahead of him at work. Focused only on that, he drove quickly to the office.

A different guard was on duty at the gate and raised his hand for Mitch to stop.

"Hi; I'm Mitch Nelson," he said. "I'm fairly new here. Haven't come in on your shift before."

"Sure, Mr. Nelson," said the guard. "Go ahead in."

Mitch parked near the building and hurried in, finding he was filled with anticipation. He was surprised at how alive he felt just wanting to get started on his work.

He was just a little surprised to see Sabrina still at her desk. He noticed that she gave him a beautiful smile. He nodded and went to his office. He noticed a line of light under Sam's door, so he was still here too.

Switching on the lights, Mitch saw his office spring to life. It made him very proud. It seemed as if he was proud more and more often.

Taking off his coat, he rolled up his shirt sleeves, removed his tie, and sat down behind his desk, already piled high with work.

He quickly found himself engrossed in the work. The ledgers were interesting and so full of information. Mitch leaned back in his chair, reading closely the ledger that listed the supplies and suppliers. He quickly got totally engrossed. He didn't even know so many different kinds of drugs existed. The list went on and on; there were things he had never even heard of, and they seemed to be in great demand because of the large quantities being shipped. Page after page of drugs began to blur in his mind. He began to feel as if his head was swimming. Leaning forward, he rested the ledger on his desktop. Would he ever be able to learn this? Was he in over his head?

No, he refused to let those thoughts take over his mind. That was his hometown talking and he refused to accept it. He was smart; his grades this term were proving that. Besides, Sam felt he could do this.

Breathing deeply, he picked up the ledger again, leaned back and started again with the first page. He took a notebook out of his desk and began to list the drugs. After filling three pages in the notebook, he again leaned forward and closed the ledger. Then, standing and stretching, he walked out of the door and down the hall.

He was relieved to see that Sabrina was still here. Glancing at his watch, he noticed that it was almost eleven o'clock.

"Do you ever go home?" he asked.

"Yes, of course," she said. "Tonight I thought Sam might need me. He is on an important conference call. By the way, I even have some free nights if you are interested."

Mitch was somewhat taken back by this statement, but it also made him feel good. She was actually coming on to him.

"Thanks, I'll keep that in mind," he said; "What I really need from you right now is a medical dictionary. Do you have one around?"

"Absolutely," she replied, rising gracefully and walking across the floor to a small room near the entryway. Mitch couldn't help but notice that she walked with a very provocative sway of her hips. Watching her walk, he wondered who wouldn't be interested in her.

As she handed him the large volume, he thanked her and headed back to his office. He again noticed the light under Sam's door.

When he got to his own office, he dropped the book on his desk and went to the bar and poured himself a tall whiskey.

Deciding he'd like to be more comfortable, he set the

whiskey on the table near the sofa, and took a breath. Then he picked up his notebook, the dictionary, and his pen and returned to the sofa. He slipped his shoes off, stretched out on the sofa, and took a deep breath. It was going to be a long night.

Starting with the first drug on the list, he looked in the dictionary, noting the way it was packaged (ie capsule, pill, powder); the coloring; the taste or lack thereof; the effects of using it; and what purpose it was developed to meet. He quickly went down his list, making notes and trying to remember as much as possible. If he could gain a strong knowledge about his product, he felt he could do a much better job for Sam and the organization. That is what he wanted to do...a good job.

When he had finished almost half of his list, he felt as if he needed a break. Sitting up, he rubbed his eyes, and then reached for his whiskey which he hadn't even touched. After downing almost all of it in a single gulp and glancing at his watch, he was almost shocked to see that it was just before three o'clock. Well, this night was shot.

Since he was in to it, he decided to finish before he left for the night, but before he could do any more work, he had to take a walk and clear his head. He headed down the hall, rubbing his eyes as he went. He was startled to see that there was still a light under Sam's door. He stopped and knocked lightly. Hearing nothing, he knocked again. Finally, he opened the door and peeked inside; the office was empty.

Shutting the door, he proceeded on down the hall, past the empty reception room, and went out the door that led to the warehouse area. The night air was cool, not cold, but very refreshing. Drinking it in deeply, he turned his face toward the twinkling stars. The quietness of the night was almost eerie. Just as he had decided to return to work, Sam and Terrance came out of the third warehouse. They were walking rapidly and appeared to be arguing. They didn't notice him until they were almost to the office complex.

"Hi there, Mitch," said Sam. "Working late?"

"Sure am, boss," replied Mitch. "There is so much I need to learn and burning a little midnight oil should help."

"Don't wear yourself out. We want to keep you around awhile," joked Sam.

They all entered the building walking toward the offices. Mitch noticed that, although Sam had spoken to him, he seemed a little distracted. Terrance didn't appear to even know he was there. Mitch decided they were just tired and said goodnight, going into his own office.

He thought about getting himself another drink, but decided he'd better just get back to work...and he did.

When he finally finished the last of his list, he put the books back on his desk and headed home.

Driving out of the gate, he waved to the guard and turned onto the quiet, empty street. As he turned into the dorm parking lot, he noticed that the sun was just starting to color the eastern sky.

Dropping into his bed, he realized he had a class in four hours. With that, he pulled the blankets over his head and immediately fell asleep.

Chapter fifteen

Remembering that day was very painful. It was certainly the doorway to his understanding of reality, and, probably the real cause of this long ride back…but back to where? "Factory Town?" To face himself? Maybe even to Peggy? No matter, at least he had to face his past and the decisions he had made. It seemed so long ago…much more than just the six years.

The clanging of the alarm clock had startled Mitch out of his sleep. He was so tired he wanted to just go back to sleep. But he couldn't. It was important…in many ways…for him to successfully complete this term.

With a great deal of effort, he forced himself into the shower. That helped; but a little of his 'product' would have really helped. Now maybe he could face the day.

All through his class, Mitch found himself thinking about all the work waiting for him at the office. He would really be glad when school was out.

The minute his last class ended, he headed for the office. It made him feel very important to be beckoned in as if he was 'somebody.' Well, maybe he was. There was that pride again.

Today he found himself looking more closely at Sabrina. She was gorgeous and maybe if he had not had Cindy…but he did…and that made him smile to himself. He loved her so much.

Sam's door was closed so Mitch went straight to his own office. His desk was piled just as he had left it early this morning. Well, no sense wasting time…he had plenty to keep him busy.

Quickly reviewing the work he had done the night before, he felt better prepared to face the first ledger…their suppliers of goods.

Mitch worked diligently, trying to understand which suppliers provided which drugs. It seemed to be an almost endless task, but finally he finished the first ledger.

Placing that ledger in the middle of his desk, he turned his chair to face the window and leaned back to admire the view. The serenity outside that window calmed his mind. He now had a good idea which of the suppliers would cause problems and have to be watched closely. He had also formed some ideas about which countries he would be visiting. As he thought about this, he really had no idea why he knew these things, he just did. Maybe this was the quality Sam had seen in him. It had to be something for Sam to offer him this job.

His reverie was broken with the sound of Sam's voice over the intercom.

"Mitch, are you there?"

Quickly hitting the transmit button he answered.

"Could you come in for a minute?" Sam asked.

"Sure, be right there," answered Mitch.

Grabbing his coat off the chair back, he went quickly to Sam's office, knocking crisply before entering.

Sam was as buried in work as he was, but he still took time to come around the desk to greet him, as usual.

After providing a drink for Mitch and pouring one for himself, he waved a hand indicating Mitch should find a seat, and then he sat behind the desk.

"How's it going?" he asked.

"Great," said Mitch. "There is sure a lot to learn, but I feel as if I'm making progress."

Sam looked a little distracted while Mitch was talking. Finally, he looked at Mitch and asked, "What were you doing out by the warehouse last night?"

Mitch was a little shocked by this question. The answer was simple, but why was Sam even asking?

"Just getting some air," said Mitch. "I was just trying to clear my head. Why?"

"I was just wondering if you had been inside the warehouse. Just want to keep up with my employees.," said Sam, seeming to relax a little.

"I won't keep you from your work any longer, but let me know if I can do anything for you," said Sam.

"Sure," said Mitch, still a little confused.

He returned to his own office wondering what that was all about. Oh, well, things seemed fine now.

Wiping all concerns from his mind, Mitch picked up the second ledger and started to study the list of local sales reps. He was completely lost in the list when he suddenly sensed someone else in the room. He looked up to see Sabrina coming toward his desk. She had shed her business-style jacket and let her neatly-coiffed hair free to fall over one eye and down her back. He saw that she was now dressed in the short, neat skirt which matched the discarded jacket and a shell blouse with a deep vee neckline. She wore stiletto heels and her legs looked as if they went on forever.

Mitch felt himself staring...and he felt a slight blush cross his face. He quickly diverted his eyes from her figure and looked up expectantly.

"Is there something you need?" asked Mitch.

"I'm about to leave for the day, Mr. Nelson," she replied in that lilting musical voice, "and I wondered if I could do anything for you...just anything?"

Mitch was a little startled and wondered if he had

misunderstood her meaning, but when he looked at her, he knew he had understood her completely. She ran the tip of her tongue over her luscious lips and she looked so sultry. He admitted he was flattered.

"No, nothing, Sabrina; not now, but thanks. Have a great evening." Mitch stammered, trying to keep his voice steady.

"Are you really sure?" she asked, coming even closer to the desk.

"I'm sure," Mitch replied, and he now knew he was stammering. He felt as if it was getting very warm in here.

After leaning slightly forward and bestowing another radiant smile upon him, she left closing the door behind her.

Mitch found that he was staring at the closed door, even several minutes after she had left the room. What was that about, he wondered? Did she really think he would be dumb enough to start an office romance? Besides, there was Peggy. Peggy? No! He meant Cindy! What was the matter with him? Was he losing his mind?

This called for a drink. He gulped down the first glass without thinking and then refilled it and carried the glass to his desk.

Sitting again, he found himself staring, unseeing, at the ledger in his hands. What was happening to him? He'd never acted like this...he had wanted Sabrina to stay. Was it the power? He hoped not. He loved the feeling of power and wanted to keep it, but he didn't want to hurt Cindy.

Okay. He refused to think about it any more. He loved his job and he definitely loved Cindy. That was it. That was the perfect life.

Now he would concentrate on work. That was important. In a few minutes, Mitch had completely forgotten the incident; he was thoroughly engrossed in his work.

He was so interested in his work, time passed quickly. As he closed the second ledger, he glanced at his watch. He was surprised to see that he had pulled another all-nighter. It was almost four o'clock.

As he left the building, he realized he was tense. He wished he had replenished his drug supply. He could use something tonight.

Well, maybe some sleep would help. When he crawled into his bed, he had one fleeting thought of Cindy...he would love to be holding her...but then he fell into a deep sleep.

The final month of school flew by for Mitch. He had replenished his drug supply, and the drugs helped him get through the long days and nights. He completed his classes and finished with a B+ average. Quite a change. He also found time to put in hours at the office. Most of the time he was still learning but he had been in contact with several of the local sales reps. He was looking forward, with some trepidation, to his first meeting with the international suppliers. That part of his job would soon start.

The one thing he regretted was that he had not had enough time to spend many hours with Cindy. She had told him she understood and she tried to make their limited time together special. She often waited at his dorm room until he got home... which could be any hour. Mitch was glad Jim was around. He could entertain her and keep her company. Jim was back in shape and limiting his booze intake. Ever since the night with the two nymphets, Jim had seemed to be changed. He was quieter and quit partying. He was almost introspective. Mitch felt a little guilty because he hadn't had time to be there for him. He had not been a very good friend. But, he told himself, he couldn't help it. After all, there were only twenty-four hours in each day, and his days were already stretched thin.

Chapter sixteen

Mitch looked out the bus window and noticed the first glimpses of light streaking the eastern sky. Time was passing quickly... and he still had some things to think about.

He remembered the summer passed quickly and he hadn't found much extra time.

Jim was staying through the summer and since the dorms weren't available, he and Mitch had found their own apartment. It was only two blocks from Cindy's apartment. Cindy was a little disappointed that he hadn't moved in with her but her roommate was still there. Anyway, when he moved in with Cindy, he wanted it to be their permanent home.

Mitch was glad to be sharing an apartment with Jim. He liked him and hoped they could again get closer since neither one had classes this summer. But even that had been a foolish dream.

As soon as classes ended, he started to work full time at the office. He tried to be at his desk no later than nine in the morning, but often he was there even earlier. He found that he was working more and more hours. It got so bad that he sometimes just slept on the couch in his office rather than going home. As his time at work increased, Sabrina became more central to his life. He counted on her to run errands, get him lunch, and place phone calls for him. It seemed as if she spent more and more time in his office and she always managed to convey her sexuality to him. He often noticed that his clothes smelled like musk…her scent. He hoped Cindy never noticed.

As fast as Sabrina's time with him increased, Cindy's decreased. This was certainly not by plan. He had wanted to spend even more time with her, not less. Every time he saw her, touched her, or smelled her, he felt the same urgent arousal she had always induced in him. However, those times seemed to be fewer and fewer. He was surprised that these rare times seemed to be enough to keep him satisfied. The shock he felt was because before he had never been able to get enough of her. Now, his passions were often fueled and satisfied by the job. It wasn't that he loved Cindy less, he just loved the power and the excitement of his job more.

His mind was so filled with work that Cindy's memory had a difficult time breaking through. And if he thought less often of Cindy, he was glad to find there was even less time to think of Peggy. She was almost completely exorcised from his memory, and that felt good.

Cindy tried to make things as easy for Mitch as she could. She wasn't demanding and never seemed to question him about the hours spent away from her. She trusted him, completely.

By the second week of his full-time work schedule, Mitch was setting up meetings with several of the over-seas suppliers. Very few of them were willing or able to meet with him in his office. This meant that Mitch had to go to them. Meetings were held in little, out-of-the way places near border cities such as Miami, Key West, San Diego, El Paso and Seattle. There were meetings at least once a week, sometimes more, and Mitch was almost overwhelmed. He met with men who actually scared him and he was glad he was never alone with them. Usually, Terrance accompanied him. Mitch began to understand that Terrance actually was serving as a bodyguard. He never spoke, but everyone seemed to be a little afraid of him. Mitch acted for Sam and for that reason, these men seemed to respect him or at least they acted as if they did when they were with him.

He met with so many people that summer that the faces started to all look the same. He would fly out early in the morning; have his meetings, many of which became intense and a little combative, especially when Mitch had to tell one of them their books were out of balance or their shipments were showing shortages; and then return home the same night. These days were long and exhausting. He was always glad to be home, but knew he would be leaving again in the next few days.

Of course, the meetings Mitch attended outside the States were even more exhausting. On most of these occasions, he would fly out one evening, meet with the supplier the next morning, and then fly home. His passport was filling up with official stamps, but he wasn't even seeing where he was...he wasn't enjoying these trips...and he wasn't learning anything about the world...except it was big.

More often than not, after a trip, Mitch chose to use his couch and not even go home. He knew sometimes that Cindy was waiting for him, either at her apartment or his, but he just couldn't find the energy to go home or even to call her. He knew he was again showing her disrespect, but he couldn't stop.

This went on for months. He began to find his days and nights becoming one, days turning into weeks, and weeks turning into months. It all became such a whirl. Every once in a while he felt some guilt about neglecting Cindy. Sometimes he felt as if he wanted to see Peggy and show her how successful he had become, to let her know what she had missed. Those thoughts triggered severe guilt and Cindy would receive, by messenger, some flowers or even jewelry, depending on how guilty he felt. He knew, though, that she didn't want the flowers or jewelry...she wanted him. Sometimes he even felt some guilt about his family but he quickly put that out of his mind. They were part of his past…not his future.

By the end of the summer, Mitch was very important to the organization. He knew, beyond a shadow of a doubt, that he was in very deep in many unlawful activities, but he continued trying to convince himself that he wasn't hurting anyone.

All of that, though, came to a grinding halt one hot August night. Mitch had just returned from one of his many meetings and was too tired to drive home. His mind was tired because he had been on the telephone all during the return flight. Sam had received his report about a local sales rep who was skimming from the money he owed the organization. The amount had continued to grow, even after Mitch had met with him. Mitch had sent a memo to Sam, suggesting they either cut him out or let Mitch and two or three 'enforcers' meet with him again. Maybe the threat of what happens to cheaters would straighten him out. Sam was upset. Nobody got away with stealing from the organization. He refused to set up another meeting although Mitch told him that the rep's client list was very profitable. Sam finally calmed down, telling Mitch he would give it more thought and they would discuss it the next day. This seemed fine to Mitch.

Lying on the couch, Mitch felt as if his office was really stuffy. Maybe a quick walk around the complex and a little fresh air, followed by a good stiff drink, would relax him and let him get some much needed sleep.

He walked slowly out of his office and down the hall, exiting from the rear of the office building. As he stood drinking in the fresh air and filling his lungs, he thought he heard a sound coming from the third warehouse. Looking back toward the offices, he didn't see any lights in any windows except his own. When he drove into the lot earlier, he hadn't noticed any other cars. Maybe he'd better have a look.

Mitch walked quietly toward the closest door of the warehouse, the one from which he had heard the noise. He pulled the door open slowly, hoping it wouldn't squeak. Thankful for well-oiled hinges, Mitch moved forward silently, listening intently to see if he could hear the noise again. A sudden sound like that of leather reins hitting a horse's flank, rang out. Mitch stood very still, but since he heard only silence, he again moved slowly forward. He began to discern a soft light and he headed in that direction. Finally, he was able to peek around a set of shelves. Mitch caught his breath and looked again, unwilling to admit he was seeing what was there. His second look confirmed his worst fears. In an open space of the warehouse, Sam, Terrance, Lonnie and Bill, two enforcers from his own staff, stood around a figure tied to a straight-back chair. The man in the chair was slumped forward and appeared to be unconscious. Sam was yelling at the man to wake up, cursing him and kicking at his legs. Mitch couldn't believe it. Sam was always so suave and friendly. He'd never heard him curse or even raise his voice. Now, the look on his face was frightening. His face was red and veins on his neck were bulging. The scowl on his face clearly showed that he was angry and out of control. He was obviously furious with the man in the chair, but who was he? What had he done?

Mitch couldn't believe he was even asking such questions. No matter what he had done, nobody deserved this treatment.

Just then, Terrance reached forward and pulled the man's head up by his hair. Mitch felt the blood drain from his face. He couldn't believe it but he found himself looking into the face of the local rep he and Sam had discussed earlier. What were they trying to prove? This wouldn't get them their money. At that moment, Sam stepped forward and backhanded the man. Blood gushed from a split lip. His whole face looked battered. Mitch thought he was going to be sick. He turned and ran as quickly and quietly as he could. Outside, he bent over, gulping fresh air to clear his head and stomach. After several gulps of air, Mitch hurried back to his office. He wasn't sure what he should do. If Sam found out he had seen that beating, would he be next? He couldn't decide if he should stay here and pretend he saw nothing or should he try to slip out and go home?

Finally he decided he would just stay here and keep quiet. If he left this late, the gate guard would log him out. It was safer just to stay here, but he was going to have that drink…a big one.

Now he wanted to talk to Cindy. He wanted her here, to hold on to…he needed her. Mitch knew he was being selfish. He was only thinking of Cindy because of his own needs. That was terrible…but he couldn't help it. He was just weak.

Mitch turned off the lamp and lay down on the couch. The full moon shining through the window gave the room an eerie glow. By moonlight, Mitch sipped his drink. His mind still wandered to that warehouse scene. What kind of mess had he gotten in to?

Well, all he had wanted to do was take care of Cindy. Maybe this was all her fault. Peggy wouldn't have let him get into such a mess.

What was he saying? This wasn't Cindy's fault. She had never asked him for anything but his love and faithfulness. He couldn't and wouldn't blame her. And why did he even think about Peggy? With her in his life he would still have been in the same mess. It was all his fault.

Mitch turned his face toward the back of the couch. He needed to get some sleep…then maybe he could think. Sleep did not come easily. Men with battered faces seemed to be drifting through his mind.

Chapter seventeen

By now, Mitch could see the bright pink in the sky to the east. It looked like the rain had gone and it was going to be a beautiful day. Well, at least in one way it would be beautiful. About the rest, he wasn't sure. Just as he was about to return to his thoughts of the past, he saw a sign saying 'Welcome to Indiana.' He was getting closer and closer to his future. He wondered just what that would be, but first, he had to know about the past. He remembered vividly the day after his discovery at the warehouse.

Mitch stirred as he woke, feeling stiff and exhausted. He knew he had slept fitfully and he felt terrible. He stumbled to his feet and went to the door. He looked out into the hallway, but it was empty and quiet. He crossed the hall and entered the men's room. What he saw in the mirror shocked him. His hair was wild, his eyes were red and swollen and he needed a shave. His clothes were rumpled, looking, as they should, like he had slept in them. He splashed his face with water and combed his hair. His electric razor and a change of clothes were in his office. That would make him look normal even if he didn't feel that way.

Crossing the hall, he quickly shaved and changed clothes. He had to keep it together today. Sam would expect a report about his trip…and would he ask Mitch about the local rep? Maybe not, and Mitch wasn't about to mention him.

It was too early for a drink, even for him, but he sure could use one. Instead, he reached into his desk and pulled out a small tin. Inside were displayed capsules and pills of many colors. He tried to be discriminating, but finally decided he couldn't make it on less than two…he might even need three. He really needed to be in control. How ironic that he would believe he was in control instead of the drugs. Real good thinking.

As he leaned back in his chair, hoping the pills would have the desired effect soon, his mind started to wander. He could see Cindy in that beautiful, sheer gown that he liked so much, her eyes shining with excitement, just because they were together.

Pushing his chair up to the desk, he picked up the phone and called Cindy's familiar number. It rang once, twice, three times. He began to feel anxious but then she answered before the fourth ring was completed.

"Hello," she said, her voice slightly throaty as if she had just awoken.

"Hi," said Mitch. "Remember me? I'm the guy who's crazy about you and stops by every once in a while."

Cindy laughed. "Oh, yes; I do recall someone like that," she said. "How are you Mitch? I've missed you."

"I'm fine," Mitch lied. "I'm sorry I've been so busy lately. Those trips to meetings are killers."

Mitch didn't know how prophetic that statement was to be.

"You know, Sweetheart, I'd love to see you," said Mitch. "In fact, I need to see you." He tried to keep his voice light but what he really wanted was to be held by Cindy and for her to tell him that everything would be okay.

But it wasn't. Nothing seemed right this morning. He wondered if it would ever be right again. He wanted to believe it would. But he wasn't sure he did.

"Oh, Mitch," said Cindy. "You know I'm here for you. Why don't you come by tonight, no matter how late you finish."

That sounded wonderful. He absolutely didn't want to wait. All he really wanted was for her to hold him.

Since he didn't want to let her know how desperate he was, he said, "You're wonderful. I'll come by as soon as possible. I've got to go now, but I love you. Don't forget it...ever."

After hanging up the phone, Mitch again thought about the day he had ahead. It was going to be very long and very hard.

Mitch decided he would just stay out of it if he could. After all, this was Sam's 'thing'...not his. He had his job and he would do it.

Feeling much better, he opened his intercom, hoping Sabrina was already here. She was and he asked her if she could bring him a cup of coffee and a couple of doughnuts. He had suddenly realized how hungry he felt.

In a very few minutes, there was a knock at the door.

"Come in," called Mitch. He admitted he enjoyed watching Sabrina as she swayed provocatively across the room. Those beautiful legs...any man would want to look at them. He found himself trying to imagine how they would feel wrapped around his body. He was sure they would be strong and exciting.

With embarrassment, Mitch realized he had been staring. He was hoping she hadn't noticed. He saw that a sly, knowing smile had crossed her face. That was even more stressful for him. She knew that he found her enticing...and that he was thinking about her. Now he would really need to be careful. He did not want to encourage her...he had Cindy, and she was all he could ever need or want. He would be faithful to her... he absolutely would.

As Sabrina came around his desk, placing the coffee and doughnuts in front of him, he felt her breast brush against his arm. Yes...she knew. He had to be very careful.

"Thank you, Miss Franklin; I appreciate the service."

"You're welcome," she responded. "I'm available for anything you need."

Getting only a small grunt in response, she left the office.

Mitch sipped his coffee and thought about what had just happened. Was he giving Sabrina the wrong message? He really hadn't meant to do that. But any man would respond in some way to her, if he was human.

Those thoughts led him to think about Cindy. She was so beautiful...and he really missed feeling her body next to his. He had been neglectful...of their mutual desires, passions and needs. That really needed to change, and soon. Pulling himself back to the present, he worked quickly at organizing his notes regarding his meeting. He needed to finish this report.

Finally, they were organized and Mitch knew he should dictate the report, but he wasn't sure he was ready to face Sabrina again so soon. Maybe he could make an oral report to Sam first.

Again he punched the intercom, this time looking for Sam. He answered quickly, somewhat surprising Mitch.

"Hi, Sam; just wanted to let you know I can give you a quick oral report on yesterday's meeting if you would like to have it."

"Give me ten minutes," said Sam, "then come on in."

"Great," replied Mitch.

He hoped his voice sounded normal to Sam...at least Sam had sounded normal. For the next ten minutes, Mitch scanned his notes. It was important for him to have a good grasp of the facts before he saw Sam. He thought about pouring himself a drink but decided it was still very early and he needed a clear head to meet with Sam.

When he knocked on Sam's door, he got an immediate response. When he entered the room, Sam greeted him as always, shaking hands and offering him a drink. He declined the drink but sat in his usual chair.

"Well, Mitch," said Sam. "How are things going? Are you still happy with us?"

What should he say now, wondered Mitch. Suddenly he heard a voice, and he realized it was his own voice, answering Sam. He was talking about how much he was learning and enjoying the responsibility. It must have sounded okay, because Sam was nodding his approval.

Finally, Mitch relaxed. Last night must have been something very unusual. It wasn't what normally went on here...he just knew it.

Since Sam had a busy schedule, Mitch gave him a thumbnail sketch of his report.

"Great," said Sam, when Mitch finished. "You are really doing a fine job. You are getting just what I want from these meetings. If you keep it up, you will be getting even more responsibility and a new position. We are really excited when we get young men like you to keep the organization strong."

Somehow, Mitch was able to thank him and excuse himself. When he was back in his office, he shut the door and leaned against it. Even more responsibility? What did that mean? He wasn't sure he could handle any more. Besides, no matter how he tried to convince himself that last night was unusual, he honestly, deep down inside, knew it was the norm.

Mitch decided he needed to finish his report so he called Sabrina into his office to take the dictation.

When she entered and sat down across from him, crossing her long legs, he tried not to notice that her skirt had slid several inches above her knee. It was very difficult not to look... temptation was strong...but he managed to keep his eyes on his notes and finished the report quickly.

"Is there anything else?" asked Sabrina.

He noticed she looked at him somewhat expectantly.

"No, that's all right now," said Mitch. "Thank you."

After she left, he felt a little guilty because of the way he was treating her. She had done nothing wrong. It was all in his mind. There wasn't anything wrong with a beautiful woman letting a single man know she was available and interested.

Mitch stood up and went to pour himself a drink. Why did he keep feeling guilty? He was doing the best he could; couldn't people see that?

He wished he had time to take a nap, but if he was going to have any time to see Cindy, he had to get his work caught up.

For the next several hours, Mitch worked diligently... making and taking phone calls, cleaning up paperwork, and trying to set up a schedule for the next week. He hurried as much as possible, wanting to get out of this place. He needed to see Cindy...she would provide him with a reality check.

Chapter eighteen

Mitch checked his watch. Almost six-o'clock and the sun was fully exposed in the eastern sky. He thought it wouldn't be long before the driver took another break. Until then, he'd try to look for answers.

He remembered that in spite of his desire to see Cindy, it had been almost eight before he left the office. The air was a little heavy, but the sky was still clear. When he started his car, he realized it had been a long time since he last arrived at the complex. Passing the guard, he waved his hand and drove out into the street. He was excited about seeing Cindy. He had almost forgotten how exciting the prospect of seeing her could be. He pushed the accelerator down harder. He couldn't get there fast enough.

When Mitch arrived at Cindy's apartment, he took the steps two at a time. He wanted just to run into the room but he did stop and knock.

He hadn't even stopped knocking before Cindy threw the door open. She had never looked more beautiful or more desirable to him. He grabbed her and pulled her to him. She felt so good. His mouth found hers and they were quickly engulfed by their passions.

Cindy leaned back, pulling Mitch in after her. Keeping her

clutched tightly to him, he kicked the door closed and managed to get her to the sofa. His hands searched her body, exploring all those beautiful spots he so enjoyed. It had not escaped him that she was wearing the gown he loved so much; it wasn't on her long. The passions he had thought were waning and controlled he found were as strong as ever. He was a little surprised, but gratified that Cindy still had the same effect on him.

Their passion was so urgent, for the first time in their relationship, they made love on the sofa. Her reaction to him was savage; she was as wild as he had ever seen her. She was his real little wildcat. That was so nice...so special.

Mitch expected to make love to her several times this night, as he had often in the past. However, he found his strength quickly left him and he felt so tired...so utterly tired. He managed to sit up and pull Cindy to him. She seemed to understand, even more than he did, the way he was feeling. She put an arm around his shoulder and pulled him to her. He kissed her full, rich mouth, but soon found he was kissing her shoulders, her full breasts, her flat stomach and her gorgeous thighs. Laying his head in her lap with his face buried in her stomach, he felt his body start to completely relax. He curled his body into a fetal position and fell instantly into a deep sleep. He felt so warm and safe with Cindy.

When he woke, he found that Cindy was caressing his face and head. He still lay with his head in her lap. This beautiful, giving woman had forsaken her own creature comforts to keep holding him. To cover her nakedness against the coolness of the room, she had pulled an afghan from the back of the sofa and covered them both.

He sat up quickly.

"Oh, Cindy, Darling. I am so sorry," he said. "I must have been so heavy for you to hold. Why didn't you wake me up?"

"I love being able to hold you," she said; "I have missed being with you."

"Me, too," said Mitch. "I love you so very much. I really needed to see you."

"I'm glad. A girl could begin to think you had lost interest," Cindy said, with a slight smile and a twinkle in her eyes. But he knew it was at least partly true.

Throughout the conversation, they had sat facing each other, their hands touching on the back of the sofa. Even with such little physical contact, Mitch could still feel the tingling shocks flowing through his body.

Looking toward the window, he thought he could see a red tinge to the clouds.

"What time is it?" he asked.

"Almost six."

He couldn't believe it. He had slept all through the night curled up on her lap. She must be exhausted.

"Cindy, please; let's go to bed. I want you to get some rest. What time do you have to be at work?"

"Eleven," she said.

"Good, we can get at least four hours of sleep."

With the final word, Mitch scooped Cindy up in his arms and carried her into the bedroom. She was clinging to his neck and he could hear her little sounds of delight. As he placed her on the bed, he again felt the passion rising in his body and the squirming of Cindy's body told him she felt the same. Sleep would have to wait.

Mitch dropped Cindy off at the bar before driving to work. He told her he wanted to see her later. They agreed that she would meet him at his apartment. Jim would keep her company until he got home. He promised to try to get home as early as possible.

When Mitch drove through the gate of the complex, he forgot the outside world. He was thrilled with the growing power; it was addictive.

As he went by Sabrina's desk, she held up some envelopes and messages and said, "These are for you, Mr. Nelson."

He was feeling a little uncomfortable because of the way he had been treating her and decided now was the time to do something about it.

"Thanks, Sabrina," he said, giving her a big smile. "I really appreciate the help you've give me. I know I've been a little testy lately. Please forgive me. I sometimes feel I'll never get the knack of things here."

"Of course, Mr. Nelson," she said with that beautiful musical voice.

"Please, Sabrina; call me Mitch."

"I'll try, Mr...er, Mitch," she said, bestowing upon him a dazzling smile. "By the way, your report is on your desk."

"Thanks; that was fast," said Mitch. "I may have more work later."

He went down the hall, looking at his mail and messages. He was so engrossed in them that he didn't even notice Sam's door was open.

"Mitch," Sam yelled. "Come on in."

Mitch stopped and went into Sam's office.

"Hi, Sam; is there something you need?"

"Not at all," said Sam. "I was just going to ask if you overslept."

Mitch flushed.

"No," he said. "I just needed a little time. Seems as if I've been here 24/7 for ages."

"I know the feeling," said Sam. "I was just joking. Have a good day."

"Thanks; you too."

Mitch sat at his desk. There was so much to do and he needed to get started.

The messages were first. All four of them were from overseas suppliers requesting meetings. He quickly looked up the profiles of each one and returned the calls. It looked like he was going to be traveling a lot in the next two weeks. Well, it couldn't be helped.

The mail contained some requests for meetings. That meant eight trips in the next two weeks. It would be rough.

Mitch looked over the report. Sabrina was good...no mistakes. He signed it, picked it up and went to Sam's office. Sam was out, so Mitch left it on his desk.

When he was back in his office, he decided to tackle his paperwork. As he studied the reports from the local suppliers, he found several areas of concern. Some were showing drops in sales. He needed to meet with them. The other problem that kept popping up was shortages in payments. He knew he'd need to meet with them. Surely, it wasn't skimming that was going on. He hoped they weren't that stupid. You didn't rip off the organization. He began leafing through his card file so he could telephone those reps he needed to meet with. Another problem was where he was going to meet with them. They never held meetings in this complex. Mitch couldn't think of any place where he could set up several meetings, no matter how hard he thought. He didn't really want to ask Sam. Maybe that was his pride talking, but he wanted Sam to think he could take care of his own responsibilities. But who would he ask?

Sabrina! She probably knew a lot more about the business than he did. In fact probably more than anyone except Sam. He was sure it wouldn't create any problems to seek her help. After all, he was more than ready to face and fight temptation.

Smiling to himself, Mitch pushed the intercom button. After all, this request would serve two purposes; one was to prove he could do his job without going to Sam; and the second was that his love for Cindy was so strong that he could resist a luscious, available woman. When Sabrina answered, he asked her if she could step into his office for a few minutes.

"Right away, Mr. Nelson," she replied. Again Mitch heard that melodic tone in her voice. He admitted he was anxious to look at her again.

Almost immediately, Mitch heard a knock.

"Come in," he called.

Sabrina walked...or rather flowed...into the room. No matter what his resolve, he had a difficult time taking his eyes off those undulating hips.

"Hello, Mitch," she purred.

Mitch felt his mouth go dry and his collar seemed to tighten.

"Have a seat, Sabrina," said Mitch. "I was wondering if you could help me with a problem?"

He was trying to keep this very business-like. He focused his eyes either on the papers on his desk or her eyes, but he had to force them not to wander.

"I'd be only too happy to help you, Mitch; anytime."

Mitch noticed that she leaned slightly forward, exposing the cleavage usually covered by her business attire. Now he knew, for sure, it was getting warmer in here.

He gulped some air, then tried to get his mind back on business.

"I have several meetings I need to hold with various local reps," said Mitch, "and I can't think of any place that is appropriate to hold them. I wondered if you might have any suggestions."

"Is that all?" she asked, sitting back in her chair. He thought he saw a look of disappointment cross her face, but he couldn't be sure because it disappeared as quickly as it had come. It was probably just his imagination.

"In the past, the organization has booked a suite in one of the larger hotels for meetings like this," she said. "Would you like me to set it up?"

"Would you?" asked Mitch. "That would be very helpful. As soon as you have the arrangements made, let me know. If possible, I will need the suite for two days, next Wednesday and Thursday. And, Sabrina, thanks."

This at least earned him another one of her smiles as she left.

Mitch sat back and watched as she left. He noticed the faint smell of musk remained in the air. She was certainly different from Cindy who smelled of lilacs...a sweet, enticing smell. Even Peggy had a different scent...that of fresh spring rain. There it was again...that memory of Peggy. Would she never leave him alone?

He knew he needed to get Sam's approval for the rental but felt confident that he would applaud his initiative. He must remember to get Sabrina a thank-you gift.

Mitch called Sam, telling him what he was planning and, as anticipated, Sam was pleased and praised him for his ingenuity. Yes, he definitely needed to get Sabrina a gift.

He completed a written request for funds, meaning to drop it off for Sam's signature in the next day or two. He also studied his lists of those with whom he needed to meet. He began to sketch out a schedule. Those in town or close by would be given the earlier appointments, leaving travel time for the others.

While he was busily trying to set up the best schedule, the intercom buzzed. It was Sabrina; she had the suite reserved.

What a fantastic girl, Mitch thought, and not only in a business sense. He couldn't help but think about that fabulous figure, those gorgeous legs, and, of course, the unbelievable smile and voice. He found himself wondering just what was hidden by the severe business attire.

He suddenly realized his body was beginning to fill with desire...how could it do that? He had left the bed of his beautiful Cindy only four hours earlier, and she was enough woman for any man. But he still felt the desire to explore Sabrina rising in him. After all, this was Cindy's fault. She was the one who showed him he could have passionate sex more often than he had believed was possible.

He had to get rid of these feelings. Besides, Cindy was not a part of this world. When he was in the compound, he felt like he was a completely different person, leading a separate life. He seemed to have forgotten that the reason for working was Cindy. Maybe his reasons had changed...he loved the power.

Mitch decided he needed a drink. He poured a large whiskey and finished it at once. He poured a second one and took it back to his desk.

Again he found himself staring out the window. The view was so serene and he felt his body begin to relax. When he finished his second drink, Mitch suddenly felt very tired. He needed a nap. It seemed as if this passion he felt was exhausting him.

He looked at his watch. It was almost five. He would start his calls to set up his meeting schedule and see how it went. He was surprised at the energy these call generated in him. Although he sometimes had to call more than once, he finally contacted everyone on his list. Some of them were a little reluctant to meet with him; these he starred so that he could try to find out why. When he finished his last call, he saw that his calendar for those two days was very tight. If he got too far behind, the meetings would go on all night. He would have to be very well prepared so that he could keep on schedule.

Realizing he hadn't eaten all day and that he was hungry, he stretched and then walked out of the office. The building was deathly silent...nobody else seemed to be here. However, when he passed Sam's office he again saw light under the door. He knocked but got no answer so he went on down the hall to the cafeteria area. There he selected some chips and candy bars from the vending machines. It wasn't much of a meal, but it would give him some energy. He needed it...he had lots more work to do.

As he walked back through the reception area, he noticed the clock. It was almost one thirty in the morning. It looked like another night on the couch.

He returned to his office, poured another stiff drink, and started to study the profiles again. Mitch was soon so wrapped up in his work, he wasn't even aware that he was nibbling on snacks or sipping his drink. It was only when his glass was empty that he realized he had been drinking. Again, looking at the time, he saw that it was almost four. He needed to get some sleep, but first he needed another drink.

After getting his drink, he stretched out on the couch. He relaxed as he drank his whiskey. He noticed it still warmed his body as it went down. When the drink was gone, Mitch switched off the lights and immediately fell asleep. He didn't even think about Cindy.

When he awoke, he wasn't sure it had been a good sleep. In fact, he had dreamt that he was running and running. Ahead of him was a huge bag of gold that seemed almost within reach, but he could never quite catch it. In addition, he was being chased...by Cindy, Peggy and Sabrina. Just as it looked as if he would be caught, he woke up. Mitch had no idea what that dream had meant. He loved Cindy and would never run away from her; and he only wanted money to share with her.

Mitch checked his watch. Almost seven. Definitely time to get back to work. He ran the electric shaver over his face and that made him feel better...but not much. He really needed a pick-me-up, so he reached for his little pillbox. It wasn't long before he felt much better. Was he making use of that pillbox more often? No, not really.

It was a very busy day for Mitch. He spent the time making notes for all the meetings he would be having in the next two weeks. He wanted to be well briefed.

Most of the afternoon was spent with Sam, specifically focused on the meetings Mitch would be having with the international suppliers. Since Mitch was representing Sam, he wanted to be clear about what Sam wanted accomplished. Sam approved the financing for the suite. Then he suggested that Mitch plan to take Sabrina with him to keep the appointments running smoothly.

"I trust her," said Sam. "She knows as much about the organization as I do and she knows how to keep her mouth shut."

Mitch agreed with Sam's suggestion and said he would talk

to Sabrina about it. Actually, the thought of spending two days with Sabrina felt good. But what had Sam meant when he said Sabrina could keep her mouth shut?

Cindy! He had completely forgotten that he was supposed to see her last night, and he hadn't even called. He needed to call her as soon as possible.

Mitch finished his conference with Sam quickly and rushed back to his office. The first number he called was Cindy's apartment. When the answering machine picked up, he hesitated. He really didn't know what to say. He was sorry, but that sounded lame. The truth was, though, that he was sorry, very sorry, even if she wouldn't forgive him. Finally, he decided.

"Hi, baby, I'm so sorry. I know you must be tired of hearing that, but it really is true. Believe me, I was working…all alone. This job may be too much for me, but I want to try. Really, Cindy; I love you so much and my life would be empty and useless without you. Please call me. I do want to see you tonight."

After hanging up, he sat thinking about the message. It was really true…and he could only hope she knew it.

His next call was to Jim. Again, he got an answering machine.

"Hi, Jim. I'm so sorry I didn't make it home last night. Thanks for taking care of Cindy. I plan to get home in the next couple of nights. I'll call."

Now he could concentrate on work. In no time, he was entirely engrossed again in his work. When his phone rang, he was startled and took a few seconds to get back to reality.

He felt a great deal of relief; it was Cindy. She sounded very cool, but at least she had called.

"Hi, Cindy; thanks for returning my call," he said.

When he got no response, he added, "As I told you, time got away from me. Please believe me, I do love you, but this job just overwhelms me, sometimes."

He paused and was so relieved when she answered.

"Mitch, I know you are telling me the truth. I love you too and I trust you, but maybe it would be better if I just got out of your life until you get established in your job."

"No!" he heard himself shout. It was just like Peggy. "Cindy, life wouldn't exist without you. Please don't leave me. I do love you so much. I'll try hard to be more responsible. Could I just see you tonight?"

"I guess so," said Cindy. "To be truthful, I want to say no, but I can't."

He thought he heard her start to cry. The last thing he wanted to do was hurt Cindy.

"Can you meet me at my apartment? I promise to be there no later than eight o'clock."

"I'll be there," she said, but her voice was so sad and listless, it broke his heart.

Before he could respond, she had hung up.

For sure he was getting out of here tonight. He would work hard until seven, three more hours, and then he would go home.

Just as he started, the intercom buzzed. Sabrina's lilting voice told he he had some mail.

"May I bring it back now?"

"Of course," replied Mitch. He realized he was looking forward to seeing her again. After all, there was nothing wrong with looking at a beautiful woman.

When she came into the office, he was disappointed to see that she was wearing a raincoat that camouflaged her figure. She crossed the room and put the mail on his desk.

"I'm sorry, Sabrina. Did I keep you from going home?" asked Mitch.

"Oh, no," she replied. "I just thought I'd try to go home early since it is a little quiet right now."

Mitch realized he wanted her company.

"I wanted to thank you for your help yesterday. I really

appreciate it," said Mitch. He wondered why he felt so stiff and awkward speaking to her.

"You're welcome, Mitch; I'm not really in a hurry," she said. "I'll be glad to stay if I can help."

"I'd appreciate it," he said. "Let me take your coat."

Mitch put her coat on one of the chairs and returned to his desk. As he sat down, he glanced up at Sabrina. She really was beautiful. Now that he was studying her, he realized she was much older than he had thought. He was just nineteen, but she must be about thirty. Imagine, a real older woman had 'come on' to him. That felt great. He started feeling so prideful. Then he brought himself up short. What was he doing? Remember... Cindy; the love of his life!

To Sabrina, he said, "I talked to Sam today about the interviews I am setting up for next week and he suggested that I take you with me to keep everything organized. Would you be interested?"

"Of course, I'd love to go with you," said Sabrina. "It sounds like fun. I am so glad you want to take me."

Mitch felt his chest tighten when she said that, because of the tone she used. It sounded so inviting...very sensual. He looked at her, and saw that she was even inviting him with her posture. That excited him...from such a fabulous woman. He tried to get his breath to return to normal. That was difficult.

"We'll talk about this later this week and solidify our plans," said Mitch, surprised he sounded so normal. "Do you have someone you need to get home to," he asked, "or do you have time for a drink?"

"I'd love a drink," she replied. "The answer is 'no,' I don't have anyone to get home to. What about you?"

This was his chance to set the limits...to let her know he was involved with a special lady...so he was really surprised when he heard himself say, "Well, no, not really. I'm not married, if that is what you mean."

What was he thinking of...now he had opened the door for

this sensual woman. Trying to cover up his embarrassment, he walked to the bar.

"What will you have?" he asked.

"Make it a gin rocks with lime, if you have it," she said.

"Coming right up; do you want tonic?"

"Just a little," she said.

This caused him to smile, but when he turned, he saw she had moved to the couch. She had her long legs curled under her, causing her skirt to rise dangerously high and her blouse appeared to be open even lower than before. She had a coquettish look on her face. He knew she was going to be trouble...and it was all his fault. Why hadn't he told her about Cindy?

Mitch poured himself a stiff drink of whiskey, drank half of it in one gulp, and then refilled his glass. Then he took both drinks to the couch. The scent of musk was strong.

"Thanks, Mitch," said Sabrina, as he handed her the glass. She sipped it and looked at him over the rim of the glass. Her eyelashes were long and thick and her eyes were so dark, they looked like two pieces of coal. Mitch felt as if he was being pulled like a magnet to her. He resisted, drinking a large gulp of his whiskey. He didn't know what to say...he knew what he should have already said...but now, it was too late.

Sabrina continued to look at him...her breasts were heavy and looked as if they wanted to burst from her blouse, and he didn't dare look at her legs. He felt as if the room was closing in on him. Now he was feeling uncomfortable with the silence.

Sabrina sipped her drink, then bent forward, offering a clear view down her blouse, and placed her glass on the coffee table. Despite his attempt to keep from looking, he found his eyes straying to her cleavage. If he hadn't known before, he would have known now, that this was a real woman, not a girl. Cindy and Peggy had beautiful and luscious breasts, but they were under-developed when compared to Sabrina. It upset him that he was comparing them. That should never occur.

As she sat back, Sabrina drug her hand lightly across his thighs. He wanted to jump out of his skin…he closed his eyes and hoped he could find the strength to keep his hands off Sabrina.

Opening his eyes, he looked into Sabrina's face, and said, inanely, "Can I freshen your drink?"

She smiled. "No, I don't think so. I think I should go."

Mitch felt like a great weight was lifted. He was glad she had the strength he lacked.

"Let me get your coat," he said.

Sabrina stood, straightening her skirt. As he helped her into her coat, he was careful not to touch her body…he felt that if he did, he wouldn't let her go.

She smiled, leaned forward, and gave him a light kiss on the cheek, and said;

"Thanks, Mitch. See you in the morning."

When she left, Mitch poured himself another drink. He finished it then went back to his desk. He felt so exhausted. He couldn't face any further work tonight. Maybe he would surprise Cindy and get there early.

Cindy…he wanted to be with her more than anything, but his body felt so exhausted, he didn't know if he could satisfy her needs tonight. He didn't want to disappoint her. The last time they were together, he had slept in her lap after their passionate sex. Tonight, he was afraid he couldn't make love to her at all. It certainly wasn't Cindy's fault. Just thinking about her made his body ache, but making love to her tonight, might be impossible. Would she think that meant he was losing interest in her; that he no longer desired and loved her? He couldn't let her even consider that, but what could he do?

Than he knew…his little box of pills. It would solve all his problems. Choosing carefully, he selected four capsules. This was more than he had ever used at one time but he needed it tonight. He knew he'd had a lot of whiskey too, but he had to get his body stimulated.

When he felt his strength returning, he grabbed his jacket and left the building. He rolled the windows down as he drove home; letting the warm, moist air hit his face. He thought about the upcoming weekend. He planned to spend every minute of it with Cindy. He would be away most of the next two weeks, so spending an entire weekend with her would help.

When he arrived home, he was glad to see that Cindy was pleased that he was there. She didn't notice that he looked a little unsteady. He did think that Jim looked at him a little suspiciously, but he just brushed that feeling off. After all, he had been working long, hard hours.

Cindy was so happy...knowing that made Mitch feel even better. His strength seemed to be returning. He hugged Cindy to him.

"Are you ready to go, baby?" he asked.

"Of course," she replied.

Waving to Jim, they left the apartment and he held her close as they walked to the car. She felt so good, and she smelled good too. Her hair and skin both smelled lightly of lilacs. He buried his face in her neck, trying to drink in this scent.

As they drove away from the apartment, Mitch looked again at Cindy, snuggled next to him. She was so wonderful...how could he ever want more.

"How about Italian?" asked Mitch.

"That would be wonderful," Cindy replied softly. "Where?"

"It's a surprise," said Mitch.

This caused Cindy to smile and snuggle closer. Yes, she really did feel good to him.

When Mitch stopped the car, Cindy's eyes grew wide, and then she smiled and threw her arms around his neck. When Mitch pulled back, he saw that there were tears in her eyes.

Worried, Mitch said, "Don't cry, Cindy. I thought you would like this."

Now smiling brightly through her tears, she replied: "I love it, darling. These are tears of joy; how sweet and romantic."

Mitch was really glad he had chosen this restaurant. It was where they had spent their first date, last Christmas Eve, when they had walked here through the snow. Mitch couldn't believe that had been only eight months earlier. Why they hadn't been back before, he didn't know. And it was great that Cindy thought he was romantic. He hadn't been doing a great job of showing her that lately. That made him feel a little sad and a little guilty. She deserved so much more.

Mama was so happy to see them. She remembered them and even sat them at the same small table. Mitch ordered the same drinks and food...but all he really wanted was to be with Cindy, to hold her, and to make love to her.

The ate slowly, picking at their food. They had such a difficult time taking their eyes off each other. When they finished, Mitch left a huge tip and they walked out, holding closely to each other. Mama smiled as they left, but said nothing.

When they reached the car, they were quiet, still just filling themselves with the sight of each other. They drove, without words, to Cindy's apartment.

This quietness disappeared as soon as the door closed behind them.

As Cindy turned to Mitch, he picked her up in his arms and carried her into the bedroom, still studying her perfection...the beauty beyond words. Love made everything perfect.

He lay Cindy on the bed and sat beside her, tracing her face with his fingers. She grabbed his hand and kissed his palm. He felt, in that kiss, her rising passion which was matching his own. There was no doubt that Cindy knew how he felt...one look would tell her.

He began to trail his fingers down her neck and throat until he reached the top button of her blouse. He felt her body shudder; he wanted to take her now, but he also wanted to drink in fully this wonderful experience. No matter how often he took this beautiful being, it was always as exciting as the first time.

With trembling hands, he unbuttoned her blouse, laying it open and pulling it from her waistband and then removing it and throwing it to the floor. He couldn't believe, that after all this time, his desire for her could still cause him to tremble. When he saw her lying there, he wondered if he could wait, but he tried to be patient. He trailed his fingers lightly through her cleavage…stopping to slide both hands under her to undo her bra. Cindy gently arched her back, making his task easy. Pulling his hands back, he brought the bra with him, slipping the straps from her shoulders so that he could release her beautiful, firm, young breasts.

His delight showed on his face and as he flung the bra away, he buried his face between her breasts, holding them against him with his hands. He knew he could never feel any better… safe, warm, comforted and loved. Cindy was caressing the back of his head and he felt her body arching, trying to press more closely to his face. He felt like he could stay here all night, but his body, and hers, were demanding more. Reluctantly pulling back, he continued tracing his fingers over her breasts and down until he reached her waistband. His touch was light and Mitch felt Cindy's body responding to it. As her responses increased, he felt his own body straining to be inside her, but …patience.

Mitch knew that by denying himself instant gratification, his end reward would be better…if he could just wait. This waiting was causing him to breathe harder and it seemed at times as if he couldn't get enough air.

Not wanting to wait much longer, Mitch unbuttoned Cindy's skirt and pushed it down her hips, catching his thumbs in the waistband of her panties as he went. Cindy raised her hips off the bed and he slid her clothing down her silky, smooth legs and over her feet. Her beauty took his breath away…and he was glad that she didn't act embarrassed or try to shield her body from his eyes. Just the sight of this fabulous body would satisfy some men...but not him. He knew how many more pleasures awaited him.

Cindy's body squirmed with delight as he kissed her from head to toe, stopping to kiss each of her ten toes. When he was doing this, Mitch felt her body shudder and stiffen with desire for him. Unable or at least unwilling to deny himself the ultimate pleasure that awaited him he pulled his own clothes off, dropping them on the floor with Cindy's. She reached and touched his hard, throbbing penis as he stood beside her. She could tell he was ready.

Mitch mounted Cindy's beckoning body and lowered himself finding her body warm and welcoming as he entered her. At that moment, he felt as if it was the start of the Fourth of July fireworks display, already exciting, but building to an even greater climax. Cindy wrapped her legs tightly around him, holding him close. With a strong, thrusting rhythm, they began their climb to the ultimate ecstasy. When they reached it, when the moans from each of them were loud and excited, they felt the ultimate culmination of such love making, the sexual fluids of their bodies mixing in a tribute to their love. Now those fireworks were exploding at their peak.

With one final thrust, Mitch pushed himself as deeply inside Cindy as he could. It was then he felt his body drain in a complete flood of pleasure. He knew from her deep moans and sighs, that Cindy had felt the same way.

Spent and exhausted, Mitch laid on top of Cindy, trying to regain his normal breathing pattern. Then he rolled over on his back, pulling her tightly against his side. Mitch knew that if he had ever taken up smoking this would have been the perfect time for a cigarette. He did wish, however, that he had some uppers to share with Cindy, hoping to rejuvenate their desires even more quickly. Of course, he didn't know if Cindy would be interested or appalled.

They lay quietly in each others arms, neither one sleeping but each lost in his own thoughts and enjoying the peace and contentment.

Finally, Mitch said;

"Cindy, Darling, I love you more every time I am with you. You seem to take me to higher heights every time and the pleasure you give me is indescribable."

Cindy didn't answer, but he felt her turn her face into his chest and he felt her warm tears falling against his skin.

She was holding him so tightly, he couldn't easily pull away, but he was concerned.

"Are you all right? Did I hurt you?"

Cindy pulled back and raised her face to his. He saw the tracks of tears down her beautiful face.

"No, you didn't hurt me...you never do...but you always make me feel so special, so desirable, so loved. You always make me feel important," said Cindy.

"You are important...and special...and particularly desirable. Don't you ever forget that. Never let anyone tell you any differently."

Again they were quiet, just enjoying each other.

Finally, Cindy said, "Are you wearing a new after shave or cologne? I smell a musk on you."

Mitch felt his body stiffen, not from desire, but from sudden fear. Sabrina! She had left her scent on him...but he hadn't done anything with her. Why would he jeopardize his wonderful relationship with Cindy, for nothing.

In response, Mitch stammered, "I don't think so...I just used what's in my kit. I'll have to check on it."

Cindy curled more closely to him and he took a deep breath. That was close. He realized it wasn't that he didn't want to be with Sabrina but that he didn't want to hurt Cindy. Did that mean he was a jerk? Maybe he was just a man.

Mitch thought they might drop off to sleep, but he soon felt Cindy's hand working magic on his body, trying to raise his level of desire. It didn't take long. Cindy continued to caress and fondle his body until he knew he had to take her again. As exhausted as he had been when he was at the office, he could not believe, even with his booze and drugs, she could get a second rise out of him so soon...but she had.

Suddenly, Cindy became the aggressor...and he liked it. She straddled his body, sitting upright so that he could not miss looking at those beautiful golden breasts, so firm and full, but not ponderous or sagging. He bet Sabrina's would sag. How could he even think of Sabrina when he was here with Cindy and she was working her magic on him, finding and satisfying his desires. Was he loosing his mind?

Cindy continued her aggressive ways, raising and lowering her buttocks, causing his desire to grow even stronger. He was writhing and moaning, almost out of control. Sparkling lights of desire and excitement blazed from Cindy's green eyes. The heat her body was exuding was almost too hot to bear. Finally, when she felt she had toyed with him long enough, she threw her body flat against him, smashing those beautiful, pillow-like breasts against his chest. They had become one, working in unison to fulfill every desire within either of them. He bucked off the bed to meet her downward thrusts. The power they generated was almost impossible to imagine. Their thrusts became even harder and faster. Moans and screams were coming from their mouths. Mitch wasn't sure he could stand much more. He wanted nothing more than to erupt, but Cindy kept him going higher and higher. Oh, the pain...but also the enjoyment. With a loud, piercing scream he had never heard from her before, she thrust her body tightly against him, forcing him even more deeply into her. She held her buttocks tightly against him as she threw her shoulders back, bending almost until her hair touched her legs, but again exposing those beautiful breast to him. His eruption had been even stronger and more powerful than their first tonight. He hadn't thought it possible...but this woman had powers he, nor anyone else, could imagine.

He felt his body leaving hers, completely spent. He wondered at that moment if he would ever again feel the hardness of desire. Reaching forward he pulled one of her breasts into his mouth. He wanted, actually really needed, the comfort and security her breasts provided for him. He had never figured out how these beautiful mounds could do that for him...but they did.

Cindy, looking completely spent and exhausted herself, rolled off to the side, pulling him with her. She held him with one arm across his shoulders and, with the other hand she guided her breast to his waiting mouth. Hungrily, he began to suck as hard as he could, pulling the hard, sensitive nipple deeply into his mouth. He fondled the other breast with his hand, kneading its fullness and pinching the nipple with his fingers. The harder he sucked and fondled, the harder and larger the nipples became. This fact did not escape Mitch. They appeared to grow with his touch. A fleeting thought crossed his mind; maybe Sabrina's breasts weren't so full from maturity but from use and stimulation. He would need to think about that...but not now. Now he wanted his full attention on Cindy's breasts.

As Mitch continued nursing and fondling, Cindy felt desire start to reenter her body. She was not sure she could contain herself, but she wasn't sure Mitch's desires met hers. She let her free hand caress the back of his head, pressing it even tighter against her breast. She allowed her fingers to caress his shoulders and travel down his arm, until they reached his hips. By sliding her had across, she knew she could tell if Mitch was also feeling this desire.

She jerked her hand back, almost as if she had been burned. She couldn't believe it, but she could tell that his desire was also building quickly.

Cindy shifted her body, bringing herself even closer to

Mitch. She felt his body twitch and knew that their desires would once more find fulfillment.

Mitch couldn't believe it either. He felt so spent, but he also could feel his body calling for more.

He began to draw more deeply as he sucked her nipple. It seemed to him that every time he sucked hard, Cindy's entire body stiffened and shuddered. Unbelievably, this reaction also caused his need to rise. Soon he would need to seek release and fulfillment again. He had no patience left.

After the third round of intensive sex, Cindy and Mitch were both completely drained and weak. They curled together on their sides, her back to him. His body fit tightly against her and one arm laid across her body, resting on her breasts. He didn't have the strength to return to fondling them. They both fell asleep quickly, completely satisfied and at ease with each other.

When the alarm sounded, it roused them both from a deep, relaxed sleep. Cindy rolled over so that she could face Mitch. He thought she looked even more beautiful in this early morning light. Her hair lay in ringlets around her face and the lovely, smooth face didn't need any make-up. It was perfect.

Mitch trailed his fingers down her side and received a smile in response.

"Good morning," she said.

"It really is," replied Mitch. "You are so lovely, I can't take my eyes off of you, but I don't know where to look first. From head to toe, you are breathtaking…perfect."

Cindy blushed, but instead of arguing with him, she reached up to give him a light kiss. As her lips lightly brushed his, he felt that electric shock again. He responded by pulling her body flat against his and turning the light kiss into a passion-filled request. Unbelievably, he wanted her again. Her response was quick and positive. She opened her mouth and their tongues met, causing even deeper desire. He knew she was ready; she was rubbing her body against his and they both knew that his manhood was responding with stiffness. He couldn't wait; he turned her onto her back and knelt between her legs. As he looked down on her waiting, desirable body, he could see his penis stiff and jerking, hovering above her. She was ready and he lowered himself into her. It was as wonderful as ever. She engulfed him, pulling him close and bucking with such force and power that she brought him to the brink of ecstasy. Mitch was almost unaware of their bucking bodies, only the feeling of pain caused by his desire. He needed to take her again. Just when he felt he couldn't stand it for another moment, he felt their bodies crash into each other in a spasmodic release. Unbelievable. Nothing could have prepared him for this woman, his desire for her, and her ability to completely satisfy him.

Mitch felt like he wanted to go back to sleep, but Cindy coaxed him out of bed and into the shower. Soaping each other's bodies was a very sensual experience, and Mitch loved it.

When they were finished, they dried each other, stopping periodically to plant kisses in special places. Finally dry, they walked into the bedroom knowing they needed to get dressed. Mitch had a difficult time attending to his own dressing because all he wanted to do was to look at Cindy. With this picture etched in his memory, he planned to keep her always in front of him, even at work. Well, he meant it...then.

Chapter nineteen

The bus slowed and, looking out the window, Mitch saw a large metropolitan area ahead. He decided it must be Indianapolis. As much as he wanted this trip to end, he dreaded his arrival.

When the bus pulled into the depot, there were lots of busses and people. This was a busy place. Mitch followed the other passengers off the bus. The air wasn't as fresh as before… too much traffic. He went into the depot, found the men's room, and then went into the restaurant. Even though he had eaten breakfast earlier, he felt a little hungry, so he decided to order a snack. When the waitress stopped at his table, he ordered coffee and doughnuts. This order reminded him of the old office; it seemed he had lots of doughnuts and coffee there.

When he had finished, he dropped some money on the table and went back to the bus. It was still at least five minutes until they were due to leave. He thought he'd just get settled. As it was, most of the passengers were already seated. Shortly, they began to move again.

Mitch returned in thought to that fateful August. It seemed like another lifetime, but was only six years ago.

After that fantastic night spent with Cindy, Mitch thought things would be wonderful for them…but that hadn't been true.

He had explained to Cindy that he would be so busy the next two weeks that meetings and travel would take all of his time. She was disappointed; after all, being with him was so exciting and satisfying. Even so, she thanked him for telling her ahead of time so she wouldn't expect to hear from him. He noticed that he did not tell her about Sabrina and that they would be spending so much time together. But it was just business. Why make Cindy unhappy or worried? He had arranged to spend Friday night with her, and hopefully all weekend. He was looking forward to that.

Typically, when he arrived at work, everything except business left this mind. Inside the complex, even thoughts of the outside world had trouble getting through. There were no thoughts of Cindy or Peggy. He wished he'd never have thoughts of Peggy, but he did. He had heard that she was working at the college library and had changed majors. Maybe she didn't want to be in any classes with him. Now she was thinking of being a librarian...that seemed to be boring, like the factory. He was lucky they weren't together. He had also heard that she was not dating anyone...she just worked and studied. The sorority even wanted her to leave...she just didn't enhance their image.

But, back at work, neither Cindy nor Peggy entered his mind. The only woman who was part of this world was Sabrina...and what a woman.

Mitch threw himself into his work. He had lots of preparation to do for the meetings he had scheduled for the next two weeks. In addition, there were lots of calls from both suppliers and sales reps. Most of their problems were minor and he handled them either on the phone or by letter. Sabrina was invaluable to him. She took messages when he was busy, took his dictation, typed his letters and notes, and even made sure he was eating. He really didn't know what he would have done without her.

Because he had so much to do, he again lost track of time. He had meant to stay at the office on Thursday night, but Friday came and went, and again, he forgot Cindy. Friday night was bad enough, but he worked straight through the weekend, catching catnaps on his couch when he could. To keep up this pace, he was drinking too much and using an unusual amount of pills...he never even considered they could have a bad effect on him...they made him feel great.

No matter what time it was, Sabrina always seemed to be at her desk, any time he needed her...and she always looked refreshed and gorgeous. He admitted his life did not lack beautiful women.

The weekend passed and he still hadn't thought to call Cindy. On Monday morning, after a long night of work, booze and drugs, he boarded the company jet for a trip to Key West. He knew he was meeting with one of the most important international suppliers for the organization. He had to be well prepared. Sam was concerned because the supplier seemed to be short-changing them...less product, more money. Mitch's job was to find out why and get him back to exclusively supplying the organization and at mutually fair prices. This particular supplier was a mountain rebel and a warlord in his country. Mitch felt that he would have to have just the right degree of authority in his voice when he spoke to him...not too weak, not too strong. He needed to work on that, but first he was just going to rest his eyes for a few minutes.

The next thing Mitch knew, the pilot announced that they were landing in Key West. Mitch rubbed his eyes. Did he look alert enough? Just in case, he downed a glass of whiskey and added two uppers. Now he could face anything or anyone.

The only other passenger was Terrance who never talked. Mitch decided it was just so quiet he had fallen asleep...drugs, booze and late nights were not to blame.

When they landed, Terrance was the first one off the plane. After checking for any problems, he motioned for Mitch to follow him. Mitch grabbed his briefcase and ran lightly down the steps. He and Terrance climbed into a nearby limo and were quickly whisked away.

Mitch relaxed in the back seat. He let his mind wander back to his first limo ride...his Senior Prom...a lifetime ago and a different world. He didn't want to go there so he forced his thoughts back to the present and the meeting coming up. Looking out the window, he saw water flashing past.

When the limo came to a stop, Mitch looked out the window. All he could see was a small, wooden house...almost a shack... that set right on the edge of the water. A second limo was parked near the building.

Mitch, for the first time, entered a meeting with a touch of fear. He didn't know if this man was more dangerous or if he was just beginning to understand the dangers. Either way, for the first time, he was grateful for the bulge under Terrance's suit coat; a definite sign that he was armed.

These plain, often trashy looking places always surprised him. On the inside, they were modern, up-to-date buildings with the newest amenities including a lot of electronic equipment. They were comfortable and had spaces for private meetings.

There were three men in the room when he and Terrance entered, all dressed in black suits. Mitch immediately identified the supplier....he was slightly older than Sam and carried himself in a regal manner.

Terrance introduced Mitch to the three men and everyone shook hands, firmly. Mitch noticed that the other two men were also armed. After the introductions, Mitch and the supplier sat at a small table, facing each other. Terrance and the other two men stepped back to the doorway, out of earshot but still visible.

Mitch began by praising the supplier for his ability to supply such excellent and high-quality products over an extended period of time. He knew he had hit just the right note when the supplier smiled and a look of pride crossed his face. Mitch added that the organization considered him an integral and important part of their set-up.

Giving him a few moments to enjoy the feeling, Mitch told him about Sam's concerns. When he first mentioned shortages, the supplier started to get agitated but Mitch quickly acknowledged there could be many reasons for this. Out of the corner of his eye, Mitch was relieved to see Terrance was alert and noticed the change in the supplier's demeanor.

When the supplier started to calm down a bit, Mitch again reiterated what an integral part of the organization they considered him and assured him that they would work closely with him to solve this problem. Now, Mitch noticed, the supplier was visibly relaxed again. Mitch felt like sighing in relief, but he didn't, at least audibly.

Things were looking good. They had broken the ice and had covered the most sensitive area of this meeting. Before he finished the meeting, Mitch had the supplier's word that the organization would be the exclusive recipient of his product, that he and they would work at trying to stop the shortage, and that if he could increase his production, the organization would increase their orders at a fair price, fully acceptable to both the supplier and the organization.

Smiling broadly, the supplier showed yellowing, jagged teeth beneath his shaggy, black mustache. It would be easy to picture this man in jungle fatigues…in fact, it would look much more natural for him than what he was now wearing.

He slapped Mitch on the back, saying he was a good boy, and ordered drinks for everyone. Mitch needed one…badly. He realized his muscles had been tight throughout the negotiations. A drink would help.

After handing Mitch his whiskey, the supplier wanted to toast their deal. This accomplished, they all prepared to leave the meeting house. Everyone seemed pleased and in a good mood.

Back in the limo, Mitch rested his head on the seatback. He

was exhausted. This non-stop work was taking its toll. These meetings, too, were intense, and tiring. Even at his young age, he could feel his energies and strengths draining; he was feeling much older, every day.

He soon felt as if someone was staring at him. He opened his eyes and saw that Terrance was looking directly at him. This was very unusual; Terrance had never looked directly at him, and he almost never even acknowledged his presence.

"That was a good job," said Terrance, in a deep, hollow voice.

Mitch couldn't believe it. Not only was Terrance looking at him and talking to him, he was praising him. In the six months he had known him, nothing like this had ever happened.

"Thanks," said Mitch. "I just want to accomplish what Sam wants done."

"You did it," said Terrance. "Can I get you a drink?"

Almost stunned, Mitch said, "Thanks, I'll have…"

"I know; a whiskey straight and tall," said Terrance, and he actually smiled. Mitch leaned back, relaxing. He was proud of the job he was doing. He felt confident that Sam was too.

Terrance handed him his drink and Mitch saw that he had a beer for himself.

"Here's to more successful trips and deals. And by the way, thanks for being there," said Mitch.

Terrance clinked his bottle against Mitch's glass. "You bet," he said.

Mitch smiled to himself. Wouldn't it be funny if he and Terrance became friends?

As soon as Mitch boarded the jet and strapped himself in, he fell asleep. In what seemed like less than five minutes, Terrance was shaking his shoulder. They were home.

Mitch retrieved his car and drove, by habit, to the office. It was okay, though, because he needed to get his notes to Sam regarding today's meeting and also pick up the things he needed for the meetings scheduled for the next two days.

When he drove through the gate, he began to feel that old excitement...the power. He noticed as he parked that Terrance also returned to the compound. He waved as Terrance drove around the building, out of sight.

Mitch was surprised, but pleasantly, to find Sabrina still at her desk. She was lovely to look at and he knew his pulse always quickened when he looked at her.

"Hi, Mitch," she said in that melodic way. "How was the trip?"

"Very successful, I think, and hopefully profitable for the organization," he said. "What are you doing here so late? It is almost nine o'clock."

"Well, I knew you were coming in and I thought you might need to dictate your report while it is all fresh, and I have a few messages for you."

"Is he still here?" asked Mitch, indicating Sam's office.

"Not tonight; his wife was having an important dinner party...real blue blood types. She insisted he be there," she replied. "Now; let's see what I can do for you."

Boy, that sounded intriguing...and could be taken so many different ways.

Together, they walked to his office. He could almost feel the heat from her body even though they weren't touching, and that scent of musk was pervading his senses.

When he thought of that scent, he thought about Cindy. He thought there was something he should remember about her, but the thought was very brief, and soon gone completely.

Flipping on the lights, he held the office door open for her. He did not miss the fact that she brushed against him as she entered.

When inside, Mitch headed straight to his desk. He knew there would be messages.

Sabrina went to the bar, first discarding her jacket and poured them both drinks. She returned to the desk and handed him his drink; then she hoisted herself onto the corner of his desk, crossing her legs and leaning slightly forward. The view was terrific.

"Here's to two great days," she toasted.

"Here, here," said Mitch, clinking his glass against hers and then downing the drink quickly. He lay back in his chair, He was so tired. Sabrina moved behind him and started to massage his temples. That felt so good…and he was very aware of her touch and scent.

After a few minutes, she asked, "Is that better?"

"It sure is," said Mitch. "You work wonders."

"Is there anything else I can do for you?" she asked.

"Let's get the report done," said Mitch, trying desperately to forget she was such a beautiful, desirable woman and that she was offering herself to him.

She went around the desk and took a seat, again crossing those long lovely legs. She was ready to take dictation.

When he had finished dictating, Mitch felt very good. He was sure that Sam would be pleased too.

Sabrina excused herself and went to type the report. Mitch spent the time packing up papers and files that he would need the next two days. Before he had finished filling his briefcase, she was back and the report was beautifully typed. He read it, signed the original which she took immediately to leave on Sam's desk, and he filed the copy in the supplier's file.

When she returned, she again sat on the corner of his desk. Her nearness was very disconcerting, Mitch thought. He wanted to be strong…no office romances…no cheating on Cindy…but it was getting very difficult. Temptation, so strong, was hard to resist.

"Sam wanted me to let you know that he thinks you should go to the hotel tonight. That way, you will be there in the morning. He arranged for the suite to be ready," she said. "He even had the clothes you keep here cleaned and packed, so you are all ready, as soon as you gather up the necessary files."

Mitch wondered about Sabrina. Was she going with him tonight? Her next sentence answered that question.

"He even had me go home and pack this afternoon, so I am all ready too," she said.

Mitch felt his heart flutter. His palms were clammy and he was sure that there were beads of sweat on his forehead.

"Well, that sounds good to me," he said. "I guess I am ready then."

"Me too," she cooed.

Mitch couldn't help but notice that as she said this, she looked straight at him. She smiled faintly, but looked deeply and unflinchingly into his eyes. He could feel the sexual tension between them. Honestly, what he really wanted to do was throw her across the desk right now, tear off her clothes, and claim that luscious body, but he fought the urge.

With a great deal of internal strength, he pushed his chair back, stood up, and said, "Let's go."

He held his hand out to her, helping her down from the desk. The heat was unbelievable. When she was standing, he helped her into her jacket, then, placing his hand against the small of her back, he accompanied her to the door. Since he was carrying his briefcase and luggage in one hand, she flipped the light switch off as they left the office.

Proceeding down the hallway, he was very aware of the feeling of his hand on her back. They picked up Sabrina's luggage in the lobby and left the building.

Mitch stored the luggage in the trunk of his car, then helped Sabrina into the passenger seat. He admitted he enjoyed the view she offered as she sat and swung her legs into the car.

He shut the door and, as he circled around to the driver's side, he realized, he was experiencing a feeling of freedom…a time for fun. Obviously he had been working too hard.

As they drove across town, Mitch felt relaxed with Sabrina. They were quiet at times, but these were peaceful, comfortable times. When they did talk, it was general small talk or business talk.

When they arrived at the hotel, a bellboy took their luggage and he handed the car keys to a valet. Then, he and Sabrina walked through the lobby to the reservation desk and he again found his hand naturally on the small of her back, and it felt wonderful.

"I believe you are holding a suite for Nelson," said Mitch, as Sabrina stood quietly next to him.

"Let me see, Mr. Nelson. Yes, we do have that reservation. It looks like it is for three nights, is that correct?" asked the desk clerk.

"That's correct," said Mitch, signing the registry.

The desk clerk motioned for the bellboy to come forward. Handing him a key, he said, "Please show Mr. and Mrs. Nelson to the Presidential Suite."

Mitch glanced at Sabrina but she didn't act as if she had even heard him. Mr. and Mrs. Nelson...it sounded nice, but Mitch felt a great sadness. That should be reserved for him and Cindy, only.

Shaking off that thought, Mitch told himself that this was business and that Cindy did not belong in this world. Business should never involve or affect her, he told himself. Sabrina was the woman in this world.

Sabrina reached out and took Mitch's arm and he felt her breast press against his arm. He felt hot...very hot.

He held his arm tighter against his side, pulling her even closer as they followed the bell boy across the lobby. There were several people in the hotel lobby and Mitch noticed, with pleasure, that most of the men followed Sabrina with their eyes as she swayed across the lobby. It made him feel proud...they were envious of him.

Going up in the elevator, Sabrina continued to hold her body close to him. On the twelfth floor, they were shown to a fabulous, two-bedroom suite. The living area, which they entered, was enormous. It was beautifully decorated with modern but comfortable furniture, expensive art, and a fabulous grand piano in the corner. Directly across from the entry, French doors led to a balcony that stretched the full length of the suite. Stepping out onto the balcony, Mitch could see the lights of the city twinkling like glittering candle lights below him. As he returned to the main room, he saw the bellboy had opened doors on either side, both leading to large master suites. He left Mitch's briefcase in the sitting room but put all the luggage in one bedroom. Neither of them said anything, in fact neither of them looked at the other. Mitch tipped the bellboy as he left, pulling the door closed behind him. As Mitch turned back, he noticed that Sabrina was watching him with a faint smile on her face.

"Well, Mr. Nelson," she said, "do you think they are trying to tell you and Mrs. Nelson something?" Then she laughed a bright, tinkly laugh. He had never heard her laugh like that and it sounded wonderful.

"If they are," he said, "maybe we should pay closer attention."

As he said this, he found himself looking expectantly at Sabrina to see how she would respond.

By this time they had both walked forward until they were standing very close together. Mitch never knew if it was the booze, the drugs, the lack of sleep, or just his desire, but at that moment, he couldn't resist this woman any longer.

Stepping even closer, he took her in his arms, sliding his hands up and down her back as he pulled her to him. Their mouths met in a passion-filled kiss...one that was filled with all the desires they had been feeling and controlling for the last six months as well as all the promises of what was possible. They clung tightly to each other and Mitch could feel shudders going up and down their bodies. The passion seemed to be flowing... like opened floodgates.

Mitch wouldn't let his mind wander...he thought only of

Sabrina. This beautiful, sensual woman actually wanted him, and he wanted her. The pride he felt at being desired by her was tremendous. He knew right now that those men in the lobby were envious of him, but they didn't know how envious they should be.

Sabrina squirmed against him and he felt his legs become weak. Sensing this, they broke apart from each other.

Sabrina looked straight at him and asked, "Do you really want me? Is this what you want to happen?"

Did he want her? What living, breathing man wouldn't want her? What amazed him was that she wanted him.

"Oh, yes," moaned Mitch. "I want this so much...but I don't want to do anything you don't want me to do."

"You know I've wanted you for a long time," she said. "I tried not to, but I did."

As he heard these words, Mitch again pulled her to him and started to explore her body. It looked as if they would collapse in the middle of the floor, but Mitch pulled back and led her to the sofa. There he held her close to him and began to kiss her beautiful face.

While he was exploring her face, she reached up and loosed her hair. It cascaded around her face and down her back. She looked younger and almost angelic...she looked like a little girl...no longer an older woman.

All Mitch really knew or cared about was this wonderful, warm, loving women he was holding. He kissed her face, her neck, and down to the top of the vee neck of her blouse. Then, slowly, he undid one button at a time, kissing the newly exposed area before going on to the next one. With each kiss, Sabrina moaned and squirmed in his arms. When the last button was undone, Mitch pulled her blouse off and tossed it on the floor. She was wearing a lacy little bra and the cups were overflowing with the beautiful ripe melons they held.

Deciding to prolong his foreplay, Mitch left these tempting, enticing breasts and proceeded to remove Sabrina's skirt, an inch at a time. As he slowly slid her skirt down from her hips, he began to follow it with his mouth, leaving tender kisses on each spot.

With each kiss, Mitch could feel her react. She had thrown her head backward and was thrusting her body upward toward his mouth. Her moans were clearly audible and they excited Mitch.

He soon found that under her skirt, Sabrina was wearing lacy thong panties. They both fascinated and intrigued Mitch who had never seen them before. Again leaving them behind, he continued pushing her skirt down her legs, planting kisses as he went. When her skirt was finally dropped on the floor, Sabrina was draped across the couch, wearing sexy, lacy underwear, a garter belt and stockings. Mitch removed her stockings very slowly and again followed them down with kisses.

Mitch admitted that he was proud that he was able to excite a mature, worldly woman. She had become putty in his hands; he had driven her desire to such a high level, he felt she would have been destroyed if he just walked away; but he knew that not only wouldn't he walk away, he couldn't. The truth was, he wanted to experience this woman; their sexual attraction had been strong; this had to happen.

He returned to his job...a labor of lust. Returning to her breasts, he sucked and kissed the exposed areas above her tiny bra. As he did so, Sabrina became wild, twining her fingers into his hair and grinding her breasts into his face. She was so wild with passion and desire, she was almost out of control.

Mitch decided he should cool her down just a little, and himself too. He wanted this to last a long time and she was getting to her climax too quickly for him.

Standing over her, he began to strip his own clothes away. He removed his coat and tie, taking the time to hang them on a chair. He kicked his shoes off and then returned to Sabrina. She was still writhing with desire and licking her lips, but her eyes were fixed on him. He slowly unbuttoned and removed his shirt. He heard a low growl escape from Sabrina. Wanting to slow her passions even more, he walked to the bar and poured them drinks which he brought with him.

He held hers toward her and began sipping his, all the time standing before her with his chest bare, his legs slightly apart, and his knees gently flexing.

Before he could finish his drink, she flew off the couch, grabbing him around his neck and wrapping those long, glorious legs around his waist.

Quickly putting the drinks down, Mitch began to kiss her mouth. She probed deeply into his while sliding her body back and forth against his.

No longer able to withstand this woman, Mitch carried her to the closest bedroom. The elegant, king-sized bed awaited them.

Still clinging to him, Sabrina was kissing him all over his face. Her eyes were glazed; she was completely lost in her passion and desire.

Mitch laid her on the bed and in one swift motion unhooked and unzipped his pants, letting them fall to the floor. As he stepped out of them, he glanced down at his briefs and knew that, if she looked, Sabrina could tell that he wanted her…soon. He looked at her; she knew.

Crawling onto the bed, he knelt beside her and, leaning forward, started to caress her breasts. He reached behind her and undid her bra which peeled away easily, and exposed two of the biggest, fullest breasts he had ever seen. Her office attire certainly did a good job of hiding them. He saw the large mounds fall slightly and he realized they were not as firm as those of the young women he had known. These were more like the women in Playboy or Hustler, magazines which had made the rounds of the dorm. In fact, to Mitch, these were what all the guys called tits, not breasts. He noticed that her nipples were already hard and seemed to be pulsating.

Almost unable to pull his eyes away from his first real tits, he was finally able to give his attention to her thong underwear. He ran his fingers under the front edges, even along the leg holes which culminated in a beautiful patch of black, curly hair. In this area, Sabrina again was more developed and advanced than the girls he had previously experienced.

Turning her over, he was delighted with the firm, rounded, exposed buttocks that greeted him. He was kissing them when suddenly he had a wild desire to spank them, and spank them he did. Never hard…he wouldn't want to hurt her, but the sound of his hand on her bare buttocks inflamed him. His penis was growing and with this woman, it must be as big as possible. After several smacks, each one followed by a sultry moan from Sabrina, he turned her over. Her eyes were glazed but still had a wild look about them.

Immediately, Mitch pulled her thong down and off her body. Now he could get a clear and full view of that wonderful curly area beckoning to him.

Mitch sat back on his heels. He just wanted to look at this woman. From the top of her head, over her mountainous tits, through the curly patch, to the end of her toes, this was a real woman…and she wanted him. With this thought, his penis literally popped out of his briefs. This fact was not lost on Sabrina. She immediately grabbed him and threw him onto the bed. She straddled him and began to kiss him from top to bottom. When she came to his briefs, she gently worked them over his buttocks and his very stiff penis. With the removal of his briefs, his penis was able to expand to its full extension.

Sabrina looked at him with such desire, he could almost feel it physically. She raised her body and lowered it over him. He thought he had great size tonight, but he was immediately engulfed by the curly, black swatch. Inside, it was hot and moist and he found his thrusting and withdrawing was smooth and exciting. No matter how large his penis had become, he was lost in this beautiful cavern. Wanting to hold on to something, he reached out for Sabrina's tits. His mouth hungrily devoured them, first one and then the other as their bodies searched for the right rhythm.

Soon Mitch felt as if he would burst, but Sabrina gave no sign that she was anywhere near that point. Her face was contorted and she reminded him of a wild animal, toying with its prey. He thought he had gone deeper and farther into this woman than he had ever gone before. In fact, he felt as if he would never escape...and he wasn't sure he wanted to.

Feeling Sabrina's excitement and desire growing toward that fever pitch, Mitch flipped her over on her back and reentered her from the top. This time, they fell easily into a satisfying rhythm that got faster and faster until they both exploded, draining their bodies both physically and mentally, of their great need and desire.

Sabrina kept her long legs wrapped around him while she gently rocked her body against his and held him tightly against those ponderous tits.

Truly spent, Mitch laid exhausted on top of Sabrina. When he finally rolled off, Sabrina situated herself in a position where he could nurse those massive tits. He really felt like a little boy at that moment and found himself sucking as if he was a baby.

While Mitch nursed, Sabrina caressed his face and head, running her fingertips along every feature. Unable to give up the comfort provided by her tits, Mitch kept nursing, getting sleepier and sleepier. He kept thinking about Sabrina and her sexy body.

He loved having sex with her...it was great sex...but all he felt was lust. He didn't love her. He kept thinking he should tell her...he didn't want to use her...but he loved her body and the sexual experience. While he was trying to find a way to say this, he fell asleep and slept soundly the entire night.

When he awoke, the morning sky was light and the sun was up. He looked at Sabrina, curled up and asleep. Those massive tits were there, still causing desire within him. They had both slept nude, without covers, but undoubtedly their body heat or maybe the heat from their sex, had kept them warm.

Mitch looked at the clock. It was almost six thirty and the first scheduled meeting was at nine o'clock. They had a lot to do before then. His talk with Sabrina about lust could wait until tonight. As a side thought, Mitch wondered if tonight would be as good as last night.

He leaned over and gave Sabrina a soft kiss on her cheek. This got no response, so the next kiss went to her mouth. The third kiss was to the tit, right on the nipple, but when this caused no response, he took the nipple in his mouth and squeezed it, first softly and then quite hard. This worked. Her eyes flew open, but with excitement and desire reflected in them, not pain. As she looked around, her eyes rested on him, and she smiled. She moved slightly and gave him a deep, enticing kiss on his mouth.

"Don't stir me up now, please!" pleaded Mitch. "It is time to get ready for work. Later for us."

She smiled sweetly and got quickly out of bed. Mitch watched her walk across the room and go into the bathroom. She looked so beautiful…just as desirable as ever.

She gave him a coy look over her shoulder and said, "I'm taking a shower. Want to join me?"

Of course he wanted to, and when he did, the experience was all that he had hoped it would be.

After dressing and setting up the rooms for the interviews, Mitch and Sabrina still had thirty minutes before the first appointment. They poured cups of coffee and sat in two easy chairs, comfortable with each other.

Mitch enjoyed just looking at her. She looked cool and professional this morning, but he knew that underneath that shell beat the heart and soul of a sexy wildcat or sex goddess. Mitch thought that she had taught him more about sex in one night than he had ever known…and yet he didn't know how or what he had learned. Maybe it was just a feeling. And maybe it was because this was pure lust, not love. Never before had he been part of pure sex, without love. For just a moment, Cindy crossed his mind, but he quickly dismissed this thought. She belonged in his other world. For now, he was in a world of big business and it included a sexy partner to fulfill his lust. He was a very lucky man. And that was another thing; Sabrina was a woman, an older woman, and she wanted him; it made him really feel like a man.

Sabrina had not looked directly at him, but she knew he was studying her, thinking about them. She liked to be admired and she loved being the object of lust. Mitch was so young, but he was also eager. He used her body for sex in a very mature and intense manner.

She thought about the first day that she had seen him. He really did look like a little boy trying to act like a man; but he had changed. Now he appeared to be a man, far beyond his years. That first day, he had looked interesting to her. She loved young, hard bodies, and even though he had acted uninterested, she knew she could get him to want her. It was interesting that she really hadn't started her campaign before Sam approached her. He liked Mitch and felt he would be a perfect fit for the organization. In fact, he felt Mitch could rise to the top echelons…something he wasn't sure even he could do; but he had one big concern about Mitch. He had a girl. Sam didn't know her but he felt she would hinder his progress. She probably didn't even know what Mitch did, so Sam asked Sabrina to seduce Mitch. Show him there was so much more out there, available for him, and he was sure the young girlfriend would be history.

Seducing Mitch hadn't been easy. It was easy enough to get him interested but he was strong and she couldn't get him to act on that interest. When she told Sam that he had given her a very hard task, he had laughed. This toughness boded well for Mitch's future with the organization. It had been Sam's idea that she join Mitch for these interviews and three nights in a luxury suite. He was sure that Mitch would see what being part of the organization could offer him and he would dump his old life.

As Sabrina thought about last night, she knew that Mitch had enjoyed her body and the sex and she was sure there would be more to follow, but that was all she felt...no real interest in her as a person; no love or romance. Mitch might be harder to conquer than she and Sam had thought. She knew that they could get Mitch's girl to witness something and then she would be gone, but Mitch was so strong, he might be gone too. This would take time, and work, and finesse. Sabrina found that she was looking forward to the challenge...and she even admitted that she would enjoy it; the fringe benefits were great. He was the first one of the conquests, though, that she wished did care about her.

As they finished their coffee, Sabrina went to check the interview room again, making sure everything was perfect. Mitch took these few minutes to just relax. The sight of Sabrina was very stimulating and he needed to be able to concentrate fully on the task before him.

The waiter arrived with juice, coffee and pastries for the morning interviewees. Mitch signed the tab, adding a large tip. That always felt so good...it was a sign he had made it.

Shortly before nine, the first rep arrived; Sabrina showed him into the second, unused bedroom which they had set up for the interviews. Mitch couldn't help but notice he watched Sabrina as she left the room. Mitch smiled...everyone wanted her...and he had her.

As the rep turned back to him, Mitch was careful not to smile. He had to impress the rep with his professional demeanor since he was so close to his own age.

Mitch glanced at his notes. This rep was doing fairly well, but Sam wanted him to increase his customer list. Mitch praised him for his accomplishments, gave him some suggestions for increasing his customer numbers, and gave him his business card, listing his private phone number; stressing to him that he should feel free to call anytime. As they shook hands and he left, Mitch felt very good. That had gone well. Now, if the rest of them went as smoothly, this would be an easy day.

Sabrina quickly brought in the next rep. Mitch felt like a doctor, solving all the ailments of the organization.

"Thank you, Miss Franklin," he said as she turned and left the room. He was thinking, yes, thank you for last night and the prospects for tonight, but he turned and introduced himself to rep number two.

The morning passed quickly. Mitch met with seven reps and only one appeared to have problems he was really concerned about. He was running a little late and wondered about lunch, but Sabrina had taken care of that. The table was set on the balcony and they enjoyed a light, refreshing lunch while talking about nothing at all. Neither of them seemed interested in getting into any subjects which might involve feelings. That was okay…tonight they would do that.

By the time they finished lunch, it was time for the next appointment. The afternoon was as busy as the morning as he met with eight additional reps. None of their problems were bad, mostly things Mitch could work out with them right there.

When the door closed behind the last man, Mitch felt exhausted. He pulled his tie off and shed his jacket, then he walked out into the main room. Sabrina was straightening up the area she was using as a reception room.

Mitch stretched out on the couch, threw an arm up across his forehead, and let out a deep sigh.

Sabrina laughed, again, in that musical way and walked toward him.

"Rough day, Mr. Nelson?" she asked in a slightly teasing manner.

"Rough and long, Mrs. Nelson," he replied, giving her a sideways glance and a smile.

Sabrina disappeared into the bedroom and she was gone so long, he almost went to sleep. When she returned, she came and placed a cold rag on his forehead.

"Thanks," he said. "You are terrific. What would I do without you?"

"Don't ever try to find out," she said.

As he took a look at her, he saw that she had changed from her business suit to a very sexy gown. It was black, sheer, and floated like a cloud. Her hair, released from it's pins, was hanging across one eye and down her back. She looked so enticing and delicious, he wanted to grab her, but he still felt so tired.

"How would you like to dictate your reports now?" she asked. "I can type them up and fax them to Sam, either tonight or tomorrow. It would be easier while they are fresh in your mind.

Mitch groaned. He knew she was right.

"Gosh, woman," he said, "what are you? A slave driver?"

She smiled at that and when he started to sit up, she pushed him back down and said, "Don't move; here are your notes. Just dictate from there."

He noticed that she crossed her legs as she prepared to take his dictation, but he was sad that her gown covered them. Maybe that was better. He should keep his mind on his work right now. Pleasure would come later.

As Mitch started dictating, he found the words came very easily. He seemed to have a knack for sizing people up and giving Sam clear, concise reports so that he could know them too.

Each of the reports was easy except for the one rep that was causing some problems. Mitch tried to convey to Sam his concerns about this man and list some possible methods for dealing with it. He added that he would be glad to discuss this when he returned to the office, later this week.

When they were all completed, Sabrina took the cloth off

his head and replaced it with a cool one. She then went to the typewriter on her temporary desk and quickly typed the reports. Her typing was so rhythmic, Mitch began to nod off.

The sound of the fax machine woke him. He was startled that he had even been sleeping. He had found with his current schedule though, that he could doze off anywhere at any time and get a few minutes sleep.

Sabrina came over and sat on the edge of the couch. She looked so beautiful looking down on him and he felt heat from her body due to her closeness.

"All finished; why don't you check them and I will fax them to Sam," she said. "Now, I've ordered dinner for us; would you like to wash up?"

He nodded and pulled himself into a sitting position. She turned and walked over to the desk to send the faxes. He loved watching her walk. It was so sensual…almost indescribable.

While she finished the faxes, he went into the bathroom to wash his hands and face. Maybe that would help.

When he looked in the mirror, he saw a very tired, almost old-looking man staring back. He splashed water on his face and combed his hair. It made a lot of difference, and he decided he would run the electric razor over his face. Sabrina was so smooth and soft, he didn't want to scratch her, and he was hoping he would be in a position later to do just that.

When he finished, he did look better; but he also looked as if he was aging.

When he finally returned to the main room, Sabrina was nowhere to be seen.

"Sabrina?" he called. "Where are you?"

"Here," she called, sticking her head in the door from the balcony. "It is so beautiful tonight, I asked them to set the table up here. Okay?"

Okay? It was wonderful. What more could he want…a beautiful, starlit sky; candlelight; champagne; and a beautiful, sexy woman. And he was getting paid for this. What a wonderful world he was living in.

He joined her on the balcony where he took her in his arms and held her tightly to him. He looked into her beautiful face for some time, then he leaned forward and gave her a deep, provocative kiss, that promised much more to follow.

When she pulled back, he thought he heard her take a quick breath, and he smiled at her. She returned his smile, and then motioned toward the champagne cooling in the bucket.

Mitch popped the cork and poured two glasses. They stood by the railing of the balcony, clinked their glasses for a silent toast, and sipped their champagne, never taking their eyes off each other.

Finally, they moved to the table where Mitch held her chair and then took his own. They ate quietly, often glancing at each other. They were so comfortable with each other. That really surprised Mitch. He didn't really believe this was possible... but it was true. He was maturing...growing.

After they finished their meal, they returned to the living area. Sabrina went to the wall and turned the lights down low so that it gave the room a very romantic glow. She returned to the couch and sat down next to Mitch, snuggling in the crook of his arm. She felt so good snuggling there, thought Mitch. In fact, it felt so natural it surprised him. How could he ever have thought she was out of his league. Here she was, actually pursuing him. It was wonderful and it made his head almost swell with pride. There was that word again. He had never had that feeling before he went to work for Sam. But was it really that bad? At least it was getting him out of the factory.

Mitch leaned back, holding Sabrina closely under his arm. This was so comfortable for him.

For several minutes, they sat quietly, just enjoying the feel of holding each other close. Then Mitch felt Sabrina start to cuddle closer to him, turning her body so that she was facing him more fully. She then started to minister to him with her fingers, beginning to find areas which would respond sensually to her touches. He felt the ache begin to grow within him and he knew that it would not be long until he felt a strong lust for this marvelous woman. He could barely wait until he could again feel every part of her body and then enter it and feel the depths of her lust too.

He felt her fingers trailing down his face and throat, continuing down to the open neck of his shirt. He was so tired and relaxed that he was really surprised when he felt the stirrings of desire spread over his body…and he loved it.

Pulling her face to his, he gave her a kiss that probed deeply into her mouth, searching for that sensual being so that he could be the means of its release. After a second or two, he felt her start to respond, not only with her fantastic, sensual mouth but with her entire body. She began to squirm and move, trying to get her body to touch as much of the surface of his body as possible. The floating gown she was wearing was deceptively sheer. It looked as if you could see through it, but you only saw shapes and shadows. Looking at her body, he searched for those wonderful heavy globes, her tits; and for that sacred triangle of curly black hair that he wanted so badly to possess. Both were only vaguely showing through the material, but he didn't know if he was really seeing these wonderful areas or if he was just imagining them. Either way, he had to be sure. He started to fondle her body through the fabric while trying to work it up her body so that he could expose this beautiful creature to full view.

Mitch realized that he wasn't the only one who was clawing at the clothes. Sabrina was clawing at his and was so excited she was impeding his movements.

Suddenly, he knew that they were becoming so filled with passion and desire, that they needed room to act out these needs, he picked Sabrina up in his arms and carried her quickly toward the bedroom. Sabrina was covering his face with kisses, even as he walked, and her squirming body was often difficult to hold. As he carried her, his excitement and desire grew rapidly because of her sensual attacks on his body. His exhaustion evaporated; he was full of energy. He couldn't believe this was the same cool, reserved woman who had handled business for him all day. This was a wildcat…unlike any he had ever seen, and he loved wildcats.

Just before reaching the bed, he felt her squirm so hard that he almost lost his balance. This bundle of lust that he was carrying was something he couldn't wait to explore. He loved the feelings she brought out in him, just by being here. He began to wonder how high she would take him. However, if she took him that high, would the fall back be too painful? It was worth the chance to him. He was ready to find out…and that night, he did.

Mitch woke from a deep sleep, trying to find his bearings. Where was he? He looked at the beautiful woman sleeping next to him and remembered. He was working…wouldn't all men like to have his job?

Staring at the sleeping Sabrina, he couldn't help but reach over and touch her beautiful, sexual body. He knew that under that calm, cool facade, resided a force more powerful than a man could contain. She could really wear you out…but the satisfactions she created were unbelievable.

Sabrina stirred as he ran his fingers along her heavy tits and her flat stomach, stopping when he began to probe the unforgettable triangle of lust.

As Sabrina opened her eyes, she smiled sweetly at him. He began to feel an ache around his heart. She was so beautiful, and just now, she seemed vulnerable.

He took her in his arms and pulled her naked body against his. The touch of skin to skin, quickly awakened his body. He knew it would not be easy to let her go and return to their work world, but he had to be strong. He just had to be.

Squeezing her more tightly against his body, he kissed her hungrily on her waiting mouth. If they only had more time.

With determination he pulled from within him, Mitch pulled his body away from Sabrina. She smiled. She knew how hard it was for him to let her go. Her smile seemed to promise more to follow...and he hoped that was true.

Quickly showering and dressing, they prepared for their last day of interviews. Sabrina was again dressed in an austere-appearing business suit and her beautiful hair was pulled severely away from her face and caught up in a bun on the back of her neck. Her make-up was light and natural and she wore horn-rimmed glasses. For a fleeting second, he wondered if she really needed them or if they were just a prop. It didn't matter; nothing could really mask her fabulous face and figure.

Mitch had just finished his coffee when the first rep arrived. Sabrina brought him into the interview room and left, closing the door behind her.

The meetings scheduled for this second day went smoothly. He felt that he was beginning to establish a rapport with the reps, something he felt was very necessary for him to succeed in his job.

By the time the last rep left, Mitch again was extremely exhausted. He rubbed his eyes and thought he would love to lie down and take a nap.

He knew this was the last day for them here. He was going to miss the close contact with Sabrina. Of course, she was at the office every day, but there she was shared. Here she was his alone.

He was thinking this as he walked into the living room. Sabrina was bending over some papers on her desk and his heart skipped a beat. She was gorgeous, no matter what she was doing. Such beauty ought to be against the law.

Seeming to sense his eyes on her, she glanced up and gave him a dazzling smile.

"Everything seemed to go well, didn't it?" she said.

"It sure did. Two good days and lots accomplished," he said.

Walking across the room he dropped onto the couch. He wasn't sure he had the energy to stand up again.

Sabrina came toward him, removing her suit jacket and releasing her hair as she approached. Mitch noticed that as she reached up to let her hair down, her huge tits pushed hard against the fabric of her blouse, stretching the buttons to their limit. He couldn't pull his eyes away. Maybe he was even hoping they would break free.

"Well, I guess we need to pack up and get out of here," said Mitch, his mouth dry."

He noticed that Sabrina looked startled at that statement.

"Why?" she asked. "We have paid for this suite until noon tomorrow, we might as well get the use out of it. We could make this such a full and exciting night, we could be sure to get the organization's monies worth."

He noticed she had a slight smile, and her eyes looked as if they were filled with longing. Why hadn't he thought of that. Of course they could stay. What man would ever turn down a night with this beauty.

Mitch realized he was smiling in response to these thoughts. In fact, he was probably leering. Tonight might be a night to remember…a once in a lifetime experience. At least that was what she was promising. But was he up to it?

He had to be. He had to get himself energized, and he knew what to do.

"I think that sounds better," said Mitch. "Another night with such wonderful company…a night to remember. I think I'll take a shower so I am refreshed for…who knows what."

Mitch realized that he was really leering now, looking forward to possessing her body so much that he found he was even licking his lips. If she excited him this much now, what would the night hold?

"Hold it, Tiger," she said, smiling. "Why not dictate your reports first. I can type them up while you take that shower."

Mitch knew she was right, but he didn't know if he could

wait; but he did. He quickly finished the reports and left Sabrina typing them as he headed for the shower.

"Why don't you order some dinner and champagne?" he asked as he left the room.

"Definitely," she replied.

When Mitch got to the bedroom, he went straight to his briefcase. He hoped he hadn't forgotten to refill the supply of drugs he always carried on his business trips. He knew he needed them tonight...he wouldn't miss the promised reward for anything.

Good, his supply was fairly full. Picking out four brightly colored capsules, four very strong narcotic uppers, he knew he would be good for the night. He would be able to match anything she threw at him. As he took them, he thought about how much knowledge he had gained. He never knew anything about drugs...and especially about combining them.

Mitch took a stinging shower and felt quite refreshed when he stepped out of the stall. He was pleasantly surprised to find a completely naked Sabrina standing in the middle of the bathroom, holding a towel for him to use to dry his body. He caught his breath...he could never get over her beauty. She began to rub his body with the towel, lingering over areas that she felt sensual about. He realized that she was awakening him already. The drugs were doing their job because he felt the strength coursing through his body...yes, it was going to be an unforgettable night...and he couldn't wait to get started. But he didn't want to let it all hang out here, so soon. He tried to pull his thoughts back so that he could calm his body down... he wanted to experience this beautiful, enchanting woman, but not now.

Sabrina, who had been kneeling in front of him, finished drying his body and stood up, handing him the towel.

"I ordered dinner," she said. "Why don't you get dressed so you can let the waiter in while I take a shower. Then we will be ready for this night."

A coquettish grin played across Sabrina's face as she turned and stepped into the shower. Mitch couldn't believe how everything she did... every move she made, every word she uttered...caused a severe physical reaction within his body. A man could start to think he had no control of his life, even his own body, if he spent too much time with this woman.

Mitch smiled to himself, shaking his head; he walked to the closet and pulled on a pair of slacks, deliberately not donning underwear which would undoubtedly be discarded shortly anyway.

Hearing a knock at the door, he grabbed his shirt, slipping it up his arms as he admitted the waiter.

After a quick look at the outside weather, he decided it was, again, a beautiful night and had the waiter set the table on the balcony once more.

Mitch signed the tab, again adding his usual big tip, and closed the door on the waiter.

He listened at the bathroom door and heard that Sabrina was still showering, so he went to the bar and poured himself a whiskey. Drinking it quickly, he felt its heat flowing through his body. He hadn't been drinking as much the last two days... too busy...but this one felt good. He knew he had taken the drugs but didn't worry about the combination. Pouring a second drink, he went into the bedroom and sat on the bed where he could hear the shower.

On the bed he saw a sheer, black negligee. Sabrina must have put it out for tonight. He felt his breath get short just thinking about her in this diaphanous material. It would hide nothing. Yes, this was going to be some night.

Just then, he heard the shower stop. He swallowed the last of the whiskey and went into the bathroom. He didn't want to miss the chance to see that beautiful body again, and drying it was a sensual experience he couldn't pass up.

Sabrina looked pleased to see him waiting for her. She stood straight and tall in the center of the room, allowing him to rub her body dry. As he was drying her mountainous tits, he felt her body arch slightly and she put her hands on his shoulders. He knew that she was so sensitive to touch that arousal was possible almost instantly. But he didn't want tonight to pass too quickly. Feeling he needed to back off, he leaned forward and kissed each nipple, then proceeded downward. When he reached the curly, black triangle that he so deeply coveted, he rubbed hard and fast, knowing that he could even arouse himself if he didn't hurry. Even so, before he finished, he felt Sabrina's body stiffen and arch and heard a soft moan escape from her. He realized he too had hardened but he had to wait.

He quickly finished drying her long, lovely legs and, throwing the towel aside, led her into the bedroom. He assisted her into the diaphanous creation she had selected. When she turned to him, he couldn't breathe.

Mitch took her into his arms and gave her a long, deep kiss. He felt the shocks go through both of their bodies…so he pulled away, knowing things could get out of hand very quickly. He didn't want to start anything until it could go on forever… without stop.

Smiling at her, he led her to the balcony where he opened the champagne and poured two glasses. This time, as they clinked their glasses, he said,

"Here's to many more business trips. You make a wonderful traveling companion."

Sabrina smiled at him, and added, "Yes, more business trips; and you too are an exciting traveling companion."

They sipped their champagne and then moved to the table. Mitch wanted to sit next to her, but he knew if he got too close he would never be able to swallow…and he needed his strength…he must eat.

They ate quietly, each sneaking glances at the other from time to time. If you had asked Mitch what he ate, he couldn't have told you. His mind was already thinking about the night to follow. Maybe even his body was there too, because he continued to feel shocks of anticipated pleasure flow through him.

When they were both finished, Mitch went around and helped Sabrina from her chair. When he took her hand, it was almost as if a shock passed between them. Each touch, each look, each word…they all caused such electric reaction.

When they entered the living room, Mitch led Sabrina to the couch. As he seated her, he glanced around the room. The lights were already dim, and the setting was extremely romantic…as if they needed any further stimulation.

Mitch looked deeply into her eyes as he pulled her onto his lap and saw glowing embers of lust shining back at him. He wanted to get lost in that glow…and he didn't think he would mind never leaving it.

Sabrina reached her arms toward him, cradling his head and pulling it toward her waiting mouth. They began to probe the depths and felt their bodies respond. They both squirmed and tried to connect their bodies as much as possible. They were both pushing toward each other with such force that nothing could have gotten between them…nothing at all.

Breaking away from her mouth, Mitch continued down her body, seeking those mountainous tits. He wanted to feel them, to suck them, to nuzzle them. He wanted to get lost in them. Sabrina's arching body told him that she too wanted this.

Suddenly, Mitch felt that he couldn't enjoy her body enough in this position. He scooped her into his arms and carried her quickly into the bedroom, laying her on her back. He knelt next to the bed and began to worship at this beautiful altar. He felt that this heavenly body deserved to be honored and worshipped, and he was just the man to do it. And he was starting…right now.

Mitch remembered that night as one that would not stop. Sabrina went from a sensual object of his ministrations to a ravenous tigress, trying to consume him. They made use of the entirety of that giant bed, first one and then the other becoming the aggressor. This led to the culmination of their coupling not once, not twice, not even three times…but a total of seven times that night. Mitch almost lost count of the number of times she brought him to the brink and then over; his eruptions came over and over that night and continued to be strong. Something he had never dreamed was possible. With Cindy, it was intense, but this was wild…completely savage. It may have been the savagery of Sabrina, or of them together that kept him strong enough to come so many times; maybe even the drugs, but whatever it was, it was wonderful. Mitch knew this night could never be duplicated.

The first lights of dawn were showing in the eastern sky before they finally fell exhausted into a deep sleep, their bodies completely spent, but also completely satisfied.

When he first opened his eyes, Mitch felt he could never move again. He moaned as he turned onto his side where he found himself looking at Sabrina's beautiful body. He couldn't believe it, but he felt a pang of desire in his groin. Impossible. He must be crazy.

Sabrina opened her eyes and smiled. His face must have shown something about the desire she was again awakening in his body, because she glanced down his body, and smiled.

"You are an insatiable animal," she said, "and I love it."

He felt himself almost blush. He knew that he wanted her again. Talk about being greedy; but he couldn't help it; she was the most desirable, intoxicating, satisfying woman he could ever imagine. In spite of his limited experience, even he knew this woman lying here with him was unusual…and most assuredly a woman to treasure.

While these thoughts were going through his mind, he was only faintly aware that Sabrina was starting to caress his body, enticing his penis to firmness again. That was something that he thought wouldn't happen for weeks after last night, but here she was, working her spell. Mitch laid back, closing his eyes, and letting his mind concentrate on Sabrina and her magic fingers. He heard some soft moans filling the room and realized they were coming from him. His body was beginning to fill with desire...he felt a stiffness in his penis that matched any he had felt earlier.

With a sudden push, he shoved his body off the bed and on to Sabrina's beautiful body. This time, his lust was so pressing, he spent no time providing Sabrina with any pleasure. He just wanted her so much...as much as he ever had...and he proceeded to take her, savagely. From the reaction of her body and the animal-like sounds she was making, he knew he was also satisfying her...she had wanted him, too.

After this violent satisfaction of their lust, Sabrina and Mitch fell asleep intertwined in each other's arms. They slept soundly. When they awoke, the clock told them it was ten o'clock. Smiling at each other, they realized they would have some explaining to do at the office.

Again they showered together. It was such a loving, giving and cleansing experience, it gave them both a glow of satisfaction and happiness for the rest of the day.

Mitch drove slowly to the compound. Sabrina sat next to him, again neatly dressed in office attire. The sign of the tigress he had possessed over the last three days was discernible, but only when she turned her deep, dark eyes toward him. A slight smile told him that she knew what he was thinking...and she liked it. Instead of a tigress, maybe she was a chameleon.

Chapter twenty

Mitch allowed a slight smile to cross his face as he watched the corn and hayfields speed past the window. How could he not smile when he thought about that three day period. It was an experience very few men ever had in their entire life, and he had been only nineteen when it happened to him. Sabrina; she was really something.

Shaking his head, Mitch thought about Sabrina. She was an angel and a devil, all at once. And he had seen and experienced all sides of her.

When they had arrived at the compound that day, Sabrina quickly took her place at the reception desk and immediately became all business. Mitch had marveled at her ability to change from one person to another so quickly.

Mitch went down the hall to his office and dropped his briefcase on the desk. Looking at his luggage sitting near the door, he thought about the long, four-day business trip he was scheduled to leave on tonight. He would need to get a quick cleaning job done on his clothes. He buzzed the intercom and asked Sabrina if she could step into his office.

Hearing her musical voice, always made Mitch feel good, and now, additionally, it brought back those wonderful memories of lust, lust, lust.

When she entered his office, she gave him a dazzling smile, but spoke in a business-like manner.

"Yes, Mr. Nelson; how can I help you?" she asked.

How could she help him? He couldn't believe it but he felt a jolt in his body. This woman really pushed his buttons.

Mitch smiled as she neared the desk.

"Miss Franklin, I need to get my clothes cleaned and back before tonight. Could you please take care of that for me?"

Sabrina continued across the room while he was speaking and by the time he finished, she was standing next to him.

"Of course," she said. "I'll be happy to take care of that for you."

Her words said one thing, quite professionally, but her body was saying something entirely different. The kind of business her body was talking about was certainly not professional. His stomach began to tighten as she leaned forward and gave him a deep, probing kiss. He felt his whole body stiffen, and he wanted more than anything to grab her in his arms and throw her to the floor, right here. As hard as it was, he fought the urge, but he certainly wasn't getting a lot of help from her.

With a sly look over her shoulder, she moved toward the door, picking up his luggage and leaving the office.

Mitch found that he had been holding his breath. She worked so many spells on him. She was dangerous.

The sound of the intercom button brought him back to the present. When he answered, it was Sam, asking if he could step into his office.

Sam seemed genuinely glad to see him. He smiled and shook his hand, offering him a drink. A glance at his watch told Mitch that it was only noon. Maybe he had better wait. Declining, he took his usual seat as Sam sat at his desk.

"Great job, Mitch," said Sam. "I couldn't have done any better myself. I hope you know how grateful I am to have you on board."

Mitch smiled. Praise from Sam was very nice. It made him

want to swell with pride to know that someone as important as Sam thought so highly of him.

"Thanks," said Mitch. "I want to thank you for letting Sabrina help me. My reports were done so much sooner than they would have been, especially with this next trip coming up so soon. She was terrific."

If he only knew how terrific she was, thought Mitch. Again, he felt a cramp in the pit of his stomach. Would he ever be able to think of her without wanting her?

"I'm glad she was so helpful," said Sam.

Mitch looked closely at Sam. Did he know? It was almost as if he was giving a double meaning to his words, or was it just his guilty conscience talking? After all, he had broken two of his own rules...to never start an office romance and to be faithful to Cindy. He kept telling himself that it was just lust and sex with Sabrina so he was being faithful to his love for Cindy, but deep down inside, he knew he was lying to himself.

Sam's voice brought him back. What was he saying?

"She was so helpful, I was wondering if you would like to take her with you on this four-day trip? You will have so much on your mind with the meetings, maybe she could keep you up to date with the reports," suggested Sam.

Would he like to take Sabrina with him? What a question. He couldn't wait to have her with him again. Of course, this trip, they would also have Terrance, but the jet did have private areas, and they could say they were working.

"That would be wonderful Sam," replied Mitch, hoping his voice was normal. "Do you think she would mind?"

Mitch was sure she wouldn't. In fact, he bet she would love to go.

"Let's check with her," said Sam, punching the button on the intercom.

When Mitch heard that voice, he again caught his breath. She was having terrible effects on him.

"Sabrina, could you step in here? Sam asked.

"Right away."

They sat quietly and in just a moment, Sabrina knocked lightly on the door and came in. Mitch thought she looked a little surprised to see him there.

"You and Mitch worked so well together," said Sam, "I was wondering if you would be interested in going with him on this four-day-trip he starts tonight? There will be lots of paperwork and you could really help with that. Of course, it is over the weekend, so you are in no way required to go."

Looking at Mitch through her thick, black lashes, she gave him a smile and then turned to Sam.

"I'd love to go," she said. "As for the weekend; you know this job is my life."

They both laughed at what must have been an inside joke. Mitch really did not take much notice of it, he couldn't keep his mind off the fact that he would have four more days with Sabrina. He hoped his body could hold up. This caused him to smile himself.

After Sabrina left the room to make her own travel arrangements, Sam and Mitch went over the items Sam wanted him to cover during the up-coming meetings. Mitch left Sam's office, feeling well prepared. Now he could use the afternoon to clear up some paper work and maybe get a little rest. It was going to be a busy night... he was sure of that.

Mitch sat at his desk but for some reason he couldn't get his mind on his work. His mind seemed to be full of beautiful floating gowns, large tits, and dazzling smiles. He needed to clear his mind, but he hated to do that. Those thoughts were nice.

For just a moment, Mitch thought about calling Cindy. He talked himself out of it because he had told her he would be busy and not able to contact her this week and next. The one thing he failed to remember was that he had stood her up Friday and never bothered to call. He was enjoying the thought that he was having his cake and eating it too. He thought he was very special.

As the day passed, Mitch buried himself in his work, keeping his mind on it as much as possible. He sent a memo to Sam regarding the rep that he had expressed concerns about. He was hopeful that Sam would meet with him about this when he returned from his trip.

About mid-afternoon, Mitch decided he had waited long enough to have a drink. He immediately downed a double whiskey and then refilled his glass. Returning to his desk, he opened the draw and took out the pillbox. He noticed that the supply was a little low. He knew the pouch he carried was low, especially after last night. He decided that he definitely needed to refill them both before he left. There was no time like the present, so he left his office and went down the hall to a special supply room, set aside for compound personnel use only. Here, on shelves, were jars filled with pills and capsules of every color, shape and size. He almost felt like a kid in a candy store when he entered this room. Working quickly, he refilled his pillbox and his pouch. In fact, since he was going to be gone, and Sabrina was going to be with him, he added some extra uppers to his travel pouch. He didn't want to take any chances of not being ready for her.

Leaving the store room, Mitch stopped by the cafeteria and picked up a sandwich. He knew that the plane would be stocked with food, but he hadn't eaten for some time, and he had used a great deal of energy. Carrying the sandwich back to his office, he was looking forward to relaxing with another whiskey. He noticed that Sabrina wasn't at her desk. He assumed she was getting ready for the trip. Just the thought of that brought a smile to Mitch's face.

Sitting on his couch, resting his feet on the coffee table, he nibbled at his sandwich and sipped on his third whiskey of the day, all the while going over the profiles of the men with whom he would be meeting in the next four days. He really didn't plan on having a lot of free time on this trip to review notes… he planned on spending any free time with Sabrina.

A knock on the door startled him.

"Come in," he called.

Sabrina peeked in, and again his heart skipped a beat. He knew that most men looking at her as she was now, dressed for business, couldn't see the unbelievable woman that existed; but he knew what was under that business-like facade…and he wanted her…right now.

Giving him a smile, she said, "Here are your clothes, all clean, pressed and packed. Where shall I put them?"

"Right there is fine," he said. "Do you have time to come in?"

"Well, just a minute. I still have to get my desk in shape if I am going to be away for four more days."

"I hope you don't mind going with me. Would you prefer not to go?"

As he said this, he knew he was holding his breath.

"No, Mitch; I am looking forward to it," she said. "Don't you want me…?"

Mitch thought she left that last question just dangling. It could mean so much more than the answer to his question.

Getting up from the couch and going to her, he took her in his arms and pulled her close.

"Doesn't this tell you that I want you?"

Smiling, she could tell she had him hooked. All she had to do was pull him in. She could feel the tenseness in his body… yes he certainly wanted her. This wasn't the first time she had used her seductive skills for Sam, but this time, she was afraid she was a little hooked herself. Mitch was so young and good looking, and he was hot. His inexperience as a lover was not a problem. He was a good student, a quick learner, and he was great at experimentation. What more could a woman want. She hadn't told Sam that it was different this time. She wondered if he would keep her from going if he knew.

"Darling, it certainly does. In fact, I hope you can wait… and I hope I can wait…at least until we take off." She smiled broadly at him as she backed away from him and, blowing him a kiss, she disappeared through the door.

She was right, thought Mitch. It would be a struggle just to wait, but wait he must. In fact, he had to find some way to handle Terrance, or they might have to wait even longer…and he didn't think he could. His patience wasn't that strong.

Returning to his paperwork, he became engrossed and the time passed quickly.

He noticed that it had grown dark outside. Looking at his watch, he saw that it was already eight o'clock. The jet was scheduled to depart at ten, so he didn't have much time. He'd better check to see that he had everything he would need to complete his job. He was very proud that Sam was pleased with his work, but he must not let down; he had to keep striving for perfection. He knew his age was something of a problem, especially when he was meeting with the suppliers, but his professional, self-assured manner was helping a great deal. He thought if they saw Sabrina on his arm, that wouldn't hurt his position either.

He gathered everything together and packed his briefcase. Just in case he really didn't have any work time on the plane, he had been careful to pack things in the order he would need them. That would save time…time he could better spend with Sabrina.

Leaving his office with his luggage and his briefcase, he turned off the lights and shut the door behind him. It would be several days before he returned to this room that was quickly becoming home to him.

When he reached the reception room, he found Sabrina was already closing up her desk, preparing to leave. Smiling, she picked up her luggage and came to meet him, reaching up and giving him a light kiss.

"Ready?" he asked, reaching for her luggage.

"Yes sir," she said. "This is going to be great."

Sabrina slipped her arm through his and they went to retrieve the car. After he loaded the luggage, he helped her into the car. Again, he noticed how beautiful her legs were as she swung them in. As he drove out of the complex, he raised a hand to the guard. Driving carefully, he headed for the airfield where the company jet was housed. Beside him, he felt the heat from her body...he had never known anyone who gave off such heat. He felt his desire growing and tried very hard to control it by not looking at her. He felt her eyes on him, but fought the urge to turn her way.

Concentrating on his driving was difficult and when he felt her hand on his thigh, he wondered if he could even keep driving. He looked at her and smiled. He loved it, but his body just became too difficult to control when this woman was around.

Taking deep breaths, he knew that she knew the effect she was having on him. It was part of her sexual-predator personality...and he was a willing prey.

He was glad to see the gate to the airfield come into sight. He gave his name to the guard and then drove to the company hangar. Parking near the main door, he got out and opened the door for Sabrina. She swung her legs around gracefully and stood next to the car as Mitch retrieved their luggage.

They entered the door and found themselves in a mostly empty hangar. The jet was in the middle of the building and there were three men going over it at this time. Mitch recognized the pilot and the two mechanics hired by the organization. He waved to them and guided Sabrina into a small office near the door.

Sabrina sat daintily on a wooden chair near the wall. The furniture here was old and scarred. Instead of beautiful paintings, the walls were covered with pin-up calendars of naked women in provocative poses. Cups with cold coffee were scattered on the desk and bookcase and an overflowing ashtray gave off a stale smell. Sabrina surely didn't belong in this setting. As he looked at her, he was sorry he had even brought her in here, but it hadn't seemed so bad until he saw her here.

"Sorry about the mess," he said.

"Don't worry, Mitch," she said. "I've certainly seen worse and I've been in even less glamorous places in my life." Her smile said she was aware of his discomfort. Was she making fun of him?

"Well, we won't be here long. I think they just about have the pre-flight checks finished," he said. "Then we'll be leaving."

Her only response was a wan smile. She looked a little uncomfortable suddenly, and he didn't know why.

Before he had time to pursue this, the door was jerked open and Terrance strode in carrying his own luggage.

"Hi," Terrance grunted. "Are they about ready?"

"I think so," said Mitch. He noticed that Terrance in no way acknowledged Sabrina. Did he not know she was going with them? He had assumed that Sam would have told him.

"Miss Franklin will accompany us on this trip," he said, looking directly at Terrance. "She will be trying to keep up on the paperwork so it won't pile up."

Terrance looked at Sabrina, nodded and then went toward the plane. Mitch wondered if he had been too strong...did Terrance know that the real work they would be doing was trying to find new ways to have sex? And, if he did, how did he feel about it?

Then Terrance was back, telling them that everything was ready. He gathered up all the luggage and went before them, leading the way to the plane.

When they arrived, Terrance handed the luggage to one of the mechanics who took it onto the plane. Mitch helped Sabrina up the steps to the plane and followed her. Inside, he directed the mechanic to put his and Sabrina's luggage in the private rooms in the back and to put Terrance's in a small room near the front of the plane. He really didn't care what Terrance or the mechanics thought. He was the boss on this flight and he was going to spend the time with Sabrina.

Soon, Terrance and the pilot boarded the plane and the mechanics closed and latched the door. Sabrina was settled into a window seat and had pulled her seat belt snuggly across her lap. Mitch took the seat next to her and strapped himself in. Terrance went forward with the pilot and sat in the co-pilot's seat.

"Don't mind him," Mitch said to Sabrina. "He hardly ever talks on these trips. It was the fifth trip before he even said one word to me."

He looked into her face and tried to read what he saw there. He wanted to say it was lust, desire…a wanting for their togetherness; but he wasn't sure. In some ways, she looked sad; but he convinced himself that wasn't true. He was just being overly sensitive. Tonight, he would show himself what she was truly thinking about. The thought of that caused him to begin to perspire…the desire in his body growing again.

The take-off was smooth and before long they had reached their cruising altitude and speed. Mitch unhooked his seat belt and went to the cockpit door.

"How long before we reach our destination?" he asked the pilot.

"About five hours before our first stop, then three or four more," he replied.

Looking at him, then at Terrance, Mitch said; "Miss Franklin and I will be in the rear compartment catching up on some work. Please call us on the intercom if plans change or you need us."

With his final word, Mitch left, not wanting a response, and returned to Sabrina. He reached down for her hand and she undid her seat belt and slid forward, taking his hand as she stood up.

"We have five hours. How about doing some 'work'?" he asked, with a somewhat lecherous smile on his lips.

"My pleasure," she said, preceding him down the hall to the back compartment.

After they entered, Mitch closed the door behind them. As he turned back, he found himself thrown back against the door with her body pressed tightly against him. She found his mouth and began, once more, to explore him. She was the tigress again...what more could he want.

Mitch reach up and unpinned her hair, letting it fall over her. He felt as if her hair falling free was a symbol of her wild side and seeing it fall seemed to ignite him, as well as her.

Putting his arms around her, he joined in the passionate kiss she had started. She was hanging onto his neck and he reached under her buttocks and picked her off the floor; walking forward, he laid her on the bed near the rear wall of the compartment. As he laid her down, she continued to hold herself near him and pulled him onto the bed on top of her. As he pressed into her lush body, he felt her beautiful, full tits pressing against his chest. In his mind, he pictured them, so full and slightly sagging, centered with hard, dark nipples that grew to great size when sucked. These thoughts coupled with the feel of this woman beneath him and her kisses and exploring hands, caused his own desire to heighten. He felt his body begin to stiffen. He was sure that if she had looked or touched the right area, she would have known he was ready for anything.

Mitch reached down to the hem of Sabrina's skirt, sliding it up her legs as he caressed her thighs. Sabrina's breath became quicker and she rolled over, throwing him onto the bed with her own body now on top. He looked into her face and saw again that glazed, non-seeing look. Her desires were so strong they were taking over her body...she was possessed...and she seemed to spread that feeling to him.

She reached down and unhooked her skirt, quickly pulling it over her head. As she lay on top of him, he reached down and squeezed and massaged her firm, round buttocks, left exposed by the thong panties. Pulling her closer and closer, he found her bucking against him, already into the throes of passion. Wanting to slow her down, he rolled her over and straddled her, holding her against the bed. Her breath was coming quickly and her head was rolling from side to side. She was so lost in passion, she hardly knew he was there. He pressed his mouth against hers and pulled her up toward him. She responded by pulling her body against his and molding it until it fit perfectly. Working his hands between them, he undid the buttons on her blouse and pulled it away and off her body. Those beautiful globes were now almost exposed. They pushed at the fabric of her bra and spilled out over the top of the cups. He buried his face in the cleavage and took several long, deep breaths. He wanted this to be his place of rest forever. It appeared that his attention to her tits was awakening even more passion in Sabrina and she started tearing at his clothing. Reluctantly releasing her wonderful body and backing off the bed, he quickly shed his shirt, pants and briefs. He stood before her completely naked, and, obviously ready to explore the depths of her body. She leaned forward and drew him to her, rubbing his hardening penis along the sides of her face. Then, she leaned forward and kissed the tip, sending shock waves through it and his entire body. Then, she pulled Mitch on top of her. He felt his penis press into the fabric of her thong. It was silky and smooth and actually felt good. While feeling this soft, smooth rubbing, he again set his sights on her tits. Reaching behind her, he undid her bra. He noticed that whenever he released her bra, her tits immediately sprung free as if they had been waiting for release. Throwing her bra away, he again buried his face in her tits. They were so warm and soft, and he loved the feel of them on his face. He saw them as great sources of peace and comfort and even nourishment in a way. They were his...his very own...and he couldn't have been happier. He loved them so much, he never wanted anyone else to ever see them, and definitely never touch them. They belonged to him. Forever. He would never share them with anyone else. He knew that he wasn't making sense. He really didn't love Sabrina...but he did love her body. He wanted to possess it, always, but it would only be for sex and lust, never for love. He really didn't know why he thought he could never love Sabrina, but he knew, deep down, that he never could. But boy, could he want her. And now, he planned to have her.

With that thought in mind, he reached down and disposed of her thong, then, as she lay there trembling with desire, he crashed his body down on top of her, pillowing his chest on her tits and pushing his penis deeply into that curly area of passion. It felt so good. She took him in deeper than he had ever thought a woman could do. No matter how big or long he became, he could not fill this woman. Even so, she kept the sides of this cavern tight against him, rubbing him rhythmically as they rocked back and forth. It was smooth and calculated, but it was intense and each time they rocked apart, they crashed together with a power that could have caused them pain, instead of the pleasure they were experiencing. Their rhythmic moves were so in sync with each other, they could easily read the other's passions and needs. In this way, they were able to reach their points of climax at the same time. This meant that they bucked together in a final throe of passion and then dropped, spent, to the bed, Mitch still lying on top of Sabrina. They stayed this way for several seconds, but Mitch eventually rolled off to the side, feeling almost too spent to even fondle those beautiful, inviting tits. Each time they had their lust-filled sex, it was better than the last time, more intense and more satisfying. He thought each time it couldn't get better, but it did. It didn't make any difference where they were...an expensive suite to an airplane compartment...it was good.

They both lay on their backs, spread-eagle on the bed, staring straight up at the ceiling, trying desperately to regain their normal breathing. Mitch wondered if you could die from having sex. He wasn't even twenty yet, so his heart was probably good enough, but what if Sabrina, or someone with ability close to hers (there was no one better), would have this kind of sex with an older man, could his heart give out? He thought it was possible...but what a way to go.

As young and firm as he was, as he looked down his body, he saw a shriveled, lax penis, completely spent. Sabrina on the other hand looked firm and exciting.

He wanted to suck those tits, but he didn't think he even had the energy to rise up and grab one. He laid there, willing his body toward that beautiful prize, but without any results.

Finally, he was able to move and cradled her in his arms. She was so beautiful, sexy and desirable...and even a little vulnerable. Why couldn't he love her? What was wrong with him? Here she was, his for the taking at any time, providing him with joy indescribable, and he couldn't tell her he loved her. He thought he might be crazy.

Mitch moved so that he was sitting up with his back against the wall. He then reached down and pulled Sabrina up so that she was sitting between his legs with her back to him. He cradled her body with his knees, squeezing his bent legs together against her body. At the same time, he closed his hands over her beautiful, full tits and squeezed and massaged. Her head rested on his chest, just below his chin. He loved holding her like this. It was almost like he was possessing her... owning her. It gave him a powerful, satisfied feeling. As he squeezed her tits, she began to rub the outer edges of his thighs with her hands. The quietness of their surroundings and the touching that they were doing, began to fuel their ardor and desire again. As spent as he had been, it was almost impossible for Mitch to believe that he could have sex with her again, but his body was telling him otherwise.

Sabrina turned her face to his and again their mouths intertwined. This just further fueled their passions and desires and Sabrina turned her body, coming around to face him. She pressed her body against his and he knew it was too late to back off. He slid down on the bed and pulled her down on top of him.

The pressure between their bodies increased their passions, quickly. Sabrina straddled Mitch, certainly not failing to see that he was rapidly reaching the point of hardness that would demand his entry into her body. She sat up straight, straddling him so that his penis was just brushing her beautiful, curly triangle, and the feel of her was increasing his size quickly. He reached up to squeeze and pinch her tits and nipples. They were bouncing in front of his face and he couldn't think of a more desirable sight.

Sabrina began to rock gently back and forth and the glazed look began to take over her face. Finally, unable to wait, Mitch reached down and raised her up by her waist and pulled her straight down on his hard penis. Again, it disappeared into that beautiful cavern and was naturally lubricated and caressed. The desire showed clearly on his face as they began to rock together in that by now familiar cadence that they fell easily into. It was so natural and it was good. He knew it could not be any better. They slowly increased the rate of their thrusts until they were crashing wildly against each other. As he thought he would literally burst with desire, Sabrina arched her back severely and clasped her thighs tightly around his body. He felt his body drain, just as hers did, and he knew that they had again reached a simultaneous culmination, thoroughly satisfying each other. This time, Sabrina fell forward on him. They were both breathing deeply, trying again to normalize their breath. Mitch put his arms around Sabrina and held her close. He turned her beautiful face to him and gave her a light kiss, then they fell asleep, feeling each other's heart beat.

Mitch was pulled out of his sleep by the intercom. The pilot was notifying them that they would be landing in ten minutes. Mitch thanked him, quickly gave Sabrina a kiss, and then threw her off the bed. He then threw himself off and started looking for his clothes. It became almost laughable as they tried to sort out which pieces of clothing were theirs. Once, when Sabrina bent over to look for her thong, Mitch couldn't help but reach out and spank her beautiful bottom. She giggled and looked at him with her hair falling over one eye...she looked beautiful

By the time they landed, both of them were back to their professional look. No one could tell that anything had happened, unless they happened to see one of the sly looks which passed between them.

Chapter twenty-one

Mitch felt the bus slowing. He knew this would probably be the last stop they made before his destination. He didn't know whether he was happy or sad about that. But it didn't matter. We all had to go on...even if we were afraid of the future. In his case, it couldn't be worse than the past.

Mitch decided he could use another cup of coffee so he got out, stretched his legs and went into the depot. Just like most depots; dirty, stale smelling, and dreary. He went to the snack bar and ordered a cup of coffee. Sipping it, he started back toward the bus. Well, at least he was beginning to understand how he got where he was now. As he settled back into his seat, he remembered how high he was that August. Great sex, good money, power, and a beautiful girlfriend. What more could anyone have wanted.

Mitch remembered that the business trip had gone well. He had been well prepared and the sexual encounters that he and Sabrina continued to have gave him a feeling of strength and power. His thinking had been that if he wasn't an important person, he wouldn't have this beautiful, luscious woman throwing herself at him. What a life.

By the time they returned from the trip, he and Sabrina were into a real pattern. Every time the plane took off, they had wild, abandoned sex. Each time it seemed better than the time before, but he could never have told you why. All he knew was that it felt better. His pride grew every time he took this woman.

In addition to the sex in the sky, if they spent a night in a hotel, the entire night was again filled with sex. To keep up with her, he kept taking pills and drinking whiskey. He needed these pick-me-ups. He was never going to admit he couldn't keep up with her. He excused the use of stimulants by saying that she got refreshed and ready while he was conducting negotiations. Of course, that wasn't true. But it sounded good at the time.

Arriving back in town, Mitch took Sabrina back to the office. It was late, almost midnight, but he wanted to finish all of the dictation before Sam arrived. Sabrina was willing to stay and work, so they went back to his office. Mitch removed his jacket, tie and shoes, and undid his collar. He wanted to be comfortable. Sabrina removed her shoes and jacket, but otherwise looked very prim and proper. Mitch walked around the office like a caged animal, dictating as fast as she could write about the negotiations he had just completed. It had been a good trip...the results would please Sam.

Once he had finished the dictation, Sabrina returned to her desk to type up the reports. Mitch fixed himself a drink and stretched out on the couch to think about the past week. It had only been a week ago tonight that he and Sabrina had first gone to the hotel...the first time for sex between them. It really seemed that more than a week had passed. She seemed so much a part of his life now. He felt a little guilty; he knew that he was using her. He didn't and couldn't love her, but he wanted to own her. Smiling, he thought the ideal solution would be to lock her up in an ivory tower where only he could see her. Then he could go to her every time he felt lust filling his body.

This thought put a smile on his face, and that is how Sabrina found him when she returned with the typed material. She asked what was funny, but he couldn't tell her. Instead, he said he was thinking how much enjoyment he had gained from the past week. That made her smile.

She said, "Me too, and I hope it continues. Maybe it isn't nice for a girl to say this, but I love sex with you. We are good together."

"You can say that any time," said Mitch, but he knew, deep down inside, that a 'good' girl wouldn't talk like that...Cindy wouldn't.

After Mitch looked over the reports, he signed them and they left them on Sam's desk. It was almost two, but they decided they needed to get away from the office. He didn't know if he should go home or not. Jim wasn't expecting him.

He drove Sabrina home and walked her to her door. For some reason, he didn't go in with her, even though he was invited.

"I'd better go home for a few minutes, anyway," he said. "Can I have a rain check?

"Of course," she said, giving him one of those dazzling smiles.

As Mitch drove home through the quiet night, he started to think about Cindy and Jim and his life away from the office. He hadn't been fair to either of them...least of all Cindy. He loved her so much, but he sure didn't treat her very well. He would have to change that soon; but he knew that he wouldn't change, at least not like he should. It wasn't fair for him to keep satisfying his lustful desires with Sabrina while he still held on to Cindy. The choice was a natural...Cindy was the keeper. It was her that he wanted in his life for all time. He had to give up Sabrina. But he couldn't think of that now. Now, he would go home. Maybe Jim could tell him how Cindy was doing.

If it was at this time that his life fell apart completely, it was in three separate, specific acts. The first was about to play out.

He turned the key in the lock as quietly as he could. Jim would no doubt be asleep and he didn't want to wake him. As he closed the door and turned the lock, he thought he heard something. He stood quietly, but heard nothing. Must be his imagination, he thought.

Walking toward his room, though, he thought he heard it again. This time, when he listened, he was sure he had heard something. Following the sound led him to Jim's door. He could hear Jim talking, softly, and then he heard a girl's voice and laughter. So, old Jim had a girl. Well, good for him. He was dying to know who she was. He bet she couldn't begin to match Sabrina in bed, but who could? Finally, he couldn't resist. He had to take a look. If he did it quietly, they wouldn't even know he was there. After all, it seemed as if they were very involved with each other.

Quietly, he turned the knob and slowly pushed the door open an inch at a time. There was a soft light on in the room. This would make spying a lot easier. When the opening was big enough, he stuck his head into the room. Jim's bed was straight ahead and Jim and the girl were so engrossed in each other, they didn't even know he was there. Smiling, he thought he could be a pretty good spy. Then, he got the biggest shock of his life. The girl giggled again, and raised up from the bed. Cindy. He couldn't believe it. His girl and his best friend.

Slamming the door back against the wall, Mitch strode into the room and right up to the bed. Cindy screamed and grabbed the sheet around her naked body. Jim sat straight up in bed; he looked scared.

Mitch glanced at his image in the mirror and knew why he looked so scared. Mitch looked like a wild man. But why shouldn't he? After all, this was the worst thing they could have done to him.

"When did you get back?" asked Jim, after he found his voice.

"Tonight, but none too soon, I guess." Said Mitch, still glaring at Cindy.

"Look, man; let me explain," said Jim.

"No, you don't owe him an explanation," said Cindy, suddenly looking very angry.

"What do you mean?" Mitch asked.

"Look, Mitch. I am a free woman. You have no ties on me. I can see anyone I want to see...and I chose Jim," said Cindy.

"But you love me," said Mitch, "at least you said you did."

"Oh, Mitch; I did love you. In fact, I probably still do love you; but I don't like you, and I can't depend on you. You are never there for me and you break your promises all the time. I know you are not dependable and I think you are probably not even faithful. Obviously something or someone means more to you than I do. I am sorry. You were the most wonderful thing that ever came into my life. But I can't take it any more."

When Cindy finished this impassioned speech, she broke down in tears, burying her face in Jim's chest.

Mitch was shocked. He couldn't believe what he was seeing or what he had heard.

"But I love you, Cindy. I am only working because I want to be able to give you everything you should have. Don't leave me," Mitch pleaded; tears running down his face.

"No, Mitch; it's over. No matter how I feel, if I can't trust you, I can't be with you," said Cindy, mumbling the words against Jim's chest.

Mitch was shocked. He stood in the middle of the room, unable to move. He couldn't understand any of this. How could Cindy say she couldn't trust him? He loved her. He always had. And what about Jim? How did they get together?

"But why Jim?" asked Mitch.

"Look, man," said Jim. "You were always sending Cindy over here to wait until you got home. Night after night, you expected me to entertain her until you could find time to get home. That is what I started out doing, but the worse you treated her, the more I came to love her. She was so true to you. One night after another, you stood her up. Oh, you always had an excuse, an apology, each time you finally called her; but most of the time you didn't even call. I guess she cried on my shoulder enough that I decided I liked having her there. You don't deserve her man. We love each other, and she can trust me."

That hurt...especially about not deserving her. But it wasn't true. He had to keep telling himself that, because he couldn't bear the thought that he had caused Cindy to leave him. But he couldn't win. He knew it was his fault...and he knew he didn't deserve her. Cindy deserved more...and, despite his protests, Jim could give her that.

Mitch turned and walked out of the apartment, not even looking back. He was hurting, really hurting, but ironically, he felt just a bit of freedom. Cindy had never fit into his new world. Maybe now, he could concentrate on Sabrina. She did fit...anywhere.

As he drove back to the office, he had convinced himself that this was all for the best. He would send a note to Jim and Cindy apologizing and wishing them well. Then he could concentrate on Sabrina.

Deep in thought, Mitch drove back to the complex. It was funny that when he drove through the gate, he felt like he was home. Work seemed to be his whole world...the staff, his family. Passing the guard, he was too deep in thought to notice his wave.

Walking slowly, with his head sagging against his chest, Mitch entered the office building and walked to his office. Instead of switching on the lights, he went to the bar, using the light of the full moon shining through the window to light his way. After pouring himself a drink, he stretched out on the couch. He was so tired, and he felt very old. How could he have thought he was on top of the world? Nothing that was his seemed tangible. Maybe it was all just a smoke screen to make him think he could get out of the factory. He really hoped that wasn't true...but the loss of Cindy made his life look empty and useless. No matter how hard he tried to convince himself she was no loss, he couldn't. Finishing his drink, he turned sideways and went to sleep. Maybe if he got some sleep, things would look better in the morning. At least he hoped they would.

Mitch woke suddenly. He thought he had heard a loud sound. Maybe it was just part of his dream. He had been dreaming about Cindy...he missed her so much. He lay staring at the ceiling trying to figure out what was happening to him. He couldn't understand why he was so upset about losing Cindy. After all, he had Sabrina. It was true that he really only lusted after her, but maybe that was enough. Every time he thought he loved a girl, really loved her, she dumped him. That hurt. Maybe with Sabrina, he couldn't be hurt. After all, he really just wanted her body...and what a body. She was quite a woman, and he saw it in the eyes of men they passed. He remembered how proud he had been when Sabrina slipped her arm through his and pressed closely to him right in front of a lot of men... gee, were they jealous...he could see their lust, too.

Mitch shook his head. Why couldn't he just forget Cindy, and Peggy, and concentrate on Sabrina. She was a fabulous woman and she belonged in his world, so why was he aching so much for Cindy?

Maybe another drink would help. As he stumbled, still somewhat sleepy, to the bar, he looked out the window. It was still dark outside. He wondered what time it was, but he was having trouble focusing on his watch. He filled his glass and returned to the couch. After he had consumed about two-thirds of his drink, his vision was a little clearer. Looking at his watch, he noticed it was only four-thirty. Still some time before anyone else came to work. He must have been dreaming when he heard the noise.

Lying back on the couch, Mitch tried to clear his head of all thoughts, especially Cindy, so that he could get some rest. Cindy...would he ever forget that tinkling laughter...and the last time he heard it? He felt sick to his stomach when he thought about her in Jim's bed. He wished he could get mad; break something; even yell; but he couldn't. He knew he couldn't be mad at them; they weren't the cause of his problems...he was. Mitch shook his head. Maybe he was growing into a maturity beyond his years, if he could even take the blame, when it might be his fault.

For some reason, this thought, that he could be responsible, allowed him to drift off to sleep, a sound sleep during which he didn't dream.

The sun was high in the sky the next time Mitch awoke. Looking at his watch, he saw it was already eight o'clock. He needed to get himself ready for another busy day. Tonight, he was leaving again, for a three-day trip, filled with meetings. Today, he needed to talk to Sam so he could find out what he wanted him to accomplish. He wished Sabrina was going with him this time; this time he really needed her...more than he could ever say.

Pushing that thought out of his mind, he tried to concentrate on business. First, he had to make himself look professional. A quick shave, a change of clothes, and cold water splashed in his face really helped. Now, as he combed his hair, he looked closely at his image in the mirror. He was pleased...he really looked professional.

Returning to his office, he sat at his desk and began to separate the reports on the suppliers he would be meeting on this trip. The reports on the past trip were already typed thanks to Sabrina. He knew that Sam would be very pleased that he was so up-to-date.

When all the information he would need to take with him was safely tucked in his briefcase, he leaned back, obviously pleased with himself. He wouldn't even think about Cindy any more. After all, she didn't belong in this life, and he did. He could do better...remember, Sabrina. Just thinking of her brought a smile to his lips. He had never imagined he could ever reach such heights of delight as he did with that woman.

She set standards for him that no one could ever match. See…
he had really outgrown Cindy. Cindy…oh, gosh; how had
he ever messed that up? He really loved her, and he knew he
always would, but he also knew that she was gone…forever…
so he had to go on. Forward. He was anxious to see if Sabrina
was in yet.

Instead of buzzing her on the intercom, Mitch walked down
the hall to the reception room. He was surprised, but also very
disappointed, to see that Sabrina was not at her desk.

Trying to throw off his disappointment, he walked on down
the hall to the cafeteria and got a cup of coffee. It tasted good,
and he got a second cup to take back to the office. On the way,
he passed the special supply cupboard. That reminded him…
he needed to resupply his travel pouch. He wondered if he
would even need so many drugs if Sabrina wasn't with him.
He might not, but he would take twice as many if it meant she
could accompany him.

As he passed through the reception area again, he was
really pleased to see Sabrina just entering the front door.

"Hi, beautiful," he said with a welcoming smile.

She responded with one of those million-dollar smiles, and
his heart took a real hit.

"Good morning, Mitch," she replied. "Did you get any rest
last night, or did that little girlfriend keep you up all night?"

She said this in a teasing tone, and he hoped she didn't
notice how quickly the smile disappeared from his face. With
a lot of will power, he returned a smile to his face and he said,
"No way, I got plenty of sleep."

"Is there anything I can do for you this morning?" she
asked.

Could she? He wanted to grab her and hold her, and fulfill,
again, all his lustful needs with her body, but he knew that
wasn't possible right now. In fact, he wondered when he would
ever get another chance. That made him sad, and he realized
that hurt almost as much as losing Cindy. He hadn't realized

that Sabrina had come to mean so much to him…or at least to his body.

"I could use some help with reports later, if you have time," he said, "and I need to have my clothes ready for another trip tonight."

"I'll see to that right away," she said, "and let me know when you need help with the reports."

With another smile, he continued on to his office.

As he passed Sam's office, it reminded him that he needed to meet with Sam today, so when he reached his office, he buzzed Sam. When Sam answered, Mitch realized he was glad to hear his voice. Everyone here, acting so normally, made him feel better all the time.

"Sam," he said, "do you have any time to meet with me today? I have reports on my meetings this week, and I also need to get some guidelines for meetings the next three days."

"Any time," said Sam. "Why don't you come in about ten o'clock and we can take all the time we need."

After ending the call, Mitch leaned back in his chair. He loved this office…and the work. Maybe he didn't need anything else; nothing, except this job and these people.

Now might be a good time to resupply his travel pouch, he thought; and besides, it would give him another chance to look at Sabrina.

He passed Sabrina at her desk, but she was busy on the phone. Well, at least he got to take a good look at her. That was a lot. After carefully selecting his array of drugs, he returned to his office. This time, he was disappointed to see that Sabrina wasn't at her desk. He wondered where she was. Seeing her was a very important part of his day.

When he passed Sam's office, he thought he heard her voice behind his door. For a minute, he felt a pang of jealousy. Boy, was that dumb. He didn't have to be jealous of Sam. After all, he had a wife.

Entering his office, he noticed his suitcase was gone. There,

Sabrina was off getting his clothes ready. She wasn't even in Sam's office.

He quickly scanned the reports he would be giving to Sam so that he was well prepared for their meeting. Then he again reviewed the men he would be meeting the next three days. Now he was all ready to meet with Sam.

Mitch spent most of the morning meeting with Sam. It was enjoyable and informative. Sam had been in touch with men at the top of the organization, and they had expressed an interest in meeting Mitch. Mitch couldn't believe that...but Sam wouldn't just say it. It had to be true.

As it turned out, Sam had told them that he would prefer to keep him in his office, at least for a while, but he promised them he would arrange a meeting in the near future.

Sam told him that he would hate to lose him, and he hoped it wouldn't be for some time. Mitch felt as if his head was swimming. He couldn't believe it. Maybe he didn't need to be successful in love...he was obviously successful in business. It never occurred to Mitch that he was getting deeper into something bad. It couldn't be bad. It made him feel too good.

When Mitch gave Sam the reports he and Sabrina had prepared, he was proud. Sam was really pleased...he couldn't believe Mitch could get complete and good reports in such a short time. Mitch told him that Sabrina had been an invaluable help to him during the trip. Without her, he told Sam, it might have been some time before he was able to complete the reports.

When he told Sam this, he got one of the best gifts he had ever received. Sam suggested that he take Sabrina on the next trip. Mitch tried not to look too pleased, but he wanted to shout. As it was, he knew he had a big smile on his face.

"So you think she would want to go again?" Sam asked.

"I don't know," said Mitch. He hoped that she would. Things would be looking up if she said yes.

"Let's get her back in here and ask her," said Sam, buzzing Sabrina.

When she entered, Mitch felt his breath catch again. She had such an effect on his body...something he couldn't control.

"Sabrina," said Sam, "the work you and Mitch did on the last trip as well as the local interviews was wonderful. He's leaving on a three-day trip tonight. Since you two work so well together, would you be interested in accompanying him?"

Mitch found he was holding his breath, waiting to hear her answer. He tried not to look at her, but the pull was so strong, it was almost physical.

"Why, I'd love to," she replied. Mitch noticed that she smiled at Sam when she was answering; and he wished it was at him.

"Good," said Sam. "I will let you two work out the details. Take all the time you need to get ready; I know you just got back."

"Thanks, Sam," she said. Turning away and looking toward Mitch, she said, "We'll talk." He noticed that she gave him a knowing look, and he began to count the minutes until they could be together again.

The rest of the day was uneventful, but it seemed to drag by. He could hardly wait to get Sabrina alone. He found that his body was filled with anticipation and he tried to concentrate on work so that his feelings and lust could be controlled. It was hard.

Finally, it was time to leave, and Sabrina knocked on his door.

"Ready?" she asked.

Was he ready; he had never been more ready in his life.

"You bet," he said, picking up his luggage and briefcase. He hoped his feelings weren't playing out on his face. That would be embarrassing; maybe it would embarrass her too. He didn't want to do that.

Driving to the airfield, they were quiet, but he was very

aware of her presence. Just having her with him, gave him a big boost. With her on his arm, he knew he wasn't a loser. If Cindy could see him now...but he knew she wouldn't really care.

As soon as the plane reached its cruising altitude, Mitch and Sabrina disappeared into the rear compartment. He thought that Terrance probably knew what was going on, but he didn't care. He really didn't care about anything except being with Sabrina, feeling her body next to his, and experiencing the joys that gorgeous body produced. Just thinking about it made his palms sweat, and his breath catch. She really had a devastating affect on him...and he loved it.

The bed in the compartment again became their lust nest. That was really the only word for it. She was still the aggressive tigress that he had learned to need. Not love...he realized... need. He knew that wasn't really fair to Sabrina, but he didn't care. All he cared about was her body...he wanted and needed her to satisfy his lust.

Mitch spent the next five hours locked in Sabrina's long, sensuous legs. She brought him again to heights that he did not think he could reach, and she made it worth the fall back to earth. He lost count of how many times he climaxed with her; but he knew they always met their climaxes together. That was one of the wonderful things about Sabrina; she matched him so closely, sexually, in every way. He couldn't even think of not visiting this altar of lust that her body offered.

Between these climbs to the heights of passion, Mitch rested comfortably on her tits, sucking and massaging them as much as he wanted. She seemed to like it; and he loved it. Sometimes, when he was thoroughly lost in the ministrations to these beautiful globes, he would think about those magazines the guys used to pass around. Not one of those centerfolds could beat Sabrina. She was the best; how could he ever do better?

The three days of meetings passed quickly. Any time he wasn't in meetings, he and Sabrina spent together. It was remarkable, but he was able to dictate all of his notes, and Sabrina typed them when he was in another negotiation, but most of the time they spent together was the sharing of their bodies and the satisfying of their lust. It went on and on, almost non-stop, and he loved it. He really believed that no other woman on Earth could bring him to such heights as many times as she did; and he didn't plan to even look for another one; Sabrina was the one he wanted. Lust was enough. He didn't need love.

When they returned to the office compound, Mitch found he didn't want her to leave him. He took her to her home and walked her to the door, he asked her if he could claim that rain check. She smiled sweetly at him and, without a word, took his hand and led him into her house. It was a beautiful house and had the look of class and money. Mitch remembered briefly wondering how she could afford it on a receptionist's salary, but that thought quickly left his mind as she led him into her bedroom and they quickly resumed their lustful activity. It was just as wonderful as ever, and he thought that he would be happy spending every minute with her, for the rest of his life.

The following morning, after a sensual, dual shower, they sat in her sunny breakfast nook and drank hot, strong coffee. He couldn't take his eyes off her. She was gorgeous...even dressed for the office. He was beginning to understand that beauty such as hers could never be disguised and that her sensual nature pervaded the air around her. She was really unbelievable...the most remarkable creature ever created.

No one was in the reception room when they entered the office complex, so he took just a minute to give her a long, deep kiss that promised there was more to follow. She seemed to enjoy it and acted as if she liked the promise of more.

He continued on to his own office and quickly lost himself in his work. He had been away from the office so much the last two weeks that he had a big stack of messages which needed his attention. Some would lead to other meetings, but some of them could be handled over the phone or with a simple letter. He worked diligently and found that the power he felt he gained from his business accomplishments was stimulating. It was what he needed to take his mind off the way his life outside had fallen apart. It also helped him not to think too much about Sabrina. That was important, because when he thought about her, he found himself with the lust she instilled in him, and the office was no place for that.

It was turning dark outside his window when he finally finished the last phone call. Of course, the calls had just led to more work, so he would be working a lot of hours in the next few days. He didn't mind, though. He got great pride out of doing a good job, and the only distraction he had in his life was Sabrina.

He leaned back in his chair. He realized he hadn't seen Sabrina all day. He wondered if she was still here; was she giving any thought to him? He hoped she was and that he was an important part of her thoughts.

He buzzed the intercom, expecting that there would be no answer. He was surprised when she answered.

"Miss Franklin, could you come in for a few minutes?" he asked.

"Right away, Mr. Nelson," she replied.

In a few minutes, Sabrina entered his office. She was still in her business attire and her hair was pulled back and pinned on top of her head. Even so, she looked absolutely gorgeous. He knew he was staring, but he just couldn't help it. In fact, he didn't want to help it.

"Is there something I can do for you?" she asked.

He noticed that she gave him a knowing smile as she asked the question.

"What do you have in mind?" he asked.

"Well," she said, "maybe this will suggest something."

During this last statement, she kicked off her shoes, and removed her jacket. Next her hair came down. This was enough to cause Mitch's lust level to rise, but when she continued by unbuttoning her blouse and exposing those beautiful tits, held captive by a staining, little, lacy bra, his lust reached such a level, he couldn't get to her quickly enough.

Even though they were in the office, he couldn't wait. He didn't know if anyone else was in the complex, but he didn't care. He grabbed her in his arms and began kissing her, deeply and sensually. Her response was immediate and he felt his body getting hotter and he couldn't wait to enter this woman again. His entry into her body was the most satisfying thing he had ever experienced, and he knew he couldn't delay this entry much longer. He put his arms around her, sliding one hand under her firm, round buttocks and picked her up. He than lay her on the carpeted floor; he was standing over her with eyes filled with lust and taking quick, short breaths. He couldn't wait and immediately stripped his clothes off, then straddled her and removed her remaining clothing. They wrapped their arms around each other and felt the lust flow through them, just as it had many times before. Even so, each time was better than the last. He didn't know when it would end. He hoped never.

When their lust was completely spent, they lay side by side on the floor, breathing deeply. He felt as if he wanted to pull her to him and find the lust building again, but his arms wouldn't move. He felt so spent and exhausted, but he knew one touch from her would excite his body again.

The longer they lay together, the darker the room became, but still neither of them seemed ready to leave. Soon, Sabrina moved closer to him and urged him to fondle and suck her tits. There was nothing he liked more than to spend his time this way. It was like being in a toy store and having the best toy reserved for him. He began to fondle and stroke those large, firm tits. He could never get used to how large and hard her nipples became when he touched or sucked them. They always inflamed his own ardor and lust and as he continued to suck and fondle, he felt the lust again growing in his loin. And it was enhanced by Sabrina's soft hand gently stroking and massaging his penis.

Again, they came together. It was unbelievable. No matter how many times they sexually satisfied each other, it was always wonderful. It always amazed him how filled with lust he could become, even after a session of sex that should have emptied him for a long time. Sabrina was really a tigress...or a witch. He didn't care which. He lusted after her over and over.

After several hours, Sabrina kissed him and told him she needed to get home. In fact, she was expecting a girlfriend for dinner, and she was already late. She quickly dressed, gave him another kiss, and left him, lying nude, on the floor of his office. He wasn't sure he could even move.

Mitch dozed off and when he awoke it was very dark and he was feeling a little cold. After all, he was completely naked. He was glad no one had come into his office and found him stretched out in this manner. It would have been very embarrassing; and he knew that anyone would know what had been going on. At least with Sabrina gone, they might not have known who his partner was, but they probably could have guessed.

Dragging himself up, he quickly dressed. He was somewhat dazed, having just expended so much energy and then slept, uncomfortably. He went to the bar and poured himself a whiskey. Downing that, he felt a little better, but he was still dazed. He picked out a capsule from his pillbox and downed it with another drink of whiskey. That should help a lot.

For the first time, he wondered where he was going to go. After all, he couldn't go back to the apartment; that belonged to Jim and Cindy now. Sabrina's house was off limits tonight, too. For the first time, Mitch felt that he was not in control. He didn't like the feeling.

Deciding he had no place to go, he planned another night on the couch. Before that, though, he would take a walk around the complex. After all, this was his entire life now.

The air was muggy outside. August was always this way.

He walked slowly, enjoying the freshness of the air, even if it was moist. He found himself outside the third warehouse where he had witnessed the man being beaten one night. He sometimes wondered if he had really seen what he thought he had seen. Nothing was ever said about it and that rep was back at work, and doing well.

He decided he would take another look in the warehouse. Maybe if he saw it was just a warehouse, he would feel better. He opened the door...no squeak. At least this complex was in good shape. If it was going to be his entire life, that was a good thing.

It was quiet when he entered the warehouse. That made him feel better and he began to walk slowly forward, toward the area he had seen earlier. As he approached the clearing, he noticed that it was lit with a dim bulb. When he got close, he heard voices. Not again. He couldn't believe it. In fact he wouldn't believe it. He had to take a look so that he would know he was wrong, even though something told him to turn around and leave.

As he approached the area, he was careful not to make any noise. Why he was acting like this, he didn't know; but he was. As he peeked through the opening in the shelf, he was shocked. It was the same scene as before. Sam, Terrance, and the two enforcers were there and another man was tied to the chair. This man was awake and alert and was trying to stammer answers to Sam's questions. Mitch wanted to take a closer look...he had to know who the man was...and he wanted to hear what they were saying.

Sam was irate again. His red face, bulging eyes and angry voice were sure signs of this. He was yelling at the man and demanding that he tell him where the money was going. Finally, Mitch began to understand. The first man that he had seen was a rep that was skimming from the organization. He knew this man, too. He was the one he had met with last week; the one he told Sam was becoming a problem.

Mitch felt sick. The two men he had told Sam he needed help with were the ones taking the beatings. It was his fault. He didn't know what to do. He couldn't stand to think that he could cause these men this kind of pain. He had told Sam he was never physical; maybe that was why Sam and the others never included him. Well, it would never happen again. He would never tell Sam another man was a problem. He would solve them all, no matter how long it took. He had learned his lesson…and he would find a way to deal with the problems.

Mitch left the warehouse as quickly as he could. He didn't want Sam to know that he had seen them. It would be his secret, but he would never cause such a thing to happen again.

When he returned to his office, Mitch poured and drank two large whiskeys. It wasn't enough. He was still feeling… and he didn't want to feel anything. He poured another drink and sat on the couch. What could he do? He had no place to go. He had to stay here tonight but he didn't want to face Sam; not yet. He finished his drink then turned out the lights. Lying on the couch, he felt as if even this world was coming apart.

Mitch finally slept, fitfully, and when he awoke, he was almost as tired as when he went to sleep. Things looked better today, though. He was going to go on doing his job, he just wouldn't involve Sam. He wondered if the men at the top of the organization knew how Sam worked. He wanted to think they didn't, but he knew they did. In fact, he was beginning to admit to himself what kind of an organization he was working for; he had known for some time, but he had refused to admit it, even to himself. Mitch wondered what he should do. He had no choice. He had to go on, but he would watch his step. He would just use them to give him the kind of life he wanted, but he wouldn't let their ways rub off on him at all. He would stay different from them…that would be his goal. After all, he had no other life.

Mitch worked quietly in his office that day. He didn't want to see Sam so he buried himself in the problems the reps were facing, determined to solve them himself. He didn't even try to see Sabrina. He felt so 'dead' inside, he was not even sure she could raise any feelings in him. He couldn't bear to know that he had reached that point, so he hoped he wouldn't see her at all.

His luck lasted until after five. He thought he had made it, but, then there was a knock at the door. It was Sabrina, and she looked as if she wanted him...now. What could he do? Sabrina sat on his desk, offering herself to him. He felt devastated. He felt nothing. He was emotionally dead.

She tried to get him interested, but he told her he had too much work to do. She looked at him quizzically. She knew what he had to do, and she knew he wasn't that busy.

"What is it, darling?" she asked. "Are you sick?"

Yes, sick. That would do it.

"I think I must be coming down with something," he said, glad to have an excuse that made sense.

"Oh, you poor darling," she said. "Can I help you?"

She was stroking his cheek while she talked, and he wished he could feel the beginning of lust; that would mean he was alive, but he didn't feel anything.

"Why don't you come home with me?" she said. "Let me take care of you."

He really didn't know what to do. Maybe this would be better. At least he would be with Sabrina.

"Okay," he said, "but I don't want to be any trouble."

"You would never be any trouble to me," she said. "Please."

Mitch smiled. Here was a beautiful woman wanting to take care of him. Then, he couldn't believe it, but he started to cry.

Sabrina slid off the desk and knelt in front of Mitch. Taking his face in her hands, she kissed his tears away.

Taking his arm, she assisted him in standing up and led him

gently to the door. As they exited, Sabrina turned off the light, still keeping her hand under his elbow.

Mitch was so empty. He had never felt so scared or so alone. He couldn't believe he was crying. That just made him feel worse. Here he was, making a fool of himself in front of this wonderful woman.

When they reached his car, Sabrina helped him into the passenger seat and asked him for his keys. Without thinking, he handed them to her and she drove them through the gate, to her house.

Mitch wasn't aware of anything. He hated this feeling and he hated to be like this, but he couldn't do anything about it.

Sabrina parked the car, then helped him out. Leading him up the steps, she opened the door and helped him into her house. He was still not seeing anything. He wasn't even aware of where he was. She led him to the bedroom. He sat on the edge of the bed while Sabrina knelt before him and removed his shoes. Standing up, she removed his tie and jacket and opened the collar button on his shirt. The last thing she did was unbuckle his belt and then she laid him down. He was so listless, he almost scared her. She pulled the comforter over him and tiptoed out of the room.

Sabrina was worried. The extreme change in Mitch scared her. She wondered if he had been working too hard, but he had seemed to thrive on work. If the work was too hard, she felt sure they couldn't have had such exciting, exhilarating sexual encounters. But what was wrong with him? Maybe he really was sick.

Sabrina returned to the bedroom. Mitch was asleep, but she went to him and put her hand on his forehead. He did not feel hot, but his face looked flushed. She decided she should let him sleep.

Returning to the living room, Sabrina stretched out on the sofa, spread an afghan over herself, and turned on the television. She wasn't sure she would sleep, but she wanted to be available if Mitch needed her. As she thought about him she realized she was really beginning to care about Mitch. She had always been cold and calculating, using her body as she needed to make gains, but this time it was different. She really cared about him; in fact, she might even be in love with him. That could be bad because she knew she was much older than him and he had a young girlfriend. She was sure that the sex they shared was better than any he was getting anywhere else, but maybe that wasn't enough. Maybe we couldn't love her. It was upsetting that she cared.

Sabrina jumped as she heard Mitch yell out in his sleep. She slipped quickly into the bedroom to look at him. He looked so peaceful and handsome lying there. He was young, but he was probably the best lover she had ever known, and it hurt deep inside to think that she could lose him. But she would. If he ever knew why she had seduced him, he would hate her.

She readjusted the comforter and returned to the living room. Stretching out on the couch again, she turned the light out, and tried to go to sleep. It was a losing battle, because all she could think about was Mitch and how she had misled him. She never thought it would catch up with her...the fact that she used her body for gain. For the first time, she felt cheap.

Sabrina awoke after a fitful night. She was glad the night was over. She crept into the bedroom to take a look at Mitch. He was just stirring, so she sat on the edge of the bed. When he opened his eyes, he looked at her. At least he looked pleased to see her. That helped.

"How do you feel, darling?" she asked.

"Better, thanks," he said. "I must have been a real dud last night. I'm sorry, Sabrina. I guess.."

"Don't give it another thought," she said. "I think you must have had a little bug...your face was flushed. I think you should stay here in bed today. If Sam asks, I'll tell him you are sick. Chances are he won't even ask. He knows you've been putting in a lot of overtime."

She leaned down and kissed him, gently, on his lips. He was glad to know that feeling was coming back...he actually felt a little desire begin deep inside. He pulled her close and kissed her, hard. He didn't know what he would do without her.

"Thanks, Sabrina," he said. "I think I will just lie around. It sounds good."

She smiled and stood up.

"I'd better get ready for work," she said. "I'll try to get home early, but if you need me, just call."

He watched as she disappeared into the bathroom. He heard the shower and wanted to join her, but he decided against it. He still wasn't sure he could get the level of desire he needed to be with her. Maybe if he rested today, tonight would be better.

Sabrina walked out of the bathroom, rubbing her hair dry with a towel. He looked at her beautiful body. He was so glad she wasn't ashamed to show it. It did cheer him up.

He watched her dress, enjoying every minute. She could entertain him any time.

She came to him and gave him another kiss.

"Goodbye, Darling. Take it easy. I love you," she said.

Then she was gone. He couldn't believe what he had heard. She said she loved him. Could that really be true? And if it was, what was he going to do about it? Could their relationship survive if she loved him while he only lusted after her? Could he learn to love her? Now he was getting a headache. He needed to give this a lot of thought, but first, he was so tired, he was going to go back to sleep.

When he awoke, he was feeling much better. He was refreshed and his eyes were clear, and his body was alive again. He was sure that he would have strong feelings of desire and lust when he saw Sabrina, because just thinking about her was causing some early stirrings.

He got out of bed, stripped off his clothes, and stepped into the shower. The stinging water really helped. Now he was really feeling better. He decided he wouldn't put on his clothes yet since the only ones he had were the ones he had worn yesterday.

He wrapped a towel around his waist and went into the kitchen. He found the whiskey, poured himself a large glass, and carried it into the living room. Looking around he found the morning paper. Sabrina had brought it in, but evidently, she hadn't read it because it was still folded.

Sitting on the sofa, he opened the paper, sipping at his whiskey. He was skimming the front page when he sat straight up. He couldn't believe it. But there it was, in black and white. The second of the events had occurred.

There, on the front page, was a picture of a man's body being pulled from a lake near town. It wasn't the picture that caught his eye, but the caption. It named the man, who had been found weighted down with concrete blocks, and it was the rep he had seen in the warehouse two nights ago. The paper said that he had obviously suffered a beating before he was killed, but that he had died of drowning; he had been thrown into the lake while he was still alive. Mitch read the story again. He knew that the blood had drained from his face. The worst thing he could imagine had happened. He had caused the death of another human being. Oh, he hadn't hit him, or thrown him into the lake, but he had singled him out to Sam. It was his fault. Now he had to face the truth. He had to go one way or the other. Either he accepted the organization as it was, including the enforcing, or he got out, now. How could he make that decision?

He didn't believe what he was thinking. Could there be any excuse for the killing of another person? He might have gone pretty far off the deep end, using and dispensing drugs, laundering money, meeting with dealers and suppliers...some of whom couldn't even enter the United States...but he didn't think he had sunk low enough to condone murder. He was sure he had reached his limit.

Before he could talk himself out of it, he dressed, called a cab, and went to the compound. He saw his car parked in its regular spot. Sabrina had driven it this morning. He noticed the keys in the ignition.

The thought of her brought a catch to his breath. She was part of the organization. When he rejected them, he would be rejecting her. But there was no other answer.

He couldn't believe where he was ending up. He'd lost his best friend; he'd lost the most wonderful girl in the world; he was leaving a job that he thought was the best in the world and was taking him out of the factory; it probably was going to cost him the most sensual, sexy woman in the world; and it was probably going to cost him his freedom. But there was no other answer. He would just have to start over...if he got the chance.

Mitch entered the reception room. It was empty; he wished Sabrina had been at her desk. He would have loved to look at her but maybe it was better this way. He might lose his resolve if he saw her.

He opened the door to his office and looked around...one last time. He loved this office...and the feeling it gave him. But nothing could replace self respect. It took him a long time to find the answer and see the real picture, but now, he had both, and he was going to follow through.

He crossed to his desk and took out the pill box. Next, he retrieved the travel pouch from his briefcase. And last, but not least, he took the two ledgers listing the suppliers and local reps. This would either be insurance, because he was afraid of what could happen to him; or it could be evidence, if he went to the authorities. Right now, he wasn't sure what he would do. He needed a little more time.

Now, the last thing he had to do was tell Sam he was leaving. He at least owed him that. It would be hard, but Mitch was trying to act mature in this matter. He stuck the ledgers in the small of his back under his belt and put the drugs in his inside jacket pocket. Then, he headed for Sam's office.

He had no way of knowing when he started to enter that office that the third event was about to take place.

He entered Sam's office for the first time without knocking. He took two steps into the office before he was able to take in the scene before him. He couldn't believe it. There on the sofa were Sam and Sabrina, locked in the throes of passion, those beautiful tits crushing into Sam's chest. As he watched in disbelief, they made one violent, matching thrust, culminating in a climax like the ones he had shared with Sabrina. He watched as Sam held her tightly to him, hoping to keep himself deep within her as long as possible, just as he had often done. Now he knew it all. Everything was a sham. He had never been mature…adult-like. He'd been a fool…used beyond belief.

They didn't even know he was there, but he must have made a sound, probably a gasp, because they both looked his way. He turned to leave; obviously he didn't owe Sam anything.

"Wait, please," yelled Sabrina. She was pulling herself away from Sam, reaching across the room toward him. He saw that beautiful, voluptuous body that he had loved to possess, but now even that seemed dirty and cheap…not perfect as he had thought.

"Please, Mitch; don't leave. Let me explain. I love you; please."

He kept walking, not looking back. He felt, rather than saw, her running down the hall after him. He knew she was naked, but he didn't even want to see her again. As he left the building, presumably for the last time, he realized he had just suffered an event that completed the destruction of his life.

Mitch was glad that Sabrina had left the keys in his car; as he drove out of the compound, he felt empty…alone. He drove listlessly, not really knowing where he wanted to go. Yes, he really did know where he wanted to go…he wanted to see Cindy.

He wanted her to hold him close and tell him that everything was going to be all right. He wanted the impossible.

Mitch found himself approaching the lake where the body had been found. He parked in the lot and sat, just looking out over the calm, smooth water. It didn't look like a place that could cause his life to fall apart, but it had. He had to think. What should he do? He wished he had someone to talk to, but he had effectively cut himself off from everyone who really cared for him.

First, his family. He had treated them the worst, and yet they were always there for him. But he couldn't go there now. He didn't want to bring this trouble down on them. They didn't deserve it. It would be better if they never saw him again.

Peggy; beautiful, loving Peggy, who had never done anything but love and encourage him. He had treated her like a betrayer...but that had been him, not her. Even if Peggy was available, he couldn't bring himself to face her. What would he say? There was nothing he could say that would make it right...blot out the past year, but he really wanted to forget this year ever happened.

Cindy...yes, Cindy was the one that had always accepted him...but he had even destroyed her love and faith. He had to stay away. She needed to go on with her life, with Jim. He wanted them both to be happy. There were his true friends, not Sam and Sabrina, the ones he had chosen. He had been a real fool.

Sitting quietly, not really seeing the lake in front of him as he stared straight ahead, he made a decision. He had to take control of his life again. It might not be in the fast lane or with the beautiful people ever again, but it would be his own, and maybe he could feel good about himself again.

Mitch drove slowly back to town. He knew what he had to do, but he was afraid. It would forever change his life, and he knew it. He still could go back to the compound, listen to Sabrina's explanation, and work again for Sam. He could probably even get Sabrina back, if he could just forget that scene in Sam's office, but it would never feel right again. No, there was only one path for him to take. He knew he would have to pay a price, but he at least thought he would feel worthy of those who had believed in him.

First, he had to have a good night's sleep; and he had a little trip to make. He hurried out of town to complete his errand and then returned and found a motel. The bed was hard and it wasn't very elegant, but it was clean and it was his, for the night.

After a good night's sleep, he left, driving toward the center of town until he found himself in front of City Hall. Parking in the lot, he got out of his car carrying the ledgers, took a deep breath, and went into the building.

In the lobby, he asked the guard where he could find the District Attorney. He was directed to the fifth floor and he grabbed an elevator before he lost his nerve.

As he rose slowly to the fifth floor, he felt much older than his nineteen years. He realized his twentieth birthday was only a week away. It was odd that he felt as if his life was ending at nineteen. He couldn't even think about being twenty. When he looked into the future, he saw nothing; nothing at all.

Chapter twenty-two

Now, the memory was complete. As Mitch sat up and looked out the bus window, he knew he was getting close to his destination. But more importantly, he was now facing the memory of events that had led to him being here, at this time. It was becoming so clear.

Mitch remembered how scared he was as he entered the District Attorney's office that day. A receptionist greeted him. She was as efficient as Sabrina, but she wasn't as beautiful. She probably wasn't as devious either.

Mitch introduced himself and asked if he could see the District Attorney. The receptionist asked if he had an appointment and he said no, but that he had some information to give him about the body found in the lake. He thought he noticed her eyes widen slightly, but in her calm voice, she asked him to have a seat.

As she disappeared into a nearby office, Mitch began to look around at his surroundings. He kept remembering the compound and the opulence on display. In contrast, this office was plain, only meeting the needs of the work done here. Maybe crime did pay. But not for him…that small-town background wouldn't let him accept the cost.

The receptionist returned and said that someone would see

him shortly. He tried to relax, but he found that he was just too wound up. He felt jumpy; he hoped he didn't look that way.

When the intercom buzzed, Mitch jumped. The receptionist looked at him and told him he could go in now.

Well, it was too late now to change his mind. He was committed.

Entering the office, he saw a neat, utilitarian office; one in which the occupant obviously spent a lot of time working.

Mitch crossed the room and shook hands with a tall, broad-shouldered man, dressed in a dark blue suit over a neat white shirt and striped tie. He was slightly graying around his temples and his face was somewhat lined, but his eyes were bright and alert, and his handshake was firm.

"Good morning, Mr. Nelson," he said, in a rich, deep voice. "My name is Richards. Won't you have a seat?"

He motioned to a chair near Mitch which he took; then he looked again at the man behind the desk.

"How can I help you, today?" he asked. "My secretary said you might have some information regarding the body found in the lake."

Mitch thought he looked a little expectant as he finished this sentence, but he was relaxed and not pressing Mitch.

Not knowing where to begin, Mitch felt his throat go dry.

After regaining his voice, he said; "I really don't know where to start. The body in the lake is just a small part of the whole picture; should I start at the beginning?"

"Yes," said Mr. Richards, relaxing in his chair but still alert, waiting to hear what Mitch had to say.

Mitch was surprised at how the story came gushing forth. He had been afraid he would not be able to tell it in a way that sounded feasible, but it all came out; every detail; and Mr. Richards was taking notes as Mitch spoke.

Mitch realized that he had started his recitation with a confession that he had been an integral part of the organization and knew that he would have to face the consequences. But he wanted to make sure that Richards understood that he would never, never condone murder. He might have been naïve, but he hoped that if he had really known what could happen, he would never have gotten involved.

At least that was what Mitch wanted to believe. He kept going over and over things in his mind. Did he really know that murders could and would take place? Did he just close his mind to it since he liked the benefits he was receiving? He hoped that wasn't true; he would hate to think that he had sunken so low.

He realized that he had been speaking for some time, with very few breaks, and that the story had just flowed out of him. He had told Richards everything he knew, or believed, or even imagined. He felt spent, exhausted, and empty.

When he finished, he leaned forward and placed the ledgers on Mr. Richards' desk, adding the pillbox and travel pouch, both filled with a variety of drugs. He never wanted to see any of them again. Right now, he knew he could use some of those drugs, but he didn't want to feel better; he didn't deserve it.

Mr. Richards was excited. He knew he had tapped a rich source that would allow him to clean up a lot of crime in his city. With Mitch's permission, he placed a call to the ATF office. He gave them a thumbnail sketch of what Mitch had told him and arranged for them to meet at the federal office in half an hour.

"Mr. Nelson," said the District Attorney, "will you accompany me to the Federal Building? There are several people there we need to speak with. In addition, I will have the local detectives working on the murder meet us there. That way, you won't have to tell your story more than once."

Mitch nodded and got up from his chair. His emptiness made him almost weak, but he followed Mr. Richards out of the office. When they reached the parking garage, Mitch was directed to a non-descript sedan parked nearby. It crossed his mind that the D.A., just like him, didn't want to attract attention with his car. That caused Mitch to smile slightly. He wished he had picked a car while joining this side, instead of the side he had chosen. But it was too late now. He had made his choices, enjoyed the fruits of those choices, and would now have to pay the price.

That scared him. He didn't know what lay ahead of him, but he knew it would be bad, and suddenly he felt like a nineteen-year-old child, not a successful business man.

When they arrived at the Federal Building, they were escorted quickly into a large room, filled with many men in black suits. They all looked quite severe. If the D.A. hadn't been behind him, he would probably have tried to flee.

Mr. Richards introduced him to those in the room. He couldn't remember their names, because he was too scared. He thought he heard that some of them were federal marshals, a federal district attorney, and a member of the commission on racketeering. He wasn't even sure he knew what all that meant.

They all sat down around a large, shiny table. Mitch knew that the chairs were comfortable, and he remembered noticing that this room was furnished more elegantly than the D.A.'s office.

He remembered that Mr. Richards encouraged him to repeat his story, just as he had told him earlier. He saw that the ledgers and drugs were on the table in front of the D.A. Mitch was glad he no longer possessed them. They felt so dirty to him. For a moment, he thought he might cry, but he couldn't, not here, in front of all these men.

So, he repeated his story. He named all of the personnel he knew that worked at the compound, unhappily including Sabrina. He described what he could remember of the times he had snuck into the warehouse as well as the trips he had taken to represent Sam. Most of the suppliers were named in the ledgers, but he described, as well as he could, the places the meetings had taken place. The federal men seemed very excited about this information. Then, he tried to answer any questions they had for him. They wanted to know where the jet was kept and he gave them the address and hangar number. They asked what part Sam and Terrance had played in the interrogations he had witnessed. And, they asked what part Sabrina had played in the process. He had a great deal of trouble answering this question. He explained that she was a receptionist but that she used her beauty and sexiness to gain favors for Sam from others; he wasn't ready to admit that he was one of her conquests. For a fleeting moment, he felt very sad, thinking about Sabrina and that beautiful body spending time in prison. From what he had heard, she would probably be very popular there, but what a waste.

Finally, after what seemed like hours, they were satisfied that they had all the information he could give them. They asked if he would be willing to testify to what he had told them. He said yes, because he knew he had to if he was ever to have a chance to have any life in the future. He hated being a stool pigeon, but why did they have to kill a man? He could have stood anything else, even Sabrina's betrayal. But murder was something he could not accept.

He vaguely heard one of the federal agents talking to him. Bringing himself back to the present, he said; "I'm sorry; did you ask me something?"

"I just asked what kind of deal we need to make with you," said the agent.

Deal? He hadn't even thought of a deal. What should he say?

"I don't know," said Mitch. "I haven't given it much thought. I just want to clear this all up."

"I'm sure we can work something out that will be satisfactory to all of us," said another one of the agents.

Actually, Mitch didn't care. He didn't feel as if he had any future, not now.

He heard them talking among themselves but he couldn't make out what they were saying.

Finally, the D. A. said, "Mitch, we are going to put you in a safe house while we are getting the necessary warrants and making the arrests. You will probably stay there until the trials. While you are there, we will put you in touch with an attorney who can represent you. You know that although you have given us all of this information, we cannot consider this, in any way, a confession. Your attorney will advise you on that and the two of you can decide what kind of a deal you want from us."

Mitch had tried to follow everything the D.A. had said, but he wasn't sure he had fully understood him. He felt as if his head would explode and that his brain, the brain that Sam so admired, had turned to cotton. Anyway, he thought they were going to give him a place to stay. That would be good. He was so tired...so very tired.

As Mitch was taken in a dark sedan from the Federal Building, accompanied by three federal agents, he thought about his own car, still parked in the lot at the D.A.'s office. He mentioned this to the agent sitting next to him. The agent promised that he would take care of the car, putting it in the impound until it was decided what would happen to it. Mitch gave him the keys and described the car. Now he could just relax and get some rest. He really needed some rest.

When the car stopped, Mitch found himself looking at a large estate with a colonial house gracing the grounds. There was a high fence around the grounds and guards patrolling the perimeter. This didn't look like a prison, but the guards made it seem like one. Of course, he was sure he wouldn't be allowed to leave, so it was a prison to him. But at least it looked nice.

Mitch walked, surrounded by the agents, into the house. It had a very large entryway and he could see a living room and library off to the sides. The agent that had been sitting beside him in the car told him that the dining room and kitchen were in the rear of the first floor but that in most cases, he would be staying on the second floor and his meals would be brought to him.

The agent indicated that Mitch should go up the broad staircase. At the top, he saw several doors leading off the hallway. He was escorted to a rear suite of rooms, including a large bedroom, an impressive sitting room which included comfortable chairs, reading lamps and shelves stocked with books of every description; and a fabulous bathroom with a sunken bathtub and a shower stall. The suite was light and airy. Mitch decided that he could be in worse prisons that this, and he probably would be, soon.

He let his mind wander for just a moment, back to the suite he and Sabrina had shared for three glorious days. They had made good use of that suite, every inch of it. The shower stall reminded him of the sensual, steamy showers he had shared with Sabrina and Cindy. He wondered why he had never shared a hot, bubbly bath with either of them.

What a thought. Here he was, facing prison and possible danger from the organization, and he was thinking about showers and baths. That was part of another world, one he would never have again.

The agent told him that they would bring him some clothes soon and that he and three other agents would be in the house at all times. They would alternate sleeping in a room down the hall. If he needed anything, he should use a bell pull near the bed. Under no circumstances was he to leave these rooms, unless accompanied by an agent. He asked if Mitch had any questions, but he couldn't think of any. He supposed that he would have some later, but he could ask them then. The agent showed him how to use the television and pointed out a huge library of video tapes. Well, at least he would have plenty to keep him entertained.

Mitch shook his hand as he left. When the door closed, he suddenly felt all alone, as if he was the only person left in the world. Throwing himself across the bed, he cried; hard sobs racked his body. He had never cried like this before, not even as a child, but that is almost what he felt like now. He was scared, and he had no one to turn to, only the agents who were strangers, protecting him because he had something they wanted. The feeling of loneliness got even stronger, but the tears did stop. He was glad. That made him feel even more like a loser. A loser…what a place to end up. Him, Mitch the wonder boy who was going to the top of the organization…a loser.

With these thoughts running through his mind, Mitch fell asleep, lying across the bed. He slept soundly, but he kept seeing beautiful women flit through his dreams, always out of his reach. He couldn't see their faces, but he knew those bodies. He knew who they belonged to…Peggy, Cindy and Sabrina. Three beautiful, caring women…he had possessed them all… but now he had lost them, forever.

When he awoke, it was getting dark in the room. He switched on a lamp next to the bed, then went into the sitting room. He turned on a lamp next to the comfortable easy chair and picked up the remote control for the television. He hadn't watched television very much in the past few months. He spent almost every minute working or in sexual encounters with one or the other of the beautiful women in his life. There hadn't been any time nor need for television.

He turned the television on, put his feet up on a hassock, and settled down to see what was playing. He came across the news. He wasn't sure he wanted to see it, but maybe he should. The retrieval of the body from the lake was still big news. The reporter was saying that word out of police headquarters was that they had a lead and were close to making an arrest. Mitch wondered how this information had reached the news media. He hoped they didn't know about him. He admitted to himself that he was worried by what the organization would do to him. He knew they had their spies everywhere. He could only hope that none of them were in the room today when he told his story. Sometimes he didn't even care. Because he couldn't see a future, ending his life didn't seem so scary. But, maybe he would have a future. Only time would tell.

After the news, Mitch switched channels, finding an old movie he hadn't seen in years. He settled down to watch it, but it made him think of that night several months ago when he and Cindy had settled down to watch "It's a Wonderful Life.' He didn't know what he had in his arms that night. He was holding a treasure without price, and he had let her get away.

No, he wouldn't think of that now. He couldn't. It hurt too much. He worked hard to get his attention on the movie. He must have been really into it, because he jumped when there was a knock at the door.

"Who is it?" he called.

"I have your dinner. Can I come in?"

He recognized the voice of the agent that had shown him to the suite.

"Sure," he yelled. "Come on in."

The agent brought in a tray, covered with delicious looking food, including a big piece of chocolate cake. It looked good and he realized that he was very hungry.

"Won't you join me?" he asked the agent as he placed the tray on a small table in a nearby alcove.

"Can't tonight," said the agent. "Maybe another time. Enjoy your meal."

With that, he was gone.

Mitch picked up the tray and carried it to the chair. He might as well be comfortable. He ate fast, and the food was good, but his mind was still wandering, causing him distress.

When he finished the meal, including the delicious cake, he put the tray outside his door. He listened but didn't hear any sounds coming from downstairs. He hoped they hadn't left him alone, but he was sure they hadn't. Actually, he felt very safe here, just not happy.

He watched television for a couple of hours. He wished he had a whiskey to drink. He would have to ask tomorrow if they would bring some in for him. But tonight, he would just go to bed. He went into the bedroom, removed his clothes, and crawled, naked, into the big, empty bed. The sheets were cool and smooth on his skin and it felt good, but he was lonely. As he thought, he realized it had been a long time since he slept alone in a bed. The only solo nights were on the couch in his office, except for the night at Sabrina's when he was so exhausted. That made him think of Sabrina and he felt the lust and desire growing in his body. He couldn't think of her. She would never again be in his arms or his bed. She belonged to Sam, and he was welcome to her. Cradling a pillow in his arms, he slept.

Chapter twenty-three

Mitch was leaning back, looking at the fly-specked ceiling of the bus. He began to feel an ache deep inside. The time he was now recalling had been very painful, and lonely. He had never felt so alone in his life.

The next morning, the agent had brought some clothes for Mitch to wear. It was a selection, mostly casual pants and shirts, but they fit perfectly. It felt good to dress so casually... it further removed him from his past.

After breakfast, Mitch had a visitor. John Sampson was an attorney who had been contacted by Mr. Richards. The D.A. had requested that he meet with Mitch, listen to his story, and, if possible, represent him in court. Mitch knew that he needed help. He wanted to tell the truth and he was willing to take his punishment, but if he had an attorney, he wouldn't feel quite so alone.

Mr. Sampson seemed to be well briefed. He didn't even ask Mitch to repeat his whole story. Instead, he looked at the notes he had and asked him specific questions about things he felt needed clarifying.

One area he concentrated on was what exactly Mitch had done for the organization. He was pleased that Mitch had never taken part in any of the rough stuff that had gone on. He told

Mitch that this would make it a lot easier for the prosecution to give him a good deal, especially since he was willingly telling all he knew.

"You don't think I'm being a real fink, telling everything, do you?" asked Mitch.

The attorney looked up from his notes, looking closely at Mitch. He saw before him a scared child, but one that wanted to do what was right.

"No, I don't think you are a fink," he said. "I think you are a young man who got himself brainwashed, and would have gone on forever if he hadn't discovered the darkest side of the organization. I admire you. A lot of people, especially your age, would have just ignored what they had seen, excusing themselves because they weren't directly involved. Just keep your chin up. You are going to come out okay, I promise."

Mitch smiled, for the first time in over twenty-four hours. All at once, he felt the gloom leave him. He actually felt alive. It was good.

"Thanks," he said. "I'm glad you came to talk to me. Will you take my case?"

"With pleasure," replied the attorney. "We're going to do just fine; hang in there."

Mitch felt so much better. He actually felt like he was breathing again, and that, maybe, somewhere out there, someday, there would be a future for him. After all, he was only nineteen.

Mr. Sampson leaned back in his chair and looked at Mitch.

"Tell me something about you," he said. "Not in relation to the organization but about you. Where are you from? What has happened to you in your life? Just anything, so I can know the real you."

This was going to be difficult. Mitch had tried so hard to forget who he really was, but he knew it was important to answer, or Mr. Sampson wouldn't have asked him.

"Well, I was born and raised in a small town. My parents and older brother still live there, but I haven't even spoken to them since Christmas. I guess I led a fairly normal life. I had fun in high school. I had a lot of friends and we had lots of fun together, just foolin' around. You know how kids are. I guess my life changed when I met a girl and she encouraged me to go to college. It wasn't her fault I got in this mess, I wasn't even seeing her by the time I got into the organization. I had a new girl by then; a beautiful, gorgeous...oh, well; I had another girl, but the mess isn't her fault either. In fact, the organization came between us and I lost her. She didn't think there was any room in my life for anything but work. She may have been right. Anyway, there was Sabrina, the receptionist at work. She was fantastic, and I had fooled myself into thinking she really cared about me, but she didn't. She was just the bait to get me in deeper and to cut me off from anyone outside the organization. I miss her, though. I guess I should have known a dumb nineteen-year-old hick kid couldn't be so successful."

When Mitch finally completed his discourse the attorney smiled.

"I don't think you're being fair to yourself, but I like the fact that you are not trying to blame anyone else for your current predicament. That bodes well for your future, and you will have a future. Tell me, Mitch, are you still nineteen?"

"Yes, I won't be twenty for a few days," he replied.

"Well, I think we have a lot going for us," said the attorney. "I won't take any more of your time now, but we will be meeting again, probably several times before you testify. You may have to face a Grand Jury even before the trial, but we will talk about everything that happens along the way. Don't worry. Get some rest. Relax."

He stood up, gathering his papers into his briefcase, shook hands with Mitch, and left the room. Mitch felt a little lonely after he left. It had been nice to have someone to talk to, but now he was alone again. He tried to decide what he wanted to do. He could always watch television or read, but neither really sounded great to him right now. He decided he wanted to write some letters. They might not let him send them, but if he wrote them, he would feel better. Looking in the desk drawer, he found some writing paper and envelopes. This could take a long time, but he felt it would be worth it.

Sitting at the desk, he first made a list of those to whom he wanted to write. This made Mitch think of the list he had started when he first saw Peggy. He couldn't even remember what had happened to that list, but it was funny how life seemed to go in circles.

The first names on the list were his parents. What could he possibly say to them. He didn't know if he could feel any worse than he did about the way he had treated them. He couldn't believe he had ever been ashamed of them. They were always there for him, working hard to give him and Carl the best life available; supporting him in every endeavor; and, most of all, loving him. Just thinking of them as he had left the house last December, brought tears to his eyes. He didn't think he had ever deliberately hurt anyone before or since that time, and just knowing he had hurt them made him feel awful. How could he have been so cruel? He hated the person he had been that day. Since then, he hadn't been much better...no phone calls, no letters. Even if he finished this letter and they let him send it, would they read it? Or did they hate him now? They really should...but he hoped they didn't...in fact, he hoped they still loved him. If they did, he would be a very lucky and successful person. He knew this now, even if he hadn't known it before. He could only hope that they were still there for him.

He knew he was daydreaming, maybe even trying to delay putting his thoughts on paper. He honestly didn't know what to say, but it was time to try. By the time he finished, he felt much better. His apology was sincere and the love he expressed for them was real. He knew it was, because it made his heart ache just to think about them. He hoped that at least this letter got mailed. They just had to know that no matter what they heard or read in the newspaper, or saw on television, he was their son and he loved them and the things they had taught him had helped him stand up against the organization.

When he finished the letter, he addressed the envelope and put the letter inside. He decided he shouldn't seal it. The agents might need to read it before it could be sent. After all, prisoners got their mail censored, didn't they?

The next letter was to Carl. He owed him...big time. He didn't even know if Carl and his girl had gotten married. If they did, he really failed Carl...after all, he wanted Mitch to be his best man. That was a laugh; he couldn't even be the best man in his family...he was a distant third. What Carl had, a life that satisfied him and about which he could have pride, really looked good to him now.

Those letters had been difficult, but the next three were painful. The first one was to Peggy. He owed her nothing but thanks. She had encouraged him to make something of himself; he was the one who chose what to become. Just because he chose badly, didn't make her wish to encourage him bad. He remembered back to when he first saw Peggy. At that moment, she was all he had ever wanted in his life. Why hadn't he kept her; worked with her to mold a future for them. There was no good answer.

Next was Cindy. He still loved her, he knew, and thought he would always love her, no matter what. He knew he was no good for her and that he had only caused her pain and heartache in the end...something he never wanted to do. The only good thing that came out of the entire mess he had made of Cindy's life was that she found Jim. He was great and would be good for her...the best.

The third of these difficult letters was to Jim. He and Jim had formed a good relationship, but he failed it, not Jim. He admitted that he and Jim had both gone off the deep end...too much partying, drinking and drugs...for a time, but Jim had straightened up. He hadn't. In fact, he had gone deeper and deeper into that life, and missed out on a good friend. At least Jim and Cindy had found each other. To Mitch, Jim was the luckiest man on Earth.

He was absolutely sure the agents would not let him send the two additional letters he planned to write, but he felt that it would help him in the cleansing of his own life to write them.

The first was to Sam. He wanted Sam to know that he had liked him, enjoyed working for him, and had gone into it with his eyes open. Sam did nothing to trap him…at first. Yes, Sam had wanted to make sure he stayed…but that was later. Mitch couldn't blame him…he had approached the liquor store clerk first. He volunteered. He also knew that, despite his protestations, he had known from the first that he was into the wrong side of life. He knew it was all illegal, but he stayed. The benefits were good. Maybe he would have stayed even longer, but the fact that they had murdered a man he had fingered made it too bad, even for him. There were no benefits that could cover that up in his mind. The murder may have been Sam's fault, but Mitch picked the victim. Only Mitch could be blamed.

The last letter was to Sabrina. Mitch felt like he hated turning her in more than anyone in the organization. He knew that she was really involved…much more than he had known… but he still cared about her. He still didn't love her, but the thought of that luscious, voluptuous body still produced feelings of lust within his own body. She was beautiful and he knew that prison would be hard on her…maybe harder than on any of them. He worried that her body would become the property of some mean inmate within the prison, or maybe even one or more of the guards. It would be terrible to see this sensual creature used until she was completely spent and her eyes became vacant windows. The only pain he felt was for her… not for Sam, or Terrance, or himself…just Sabrina. He wrote of his feelings for her, the hours of enjoyment she had given him, and the feeling that he must be important if she lusted after him. He begged her to forgive him. The physical lusting and the satisfaction they had enjoyed together was memorable, so maybe that part of her could forgive him; but the other part, the part that knew what was awaiting her in prison, would hate him, and he couldn't blame her for not forgiving him for that.

When he had finished the last letter, he realized he was exhausted; spent just as if he had been romping with Sabrina in a big, king-sized bed. But this exhaustion was different; his lust would remain, although it was not very strong, but his energy was gone. He returned to the bedroom and fell into bed. He was asleep in a few minutes. This time he slept well, dreamless. Maybe the writing of the letters had cleansed his heart and mind. He hoped so.

The days had begun to run together. He never left his suite, seeing only his attorney, the agents guarding him, and sometimes one of the prosecutors. Mr. Sampson had told him not to talk to anyone about his testimony until the deal and the testimony was perfected. He would tell everything to the Grand Jury first, not leaving out anything, even his own involvement; and then he would testify in two court hearings…a federal case about the racketeering, and a state case about the murder. He knew these cases would be hard. Reporters were sure to print a lot and his parents would be hurt. He had hurt them enough, but the hurt and pain was not finished. He wished that he was farther from his home town, then maybe the news wouldn't get to them…but he knew it would.

His attorney and the prosecutors had reviewed the letters he had written. They agreed to let him mail the ones to his parents, Carl, Peggy, Cindy and Jim. The ones to Sam and Sabrina were being held. They had agreed to send them after the cases were closed and sentences had been handed down. Since he sent the letters he had not had any responses. He knew that deep down he had hoped at least one of them would respond, letting him know they understood and were still there for him. But, he knew he really didn't deserve it.

The day before his testimony, John spent most of the day going over with him the testimony he would give. Since John could not be in the Grand Jury room, he wanted Mitch to know exactly what to say and how to say it. By that night, Mitch felt he knew everything John wanted him to know, but he felt exhausted. He hoped he would have good night's sleep, but he slept fitfully anxious about what was about to happen.

The next morning, he was whisked to the Court House in a dark sedan, again surrounded by agents. They took him up the back way from the parking garage and kept him in a guarded room until he was called to testify. After his testimony, they reversed their route, returning him quickly to the safe house. Mitch felt that he had done a good job of testifying. He knew he looked as bad as any of the accused, but he didn't care…he was. That night he ate a good dinner, watched a little television, and then slept well.

The time before the first trial, the racketeering trial was to start, was long to him. In reality, it was only six weeks after his first testimony, but he was anxious to get it over with. He was not looking forward to testifying against Sam and Sabrina while they were watching him, but he knew he had to do it.

John had worked long and hard with the prosecutors and they had worked out a deal for him. Due to his young age and the fact that he had willingly come forward, Mitch would receive ten years in a federal prison for racketeering. Ten years…and serve five with good behavior. It sounded like a lifetime, but John told him it was a good deal. The others would probably get life sentences. His heart jumped a little. Did he mean everyone? Sam and Terrance he could understand, but what about Sabrina? John assured him that Sabrina had a good attorney and that she would probably get off with less time. After all, the jury would probably see her as a victim too, and she was a beautiful woman. It didn't help though…he knew that he was going to be the means of sending her to prison.

In the state case for murder, Sabrina was not named as a defendant. That helped. The four men involved were probably looking at a minimum of life without parole.

As the day of his first court appearance dawned, Mitch woke early. He was nervous. He knew that the prosecutor would be there as well as his own attorney to protect him, but he was still nervous. It would be the first time he had come face to face with Sam since that day he found him and Sabrina having sex on the couch. He hadn't spoken to him since then.

He dressed carefully in a suit, shirt, and tie that John picked out for him. It wasn't flashy. In fact, he blended right into the group of agents surrounding him. Riding in the back seat of that familiar sedan, he felt his palms getting clammy and his mouth was dry. He hoped he would be able to talk by the time he got to court.

He waited in a room near the courtroom until it was his time to testify. As he was leaving the room, the agent that had been the most friendly, shook his hand and wished him good luck. That helped…more than anyone could know. As he entered the courtroom, he did not feel so alone, thanks to that simple gesture. Just before he was called to the witness stand, he expelled a deep breath. He hoped that he could keep his breathing normal.

As he took the oath, swearing to tell the truth, he knew that this was his chance to start on the road to making things up to everyone that had cared about him. When he took the witness stand, he looked around. He couldn't believe it. There, in the front row, just behind the prosecutor, were his parents, Carl and a girl he assumed was his wife, Peggy, Cindy and Jim. As he looked at them, he wanted to yell out that life was good again. They believed in him; they were supporting him.

As the prosecutor approached, Mitch knew that everything was going to be all right. He concentrated on the prosecutor's questions, answering them completely and clearly. He did not try to hide anything. Today was the day for the complete truth, and nothing but the truth. When the prosecutor asked if he could identify Sam, Sabrina and Terrance, he pointed to them at the defendants' table, identifying them individually. He looked them straight in the eye, never flinching. Sam and Terrance glared at him as he identified them; Sabrina wouldn't even look at him, keeping her head down. Even so, it felt good to do the right thing.

When the defense attorneys tried to get Mitch to change his testimony, he found a resolve that he was not sure existed in him. He was able to look at them and continue to tell the truth. The attorneys tried to get him to say that he was the one doing the trafficking and dealing without the knowledge of Sam or Terrance or any of the people involved in the organization. He restated that he admitted trafficking and dealing, but he had done it for and with the full knowledge of Sam, and that Terrance had accompanied him as Sam's muscle.

Even though he was asked the same questions over and over in all different ways, he stuck to his story. He never wavered. Finally, almost four hours after he had taken the stand, he was excused. As he walked to the side room, he glanced at his supporters in the front row. Although his mother, Peggy and Cindy had tears in their eyes, they were smiling at him. He felt the glow of love in a way he had never felt before. It was wonderful.

Before he was returned to the safe house, John Sampson came into the witness waiting room.

"You did a great job," he said. "I haven't been so proud of a client for years. One more to go, then you can finish paying your debt to society. It is going to work out Mitch. There is life ahead for you."

He shook Mitch's hand. It felt good. For the first time, he believed that.

"By the way," said John, "I have received permission for

your family to visit you before you go back to the safe house, that is, if you'd like to see them."

Would he like to see them? He had never wanted anything more in his whole life.

"Yes! Please bring them in!" he said, obvious excitement in his voice.

John left the room and when the door opened again, he looked up. He wanted to run to them, but would they want that?

His mother was the first to enter the room. She held out her arms and he literally fell into them.

"My baby, my baby," she murmured. "We have missed you so much."

She was crying and Mitch realized he was crying too.

After holding his mother close for several minutes, he released her and looked at his father. He looked older and more worn than when he had last seen him. He didn't want to think that he was the cause of that...but he probably was.

His father threw his arms around him, hugging him tightly. He couldn't remember his father ever hugging him.

As the dam seemed to open and the tears flowed freely, Mitch hugged Carl; was introduced to his new wife, Grace; hugged Peggy, loving to feel her in his arms again; hugged Cindy who whispered that she still loved him; and even hugged Jim.

As they stood around, now just exchanging pleasantries, they each, in their own way, told him how proud they were of him for testifying. None of them admonished him for getting into this mess in the first place, but he knew they were thinking about it...at least he was. Peggy looked drawn. Her beautiful face was tired looking and her hair no longer shone. He hoped she wasn't sick. Cindy, on the other hand, looked radiant as she clung to Jim. They told Mitch they planned to be married in a few months and Cindy showed him the engagement ring she was wearing. He wished them nothing but the best and asked them to keep in touch with him. They promised, but he wondered if they would. Each of them thanked Mitch for his letters. That had made a difference to each of them. He was very glad he had written them.

Soon, an agent entered and said it was time to go. Mitch hugged everyone again, saving special hugs for Peggy and his mother. He thanked each of them for coming and their support. He told them that he knew it would be a long time before he could see them again, but that he would be thinking of them, every day. As the door closed behind them, he felt his chest swell, not with pride, but with thanks that he had such special people in his life. Despite all of the mistakes he had made, he was a lucky man…a very lucky man.

On the ride back to the safe house, he received congratulations from the agents for the good job he had done on the stand. That felt good. He was trying, as hard as he could, to make up for all the bad choices he had made and acts he had committed. It would take a long time, he knew.

Back at the safe house, he enjoyed his meal and watched television, very relaxed. Just knowing someone cared for you made a wonderful difference.

It didn't take the jury long to return guilty verdicts in the racketeering case. When the sentences were handed down, Mitch was not in the courtroom. The judge and the prosecutor had agreed to let him be represented by John Sampson. Sam, Terrance, and several of the henchmen were given life sentences in a maximum security federal prison without the chance of parole; Sabrina was given fifteen years in a federal women's prison. Mitch later learned that she had broken down in tears when she heard the sentence. Mitch was given ten years in federal prison, not to be the same as where any of the others were incarcerated.

Well, at least it was over. He wanted to get on with paying his debt, so that he could get on with his life. During this stressful period, he had turned twenty...now he wanted to act like an adult.

Shortly after the end of the federal trial, Sam, Terrance, Lonnie and Bill went on trial for murder in state court. Again, Mitch was the star witness, and, again, he had his cheering section in the front row. The only concern he had was how bad Peggy looked. Her natural beauty couldn't compete with the sadness covering her entire being. Her eyes looked sad and her beautiful figure was wasting away to nothing. He wondered if she was sick. Maybe he could write to her and she would tell him.

As in the racketeering trial, Mitch made an excellent witness, unshakable on cross examination. When he left the stand that day, he knew that he had done all he could to make sure these men hurt nobody else.

Again he was given a short visit with his family and friends. It wasn't quite as emotional as the first meeting, until it came time to leave. Then, he knew it would be a long time until he saw them. He was leaving tonight for prison.

Just before they all left, John came into the room. He told them that this would be the last contact they could have with Mitch until his release. They had reached an agreement where he would be housed in a minimum security prison under an assumed name. That meant that nobody could know where he was or what name he was using. The government felt that this was the only way they could protect him.

This was a devastating blow to them all. They had just found each other, and now they were being pulled apart again, this time, unwillingly. After the tears stopped, they hugged and kissed each other goodbye. He asked them to continue writing so he could keep up with their lives, but not to mail the letters. He wanted all the letters when he returned home and it would let him be a part of their lives during the next few years. He promised that he would write letters to each of them too.

As they left, he whispered to his mother to watch over

Peggy. He told her he was worried about her. She squeezed his hand. He knew she would do it.

When they had left, Mitch said goodbye to John. He had been an excellent attorney for him. He wasn't sure when he could ever repay him. After all the government had confiscated all of his bank accounts. John told him not to worry. It was worth it to see justice done. Even so, Mitch would always be in his debt.

On the drive to the prison, everyone was pretty quiet. The agent who had become his close friend, seemed sad and withdrawn. It took all night and part of the morning for them to reach the prison, his home for the next few years.

He soon found out that it was located in eastern Oklahoma. It wasn't where he would have chosen to spend the next few years because it was prison, but as prisons go, it was okay. In the warden's office, he was given his new name, Rod Fisher, and his prison clothes. As he was being led into the cell area, he shook hands with the agents who had driven him here, the same ones who had protected him for the last few months.

"Thanks," he said. "I hope I wasn't too much trouble for you."

"No; no you weren't," said his friend. "It has been a pleasure. By the way, my name is Scott Collins. Look me up when you get out. We all hope things go well for you from now on."

"Me too," said Mitch. "I am going to do my best."

Turning, Mitch entered the cell block which would become his home for the next five years.

Now he was free, and he was going home...home.

Chapter twenty-four

His timing had been great. He had reached the end of his reminiscence just as they arrived at the outskirts of his hometown. Well…he was almost home. Now what was he going to do? Would he be welcomed? Or would they wish he was gone again? Only time would tell. He hadn't been able to notify anyone of his arrival. Maybe he really hadn't wanted to anyway. In his knapsack next to him on the bus seat were packets of letters he had written to his friends and family over the past five years. He wondered if they had written to him, or if they would be interested in what he had written.

Mitch realized that the five years behind bars had changed him. He was not the self-assured young entrepreneur he had been before his world came crashing down, nor was he the determined young witness he had been during the trials. In fact, he felt very old and very insecure…he was afraid.

Maybe he had been behind bars too long. After all, prison was full of stories of men who could no longer function in the outside world. They always found a way to get back to prison when they were released because prison had become their only home. He hoped he wasn't like that…but he did know that he was jumpy…even a little scared.

As the bus pulled into the depot, the driver yelled that they would be stopping here for fifteen minutes.

Mitch knew he would be stopping for longer than that. He just didn't know how long. He hoped it would be forever, but only time would tell. Mitch smiled to himself. Imagine, him hoping to stay in this town forever.

That would make everyone that knew him laugh. It even made him laugh to himself.

Stepping down from the bus, he hoisted his knapsack over his shoulder. Looking around, he felt like he was in an unfamiliar place. Maybe he had tried so hard to get out of this town seven years ago, he had wiped the memories from his mind. He hoped not. He wanted to belong.

Mitch started to walk down the street, headed toward the railroad tracks. The special spot along the railroad track was his destination. He had made a quick trip back here one night several years ago, the night he had realized that things were not going to turn out well. Anyway, that late night he had slipped in and out of town without being seen. He had chosen a flat area near the train tracks where a small lane crossed them. When he arrived, it took him some minutes to find the right spot. His measurements had been exact; all he had to do was remember them. He knelt next to the spot, brushing away all the trash and weeds around it. He found a piece of metal that would serve as a shovel. He began digging, looking around to make sure no one was watching. He didn't see anyone. That was one reason he had chosen this spot; it was so private.

Digging quickly, he managed to dig down the necessary twelve inches. There, just where he had put it, was a small metal box. He pulled it out and blew the dirt off the top. It wasn't locked; after all, if anyone had found it, why worry about a lock? He set it on the ground in front of him and, while still on his knees, he opened the little box.

Inside was his stash. A smile crossed Mitch's lips. Years

ago, his stash would have been pretty colored pills and capsules, but this was entirely different.

He gently lifted the first item out of the box. He got tears in his eyes as he looked at the beautiful id bracelet that Peggy had given him on their first Christmas together. He slipped it on his wrist. It felt good there.

The next thing he lifted from the box was a small diary listing some of the main people in the organization, those even above Sam; this was his insurance. As long as he had this, he could get them to leave him alone. This was going into a safe-deposit box immediately, with instructions for opening it if something unforeseen should happen to him.

The third and last thing in the box was a plain envelop. Inside was a small wad of money...$500.00. He knew it was drug money, but he didn't want to be dependent on his family. This would help him get started. He really didn't know what he would do with it, but it would be good...not evil.

Mitch stuffed the diary and the money into his knapsack and stood. He brushed off his knees and started walking back toward the center of town. He dropped the little box in a sidewalk trash can and kept on walking.

In town, he stopped at the bank. It was one he had never been in before. He hoped they wouldn't know who he was.

He went to the information desk and asked where the safety deposit boxes could be found. After receiving directions, he went directly to the desk that had been pointed out to him.

When he told the lady at the desk he wanted to rent a box, she asked him his name. It was difficult not to answer Rod Fisher. He had used the name exclusively for the last five years, but he was glad to get rid of it.

"Mitch Nelson," he replied.

Noticing her handwriting was small and neat, like Peggy's, he saw her fill out a card with all the information. He gave his address as 783 Elm Street, his parents' address, and gave their phone number. When she had completed the card she asked him to sign on the signature line. After he had signed, she handed him a key and a card with the box information. She asked him if he wanted to put something in the box today and when he said yes, she asked that he accompany her. When they reached the vault area, she removed the box, using both keys, and handed it to him. Returning his key to him, she returned to her desk. He put the diary into the box and returned it to the slot, turning the key.

When he passed the clerk, she was waiting on someone else, but he gave her a smile and a small wave. In return, she smiled, but kept talking to the new client.

As he left the bank, the noonday sun was shining brightly. He loved the feel of the sun on his face. It had been too long since he could enjoy this feeling of freedom.

Mitch walked slowly, swinging his knapsack at his side, enjoying the feeling and taking in all the sights, sounds and smells around him. As he walked toward his parents' house, he passed close to Peggy's house. That caused a little pang in his heart as he thought about those days a lifetime ago, when they were the perfect couple. He regretted several things in his life, but the way he had treated Peggy and Cindy were the biggest regrets. Neither one had deserved the treatment they got; maybe the truth was he never deserved either one of them.

Turning before he reached Peggy's house, he walked a little faster as he neared home. He wondered how they would feel about him coming home. After all, this had never been discussed. Well, if it made them uncomfortable for him to be there, he would leave. He didn't intend to hurt anyone else, ever. He had done enough of that to last a lifetime.

He stopped in front of the house. How had he ever believed this was not a good place to be? It looked great to him right now.

Going up the front walk, onto the porch, he knocked on the door. He realized he was a little nervous.

His mother answered the door. If he had ever had any doubt

about his welcome, it disappeared with the look on her face.

"Mitch, oh Mitch," she cried, hugging him to her. "I'm so glad you are home. We have missed you so much and we've been counting the days."

He hugged her back and he wasn't sure he would ever let her go. He never knew that being hugged by his mother could feel so good.

"Come in; come in," she said, leading him into the familiar, comfortable living room.

"Thanks, Mom," he said. "I wasn't sure I should come here or..."

"Not come here? Where else would you go? This is your home," she said and he felt such a good feeling come over him.

They sat together on the sofa. It felt so comfortable, he thought he wanted to stay here for the rest of his life.

"Is dad at work?" he asked.

"Yes, but he will be home soon. He will be so glad to see you. So will Carl. He and Carol are expecting in three months; this will be their second child," she said.

"I'm an uncle?" he asked?

"Yes; they have an adorable little boy. You will love him," she replied.

As she spoke, he felt real envy of his brother. He had ended up with just what he wanted, the honest way. He was a lucky man.

"Are you hungry?" she asked. "I could fix you something to eat."

"No, I'll be fine until supper," he said. "Would you mind if I lied down for a while?"

"Of course not; go right ahead. Your room is just as you left it," she said smiling. "I am so happy that you are home."

Mitch gave her a kiss on her cheek, and then picking up his knapsack, he a walked down the hall to his old room. When he opened the door and turned on the light, he felt like he was back in high school. He dropped his knapsack on the desk chair and lay down across the bed. To him, this was Heaven. He was never going to forget how good a life this was; never.

Mitch woke to the sounds of laughter. He got up, somewhat dazed, and went to the hall. Looking toward the living room, he saw his mother hugging his father. They were laughing and crying at the same time.

Mitch went into the living room and his father, seeing him, broke away from the embrace of his mother and came toward him. Throwing his arms around him, he said;

"Welcome home, Son. We have missed you so much."

Mitch could hardly believe it; how could they welcome him home after what he had done; he brought them shame, after they had lived all their lives with good reputations. Even so, he was being welcomed home; it was a miracle.

When his father stepped back, Mitch guided him to an easy chair, one he knew his father had always loved. When he was seated, he turned back to his mother.

"Here, Mom; sit here," he said, guiding her to the sofa. She was smiling at him, obviously happy to have him home. He could never remember feeling like this. It was the first time his parents had really let him see their feelings. He knew that they were opening up to him in a way that was not usual for them and their generation. He felt like the Prodigal Son being welcomed home.

The time seemed to fly as they talked about the last few years. He wanted to know everything that had been happening; and they just wanted to know that he was okay.

When supper was ready, they moved into the dining room, still just enjoying being together.

After supper, while his father relaxed and read the paper, Mitch helped his mother with the dishes. He noticed that she couldn't stop smiling. He couldn't remember the last time he had helped his mother do anything. He couldn't believe he had been such a useless son to them.

When the dishes were done, they joined his father in the living room. After a little discussion, they decided they should let Carl know that he was back so his mother called him. Carl was as happy as his parents were to have him back. They talked for a long time on the phone and before they hung up they had arranged for all of them to go to Carl's house for supper the next day. It would give Mitch a chance to really meet his sister-in-law and, for the first time, meet his nephew. Carl said he looked just like Mitch did when he was a baby. Mitch couldn't help but hope he was a better son, and a lot smarter, than he was.

After a good nights sleep, Mitch decided he'd better start making plans for a future. He knew his education was limited to two semesters in college, none of which would probably help him in seeking work; and, of course, he couldn't list his last employer either as experience or as a reference. He really was starting at zero, or maybe even less, sine he now had a prison record. He really didn't know where to start.

After finishing breakfast, the old favorite, a bowl of cereal, he kissed his mother and left the house, telling her he wanted to take a walk. He really didn't know what he wanted to do, but he had to walk and think. Before he knew it, he found himself across the street from Peggy's house. He didn't know what had brought him here, but he thought it was one of the dumbest things he had ever done. If someone saw him hanging around here, they would probably think he was a stalker. All he had to do was get picked up; with his record they would probably throw away the key.

He walked faster, trying to get away from the neighborhood. Peggy probably didn't even live there any more. He was sure she was married by now…she was too special to be single and alone. She had so much to give to a relationship…he should know.

Before long, he found himself in front of the Public Library. Maybe they had the local want ads here and he could look into a job. Before he looked though, he wanted to make a call.

Finding a pay phone, he dialed the operator and asked for a number; then he dialed. When a secretary answered, he asked if he could please speak to John Sampson. When she asked if he would know what he was calling about, Mitch said to just tell him an old friend wanted to speak to him.

The next voice he heard was familiar.

"This is John Sampson; may I help you?"

"You already did," said Mitch. "I just wanted to call and thank you once again."

"Mitch! When did you get back?" The questions tumbled out of John.

"Just got in yesterday," said Mitch.

"Well, what are you doing?" he asked.

"Just trying to decide what I should do," Mitch said. "I want to find a job, but I really don't have any experience I can list on an application."

John laughed. "No, I guess you don't. Listen, Mitch, you are a very bright young man; would you be interested in doing leg work for a group of attorneys I know? The pay might not be as much as you want, but I'm sure you'd find the work interesting."

Would he be interested? Of course he would be interested.

"I think it would be great. Where do I go? Who do I contact?"

"Let me make some phone calls," said John. "Is there some place I can reach you later today, or tomorrow?"

"Yes, I'm staying with my parents for the time being," he said, adding the phone number. "And, thanks, John. I didn't call to ask you for a job, but I really do appreciate it."

When he hung up, he felt much better. Maybe doing the right thing five years ago would have some good results besides the good feelings it gave him. As he left the phone booth, he thought he was walking just a little lighter.

He really didn't want to go home yet. It wasn't for the

old reason… that he didn't want to be with his family; it was because he liked being outdoors. Now there really wasn't any reason to go into the library. He had been inside as much as he wanted to be for a long time.

He walked all over town; past the high school, the football field, the local malt shop, and the movie theater. So much of his childhood and teen years could be found in these places. He wished he could start all over…with the knowledge he had now. But he knew it couldn't be. What had been, had been. Today was a new beginning.

It was funny that he considered this town to be a new beginning. He had always thought that it was the old trap. It was really odd what a different outlook seven years could bring.

Mitch stopped at a local coffee shop and ordered a burger and coffee. It felt wonderful to have the freedom to do these simple things.

While he was eating, he began to wonder what had happened to the people in his past. Of course, he hadn't been able to be in touch with them, but maybe he could try to contact them now. He would love to know if Cindy and Jim had gotten married. He hoped they had and that they were happy. They both deserved it. And then there was Peggy. He really wondered what had happened to her. Had she met the man of her dreams? She should have. She deserved happiness and she would be a wonderful mother. Then, as he sipped his second cup of coffee, he admitted he wanted to know what was happening with Sabrina. He still didn't love her, but she had given him so much carnal joy, he thought he owed her at least some thought. Was she still in prison? Had it changed her? He really wanted to know. Finally, he made a decision. Tomorrow, he would go back to where it all came apart for him…the college campus. Maybe he could find out where everyone ended up if he started there.

With a plan in mind, he paid his bill, left a tip and then headed home. It helped to know what he was going to do.

One the way home, he passed the DMV. Remembering his license must be expired, he stopped by and got it renewed. He was feeling like a normal citizen again.

That evening was wonderful. Carl and Grace both seemed so happy to have him home, and their little boy, Jacob, was a joy. He was a happy, active two-year-old who seemed to have everything he could ever want. He seemed happy with his two loving parents. Mitch hoped he never changed. If he could do anything about it, Jacob would remain the same happy child he saw here tonight, even if he had to eventually tell him the truth.

When he got home, he told his parents he was planning to go on a hunting trip...a hunt for past friends. They laughed because they knew he was getting involved with life...the best thing that could happen to him.

Chapter twenty-five

The sun was bright the next morning as Mitch left. His father had loaned him his car and it felt good to be driving along the highway with the fresh air blowing through the open window. He turned on the radio. He didn't recognize any of the popular songs. He guessed that five years had made a lot of changes in the music business. Turning the dial, he came to a station that played Oldies. Believe it or not, he felt more comfortable with them.

When he arrived at campus, he wondered where he should start. Cindy had never been a student, but Jim had been. If they were together, all he had to do was trace Jim. Peggy, too, had been a student. The first stop needed to be the registrar's office.

When he walked up to the counter, a perky, young student asked if she could help him. He noticed she gave him a quick once-over and seemed to be flirting with him. That made him smile. If she knew what he did to the women in his life, not only would she never flirt with him, she'd run as fast as she could.

Shaking off the thought, Mitch told her that he was a former student, just passing through town, and was interested in looking up some old friends that he had lost contact with over the years. He gave her Jim's and Peggy's names and asked if she could help him.

She frowned, looked at the names, and then looked back at him.

"We're not really supposed to give out addresses," she said, "but if they are friends of yours, I don't guess it would hurt. Just a minute and I'll see if I can find them."

She disappeared into the back room, and he took the time to look around the office. It looked about the same as he remembered; things here didn't seem to change; just the faces. He noticed an older woman at the counter and was glad he hadn't approached her. She would have probably told him 'no.'

In just a few minutes, the girl returned and handed him a card. On the card he saw that she had noted the last known addresses under the names. He gave her a smile and thanked her, telling her he owed her. She smiled and said, "Just come by when we close and I'll let you thank me properly."

Mitch smiled as he left. He should just do that. He would probably scare her to death. At least it might stop her from flirting with strangers.

As he went down the steps, he glanced at the card. The first address was for Jim. He was pleased to see that it was right here in town. He decided to try to look him up first. And, if he was lucky, he would also get to see Cindy.

Returning to the car, he dug a street map out of the glove compartment. He located the street he was looking for and headed that way. The closer he got to the address, the more nervous he became. What if Jim didn't want to see him? After all, it had been five years. He reached into his jacket pocket and felt the packets of letters he had written to Jim and Cindy over the years. He had told them a lot of things in these letters and had, in more ways than he could have imagined existed, asked for their forgiveness. But would they give it? Well, he wasn't going to find out unless he contacted them.

He stopped the car in front of a small but neat house. It had a beautiful flower garden in the side yard and a white picket fence surrounding it. It looked perfect. Taking a deep breath, he got out of the car and went to the front door. He knocked sharply, before he had time to change his mind. He could hear someone coming to the door. Suddenly, his mouth was very dry.

When the door opened, he knew he was in the right place. He was looking into the beautiful face of Cindy. She didn't look as if she had aged at all. It was obvious that she was happy and that life had been good to her.

"May I help you?" she said, seemingly distracted from the person standing in front of her.

"Hi, Cindy; don't you recognize an old friend?"

She looked at him, and yelled.

"Mitch! When did you get back in town?" she said, opening the door wide and giving him a warm, welcoming hug.

It felt so good to have Cindy in his arms again that he had to force himself to give her a small kiss and stand back. He liked the fact that she had not asked him when he got out. He should have known she had too much class to make him feel uncomfortable.

"Just a couple of days ago," he said.

"Well, come on in," she said, opening the door wider for him to enter.

When he got inside, he saw that the house, although small, was nicely furnished. It looked comfortable and happily enjoyed. Before he could take a seat, he was almost knocked off his feet. A boy, probably about three, was tearing around the room on a tricycle and a little girl was chasing him. They were beautiful kids.

"Yours?" he asked.

"Yes," said Cindy. "Children, this is your Uncle Mitch. Remember, Mommy and Daddy have told you all about him."

They quickly abandoned the tricycle and started to climb on him. They were absolutely wonderful.

Sitting down quickly, he found himself with a lapful of wiggling kids. He couldn't believe that Cindy and Jim had told them about him.

"You lived with my daddy," said the little boy.

"That's right," said Mitch; "a long time ago."

"My daddy said you were his best friend; you gave him mommy. Where have you been?" said the precocious little boy.

"That's enough for now," said Cindy, rescuing him from the interrogation. "You two scat; I want to talk to Uncle Mitch. Please go and play in your rooms."

They crawled to the floor, but the little girl, the image of Cindy, took time to give him a kiss on his cheek. They were terrific...Jim was a lucky man.

"I'm sorry about that," said Cindy. "It is just that they have heard Jim talk about you so much, that they think they already know you."

"It's okay," said Mitch. "They are terrific. You look happy. Are you?"

"Yes," said Cindy, smiling. "I'm very happy."

"What is Jim doing now?" asked Mitch, trying to get his mind off Cindy.

"He's a football coach and teacher at a high school. Would you have ever believed he would coach high school kids?" she asked. He heard that tinkling laugh again and it caused him a pang of memory.

"No, but we've all changed, I guess," said Mitch. "I hope I get the opportunity to see him. What time does he get home?"

"During the season, he is usually late," she said, "but you could drop by the practice field after school or come here on Saturday. That is the day he tries to stay home with the kids."

"I'll try to get back in the next week or so," said Mitch. "Please tell him I came by."

"I will, Mitch. He will be so happy to know you are home. Please do come back. We both care for you so much."

As she said this, Mitch noticed a sadness in Cindy's eyes, and he knew it was for him and his lost opportunities.

As he started to leave, he felt the letters he had put in his pocket.

"Oh, here," he said. "These are the letters I wrote to you and Jim while I was away. I did appreciate your support, you know. It was important."

"Thanks, Mitch; you will always have our support. Wait just a minute."

She went to a little desk near the door and took a packet of letters from the drawer.

"You didn't think we'd forget, did you?"

He gave Cindy a kiss and then, taking the letters, he left.

"Kiss the kids for me," he said, "and tell Jim he's the luckiest guy I ever knew."

Before he reached the car, Cindy ran after him and gave him another kiss.

"Come back; please," she said.

"Okay," he said, smiling.

He slid behind the wheel, waved, and drove away. Jim really was a lucky guy. What a waste he had made of his life. Jim had a beautiful family; Carl had a beautiful family; and he had...nothing.

Looking at the card again, he noticed that Peggy's address was still listed as her parents' house. He couldn't believe she still lived there. Maybe she just hadn't sent in a change of address. He wasn't sure he would be very welcome if he contacted Dr. or Mrs. Johnson, but he sure would love to see Peggy and know how she was doing. He remembered the last time he had seen her. She hadn't looked good. He hoped she was okay.

Mitch was about to leave town when he remember the

agents had put his car in lock-up. He wondered if it was still there or if it had been confiscated like everything else.

Well, the only way he could find out would be to contact the federal agents at their office. Driving to the Federal Building, he parked his dad's car in the lot and went up to the office. He had no idea if any of the same agents were still stationed here, but he was anxious to find out.

He went directly to the receptionist, who appeared to be quite busy, and asked her if Scott Collins was still working out of this office.

Looking up, she said, "Yes, he is. Whom may I say is asking?"

"Mitch Nelson," he replied. "Could you ask him if he has a few minutes?"

"Have a seat," she said, and picked up a telephone.

Mitch waited quietly but he was anxious. Mitch remembered the labyrinth of offices that lay behind the wall. Suddenly he was there.

"Mitch," he said, shaking his hand. "Welcome back."

"Thanks," he said. "It's good to be back. I never knew that freedom could feel so good."

Leading Mitch back into the labyrinth to a small office, he showed him to a chair and sat down himself behind the desk.

"It's good to see you," he said. "I hope things weren't too hard for you."

"No," said Mitch, with a wry smile. "Not as bad as I deserve, I am sure."

"What are you going to do now? Any prospects?"

"Some, but I am not sure yet," said Mitch. "I just want to get on with my life. And that brings me to a question. I just wondered if the government confiscated my car. I really loved that car."

"Yes, and no," said Scott, smiling. "Usually they take the cars to auction, but since you were a willing witness, I pulled a couple of strings and bought the car myself. I have your car on blocks…in my garage."

Mitch couldn't believe it. He never knew people could be so nice to strangers.

"I don't know how to thank you," said Mitch, his voice catching in his throat. "I don't know when I can pay you for it and for your trouble, but I will."

"Forget it," said Scott. "Can you come by next weekend to get it? I could use that garage space."

Mitch saw him smile as he said this.

"You bet," said Mitch. "How about Saturday?"

Mitch arranged to meet Scott at his house on Saturday morning at eleven.

As he shook hands and said goodbye, Mitch had such a warm feeling inside, he wondered why he had ever thought his old life made him feel good.

Chapter twenty-six

His third full day of freedom dawned clear and sunny. Things had been great since he got home. It was nice being around his parents. He hadn't known they were such great people. He must have been blind.

He left right after breakfast with the purpose of tracking Peggy down. He really didn't know where to start. He was afraid to go to the house. The Johnsons would probably call the police on him. As he walked, he thought.

He found himself in front of the Public Library again. He remembered the afternoons he and Peggy had studied here. Those were really good days.

For some reason, he went in. Maybe he could find the answer here. After all, they did have old newspaper files; maybe, if she got married, he could find her married name in the news files.

He found his way to the reference desk and asked the elderly woman manning it how he could look up a person in back issues of the newspapers. She looked a little shocked that he did not know how to do this, but she told him and sent him to a general file.

Sitting in front of a screen, he typed the name...Johnson, Peggy. When he hit the button that read 'locate,' he sat, finding himself very tense and apprehensive. It was surprising how much information was in these files, but eventually he was given a screen listing all the back issues of the paper in which Peggy Johnson was mentioned. He wondered if they were all about his Peggy; but if he needed to, he would read each one.

Starting with the papers dated closest to the time of his incarceration and coming forward, he was able to follow Peggy's life, just as if he had been there.

There were articles about her sorority activities, her scholastic achievements, and finally her college graduation, but no information on an engagement or a marriage. He was frustrated. She seemed to disappear after graduation. What had happened to her? He knew if she had gotten really sick, that would have been here, so, hopefully, she was alive and well; but where?

Returning to the files he had already scanned, he began to read them more closely. She had changed her major in college, just as he had heard, and her degree was in library science. Maybe she was working in a library around here…maybe even this one.

He returned to the lady at the reference desk and asked if she knew if Peggy Johnson worked at this library.

She looked over the top of her glasses at him, seemingly sizing him up.

"Why do you want to know?" she asked.

"She is an old friend of mine," he said. "I've been away and I just wanted to look her up now that I'm back in town."

"Well, she used to work here," said the woman, "but she left."

"Do you know where she went?" he asked, suddenly very excited.

"No, not really," she said. "I think she went to work for a school somewhere, but I don't know which one."

"Thanks, anyway," said Mitch, trying to hide his disappointment.

Returning home, Mitch looked up all the schools in the area and called, asking if Peggy worked in their library. She didn't...none of them. He was very discouraged.

Later, he got a call from John Sampson. He had arranged for Mitch to meet with a group of attorneys in town to interview for a possible job. Everything was looking good. If only he knew what had happened to Peggy.

That night, Jim called. It was really good to hear his voice. He asked Mitch to come on Saturday and spend the day with his family. He wanted to have the time to catch up. Mitch was happy about the prospect of spending a day with Jim and Cindy and their children. He was glad to know he could spend time with Cindy and accept her as Jim's wife. He was happy for them...really happy for them.

He told Jim he'd be there about noon. After a little more small talk, they hung up.

During the week, Mitch met with the attorneys and they were very interested in him. They offered him a job doing leg work for them. They knew with his record, he couldn't move up much, but he could, maybe, be an aide in the office eventually. Mitch thought about how this time he would really need to work to move up in an organization. At least he had learned his lesson...you got nothing for free...nothing but trouble.

At home, Mitch talked to his dad about the offer. It was steady and reputable, and it might be difficult to get a position with his record, but he wasn't sure this was the answer. He had asked them to give him a week to make a decision. If nothing else came along that seemed more appropriate, he would take the job. After all, he wasn't going to lay around for the rest of his life. Five-hundred dollars wouldn't last long. Carl and Jim were working hard, but they had both earned the respect and love of really wonderful wives and great kids. That was what he wanted. For the first time in his life, a simple family life was what he wanted. He knew he would never be rich financially, but there were other ways of being rich. While he was working for Sam, he had forgotten that. Now he wanted to remember it, and live it, always.

Saturday morning, Carl drove him to Scott's house to pick up his car. It was nice spending time with Carl and he seemed genuinely happy to help Mitch.

After he picked up his car and said goodbye to Carl, he drove over to Jim's house. When he arrived, Jim rushed out. It was great to see him. Mitch was so happy to be with friends again, and he envied them so much. He didn't want Cindy any more; she truly belonged to Jim; but he wanted what they had. And he didn't even have any prospects at the moment.

He told Jim about the job offer and they talked about it for some time. He explained that he really didn't know what he wanted to do, but he didn't think the law was the right area for him. He knew that he had something to give back, but what?

Jim told him not to worry; that something would show up for him, especially if he was open to ideas and offers.

They cooked out in Jim's back yard. He really was domesticated...a long way from their booze and drug fueled partying days that first year. And he knew this was the way it should be...for everyone.

After lunch, he and Jim sat in lawn chairs in the back yard while Cindy put the children down for a nap.

"Your family is terrific," said Mitch. "I am jealous."

He said this with a laugh, but he and Jim both knew he was serious.

"Hey, Mitch; you can have the same thing," said Jim. "Don't you have any girl in mind for the position of Mrs. Mitch Nelson?"

"Not really," he said. "You know what a mess I made of any good relationship that ever came along. And the one that might have lasted, until I sent her to prison, was not built on everlasting love."

They sat quietly, comfortable with each other, for some time. When Cindy joined them, she seemed full of excitement.

"What's the matter with you?" Jim asked. "I haven't seen you this excited for some time."

"Oh, nothing," said Cindy, a smile crossing her face.

Mitch looked at her. She was as beautiful as ever. He remembered those wonderful nights in her arms, sharing themselves with each other, but he found that his feelings for Cindy, thankfully, were much different now. She was a friend, and the wife of his best friend…nothing more. He was relieved to know that.

He wasn't sure he could say the same thing about Peggy. He guessed he had never really gotten her out of his system. Maybe first love never leaves you…that was the excuse he gave himself.

He knew first lust left you. He rarely thought of Sabrina any more. He felt sorry for her, but he had no desire for her, even when he thought of her beautiful, luscious body. He was completely cured of her.

As these thoughts were going through his mind, he felt Cindy's eyes on him. What was she thinking? Could she read his mind?

"Mitch, do you have a job yet?"

"Hey, Cindy; lay off the guy," said Jim. "You know he isn't a slacker."

"No, Honey; that's not it," she said. "I just heard of a position I think he would be great for…and it is right here in town, so we could see a lot of him. It would give his 'nephew and niece' a chance to get to know him.

"What job?" asked Mitch. "And what makes you think they would be interested in me…remember my past."

"Oh, Mitch, don't be silly," she said. "I would never even mention it if I didn't think it would be perfect for you. Of course, you wouldn't make much money…definitely not like you used to…but it is a job I think you would feel good about. You would be helping people…while still using all that special talent you have for running a business. At least you could take a look at it. In fact, I told the person who is looking for someone about you, and she would love to interview you."

Mitch shook his head. Cindy was really something. Well, it wouldn't hurt to at least find out about it. After all, he didn't have many offers.

"Tell me about it," he said.

Jim shook his head. "Here she goes again. She is 'Little Miss Fixit.' She can't stand to see a need that isn't filled…and if you might fill it, Heaven help you."

Mitch smiled. "That isn't so bad. At least she cares. That's something I want to do. In fact, I have to," he said.

"Well, Mitch," said Cindy, "it is a small, private school that provides for kids who have problems caused by a history of drug use. The purpose is to educate and change them. I know you know about drugs from a different perspective, but I think you would be great with the kids. I think they would really respond to you. It has a small staff: three teachers, a director, and an assistant director who also serves as a secretary, librarian, and general 'Girl Friday.' Right now, they need a director. Won't you at least take a look at them?"

Mitch laughed out loud. "Does she ever run down?" he asked Jim.

"Not often," he answered, "but I have learned to live with it. Sometimes she even talks in her sleep, all night."

"Oh, be quiet," she said, smiling at Jim and throwing him a kiss. "Well, Mitch; what do you say? Will you at least meet with the assistant director.?"

"Why not?" said Mitch, entering into the gentle bantering that was going on.

"Lead the way."

"Hurray, I knew you'd do it," she said. "I know you will love the program, and the staff is terrific."

In her exuberance, she leaned forward and gave Mitch a kiss on the cheek. He was startled, but it felt good, but only in a friendly way. Life was beginning to look good again.

As Mitch thought about it, he realized that he had a chance at a good life again because he had faced up to his wrong doings, paid a price, and regained his friends and family. Now he was free to build a good life. It could be good. Maybe this position, one where he could give something back, where he could influence kids not to end up where he had previously encouraged people to go, would be a start. Then all he'd need would be a wonderful woman to share that life with him. But would that ever happen?

"Well, Cindy, when do I meet this wonder woman?" asked Mitch.

"Any minute now," she replied. "I asked her to stop by here this afternoon. I knew that you would agree to a meeting. Just relax."

While she was talking, he heard the doorbell ring. Well, no time like the present. At least he had no time to rethink this decision.

"That must be her," said Cindy. "Relax fellows; I'll bring her out here."

As she disappeared into the house, Jim said; "Hey, I'm sorry Buddy. She just has to try to fix everyone up. I hope you don't mind; you can just say 'no' to this woman. At least you will have had your meeting."

"No," said Mitch. "This sounds right. I think this would meet my needs, and I might do some good too. Maybe I'll find a girl and settle down like you; but you've got a bit of a head start on me."

They were laughing as Cindy returned to the backyard. When the screen door slammed behind her, they both stood, looking toward her and her guest.

"Mitch, Jim; this is the lady I wanted you to meet," she said.

As Cindy stood aside, Mitch almost fainted. He already knew her...standing before him was his beautiful goddess, Peggy. He had found his future...and an 'old' beginning.

About the Author

Born and raised in Indiana, I met and married a farmer at the age of 19. After his death at the age of 22, I received my BA and MA degrees from Indiana University and worked for the next thirty plus years as a social worker, mostly with children and families and for the last ten years as an investigator of the abuse and neglect of children. Writing court reports on these cases became the telling of their stories so the understanding of the family members was important and necessary and often involved life and death situations. After a severe back injury forced me to retire, I worked as a travel agent and then, after again retiring, began to write based on my observations and experiences with a variety of people. Currently I divide my time between Puerto Vallarta, Mexico and Sonoma, California.